"Master enchanter Peter S. Beagle is best known for his novel *The Last Unicorn*, a book which has charmed generations of readers. But the briefer enchantments collected in these two volumes also brim with the deepest and truest of his magical powers: with laughter, with wisdom, and with the ineffable pleasure of the imaginary memories he shares. From the gradually refined focus of 'Professor Gottesman and the Indian Rhinoceros' to the crankily slipped-and-skewed perspective of 'Vanishing,' these are visions of an inner world all of us need to visit again and again. Each tale is a spell welcoming our hearts to their real home: wonder."
—Nisi Shawl, author of *Everfair*

"Stepping into a Peter Beagle story is like stepping out your front door into an alternate, but entirely logical, world: Your girlfriend seems to be a werewolf, the evening news is anchored by the Angel of Death, dreadful poetry is a lethal weapon, and a Berkeley traffic cop has to negotiate a depressed dragon out of an intersection. But then, what else to expect from a wizard of mischief like Beagle? Two perfect volumes that should come with a warning: When you try and go back inside your house, all its rooms will have changed."
—Laurie R. King, author of *The Beekeeper's Apprentice*

"Having all these Peter Beagle stories collected together is pure joy. His writing has amazed me my whole life. You'd think I'd be used to it by now, but the amazement is ongoing."
—Carrie Vaughn, author of the Kitty Norville series

"This was an amazing collection, and I cannot recommend it enough for existing fans of Mr. Beagle or fans of fantasy shorts or cozy fantasy."
—*All Booked Up*

"Peter S. Beagle's short stories tap into the sweetest sap of the soul and leave their mark forever. He always makes me cry in the most wonderful and necessary way."
—Delilah S. Dawson, author of *Wicked as They Come*

"*The Essential Peter S. Beagle Volumes I & II* are everything I hoped for and wanted them to be. Beagle's clever and utterly whimsical storytelling is evident in every story, and I love jumping from tale to tale and exploring the facets of his mind. The writing is fun and explores the unique while keeping one foot in the familiar, making it perfect for readers of all ages. I highly recommend these charming volumes!"
—Charlie N. Holmberg, author of *Keeper of Enchanted Rooms*

Praise for Peter S. Beagle

"One of my favorite writers."
—Madeleine L'Engle, author of *A Wrinkle in Time*

"Peter S. Beagle illuminates with his own particular magic such commonplace matters as ghosts, unicorns, and werewolves. For years a loving readership has consulted him as an expert on those hearts' reasons that reason does not know."
—Ursula K. Le Guin, author of *A Wizard of Earthsea*

"Peter S. Beagle has both opulence of imagination and mastery of style."
—*New York Times Book Review*

"At his best, Peter S. Beagle outshines the moon, the sun, the stars, the entire galaxy."
—*Seattle Times*

"Peter Beagle deserves a seat at the table with the great masters of fantasy."
—Christopher Moore, author of *Lamb* and *The Serpent of Venice*

"Not only one of our greatest fantasists, but one of our greatest writers, a magic realist worthy of consideration with such writers as Marquez, Allende, and even Borges."
—*The American Culture*

"We all have something to learn—about writing, about humanity, about hope—from Peter Beagle."
—Seanan McGuire, Hugo Award-winning author of the Wayward Children series

"Peter S. Beagle is (in no particular order) a wonderful writer, a fine human being, and a bandit prince out to steal readers' hearts."
—Tad Williams, author of *Tailchaser's Song*

"Peter S. Beagle is a master of the magical."
—Kurt Busiek, author of *Astro City* and *The Avengers*

"[Beagle] has been compared, not unreasonably, with Lewis Carroll and J. R. R. Tolkien, but he stands squarely and triumphantly on his own feet."
—*Saturday Review*

"Peter S. Beagle is the magician we all apprenticed ourselves to."
—Lisa Goldstein, author of *The Red Magician*

"One of the all-time greats."
—*The Guardian*

"There are other authors who can write a sentence as well as Beagle, but there are very few who keep inventing sparkling fantasy ideas for decade after decade."
—*SF Commentary*

Praise for *The Overneath*

[Starred] "Beagle's latest collection of short stories includes 13 fantasy gems and features many previously uncollected and never-before-published works. . . . A masterful collection from a short story master—a must-read for Beagle fans."
—*Kirkus*

[Starred] "With sharp, lean elegance, Beagle effortlessly chronicles the lives of unicorns, trolls, magicians, and adventurers in 13 poignant stories, many of which caution readers about magic gone awry and temperamental creatures. . . . This enchanting collection employs simple humor and affectionate sarcasm and will enchant any reader who still believes in magic."
—*Publishers Weekly*

[Starred] "Beagle's strong and versatile talent is well on display here, and fantasy readers will be missing out if they don't give it a look."
—*Booklist*

"Verdict: For fantasy fans, Beagle should be a staple."
—*Library Journal*

Praise for *Sleight of Hand*

"Wise, warm and deep."
—*The New York Times*

"This 13-story anthology will entice even the most jaded reader to read long hours into the night . . . *Sleight of Hand* will beguile and enchant."
—*New York Journal of Books*

"Beagle still has the power to surprise . . . a new collection of stories by one of the all-time greats."
—*The Guardian*

Also by Peter S. Beagle

Fiction

A Fine and Private Place (1960)

The Last Unicorn (1968)

Lila the Werewolf (1969)

The Folk of the Air (1986)

The Innkeeper's Song (1993)

The Unicorn Sonata (1996)

Tamsin (1999)

A Dance for Emilia (2000)

The Last Unicorn: The Lost Version (2007)

Return (2010)

Summerlong (2016)

In Calabria (2017)

The Way Home (2023)

Short fiction collections

Giant Bones (1997)

The Rhinoceros Who Quoted Nietzsche and Other Odd Acquaintances (1997)

The Line Between (2006)

Your Friendly Neighborhood Magician: Songs and Early Poems (2006)

We Never Talk About My Brother (2009)

Mirror Kingdoms: The Best of Peter S. Beagle (2010)

Sleight of Hand (2011)

The Overneath (2017)

Nonfiction

I See By My Outfit (1965)

The California Feeling (with Michael Bry, 1969)

The Lady and Her Tiger (with Pat Derby, 1976)

The Garden of Earthly Delights (1982)

In the Presence of Elephants (with Pat Derby and Genaro Molina, 1995)

As editor

Peter S. Beagle's Immortal Unicorn (with Janet Berliner, 1995)

The Secret History of Fantasy (2010)

The Urban Fantasy Anthology (with Joe R. Lansdale, 2011)

The New Voices of Fantasy (with Jacob Weisman, 2017)

The Unicorn Anthology (with Jacob Weisman, 2019)

THE ESSENTIAL
PETER S. BEAGLE
VOLUME II

TACHYON PUBLICATIONS

SAN FRANCISCO

The Essential Peter S. Beagle: Volume II
© 2023 by Peter S. Beagle

Introduction © by Meg Elison
Cover art and interior illustrations by Stephanie Law
Cover design and interior layout by Elizabeth Story

Tachyon Publications LLC
1459 18th Street #139
San Francisco, CA 94107
415.285.5615
www.tachyonpublications.com
tachyon@tachyonpublications.com

Series editor: Jacob Weisman
Project editor: Jaymee Goh

Print ISBN: 978-1-61696-390-3
Digital ISBN: 978-1-61696-391-0

Printed in the United States by Versa Press, Inc.

First Edition: 2023
9 8 7 6 5 4 3 2 1

"Sleight of Hand" © 2009 by Peter S. Beagle. First published in *Eclipse Three: New Science Fiction and Fantasy* (Night Shade Books), edited by Jonathan Strahan. | "Oakland Dragon Blues" © 2009 by Peter S. Beagle. First published in *The Dragon Book: Magical Tales from the Masters of Modern Fantasy* (Ace), edited by Jack Dann and Gardner Dozois. | "The Rock in the Park" © 2010 by Peter S. Beagle. First published in *Sleight of Hand* (Tachyon). Derived from an original podcast performance recorded for *The Green Man Review*. | "The Rabbi's Hobby" © 2008 by Peter S. Beagle. First published in *Eclipse Two: New Science Fiction and Fantasy* (Night Shade Books), edited by Jonathan Strahan. | "The Way It Works Out and All" © 2011 by Peter S. Beagle. First published in *The Magazine of Fantasy & Science Fiction*, July–August 2011. | "The Best Worst Monster" © 2011 by Peter S. Beagle. First published in *Sleight of Hand* (Tachyon). | "La Lune T'Attend" © 2010 by Peter S. Beagle. First published in *Full Moon City* (Pocket), edited by Darrel Schweitzer and Martin H. Greenberg. | "The Story of Kao Yu" © 2016 by Peter S. Beagle. First published by Tor.com. | "Trinity County, CA: You'll Want to Come Again and We'll Be Glad to See You!" © 2001 by Peter S. Beagle. First published in *Orson Scott Card's Intergalactic Medicine Show*, August 2010. | "Marty and the Messenger" © 2005 by Peter S. Beagle. Derived from an original podcast performance recorded for *The Green Man Review*. | "The Mantichora" © 2023. Original to this collection. | "Mr. McCaslin" © 2005 by Peter S. Beagle. Derived from an original podcast performance recorded for *The Green Man Review*. | "The Fifth Season" © 2005 by Peter S. Beagle. Derived from an original podcast performance recorded for *The Green Man Review*. | "Tarzan Swings by Barsoom" © 2012. First appeared as "The Ape Man of Mars" in *Under the Moon of Mars: New Adventures in Barsoom* (Simon & Schuster), edited by John Joseph Adams. | "The Bridge Partner" © 2011 by Peter S. Beagle. First published in *Sleight of Hand* (Tachyon). | "Vanishing" © 2010 by Peter S. Beagle. First appeared in *Orson Scott Card's Intergalactic Medicine Show*, March 2009.

THE ESSENTIAL
PETER S. BEAGLE

VOLUME II
OAKLAND DRAGON BLUES
AND OTHER STORIES

Table of Contents

EATING THE HEART OF PETER S. BEAGLE

by Meg Elison

IT IS THE MISTAKE of a rank amateur reader to assume they know the author by their work.

The author is feeding us pieces of his heart, but we can't know how he cut them, how he changed them first. What we taste is not the whole truth. This was something I understood long before I met Peter S. Beagle; I knew better than to believe him the devilishly clever, compassionate and grandfatherly figure I imagined as I read his books and stories, as I received the pulverized bits of his heart he had carved off and reconstituted into *Star Trek* and books like the luminous *Summerlong*. I knew the Beagle in my mind was the wine and not the fruit. I should expect the usual experience of the author on tour; a tired and grumpy person who has been in too many cars and airplanes and is either getting a cold or getting over one and would like very much not to shake any more hands.

Instead, the man fed me his heart.

The Essential Peter S. Beagle: Volume II is another opportunity for readers to taste Peter S. Beagle. His unmatched capacity for fantasy is on display here, with dragons guarding the lairs of drug dealers and the kind of inexplicable slides through time and space that inspire us to imagine the people we might have come from and the people we might have been, had history run just a little bit differently. His turbulence of emotion and depth of connection appears in "The Rabbi's Hobby," an unforgettable jewel of a story about loss and what it means to be haunted, to never forget. In each of these, the author's heart is cut up and fed to us, bite by bite. In a career this long, we know that he has to grow it back each time. There are so many of us to feed. And in this body of work, no one goes without.

Not content with being a master of fantasy, Beagle also brings that same macerated heart to tales of science fiction like "Marty and the Messenger," a playful tale of food that speaks up and finds the author himself in the cosmos, spoon poised, ready to eat and be eaten in his eagerness to know what new life forms are like. As always, Beagle's heart brings distinct flavor to the voice of a fairy tale and a legend, and "The Mantichora" is another entry in that never-ending story that every author takes up their chance to tell.

Reading Peter S. Beagle is so like meeting him that I struggle to keep the two separate in my mind. In stories like "Marty and the Messenger," and "The Fifth Season," when the author is present as a character, it is literary and correct to assume that the character is not the man. The author has been safely solipsized into an untouchable version of the man himself, a figure of speech rather than the speaking figure himself.

Yet I cannot help but feel that same beating heart in his work as I felt in his presence. His voice is so utterly the same on the page as it is on the stage. The night that I met Peter, he told stories about the authors he knew, famous and infamous, with a collegial wit and a need to reveal them as he revealed himself. He sat for hours with an endless line of people wanting their works signed, some of them getting the maximum number inscribed and getting back in line to complete their quest. Some of them mentioned only his earliest works, having read nothing since The Last Unicorn (1968) and he was unfailingly kind to each.

The moment I remember best from that long night is one wherein a fan asked Peter to record a talking head video for some grandchildren who could not attend, kids who loved his work and would get a kick out of hearing from the man himself. Peter hesitated not one second but put on his best grin and spoke into the lens as if he could see the favored children there, finishing with a flourish and wishing them adventures and joy.

As the man turned his phone around, his face fell as he realized he hadn't been recording at all during that time.

Peter again, without hesitation, said, "that was just a dress rehearsal!" With the same energy, he addressed the children he would never meet, wishing them good stories and deep down-filled pillows to support their dreams. He didn't complain, he didn't so much as roll an eye at the man's lack of savvy or tact. He simply gave his heart away, one beat at a time. Everyone watching could taste it. The man with the grandkids took it home in a doggy bag.

I'm not encouraging rank amateurism in you, reader. I'm not trying to tell you that you know this man from top to bottom when you read his work. There's more to any person than what can be pressed between the pages of a book, or revealed in any brief couple of meetings. We cannot swallow him whole; we can only have a taste here and there.

This collection is another series of tastes of Peter S. Beagle's heart. It is sweet and it is bitter. It is served up for you in a dozen different ways. It is a taste you will never forget. It is cut from him and from the whole of his work; you won't know all of him through reading just this.

But what you know will be true.

SLEIGHT OF HAND

This story was crafted out of childhood memories, a chance encounter with a preposterous ad in an even more preposterous location, and the raw, constant terror I felt when my closest cousin was about to go into surgery for a brain aneurysm. At the time I was too paralyzed by fear for her to do anything but call her husband twice a day for news of her condition. Afterward, when she came out of the operation in fine shape, and I could think again, I found myself writing what follows.

S HE HAD NO IDEA where she was going. When she needed to sleep she stopped at the first motel; when the Buick's gas gauge dropped into the red zone she filled the tank, and sometimes bought a sandwich or orange juice at the attached convenience store. Now and then during one of these stops she spoke with someone who was neither a desk clerk nor a gas-station attendant, but she forgot all such conversations within minutes, as she forgot everything but the words of the young policeman who had come to her door on a pleasant Wednesday afternoon, weeks and worlds ago. Nothing had moved in her since that point except the memory of his shakily sympathetic voice, telling her that her husband and daughter were dead: ashes in a smoking, twisted, unrecognizable ruin, because, six blocks from their home, a drowsy adolescent had mistaken his accelerator for his brake pedal.

There had been a funeral—she was present, but not there—and more police, and some lawyer; and Alan's sister managing it all, as always, and for once she was truly grateful to the interfering bitch. But that was all far away too, both the gratitude and the old detestation, made nothing by the momentary droop of a boy's eyelids. The nothing

5

got her snugly through the days after the funeral, dealing with each of the endless phone calls, sitting down to answer every condolence card and e-mail, informing Social Security and CREF of Alan's death, going with three of his graduate students to clean out his office, and attending the memorial on campus, which was very tasteful and genuinely moving, or so the nothing was told. She was glad to hear it.

The nothing served her well until the day Alan's daughter by his first marriage came to collect a few of his possessions as keepsakes. She was a perfectly nice girl, who had always been properly courteous in an interloper's presence, and her sympathy was undoubtedly as real as good manners could make it; but when she had gone, bearing a single brown paper grocery bag of photographs and books, the nothing stepped aside for the meltdown.

Her brother-in-law calmed her, spoke rationally, soothed her out of genuine kindness and concern. But that same night, speaking to no one, empty and methodical, she had watched herself pack a small suitcase and carry it out to Alan's big old Buick in the garage, then go back into the house to leave her cell phone and charger on Alan's desk, along with a four-word note for her sister-in-law that read *Out for a drive*. After that she had backed the Buick into the street and headed away without another look at the house where she used to live, once upon a time.

The only reason she went north was that the first freeway on-ramp she came to pointed her in that direction. After that she did not drive straight through, because there was no *through* to aim for. With no destination but away, without any conscious plan except to keep moving, she left and returned to the flat ribbon of the interstate at random intervals, sometimes wandering side roads and backroads for hours, detouring to nowhere. Aimless, mindless, not even much aware of pain—that too having become part of the nothing—she slogged onward. She fell asleep quickly when she stopped, but never for long, and was usually on her way in darkness, often with the moon still high. Now and then she whistled thinly between her teeth.

The weather was warm, though there was still snow in some of the higher passes she traversed. Although she had started near the coast, that was several states ago: now only the mountains were constant. The Buick fled lightly over them, gulping fuel with abandon but cornering like a deer, very nearly operating and guiding itself. This was necessary, since only a part of her was behind the wheel; the rest was away with Alan, watching their daughter building a sandcastle, prowling a bookshop with him, reaching for his hand on a strange street, knowing without turning her head that it would be there. At times she was so busy talking to him that she was slow to switch on the headlights, even long after sunset. But the car took care of her, as she knew it would. It was Alan's car, after all.

From time to time the Buick would show a disposition to wander toward the right shoulder of the road, or drift left into the oncoming lane, and she would observe the tendency with vague, detached interest. Once she asked aloud, "Is this what you want? I'm leaving it to you— are you taking me to Alan?" But somehow, whether under her guidance or its own, the old car always righted itself, and they went on together.

The latest road began to descend, and then to flatten out into farm and orchard country, passing the occasional township, most of them overgrown crossroads. She had driven for much of the previous night, and all of today, and knew with one distant part of herself that it would soon be necessary to stop. In early twilight, less than an hour later, she came to the next town. There was a river winding through it, gray and silver in the dusk, with bridges.

Parking and registering at the first motel with a VACANCY sign, she walked three blocks to the closest restaurant, which, from the street, looked like a bar with a 1950s-style diner attached. Inside, however, it proved larger than she had expected, with slightly less than half of the booths and tables occupied. Directly to the left of the PLEASE WAIT TO BE SERVED sign hung a poster showing a photograph of a lean, hawknosed man in late middle age, with white hair and thick eyebrows, wearing evening dress: tailcoat, black bowtie, top hat. He was smiling slightly and fanning a deck of playing cards between long, neat fingers. There was no name under the picture; the caption read only DINNER MAGIC. She looked at it until the young waitress came to show her to her booth.

After ordering her meal—the first she had actually sat down to since leaving home—she asked the waitress about Dinner Magic. Her own voice sounded strange in her ears, and language itself came hard and hesitantly. The girl shrugged. "He's not fulltime—just comes in now and then, does a couple of nights and gone again. Started a couple of weeks ago. Haven't exchanged two words with him. Other than my boss, I don't know anybody who has."

Turning away toward the kitchen, she added over her shoulder, "He's good, though. Stay for the show, if you can."

In fact, the Dinner Magic performance began before most of the current customers had finished eating. There was no stage, no musical flourish or formal introduction: the man in evening dress simply walked out from the kitchen onto the floor, bowed briefly to the diners, then tossed a gauzy multicolored scarf into the air. He seized it again as it fluttered down, then held it up in front of himself, hiding him from silk hat to patent-leather shoes . . .

. . . and vanished, leaving his audience too stunned to respond. The applause began a moment later, when he strolled in through the restaurant's front door.

Facing the audience once more, the magician spoke for the first time. His voice was deep and clear, with a certain engaging roughness in the lower range. "Ladies, gentlemen, Dinner Magic means exactly what it sounds like. You are not required to pay attention to me for a moment, you are free to concentrate on your coffee and pie—which is excellent, by the way, especially the lemon meringue—or on your companion, which I recommend even more than the meringue. Think of me, if you will, as the old man next door who stays up all night practicing his silly magic tricks. Because that, under this low-rent monkey suit, is exactly what I am. Now then."

He was tall, and older than the photograph had suggested—how old, she could not tell, but there were lines on his cheeks and under his angled eyes that must have been removed from the picture; the sort of thing she had seen Alan do on the computer. From her booth, she watched, chin on her fist, never taking her eyes from the man as he ran through a succession of tricks that bordered on the miraculous even as his associated patter never transcended a lounge act. Without elephants or tigers, without a spangled, long-legged assistant, he worked the room. Using his slim black wand like a fishing rod he reeled laughing diners out of their seats. Holding it lightly between his fingertips, like a conductor's baton or a single knitting needle, he caused the napkins at every table to lift off in a whispering storm of thin cotton, whirl wildly around the room, and then settle docilely back where they belonged. He identified several members of his audience by name, address, profession, marital status, and, as an afterthought, by driver's license state and number. She was never one of these; indeed, the magician seemed to be consciously avoiding eye contact with her altogether. Nevertheless, she was more intrigued—more *awakened*—than she had meant to let herself be, and she ordered a second cup of coffee and sat quite still where she was.

Finishing at last with an offhanded gesture, a bit like an old-fashioned jump shot, which set all the silverware on all the tables chiming applause, the magician walked off without bowing, as abruptly as he had entered. The waitress brought her check, but she remained in her booth even after the busboy cleared away her dishes. Many of the other diners lingered as she did, chattering and marveling and calling for encores. But the man did not return.

The street was dark, and the restaurant no more than a quarter full, when she finally recollected both herself and her journey, and stepped out into the warm, humid night. For a moment she could not call to mind where she had parked her car; then she remembered the motel and started in that direction. She felt strangely refreshed, and was seriously considering the prospect of giving up her room and beginning to drive again. But after walking several blocks she decided that she must have somehow gone in the wrong direction, for there was no motel sign in sight, nor any landmark casually noted on her way to the restaurant. She turned and turned again, making tentative casts this way and that, even starting back the way she had come, but nothing looked at all familiar.

Puzzlement had given way to unease when she saw the magician ahead of her, under a corner streetlamp. There was no mistaking him, despite his having changed from evening clothes into ordinary dress. His leanness gave him the air of a shadow, rather than a man: a shadow with lined cheeks and long bright eyes. As she approached, he spoke her name. He said, "I have been waiting for you." He spoke more slowly than he had when performing, with a tinge of an accent that she had not noticed.

Anxiety fled on the instant, replaced by a curious stillness, as when Alan's car began to drift peacefully toward the guardrail or the shoulder and the trees. She said, "How do you know me? How did you know all about those other people?"

"I know nearly everything about nearly everyone. That's the curse of my position. But you I know better than most."

She stared at him. "I don't know you."

"Nevertheless, we have met before," the magician said. "Twice, actually, which I confess is somewhat unusual. The second time was long ago. You were quite small."

"That's ridiculous." She was surprised by the faint touch of scorn in her voice, barely there yet still sharp. "That doesn't make any sense."

"I suppose not. Since I know how the trick's done, and you don't, I'm afraid I have you at a disadvantage." He put one long finger to his lips and pursed them, considering, before he started again. "Let's try it as a riddle. I am not entirely what I appear, being old as time, vast as space, and endless as the future. My nature is known to all, but typically misunderstood. And I meet everyone and everything alive at least once. Indeed, the encounter is entirely unavoidable. Who am I?"

She felt a sudden twist in the nothing, and knew it for anger. "Show's over. I'm not eating dinner anymore."

The magician smiled and shook his head very slightly. "You are lost, yes?"

"My motel's lost, I'm not. I must have taken a wrong turn."

"I know the way," the magician said. "I will guide you."

Gracefully and courteously, he offered his arm, but she took a step backward. His smile widened as he let the arm fall to his side. "Come," he said, and turned without looking to see whether she followed. She caught up quickly, not touching the hand he left open, within easy reach.

"You say we've met before. Where?" she asked.

"The second time was in New York City. Central Park," the magician said. "There was a birthday party for your cousin Matthew."

She stopped walking. "Okay. I don't know who you are, or how you knew I grew up in New York City and have a cousin named Matthew. But you just blew it, Sherlock. When we were kids I *hated* stupid, nasty Matthew, and I absolutely never went to any of his birthday parties. My parents tried to make me, once, but I put up such a fuss they backed down. So you're wrong."

The magician reached out abruptly, and she felt a swift, cool whisper in her hair. He held up a small silver figure of a horse and asked with mock severity, "What are you doing, keeping a horse up in there? You shouldn't have a horse if you don't have a stable for it."

She froze for an instant, wide-eyed and open-mouthed, and then clutched at the silver horse as greedily as any child. "That's *mine!* Where did you get it?"

"I gave it to you." The magician's voice sounded as impossibly distant as her childhood, long gone on another coast.

And then came his command: "*Remember.*"

∞

At first she had enjoyed herself. Matthew was fat and awful as usual, but his birthday had been an excuse to bring together branches of the family that rarely saw one another, traveling in to Central Park from places as whispered and exotic as Rockaway and Philadelphia. She was excited to see her whole family, not just her parents and her very small baby brother, and Matthew's mother and father, but also uncles and aunts and cousins, and some very old relatives she had never met before in her life. They all gathered together in one corner of the Sheep Meadow, where they spread out picnic blankets, coverlets, beach towels, anything you could sit down on, and they brought out all kinds of old-country dishes: piroshki, pelmeni, flanken, kasha, rugelach, kugel mit mandlen, milk bottles full of borscht and schav—and hot dogs and hamburgers too, and baked beans and deviled eggs, and birthday cake and candy and cream soda. It was a hot blue day, full of food.

But a four-year-old girl can only eat and drink so much . . . and besides, after a while the uncles all began to fall asleep on the grass, one by one, much too full to pay attention to her . . . and all the aunts were sitting together telling stories that didn't make any sense . . . and Matthew was fussing about having a "stummyache," which she felt he certainly deserved. And her parents weren't worth talking to, since whenever she tried they were busy with her infant brother or the other adults, and not really listening. So after a time she grew bored. Stuffed, but bored.

She decided that she would go and see the zoo.

She knew that Central Park had a zoo because she had been taken there once before. It was a long way from the picnic, but even so, every now and then she could hear the lions roaring, along with the distant sounds of busses and taxis and city traffic that drifted to her ears. She was sure that it would be easy to find her way if she listened for the lions.

But they eluded her, the lions and the zoo alike. Not that she was lost, no, not for a minute. She walked along enjoying herself, smiling in the sunlight, and petting all the dogs that came bouncing up to her.

If their owners asked where her parents were, she pointed firmly in the direction she was going and said "right up there," then moved on, laughing, before they had time to think about it. At every branching of the path she would stop and listen, taking whatever turn sounded like it led toward the lions. She didn't seem to be getting any closer, though, which eventually grew frustrating. It was still an adventure, still more exciting than the birthday picnic, but now it was beginning to annoy her as well.

Then she came around a bend in the path, and saw a man sitting by himself on a little bench. To her eyes he was a very old man, almost as old as her great-uncle Wilhelm—you could tell that by his white hair, and the deep lines around his closed eyes, and the long red blanket that his legs stretched out in front of him. She had seen other old men sitting like that. His hands were shoved deep into his coat pockets, and his face lifted to the angle of the afternoon sun.

She thought he was asleep, so she started on past him, walking quietly, so as not to wake him. But without opening his eyes or changing his position, he said in a soft, deep voice, "An exceptional afternoon to you, young miss."

Exceptional was a new word to her, and she loved new words. She turned around and replied, trying to sound as grown up as she could, "I'm very exceptional, thank you."

"And glad I am to hear it," the old man said. "Where are you off to, if I may ask?"

"I'm going to see the lions," she told him. "And the draffs. Draffs are excellent animals."

"So they are," the old man agreed. His eyes, when he opened them, were the bluest she had ever seen, so young and bright that they made the rest of him look even older. He said, "I used to ride a draff, you know, in Africa. Whenever I went shopping."

She stared at him. "You can't ride a draff. There's no place to *sit*."

"I rode way up on the neck, on a little sort of platform." The old man hadn't beckoned to her, or shifted to make room for her on the bench, but she found herself moving closer all the same. He said, "It was like being in the crow's-nest on the mast of a ship, where the lookout sits. The draff would be swaying and flowing under me like the sea, and the sky would be swaying too, and I'd hang onto the draff's neck with one hand, and wave to all the people down below with the other. It was really quite nice."

He sighed, and smiled and shook his head. "But I had to give it up, because there's no place to put your groceries on a draff. All your bags and boxes just slide right down the neck, and then the draff steps on them. Draffs have very big feet, you know."

By that time she was standing right in front of him, staring into his lined old face. He had a big, proud nose, and his eyebrows over it were all tangly. To her they looked mad at each other. He said, "After that, I did all my shopping on a rhinoceros. One thing about a rhinoceros"— and for the first time he smiled at her—"when you come into a store, people are always remarkably nice. And you can sling all your packages around the rhino's horn and carry them home that way. *Much* handier than a draff, let me tell you."

He reached up while he was talking and took an egg out of her right ear. She didn't feel it happen—just the quick brush of his long fingers, and there was the egg in his hand. She grabbed for her other ear, to see if there might be an egg in there too, but he was already taking a quarter out of that one. He seemed just as surprised as she was, saying, "My goodness, now you'll be able to buy some toast to have with your egg. Extraordinary ears you have—my word, yes." And all the time he was carrying on about the egg, he was finding all kinds of other things in her ears: seashells and more coins, a couple of marbles (which upset him—"You should *never* put marbles in your ears, young lady!"), a tangerine, and even a flower, although it looked pretty mooshed-up, which he said was from being in her ear all that time.

She sat down beside him without knowing she was sitting down. "How do you *do* that?" she asked him. "Can *I* do that? Show me!"

"With ears like those, everything is possible," the old man answered.

"Try it for yourself," and he guided her hand to a beautiful cowrie shell tucked just behind her left ear. Then he said, "I wonder . . . I just wonder . . ." And he ruffled her hair quickly and showed her a palm full of tiny silver stars. Not like the shining foil ones her preschool teacher gave out for good behavior, but glittering, sharp-pointed metal stars, as bright as anything in the sky.

"It seems your hair is talented, too. *That's* exceptional."

"More, please!" she begged him.

The old man looked at her curiously. He was still smiling, but his eyes seemed sad now, which confused her.

"I haven't given you anything that wasn't already yours," he said. "Much as I would otherwise. But *this* is a gift. From me to you. Here." He waved one hand over his open palm, and when it passed she saw a small silver figure of a horse.

She looked at it. It was more beautiful, she thought, than anything she had ever seen.

"I can keep it? Really?"

"Oh yes," he said. "I hope you will keep it always."

He put the exquisite figure in her cupped hands, and closed her fingers gently over it. She felt the curlicues of the mane, blowing in a frozen wind, against her fingertips.

"Put it in your pocket, for safekeeping, and look at it tonight before you go to bed." As she did what he told her, he said "Now I must ask where your parents are."

She said nothing, suddenly aware how much time had passed since she had left the picnic.

"They will be looking everywhere for you," the old man said. "In fact, I think I can hear them calling you now." He cupped his hands to his mouth and called in a silly, quavering voice, "Elfrieda! *Elfrieda!* Where are you, Elfrieda?"

This made her giggle so much that it took her a while to tell him, "That's not my name." He laughed too, but he went on calling, "Elfrieda! Elfrieda!" until the silly voice became so sad and worried that she stood up and said, "Maybe I ought to go back and tell them I'm all right." The air was starting to grow a little chilly, and she was starting to be not quite sure that she knew the way back.

"Oh, I wouldn't do that," the old man advised her. "If I were you, I'd stay right here, and when they come along you could say to them, 'Why don't you sit down and rest your weary bones?' That's what I'd do."

The idea of saying something like that to grownups set her off giggling again, and she could hardly wait for her family to come find her. She sat down by the old man and talked with him, in the ordinary way, about school and friends and uncles, and all the ways her cousin Matthew made her mad, and about going shopping on rhinoceroses. He told her that it was always hard to find parking space for a rhino, and that they really didn't like shopping, but they would do it if they liked you. So after that they talked about how you get a rhinoceros to like you, until her father came for her on the motorcycle.

"I lost it back in college." She caressed the little object, holding it against her cheek. "I looked and looked, but I couldn't find it anywhere." She looked at him with a mix of wonder and suspicion. She fell silent then, frowning, touching her mouth. "Central Park . . . there was a zoo in Central Park."

The magician nodded. "There still is."

"Lions. Did they have lions?" She gave him no time to answer the question. "I do remember the lions. I heard them roaring." She spoke slowly, seeming to be addressing the silver horse more than him. "I wanted to see the lions."

"Yes," the magician said. "You were on your way there when we met."

"I remember now," she said. "How could I have forgotten?" She was speaking more rapidly as the memory took shape. "You were sitting with me on the bench, and then Daddy . . . Daddy came on a motorcycle. I mean, no, the *policeman* was on the motorcycle, and Daddy was in the . . . the sidecar thing. I remember. He was so furious with me that I was glad the policeman was there."

The magician chuckled softly. "He was angry until he saw that you were safe and unharmed. Then he was so thankful that he offered me money."

"Did he? I didn't notice." Her face felt suddenly hot with embarrassment. "I'm sorry, I didn't know he wanted to give you money. You must have felt so insulted."

"Nonsense," the magician said briskly. "He loved you, and he offered what he had. Both of us dealt in the same currency, after all."

She paused, looking around them. "This isn't the right street either. I don't see the motel."

He patted her shoulder lightly. "You will, I assure you."

"I'm not certain I want to."

"Really?" His voice seemed to surround her in the night. "And why would that be? You have a journey to continue."

The bitterness rose so fast in her throat that it almost made her throw up. "If you know my name, if you know about my family, if you know things I'd forgotten about, then you already know why. Alan's dead, and Talley—my Mouse, oh God, *my little Mouse*—and so am I, do you understand? I'm dead too, and I'm just driving around and around until I rot." She started to double over, coughing and gagging on the rage. "I wish I were dead with them, that's what I wish!" She would have been desperately happy to vomit, but all she could make come out were words.

Strong old hands were steadying her shoulders, and she was able, in a little time, to raise her head and look into the magician's face, where she saw neither anger nor pity. She said very quietly, "No, I'll tell you what I really wish. I wish *I* had died in that crash, and that Alan and Talley were still alive. I'd make that deal like a shot, you think I wouldn't?"

The magician said gently, "It was not your fault."

"Yes it was. It's my fault that they were in my car. I asked Alan to take it in for an oil change, and Mouse . . . Talley wanted to go with him. She loved it, being just herself and Daddy—oh, she used to order him around so, pretending she was me." For a moment she came near losing control again, but the magician held on, and so did she. "If I hadn't asked him to do that for me, if I hadn't been so selfish and lazy and sure I had more important things to do, then it would have been me that died in that crash, and they'd have lived. They *would* have lived." She reached up and gripped the magician's wrists, as hard as she could, holding his eyes even more intently. "You see?"

The magician nodded without answering, and they stood linked together in shadow for that moment. Then he took his hands from her shoulders and said, "So, then, you have offered to trade your life for the lives of your husband and daughter. Do you still hold to that bargain?"

She stared at him. She said, "That stupid riddle. You really *meant* that. What *are* you? Are you Death?"

"Not at all. But there are things I can do, with your consent."

"My consent." She stood back, straightening to her full height. "Alan and Talley . . . nobody needed *their* consent—or mine, either. I meant every word."

"Think," the magician said urgently. "I need you to know what you have asked, and the extent of what you think you mean." He raised his left hand, palm up, tapping on it with his right forefinger. "Be very careful, little girl in the park. There *are* lions."

"I know what I wished." She could feel the sidewalk coiling under her feet.

"Then know this. I can neither take life nor can I restore it, but I *can* grant your wish, exactly as it was made. You have only to say—and to be utterly certain in your soul that it *is* your true desire." He chuckled suddenly, startlingly; to her ear it sounded almost like a growl. "My, I cannot recall the last time I used that word, *soul.*"

She bit her lip and wrapped her arms around herself, though the night continued warm. "What can you promise me?"

"A different reality—the exact one you prayed for just now. Do you understand me?"

"No," she said; and then, very slowly, "You mean, like running a movie backward? Back to . . . back to *before*?"

The old man shook his head. "No. Reality never runs backward; each thing is, and will be, as it always was. Choice is an uncommon commodity, and treasured by those few who actually have it. But there *is* magic, and magic can shuffle some possibilities like playing cards, done right. Such craft as I control will grant your wish, precisely as you spoke it. Take the horse I have returned to you back to the place where the accident happened. The *exact* place. Hold it in your hand, or carry it on your person, and take a single step. One single step. If your commitment is firm, if your choice is truly and finally made, then things as they always were will *still* be as they always were—only now, the way they always were will be forever different. Your husband and your daughter will live, because they never drove that day, and they never died. *You* did. Do you understand now?"

"Yes," she whispered. "Oh, yes, yes, I do understand. Please, do it, I accept, it's the only wish I have. Please, *yes*."

The magician took her hands between his own. "You are certain? You know what it will mean?"

"I can't live without them," she answered simply. "I told you. But . . . how—"

"Death, for all His other sterling qualities, is not terribly bright. Efficient and punctual, but not bright." The magician gave her the slightest of bows. "And I am very good with tricks. You might even say exceptional."

"Can't you just send me there, right this minute—transport me, or e-mail me or something, never mind the stupid driving. Couldn't you do that? I mean, if you can do—you know—*this*?"

He shook his head. "Even the simplest of tricks must be prepared . . . and this one is not simple. Drive, and I will meet you at the appointed time and place."

"Well, then." She put her hands on his arms, looking up at him as though at the sun through green leaves. "Since there are no words in the world for me to thank you with, I'm just going to go on back home. My family's waiting."

Yet she delayed, and so did he, as though both of them were foreigners fumbling through a language never truly comprehended: a language of memory and intimacy. The magician said, "You don't know why I am doing this." It was not a question.

"No. I don't." Her hesitant smile was a storm of anxious doubt. "Old times' sake?"

The magician shook his head. "It doesn't really matter. Go now."

The motel sign was as bright as the moon across the street, and she could see her car in the half-empty parking lot. She turned and walked away, without looking back, started the Buick and drove out of the lot. There was nothing else to collect. Let them wonder in the morning at her unruffled bed, and the dry towels never taken down from the bathroom rack.

The magician was plain in her rear-view mirror, looking after her, but she did not wave, or turn her head.

Free of detours, the road back seemed notably shorter than the way she had come, though she took it distinctly more slowly. The reason, to her mind, was that before she had been so completely without plans, without thought, without any destination, without any baggage but grief. Now, feeling almost pregnant with joy, swollen with eager visions—*they will live, they will, my Mouse will be a living person, not anyone's memory*—she felt a self that she had never considered or acknowledged conducting the old car, as surely as her foot on the accelerator and her hands on the wheel. A full day passed, more, and somehow she did not grow tired, which she decided must be something the magician had done, so she did not question it. Instead she sang nursery songs as she drove, and the sea chanteys and Gilbert and Sullivan that Alan had always loved. *No, not loved. Loves! Loves now, loves now, and will go on loving, because I'm on my way. Alan, Talley, I'm on my way.*

For the last few hundred miles she abandoned the interstate and drove the coast road home, retracing the path she and Alan had taken at the beginning of their honeymoon. The ocean was constant on her right, the massed redwoods and hemlocks on her left, and the night air smelled both of salt and pinesap. There were deer in the brush, and scurrying foxes, and even a porcupine, shuffling and clicking across the road. Once she saw a mountain lion, or thought she had: a long-tailed shadow in a shadow, watching her shadow race past. *Darlings, on my way!*

It was near dawn when she reached the first suburbs of the city where she had gone to college, married, and settled without any control—or the desire for control—over very much of it. The city lay still as jewels before her, except when the infrequent police siren or fire-engine clamor set dogs barking in every quarter. She parked the Buick in her driveway, startled for a moment at her house's air of abandonment and desolation. *What did you expect, disappearing the way you did, and no way to contact you?* She did not try the door, but stood there for a little, listening absurdly for any sound of Alan or Talley moving in the house. Then she walked away as calmly as she had from the magician.

Six blocks, six blocks. She found the intersection where the crash had occurred. Standing on the corner angle of the sidewalk, she could see the exact smudge on the asphalt where her life had ended, and this shadowy leftover had begun. Across the way the light grew beyond the little community park, a glow as transparent as seawater. She drank it in, savoring the slow-rising smells of warming stone and suburban commuter breakfasts. *Never again . . . never again*, she thought. Up and down the street, cars were backing out of garages, and she found herself watching them with a strange new greed, thinking, *Alan and Mouse will see them come home again, see the geese settle in on the fake lake for the night. Not me, never again.*

The street was thickening with traffic, early as it was. She watched a bus go by, and then the same school van that always went first to the farthest developments, before circling back to pick up Talley and others who lived closer to school. *He's not here yet,* she thought, fingering the silver horse in her pocket. *I could take today. One day—one day only, just to taste it all, to go to all the places we were together, to carry that with me when I step across that pitiful splotch—tomorrow? My darlings will have all the other days, all their lives . . . couldn't I have just the one? I'd be right back here at dawn, all packed to leave—surely they wouldn't mind, if they knew? Just the one.*

Behind her, the magician said, "As much as you have grieved for them, so they will mourn you. You say your life ended here; they will say the same, for a time."

Without turning, she said, "You can't talk me out of this."

A dry chuckle. "Oh, I've suspected that from the beginning."

She did turn then, and saw him standing next to her: unchanged, but for a curious dusk, bordering on tenderness, in the old, old eyes. His face was neither pitying nor unkind, nor triumphant in its foreknowledge, but urgently attentive in the way of a blind person. "There she was, that child in Central Park, stumping along, so fierce, so determined, going off all alone to find the lions. There was I, half-asleep in the sun on my park bench . . ."

"I don't understand," she said. "Please. Before I go, tell me who you are."

"You know who I am."

"I don't!"

"You did. You will."

She did not answer him. In silence, they both turned their heads to follow a young black man walking on the other side of the street. He was carrying an infant—a boy, she thought—high in his arms, his round dark face brilliant with pride, as though no one had ever had a baby before. The man and child were laughing together: the baby's laughter a shrill gurgle, the father's almost a song. Another bus hid them for a moment, and when it passed they had turned a corner and disappeared.

The magician said, "Yet despite your certainty you were thinking, unless I am mistaken, of delaying your bargain's fulfillment."

"One day," she said softly. "Only to say goodbye. To remind myself of them and everything we had, before giving it all up. Would that . . . would it be possible? Or would it break the . . . the spell? The charm?"

The magician regarded her without replying immediately, and she found that she was holding her breath.

"It's neither of those. It's just a trick, and not one that can wait long on your convenience." His expression was inflexible.

"Oh," she said. "Well. It would have been nice, but there—can't have everything. Thank you, and goodbye again."

She waited until the sparse morning traffic was completely clear. Then deliberately, and without hesitation, she stepped forward into the street. She was about to move further when she heard the magician's voice behind her. "Sunset. That is the best I can do."

She wheeled, her face a child's face, alight with holiday. "*Thank* you! I'll be back in time, I promise! Oh, *thank* you!"

Before she could turn again the magician continued, in a different voice, "I have one request." His face was unchanged, but the voice was that of a much younger man, almost a boy. "I have no right to ask, no claim on you—but I would feel privileged to spend these hours in your company." He might have been a shy Victorian, awkwardly inviting a girl to tea.

She stared back at him, her face for once as unreadable as his. It was a long moment before she finally nodded and beckoned to him, saying, "Come on, then—there's so little time. Come on!"

In fact, whether or not it was due to his presence, there was time enough. She reclaimed the Buick and drove them first up into the hills, to watch the rest of dawn play itself out over the city as she told him stories of her life there. Then they joined an early-morning crowd of parents and preschoolers in the local community playground. She introduced the magician to her too-solicitous friends as a visiting uncle from Alan's side of the family, and tried to maintain some illusion of the muted grief she knew they expected of her; an illusion that very nearly shattered with laughter when the magician took a ride with some children on a miniature train, his knees almost up to his ears. After that she brought them back down to the bald flatlands near the freeway, to the food bank where she had worked twice a week, and where she was greeted with cranky affection by old black Baptist women who hugged her and warned her that she needn't be coming round so soon, but if she was up to it, well, tomorrow was likely to be a particularly heavy day, and Lord knows they could use the extra hand. The magician saw the flash of guilt and sorrow in her eyes, but no one else did. She promised not to be late.

Time enough. They parked the car and took a ferry across the bay to the island where she had met Alan when they were both dragged along on a camping trip, and where she and Alan and Talley had picnicked often after Talley was born. Here she found herself chattering to the magician compulsively, telling him how Alan had cured their daughter of her terror of water by coaxing her to swim sitting up on his back, pretending she was riding a dolphin. "She's become a wonderful swimmer now, Mouse has, you should see her. I mean, I guess you *will* see her—anyway you *could* see her. I won't, but if you wanted to . . ." Her voice drifted away, and the magician touched her hand without replying.

"We have to watch the clock," she said. "I wouldn't want to miss my death." It was meant as a joke, but the magician did not laugh.

Time enough. Her vigilance had them back at the house well before sunset, after a stop at her family's favorite ice-cream shop for cones: coffee for herself—"Double scoop, what the hell?"—and strawberry, after much deliberation, for the magician. They were still nibbling them when they reached the front door.

"God, I'll miss coffee," she said, almost dreamily; then laughed. "Well, I guess I won't, will I? I mean, I won't know if I miss it or not, after all." She glanced critically up at the magician beside her. "You've never eaten an ice-cream cone before, have you?"

The magician shook his head solemnly. She took his cone from him and licked carefully around the edges, until the remaining ice-cream was more or less even; then handed it back to him, along with her own napkin. "We should finish before we go in. Come on." She devoted herself to devouring the entire cone, crunching it up with a voracity matching the sun's descent.

When she was done she used her key to open the door, and stepped inside. She was halfway down the front hall, almost to the living room, when she realized the magician had not followed.

"Hey," she called to him. "Aren't you coming?"

"I thank you for the day, but this moment should be yours alone. I will wait outside. You needn't hurry," he said, glancing at the sky. "But don't dawdle, either."

With that he closed the door, leaving her to the house and her memories.

Half an hour later, six blocks away, she stood slightly behind him on the sidewalk and studied the middle of the intersection. He did not offer his hand, but she lifted it in both of hers anyway. "You are very kind."

He shook his head ruefully. "Less than you imagine. Far less than I wish."

"Don't give me that." Her tone was dismissive, but moderated with a chuckle. "You were waiting for me. You said so. I would have bumped into you wherever I drove, wouldn't I? If I'd gone south to Mexico, or gotten on a plane to Honolulu or Europe, sooner or later, when I was ready to listen to what you had to say, when I was ready to make this deal, I'd have walked into a restaurant with a sign for Dinner Magic. Right?"

"Not quite. You could only have gone the way you went, and I could only have met you there. Each thing is, and will be, as it always was. I told you that."

"I don't care. I'm still grateful. I'm still saying thanks."

The magician said softly, "Stay."

She shook her head. "You know I can't."

"This trick . . . this misdirection . . . I can't promise you what it will buy. Your husband and daughter will live, but for how long cannot be known by anyone. They might be killed tomorrow by another stupid, sleepy driver—a virus, a plane crash, a madman with a gun. What you are giving up for them could be utterly useless, utterly pointless, by next sunrise. Stay—do not waste this moment of your own choice, your own power. *Stay.*"

He reached out for her, but she stepped away, backing into the street so suddenly that a driver honked angrily at her as he sped by. She said, "Everything you say is absolutely true, and none of it matters. If all I could give them was one single extra second, I would."

The old man's face grew gentle. "Ah. You are indeed as I remembered. Very well, then. I had to offer you a choice. You have chosen love, and I have no complaint, nor would it matter if I did. In this moment you are the magician, not I."

"All right, then. Let's do this."

The huge red sun was dancing on tiptoe on a green horizon, but she waited until the magician nodded before she started toward the intersection. Traffic had grown so heavy that there was no way for her to reach the stain that was Alan and Talley's fading memorial. The magician raised his free hand, as though waving to her, and the entire lane opened up, cars and drivers frozen in place, leaving her free passage to where she needed to be. Over her shoulder she said, "Thank you," and stepped forward.

The little girl shook her head and looked around herself. She was confused by what she saw, and if anyone in the park other than the old man had been watching, they would have wondered at the oddly adult way that she stood still and regarded her surroundings.

"Hello," the magician said to her.

"This . . . isn't what I expected."

"No. The audience sees a woman cut in half, while the two women folded carefully within separate sections of the magic box experience it quite differently. You're in the trick now, so of course things are different than you expected. It's hardly magic if you can guess in advance how it's done."

She looked at her small hands in amazement, then down the short length of her arms and legs. "I *really* don't understand. You said I would die."

"And so you will, on the given day and at the given time, when you think about asking your husband to take care of your oil change for you and then decide—in a flickering instant, quite without knowing why—that you should do this simple errand yourself, instead." He looked enormously sad as he spoke. "And you will die now, in a different way, because that one deeply buried flicker is the only hint of memory you may keep. You won't remember this day, or the gifts I will give you, or me. The trick won't work, otherwise. Death may not be bright, but he's not stupid, either—all the cards have to go back in the deck, or he *will* notice. But if you and I, between us, subtly mark one of the cards . . . that should slip by. Just."

He stopped speaking; and for a little it seemed to the woman in the girl, staring into the finality of his face as though into a dark wood, that he might never again utter a word. Then he sighed deeply. "I told you I wasn't kind."

She reached up to touch his cheek, her eyes shining. "No one could possibly be kinder. You've not only granted my wish, you're telling me I'll get to see them again. That I'll meet Alan again, and fall in love again, and hold my little Mouse in my arms, exactly as before. That *is* what you are saying, isn't it?"

He held both his hands wide, elegant fingers cupped to catch the sun. "You are that child in Central Park, off to see the lions. And I am an old man, half-asleep on a bench . . . from this point on the world proceeds just as it ever was, and only one thing, quite a bit ahead of today and really not worth talking about, will be any different. Please look in your pocket, child."

She reached into the front of her denim coverall, then, and smiled when she felt her four-year-old hand close around the silver horse. She took it out, and held it up to him as if she were offering a piece of candy.

"I don't know who you are, but I know what you are. You're something good."

"Nonsense," he said, but she could see he looked pleased. "And now . . ." The magician placed his vast, lined hands around hers, squeezed once, gently, and said, *"Forget."* When he took his hands away the silver horse was gone.

The little girl stood on the green grass, looking up at the old man with the closed eyes. He spoke to her. "Where are you off to, if I may ask?"

"I'm going to see the lions," she told him. "And the draffs. Draffs are excellent animals."

"So they are," the old man agreed, tilting his head down to look at her. His eyes, when he opened them, were the bluest she had ever seen.

OAKLAND DRAGON BLUES

Once upon a time I tried to do a straight-up trade with Ursula K. LeGuin—my unicorns for the dragons from her Earthsea series—because Ursula's dragons are *just that good*. Pretty much the definitive article, in fact, and there's an end on't.

She declined to accept my offer, of course. Smart woman. I mean, I'm happy enough with my unicorns these days; but I'm convinced that dragons should have been put off-limits to fantasists after Earthsea.

So you can imagine my surprise a couple of years ago when I found myself writing an entire novel full of dragons, just because an idea came along that intrigued me too much to ignore. Then, as if stepping over the line once wasn't risky enough, in a moment of rash confidence I agreed to tackle a story for a dragon-themed original anthology. I started by consciously resolving to go for something as different as possible from anything of Ursula's. My chosen setting was the forests of rural northern California. My chosen time was right now. My invented gimmick: the notion that if dragons existed, then the illegal meth labs and marijuana farms that hide in the forests of rural northern California would certainly find them more useful than mere pit bulls or Dobermans . . . but the story I wrote, about the animal control officers who have to handle such things, refused to come into sharp focus. A week before my deadline I knew I couldn't solve it in time, and prepared to send my friendly, patient editor an apologetic admission of defeat.

Then—as I'm always quoting Samuel Johnson's "When a man knows that he is to be hanged within a week, it concentrates his mind wonderfully"—I remembered that when I was 22, and taking my first failed crack at what eventually became *The Last Unicorn*, I'd included a particularly morose and colorful dragon in the opening chapter: a dragon that I had ruthlessly excised when I returned to work on the manuscript three years later.

With that thought, this story was born.

I've lived in the Oakland/Berkeley area for some years now, but I've loved it since I wandered in from Stanford (where I was *supposed* to be) around 1961. Under the *nom de l'imaginaire* of Avicenna, it has come to be a regular literary landscape of mine. The dragon of this story sets events in motion by plopping down at a particular intersection that I frequently walk to from my apartment. Now when I pass that crossroads I tend to stand for a little while on the corner and literally see him there: a part of my world that wasn't there before, and won't be going away.

As for the failed Dragon Control piece, the one set in modern-day Northern California, that took two more years of mulling to finally complete and publish. Stories have lives of their own, and we authors have less power over them than we'd like to imagine.

"I AM HAPPY TO REPORT," Officer Levinsky said to Officer Guerra, pointing to the dragon sprawled across the Telegraph and 51st Street intersection, "that this one is all yours. I've been off shift for exactly seven minutes, waiting for your ass to get here. Have a nice day."

Guerra stared, paling visibly under his brown skin. Traffic was backed up in all four directions: horns were honking as madly as car alarms, drivers were screaming hysterically—though none, he noticed, were getting out of their cars—and a five-man road crew, their drills, hoses, sawhorses and warning signs scattered by a single swing of the dragon's tail, were adding their bellows to the din. The dragon paid no attention to any of it, but regarded the two policemen out of half-closed eyes, resting its head on its long-clawed front feet, and every now and then burping feeble, dingy flames. It didn't look well.

"How long's it been here?" Guerra asked weakly.

Levinsky consulted his watch again. "Thirty-one minutes. Just plopped out of the sky—damn miracle it didn't crush somebody's car, flatten a pedestrian. Been lying there ever since, just like that."

"Well, you called it in, right?" Guerra wondered what the police code for a dragon in the intersection would be.

Levinsky looked at him as though he had suggested a fast game of one-on-one with an open manhole. "You *are* out of your mind—I always thought so. No, I didn't call it in, and if you have the sense of a chinch bug, you won't either. Just get rid of it, I'm out of here. Enjoy, Guerra."

Levinsky's patrol car was parked on the far side of the intersection. He skirted the dragon's tail cautiously, got in the car, slapped on his siren—for pure emotional relief, Guerra thought—and was gone, leaving Guerra scratching his buzz-cut head, facing both a growing traffic jam and a creature out of fairy tales, whose red eyes, streaked with pale yellow, like the eyes of very old men, were watching him almost sleepily, totally uninterested in whatever he chose to do. But watching, all the same.

The furious chaos of the horns being harder on Guerra's normally placid nerves than the existence of dragons, he walked over to the beast and said, from a respectful distance, "Sir, you're blocking traffic, and I'm going to have to ask you to move along. Otherwise you're looking at a major citation here."

When the dragon did not respond, he said it again in Spanish; then drew a deep breath and started over in Russian, having taken a course that winter in order to cope with a new influx of immigrants. The dragon interrupted him with a brief hiccup of oily, sulphurous flame halfway through. In a rusty, raspy voice with a faint accent that was none of the ones Guerra knew, it said, "Don't start."

Guerra rested his hand lightly on the butt of the pistol that he was immensely proud of never having fired during his eight years on the Oakland police force, except for his regular practice sessions and annual recertifications at the Davis Street Range. He said, "Sir, I am not trying to start anything with you—I'm having enough trouble just believing in you. But I've got to get you out of this intersection before somebody gets hurt. I mean, look at all those people, listen to those damn *horns*." The racket was already giving him a headache behind his eyes. "You think you could maybe step over here to the curb, we'll talk about it? That'd work out much better for both of us, don't you think?"

The dragon raised its head and favored him with a long, considering stare. "I don't know. I like this place about as well as I like any place in this world, which is not at all. Why should I make things easier for you? Nobody ever cares about making anything easier for *me*, let me tell you."

Guerra's greatest ambition in law enforcement was to become a hostage negotiator. He had been studying the technique on and off for most of his tenure on the force, both on site and through attending lectures and reading everything he could find on the subject. The lecturers and the books had a good deal to say concerning hostage-takers' tendency to self-pity. He said patiently to the dragon, "Well, I'm really trying to do exactly that. Let's get acquainted, huh? I'm Officer Guerra—Michael Guerra, but people mostly call me Mike-O, I don't know why. What's your name?" *Always get on a first-name basis, as early as possible. It makes you two human beings together—you'll be amazed at the difference it makes.* Now if only one of those books had ever covered the fine points of negotiating with a burping mythological predator.

"You couldn't pronounce it," the dragon replied. "And if you tried, you'd hurt yourself." But it rose to its feet with what seemed to Guerra an intense and even painful effort, and with some trepidation he led it away from the intersection to the side street where he had parked his blue-and-white patrol car. The traffic started up again before they were all the way across, and if people went on honking and cursing, still there were many who leaned out of their windows to applaud him. One driver shouted jovially, "Put the cuffs on him!" while another yelled, "Illegal parking—get the boot!" The dragon half-lumbered, half-slithered beside Guerra as sedately as though it were on a leash; but every so often it cocked a red eye sideways at him, like a wicked bird, and Guerra shivered with what felt like ancestral memory. *These guys used to hunt us like rabbits. I know they did.*

The phone at his waist made an irritable sound and rattled against his belt buckle. He nodded to the dragon, grunted, "My boss, I better take this," and heard Lieutenant Kunkel's nasal drone demanding, "Guerra, you there? Guerra, what the fuck is going on up in Little Ethiopia?" Lieutenant Kunkel fully expected Eritrean rebels to stage shootouts in Oakland sometime within the week.

"Big, nasty traffic jam, Lieutenant," Guerra answered, consciously keeping his voice light and level, even with a dragon sniffing disdainfully at his patrol car. "All under control now, no problem."

"Yeah, well, we've been getting a bunch of calls about I don't know what, some sort of crazy dragon, UFO, whatever? You know anything about this shit?"

"Uh," Guerra said. "Uh, no, Lieutenant, it's just the time of day, you know? Rush hour, traffic gets tied up, people get a little crazy, they start seeing stuff. Mass hysteria, shared hallucinations, it's real common. They got books about it."

Lieutenant Kunkel's reaction to the concept of shared hallucinations was not at first audible. Then it became audible, but not comprehensible. Finally coherent, he drew on a vocabulary that impressed Guerra so powerfully for its range and expressiveness that at a certain point, phone gripped between his ear and his shoulder, he dug out his notebook and started writing down the choicest words and phrases he caught. If anything, Guerra was a great believer in self-improvement.

The lieutenant finally hung up, and Guerra put the book back in his pocket and said to the dragon, "Okay. He's cool. You just go on away now, go on home, back wherever you . . . well, wherever, and we'll say no more about it. And you have an extra-nice day, hear?"

The dragon did not answer, but leaned against his car, considering him out of its strange red-and-yellow eyes. Huge as the creature was— Guerra had nothing but military vehicles for comparison—he thought it must be a very old dragon, for the scales on its body were a dull greenish-black, and its front claws were worn and blunt, no sharper than a turtle's. The long low purple crest running along its back from ears to tail tip was torn in several places, and lay limp and prideless. The spikes at the end of its tail were all broken off short; and in spite of the occasional wheeze of fire, there was a rattle in the dragon's breath, as though it were rusty inside. He supposed the great purple wings worked: it was hard to see them clearly, folded back along the body as they were, but they too looked . . . *ratty,* for lack of a better word. Spontaneously, he blurted out, "You've had kind of a rough time, huh? I get that."

"Do you?" The dragon's black lips twitched, and for a moment Guerra thought absurdly that it was going to cry. "Do you indeed, Mike-O? Do you *get* that my back's killing me—that it aches all the time, right there, behind the hump, because of the beating it takes walking the black iron roads of this world? Do you *get* that the smell of your streets—even your streams, your rivers, your bay—is more than I can bear? That your people taste like clocks and coal oil, and your children are bitter as silver? The children used to be the best eating of all, better than antelope, better than wild geese, but now I just can't bring myself to touch another one of them. Oh, it's been dogs and cats and mangy little squirrels for months, *years*—and when you think how I used to dine off steamed knight, knight on the half shell, broiled in his own armor with all the natural juices, oh . . . excuse me, excuse me, I'm sorry . . ."

And, rather to Guerra's horror, the dragon did begin to cry. He wept very softly, with his eyes closed and his head lowered, his emerald-green tears smelling faintly like gunpowder. Guerra said, "Hey. Hey, listen, don't do that. Please. Don't cry, okay?"

The dragon sniffled, but it lifted its head again to regard him in some wonder. Surprisingly severe, it said, "You are a witness to the rarest sight in the world—a dragon in tears—and all you can say is *don't do that?* I don't *get* you people at all." But it did stop crying; it even made a sound like rustling ashes, which Guerra thought might be a chuckle. It said, "Or did I embarrass you, Mike-O?"

"Listen," Guerra said again. "Listen, you've got to get out of here. There's going to be rumors for days, but I'll cover with the lieutenant, whoever, whatever I have to say. Just *go,* okay?" He hesitated for a moment, and then added, "Please?"

The dragon licked forlornly at its own tears with its broad forked tongue. "I'm tired, Mike-O. You have no idea how tired I am. I have one task to complete in this desolate world of yours, and then I'm done with it forever. And since I'll never, never find my way back to my own world again, what difference does anything make? Afterward . . . *afterward*, you and your boss can shoot me, take me to prison, put me in a zoo . . . what wretched difference? I just don't care anymore."

"No," Guerra said. "Look, I'll tell you the truth, I do not want to be the guy who brings you in. For starters, it'll mean more reports, more damn *bookkeeping* than I've ever seen in my life. I *hate* writing reports. And besides that . . . yeah, I guess I'd be famous for a while—fifteen minutes, like they say. The cop who caught the dragon . . . newspapers, big TV shows, fine and dandy, maybe I'd even meet some girls that way. But once it all died down, that's all I'd ever be, the guy who had the thing on the street with the dragon. You think that's a résumé for somebody wants to be a hostage negotiator? I don't think so."

The dragon was listening to him attentively, though with a slightly puzzled air. Guerra said, "Anyway, what's this about finding your way back to your own world? How'd you get here in the first place?"

"How did I *get* here?" To Guerra's astonishment and alarm, the dragon rumbled croupily, deep in its chest, and the ragged crest stood up as best it could, while the head seemed to cock back on its neck like the hammer on a pistol. A brief burst of fire shot from the fang-studded mouth, making Guerra scramble aside.

"That's easy," it said, tapping its claws on the asphalt. "I got written here."

Guerra was not at all sure that he had heard correctly. "You got . . . *written?*"

"Written *and* written out," the dragon rasped bitterly. "The author put me in his book right at the beginning, and then he changed his mind. Went back, redid the whole book, and *phhffttt*." More fire. Guerra ducked again, barely in time. "Gone, just like that. Not one line left—and I had some good ones, whole paragraphs. All gone."

"I'm having a very hard time with this," Guerra said. "So you're in a book—"

"*Was.* I *was* in a book—"

"—and now you're not. But you're real all the same, blocking traffic, breathing fire—"

"Art is a remarkable creative force," the dragon said. "I exist because a man made up a story." It mentioned the writer's name, which was not one Guerra knew. "I'm stranded here, loose and wandering in his world because he decided not to write about me after all." It bared double rows of worn but quite serviceable teeth in a highly unpleasant grin. "But I'm real, I'm here, and I'm looking for him. Followed him from one place to another for years—the man does move around—and finally tracked him to this Oakland. I don't know exactly where he lives, but I'll find him. And when I do he is going to be one crispy author, believe me." It snorted in anticipation, but Guerra had already taken refuge behind the patrol car. The dragon said, "I told you, after that I don't care what happens to me. I can't ever get home, so what does it matter?"

Its voice trembled a little on the last words, and Guerra worried that it might be about to start weeping again. He edged cautiously out from the shelter of the car and said, "Well, you sure as hell won't get back home if you fry up the one guy who maybe can help you. You ever think about that?"

The long neck swiveled, and the dragon stared at him, its eyes red and yellow, like hunters' moons. Guerra said, "He lives in Oakland, this writer? Okay, I'll find out the address—that's one thing cops are really good at, tracing people's addresses—"

"And you'll tell me?" The dragon's whole vast body was quivering with eagerness. "You would do that?"

"No," Guerra said flatly. "Not for a minute. Because you'd zip right off after him, and be picking your teeth by the time I got off my shift. So you're going to wait until I'm done here, and we'll find him together. Deal?" The dragon was clearly dubious. Guerra said, "Deal—or I won't give you his address, but I *will* tell him you're looking for him. And he'll move again, sure as hell—I would. Think about it."

The dragon thought. At last it sighed deeply, exhaling tear-damp ashes, and rumbled, "Very well. I'll wait for you on that sign." Guerra watched in fascination as the shabby purple wings unfolded. Worn claws scrabbling on the sidewalk, the beast took a few running steps before it lifted into the air. A moment later it landed neatly on the top frame of a billboard advertising a movie that apparently had a mermaid, a vampire and a giant octopus in the cast. The dragon posed there all during Guerra's shift, looking like part of the promotion, and if it moved even an inch he never saw it.

The road crew was back at work, and the intersection was in serious need of a patrolman. Both streets were torn up, the traffic lights were all off, and Guerra had his hands full beckoning cars forward and holding them up, keeping drivers away from closed-off lanes and guiding them around potholes. It kept his mind, as nothing else could have, almost completely off the dragon; although he did manage, during a comparative lull, to call in for the current address of the writer who had carelessly created the creature and then forgotten about it. *Like God, maybe*, Guerra thought, then decided he might not mention that notion to Father Fabros on Sunday.

His shift ended in twilight; the traffic had noticeably thinned by then, and he felt comfortable turning the intersection over to Officer Colasanto, who was barely in his second year. Walking to his car, Guerra gestured to the dragon, and it promptly took off from the billboard, climbing toward the night clouds with a speed and elegance he had never imagined from those ragged wings and age-tarnished body. Once again the bone-image came to him of such creatures stooping from the sky at speeds his ancestors could not have comprehended before it was too late. He shivered, and hurriedly got into the patrol car.

He checked in at the police station, joking amiably with friends about the morning's dragon alarm—neither Lieutenant Kunkel nor Officer Levinsky was present—changed into civilian clothes, and hurried back out, anxious lest the dragon should become anxious. But he saw no sign of it, and had to assume that it was following him beyond his sight, hungry enough for revenge that it was not likely to lose track of him. Not for the first time, Guerra wondered what had possessed him to take sides in this mess, and which side he was actually on.

The dragon's author lived in North Berkeley, past the chic restaurants of the Gourmet Ghetto, and on out into the classic older houses, "full of character," as the real-estate agents liked to put it, if a little short on reliable plumbing. Guerra found the house easily enough—it had two stories, a slightly threadbare lawn and a tentative garden—and pulled into the driveway, expecting the dragon, in its fury and fervency, to land beside him before he was out of the car. But he only glimpsed it once, far above him, circling with chilling patience between the clouds. A motion-detector floodlight came on as Guerra walked up the driveway and rang the bell.

The author answered with surprising quickness. He was a middle-sized, undistinguished-looking man: bearded, wearing glasses, and clad in jeans, an old sweatshirt, and sneakers that had clearly been through two or three major civil conflicts. He blinked at Guerra and said "Hi? What can I do for you?"

Guerra showed his badge. "Sir, I'm Officer Michael Guerra, Oakland Police, and I need to speak with you for a moment." He felt himself blushing absurdly, and was glad that the light was gone.

The author was sensibly wary, checking Guerra's badge carefully before answering. "I've paid that Jack London Square parking ticket."

Guerra had just started to say, "This isn't exactly a police matter," when, with a terrifyingly silent rush—the only sound was the soft whistle of wind through the folded wings—the dragon landed in the tentative garden and hissed, "Remember me, storyteller? Scribe, singer, sorcerer—*remember me?*"

The author froze where he stood in the doorway, neither able to come forward nor run back into his house. He whispered, "No. You can't be here . . . you can't *be* . . . " He did not seem able to close his mouth, and he was hugging himself, as though for protection.

The dragon sneered foul-smelling flames. "Come closer, you hairy hot pocket. I'd rather not singe your nice house when I incinerate you."

Guerra said, "Wait a minute now, just a minute. We didn't talk about any incineration. No incineration here."

The dragon looked at him for the first time since it had landed. It said, "Stop me."

Guerra's gun was in the car, but even if he could have reached it, it would have been no more practical use than a spitball. His mouth was dry, and his throat hurt.

Remarkably, the author stood his ground. He spoke directly to the dragon, saying, "I didn't write you out of the book. I dropped the damn book altogether—I didn't know how to write it, and I was making an unholy mess out of it. So I dropped a lot of people, not just you. How come you're the only one hunting me down and threatening my life? Why is this all about *you?*"

The dragon's head swooped low enough to be almost on a level with the writer's, and so close that a bit of his beard did get singed. But its voice was colder than Guerra had ever heard it when it said, "Because you wrote enough life into me that I deserved more. I deserved a *resolution*—even if you killed me off in the end, that would have been *something*—and when I didn't get it, I still had this leftover life, and no world to live it in. So of course, of course I have been trapped in your world ever since—miserable dungheap that it is, there is no other place for me to exist. And no other emotion, out of all I might have had . . . but revenge."

Its head and neck cocked back then, as Guerra had seen them do before, and he turned and sprinted for his car and the useless gun. But he tripped over a loose brick from the garden border, fell full length, and lay half-stunned, hearing—to his dazed surprise—the voice of the author saying commandingly, "Hold it, just hold the phone here, before you go sautéing people. You're angry because I didn't create a suitable world for you, is that it?"

The dragon did not answer immediately. Guerra struggled wearily to his feet, looking back and forth between the house and his car. A family across the street—a man in a bathrobe, his small Indian wife in a sari, and a young boy wearing Spider-Man pajamas—were standing barefoot on their own lawn, clearly staring at the dragon. The man called out, loudly but hesitantly, "Hey, you okay over there?"

Guerra was still trying to decide on his response, when he heard the dragon say in a different tone, "No, I'm angry because you did. You made up a fairy tale that I belonged in, and then you destroyed it and left me *outside*, in this terrible, terrible place that I can't escape. And I never *will* escape it, I know, except by dying, and we dragons live such a long time. But if I avenge myself now, as you deserve"—it swung its head briefly toward Guerra—"then policemen like *him* will in turn kill me, sooner or later. And it will be over."

"SWAT teams," Guerra said, trying to sound stern and ominous. "Whole patrols. Divisions. Bomb Squad, FBI, the Air Force—"

"Hold it!" The author was very nearly shouting. "That's it? That's your problem with me?" He held his hands up, palm out, looked at them, and began rubbing them together. "Give me five minutes—*three* minutes—I'll be right back, I'll just get something. Right back."

He turned and started toward the house, but a fireball neatly seared a stripe of lawn at his feet. The dragon said, "You stay. *He* goes."

The author looked down at the crumbling, crackling grass, then turned to Guerra. "Through the door—sharp left—turn right, straight through the other door. My office. Notebook beside the laptop, Betty Grable on the cover, you can't miss it. Grab that, grab a couple of pens, get back out here before he trashes the landscaping. You know how much it cost to put this lawn in?"

But Guerra was already at the door. He hurried through to the office as directed, snatched up notebook and pens, paused for a moment to marvel at the books and electronics, the boxes of paper and printer cartridges, the alphabetized manuscripts in their separate folders— *this is how they live, this is a real writer's workroom*—and raced back out to the lawn, where the author and his creation were eyeing each other in wary silence. Guerra was relieved to see that the dragon's head and neck were relaxed from the attack position, and horrified to realize that the neighboring family—with the addition of a smaller boy in Batman pajamas—were now standing at the edge of their lawn, while a girl coasting on in-line skates was gliding up the driveway, and a large man with a pipe in his mouth, who looked like a retired colonel in a movie, was striding across the street as though to direct the catapults. The larger of the two boys was telling his brother learnedly, "That's a *dragon*. I saw one on the Discovery Channel." *I could have switched shifts with Levinsky, like we were talking about the other day . . .*

"Thanks," the author said, taking the writing materials from Guerra's hands. Ignoring the growing assembly on his lawn and his driveway, and the cricketlike chirps of cell-phone cameras, he sat down cross-legged on his own doorstep and propped the open notebook on his knee. "I did this in Macy's window one time," he remarked conversationally. "For the ERA or the EPA, one of those." He rubbed his chin, muttered something inaudible, and began to write, reading aloud as he went.

Once upon a time, in a faraway place, there lived a king whose daughter fell in love with a common gardener. The king was so outraged at this that he imprisoned the princess in a high tower and set a ferocious dragon to guard her.

The dragon slithered closer and craned its neck, reading over his shoulder. The author continued.

But the dragon, fierce as it was, had a tender, sympathetic heart, greatly unlike the rest of its kind—

"I don't like that," the dragon interrupted. "'The rest of its kind'—it sounds condescending, even a touch bigoted. Why not just say *family*, or 'the rest of its kinfolk'? Much better tone, *I* think."

"Everybody's a critic," the author mumbled. "All right, all right, *kinfolk*, then." He made the correction. The man who looked like a colonel was standing beside another man who looked like a hungover Santa Claus, and the Indian mother was gripping her sons' shoulders to hold both boys exactly where they were.

The author continued.

Now the dragon could not set the princess free against her father's orders, but it did what it could for her. It kept her company, engaging her in cheerful, intelligent conversation, comforting her when she was sad, and even singing to her in her most depressed moments, which would always make her laugh, since dragons are not very good singers.

He hesitated, as though expecting some argument or annoyed comment from the dragon, but it only nodded in agreement. "True enough. We love music, but not one of us can sing a lick. Go on." Its voice was surprisingly slow and thoughtful, and—so it seemed to Guerra—almost dreamy.

> *But what the princess valued most, of all the dragon's kindnesses, was that when her gardener lover had managed to smuggle a letter to her, the dragon would at once fly up to her barred window and hover there, like any butterfly or hummingbird, to pass the letter to her and wait to carry her rapturous reply.*

He paused again and looked up at the dragon. "You won't mind if I make you a little bit smaller? Just for the sake of the hovering?"

With a graciousness that Guerra would never have expected, the dragon replied, "You're the artist—do as you think best." After a moment it added, a bit shyly, "If you wanted, you could do something with my crest. That would be all right."

"Easy. Might touch up your scales some, too—nobody's quite as young as they used to be." He worked on, still reading softly, as much to himself as to them. What struck Guerra most forcefully was that his was very nearly the only voice in the crowded darkness, except for one of the small boys—"Dragons *eat* people! He eat those men *up!*"— and the roller-skating girl sighing to a boy who had joined her, "This is *so* cool . . ." Guerra gestured at them all to move back, but no one appeared to notice. If anything, they seemed to be leaning in, somehow yearning toward the magnificently menacing figure that loomed over the man who still sat tailor-fashion, telling it a story about itself.

> *Now when the king came to visit his imprisoned child— which, to be as fair to him as possible, he did quite often— the dragon would always put on his most terrifying appearance and strut around the foot of the tower, to show the king how well he was fulfilling his charge . . .*

43

To Guerra's astonishment the dragon appeared not only somewhat smaller, but younger as well. Before his eyes, slowly but plainly, the faded greenish-black scales were regaining their original dark-green glitter, and the tattered crest and drab, frayed wings were springing back to proud fullness. The dragon rumbled experimentally, and the fire that lapped around its fangs—like the great claws, no longer worn dull—was the deep red, laced with rich yellow, that such fire should be. Guerra stared back and forth between this new glory and the ball-point pen on the Betty Grable notebook, and no longer wished to have switched shifts with Officer Levinsky.

But beyond such wonders, the most marvelous change of all was that the dragon was beginning to fade, to lose definition around the edges and grow steadily more transparent until Guerra thought he could see his car through it, and the lights of houses across the street, and the rising moon. After a moment, though, he realized he was wrong. The lights were plainly coming from a number of low-roofed huts that clustered in the shadows at the base of a soap-bubble castle, and what he had taken for his car was in fact nothing but a rickety haywagon. The vision extended on all sides: whichever way he turned, there was only the reality of the huts and the castle and the deep woods beyond. And one of the castle towers had a single barred window, with a face glimmering behind it. . . .

"Yes," said the dragon. For all its increasing dimness, its voice had grown as powerful and clear as a mountain waterfall. "Yes . . . yes . . . that was just how it was. *How it is . . .*"

The sense of one common breath being drawn and exhaled was abruptly broken by a soft wail, "Dragon gone!" and the little boy in the Batman pajamas suddenly shrugged free of his mother's grip and came racing across the street and the lawn. "*Dragon gone!*" Guerra made a dive for him, but missed, and was almost trampled by the boy's father. The whiskey-faced Santa Claus came charging after.

With the persistence and determination of a rabbit heading for his hole, the boy shot between several sets of legs straight for the splendid shadow that was fading so swiftly now. He tripped, skidded on his seat and looked up at the mighty head and neck, wings and crest, fading so swiftly against a sky of castles and stars. "Dragon gone?" It was a forlorn question now.

The head came slowly down, lowering over the boy, who sat unafraid as the dragon studied him lingeringly. Guerra remembered—shadow or no shadow—the dragon's comments on the heart-melting tastiness of children. But then the boy's father had him in his arms and was sweeping him off, darkly threatening to sue *somebody*, there had to be *someone*. And the dragon was indeed gone.

The castle was gone too; and so, in time, went most of the author's neighbors, hushed and wondering. But some stayed a while, for no reason they could have explained, coming closer to the house merely to stand where the dragon had been. Several of those spoke diffidently to the author; Guerra saw others surreptitiously pluck up grass blades, both burned and untouched, plainly as souvenirs.

When the last of that group had finally wandered off, the author closed the notebook, capped the pen, stood up, stretched elaborately and said, "Well. Coffee?"

Guerra rubbed his aching forehead, feeling the way he sometimes did when, falling asleep, he suddenly lunged awake out of a half-dream of stumbling down a step that wasn't there. He said feebly, "Where did he go?"

"Oh, into that story," the author answered lightly. "The story I was making up for him."

"But you didn't finish it," Guerra said.

"He will. It's his fairy tale world, after all—he knows it better than I do, really. I just showed him the way back." The author smiled with a certain aggravating compassion. "It's a bit hard to explain, if you don't— you know—*think* much about magic."

"Hey, I think about a lot of things," Guerra said harshly. "And what I'm thinking about right now is that that's wasn't a real story. It's not in any book—you were just spitballing, improvising, making it up as you went along. Hell, I'll bet you couldn't repeat it right now if you tried. Like a little kid telling a lie."

The author laughed outright, and then stopped quickly when he saw Guerra's expression. "I'm sorry, I'm not laughing at you. You're quite right, we're all little kids telling lies, writers are, hoping we can keep the lies straight and get away with them. And nobody lasts very long in this game who isn't prepared to lie his way out of trouble. Absolutely right." He regarded the ruined strip of lawn and winced visibly. "But you make the same mistake most people do, Officer Guerra. The magic's not in books, not in the publishing—it's in the telling, always. In the old, old telling."

He looked at his watch and yawned. "Actually, there might *be* a book in that one, I don't know. Have to think about it. What about that coffee?"

"I'm off duty," Guerra said. "You got any beer?"

"I'm off duty too," the author said. "Come on in."

THE ROCK IN THE PARK

In 2008 *The Green Man Review*, a delightful online magazine of fantasy, music, folklore, and much indescribable else, asked me to create and record four seasonally-themed podcasts. I wound up writing five, all of them revisiting the world of my Bronx 1950s childhood, taking my three oldest friends and myself from the age of eleven or so to the summer we all turned fifteen, with inevitable separation and the great world beyond Gunhill Road looming ahead.

This story was the Fall entry in the series, and I'll swear to my grave that it really did happen just like this, back when Phil Sigunick and I were thirteen. Some things you can't make up.

V AN CORTLANDT PARK begins a few blocks up Gunhill Road: past the then-vacant lot where us neighborhood kids fought pitched battles over the boundaries of our parents' Victory Gardens; past Montefiore Hospital, which dominates the entire local skyline now; past Jerome Avenue, where the IRT trains still rattle overhead, and wicked-looking old ladies used to sit out in front of the kosher butcher shops, savagely plucking chickens. It's the fourth-largest park in New York City, and on its fringes there are things like golf courses, tennis courts, baseball diamonds, bike and horse trails, a cross-country track and an ice-skating rink—even a cricket pitch. That's since my time, the cricket pitch.

But the heart of Van Cortlandt Park is a deep old oak forest. Inside it you can't hear the traffic from any direction—the great trees simply swallow the sound—and the place doesn't seem to be in anybody's flight path to JFK or LaGuardia. There are all sorts of animals there, especially black squirrels, which I've never seen anywhere else; and possums and rabbits and raccoons. I saw a coyote once, too. Jake can call it a dog all he likes. I know better.

It's most beautiful in fall, that forest, which I admit only grudgingly now. Mists and mellow fruitfulness aren't all that comforting when bloody school's starting again, and no one's ever going to compare the leaf-changing season in the Bronx to the shamelessly flamboyant dazzle of October New Hampshire or Vermont, where the trees seem to turn overnight to glass, refracting the sunlight in colors that actually hurt your eyes and confound your mind. Yet the oak forest of Van Cortlandt Park invariably, reliably caught fire every year with the sudden *whoosh* of a building going up, and it's still what I remember when someone says the word *autumn*, or quotes Keats.

It was all of Sherwood to me and my friends, that forest.

Phil and I had a rock in Van Cortlandt that belonged to us; we'd claimed it as soon as we were big enough to climb it easily, which was around fourth grade. It was just about the size and color of an African elephant, and it had a narrow channel in its top that fit a skinny young body perfectly. Whichever one of us got up there first had dibs: the loser had to sit beside. It was part of our private mythology that we had worn that groove into the rock ourselves over the years, but of course that wasn't true. It was just another way of saying *get your own rock, this is ours.* There are whole countries that aren't as territorial as adolescent boys.

We'd go to our Rock after school, or on weekends—always in the afternoons, by which time the sun would have warmed the stone surface to a comfortable temperature—and we'd lie on our backs and look up through the leaves and talk about painters Phil had just discovered, writers I was in love with that week, and girls neither of us quite knew how to approach. We never fixated on the same neighborhood vamp, which was a good thing, because Phil was much more aggressive and experienced than I. Both of us were highly romantic by nature, but I was already a *princesse lointaine* fantasist, while Phil had come early to the understanding that girls were human beings like us. I couldn't see how that could possibly be true, and we argued about it a good deal.

One thing we never spoke of, though, was our shared awareness that the oak forest was magic. Not that we ever expected to see fairies dancing in a ring there, or to spy from our warm, safe perch anything like a unicorn, a wizard or a leprechaun. We knew better than *that*: as a couple of New Yorkers, born and bred, cynicism was part of our bone marrow. Yet even so, in our private hearts we always expected something wild and extraordinary from our Rock and our forest. And one hot afternoon in late September, when we were thirteen, they delivered.

That afternoon, I had been complaining about the criminal unfairness of scheduling a subway World Series, between the Yankees and the Dodgers, during school hours, except for the weekend, when there would be no chance of squeezing into little Ebbets Field. Phil, no baseball fan, dozed in the sun, grunting a response when absolutely required ("Love to do a portrait of Casey Stengel; *there's* a face!"). I was spitballing ways to sneak a portable radio and earpiece into class, so I could follow the first game, when we heard the hoofbeats. In itself, that wasn't unusual—there was a riding stable on the western edge of the Park—but there was a curious hesitancy and wariness about the sound that had us both sitting up on our Rock, and me saying excitedly, "Deer!"

These days, white-tail deer dropping by to raid your vegetable garden are as common in the North Bronx as rabbits and squirrels. Back then, back when I knew Felix Salten's *Bambi* books by heart, they were still an event. But Phil shook his head firmly. "Horse. You don't hear deer."

True enough: like cats, deer are just *there*, where they weren't a moment before. And now that it was closer, it didn't sound like a deer to my city ears—nor quite like a horse, either. We waited, staring toward a grove of smaller trees, young sycamores, where something neither of us could quite make out was moving slowly down the slope. Phil repeated, "Horse—look at the legs," and lay back again. I was just about to do the same when the creature's head came into view.

49

It didn't register at first; it couldn't have done. In that first moment what I saw—what I allowed myself to see—was a small boy riding a dark-bay horse not much bigger than a colt. Then, somewhere around the time that I heard myself whisper "Jesus *Christ,*" I realized that neither the boy nor the horse was *that* small, and that the boy wasn't actually riding. The two of them were *joined,* at the horse's shoulders and just below the boy's waist. In the Bronx, in Van Cortlandt Park, in the twentieth century—in our little lives—a centaur.

They must operate largely on sight, as we do, because the boy only became aware of us just after we spotted him. He halted instantly, his expression a mix of open-mouthed curiosity and real terror—then whirled and was gone, out of sight between the great trees. His hoof-beats were still fading on the dead leaves while we stared at each other.

Phil said flatly, "Just leave me out of your hallucinations, okay? You got weird hallucinations."

"This from a person who still thinks Linda Darnell's hot stuff? You know what we saw."

"I never. I wasn't even here."

"Okay. Me neither. I got to get home." I slid down off the Rock, picking up my new schoolbook bag left at its base. Less than a month, and already my looseleaf notebook looked as though I'd been teething on it.

Phil followed. "Hell, no, it was your figment, you can't just leave it on a doorstep and trust to the kindness of strangers." We'd seen the Marlon Brando *Streetcar Named Desire* a year earlier, and were still bellowing "STELLA!!!" at odd moments in the echoing halls of Junior High School 80. "You saw it, you saw it, I'm gonna tell—Petey saw a centaur—*nyaahh, nyaahh,* Petey saw a centaur!" I swung the book bag at him and chased him all the way out of the Park.

On the phone that evening—we were theoretically doing our biology homework together—he asked, "So what do the Greek myths tell you about centaurs?"

"Main thing, they can't hold their liquor, and they're mean drunks. You don't ever want to give a centaur that first beer."

"I'll remember. What else?"

"Well, the Greeks have two different stories about where they came from, but I can't keep them straight, so forget it. In the legends they're aggressive, always starting fights—there was a big battle with the Lapiths, who were some way their cousins, except human, don't ask, and I think most of the centaurs were killed, I'm not sure. But some of them were really good, really noble, like Cheiron. Cheiron was the best of the lot, he was a healer and an astrologer and a teacher—he was the tutor of people like Odysseus, Achilles, Hercules, Jason, Theseus, all those guys." I paused, still thumbing through the worn Modern Library Bulfinch my father had given me for my tenth birthday. "That's all I know."

"Mmmff. Book say anything about centaurs turning up in the Bronx? I'll settle for the Western Hemisphere."

"No. But there was a shark in the East River, a couple of years back, you remember? Cops went out in a boat and shot at it."

"Not the same thing." Phil sighed. "I still think it's your fault, somehow. What really pisses me off, I didn't have so much as a box of Crayolas to draw the thing with. Probably never get another chance."

But he did: not the next day, when, of course, we cut P.E. and hurried back to the Park, but the day after that, which was depressingly chilly, past pretending that it was still Indian Summer. We didn't talk much: I was busy scanning for centaurs (I'd brought my Baby Brownie Special camera and a pair of binoculars), and Phil, mumbling inaudibly to himself, kept rummaging through his sketch pads and colored pencils, pastels, gouaches, charcoals and crayons. I made small jokes about his equipment almost crowding me off the Rock, and he glared at me in a way that made me uneasy about that "almost."

I don't remember how long we waited, but it must have been close to two hours. The sun was slanting down, the Rock's surface temperature was actually turning out-and-out cold, and Phil and I were well past conversation when the centaurs came. There were three of them: the young one we had first seen, and the two who were clearly his parents, to judge by the way they stood together on the slope below the sycamore grove. They made no attempt to conceal themselves, but looked direct-ly at us, as we stared back at them. After a long moment, they started down the slope together.

Phil was shaking with excitement, but even so he was already sketching as they came toward us. I was afraid to raise my camera, for fear of frightening the centaurs away. They had a melancholy dignity about them, even the child, that I didn't have words for then: I recall it now as an air of royal exile, of knowing where they belonged, and knowing, equally, that they could never return there. The male—no, the *man*—had a short, thick black beard, a dark, strong-boned face, and eyes of a strange color, like honey. The woman . . .

Remember, all three of them were naked to the waist, and Phil and I were thirteen years old. For myself, I'd seen nude models in my uncles' studios since childhood, but this woman, this *centauride* (I looked the word up when I got home that night), was more beautiful than anyone I knew. It wasn't just a matter of round bare breasts: it was the heart-breaking grace of her neck, the joyous purity of the line of her shoulders, the delicacy of her collarbones. Phil had stopped sketching, which tells you more than I can about what we saw.

The boy had freckles. Not big ones, just a light golden dusting. His hair was the same color, with a kind of reddish undercoloring, like his mother's hair. He looked about ten or eleven.

The man said, "Strangers, of your kindness, might either of you be Jersey Turnpike?"

He had a deep, calm voice, with absolutely no horsiness in it—noth-ing of a neigh or a whinny, or anything like that. Maybe a slight sort of funny gurgle in the back of the throat, but hardly noticeable—you'd really have to be listening for it. When Phil and I just gaped, the woman said, "We have never come this way south before. We are lost."

Her voice was low, too, but it had a singing cadence to it, a warm offbeat lilt that entranced and seduced both of us even beyond her innocent nudity. I managed to say, "South . . . you want to go south . . . um, you mean south like down south? Like *south* south?"

"Like Florida?" Phil asked. "Mexico?"

The man lifted his head sharply. "Mexico, yes, that was the name, I always forget. It is where we go, all of us, every year, when the birds go. *Mexico.*"

"But we set out too late," the woman explained in her soft, singing voice. "Our son was ill, and we traveled eastward to seek out a healer, and by the time we were ready to start, all the others were gone—"

"And Father took the wrong road," the boy broke in, his tone less accusatory than excited. "We have had such adventures—"

His mother quelled him with a glance. Embarrassment didn't sit easily on the man's powerful face, but he flushed and nodded. "More than one. I do not know this country, and we are used to traveling in company. Now I am afraid that we are completely lost, except for that one name someone gave me—Jersey Turnpike. Can Jersey Turnpike lead us to Mexico?"

We looked at each other. Phil said, "Jersey Turnpike isn't a person, it's a road, a highway. You can go south that way, but not to Mexico— you're way off course for Mexico. I'm sorry."

The boy mumbled, "I *knew* it," but not in a triumphant, wise-ass sort of way; if anything, he appeared suddenly very weary of adventures. The man looked utterly stricken. He bowed his head, and the color seemed to fade visibly from his bright chestnut coat. The woman's manner, on the other hand, hardly altered with Phil's news, except that she moved closer to her husband and pressed her light-gray flank against his, in a gesture of silent trust and confidence.

"You're too far east," I said. "You have to cut down through Texas." They stared uncomprehendingly. I said, "Texas—I *think* you'd go by way of Pennsylvania, Tennessee, maybe Georgia . . ." I stopped, because I couldn't bear the growing fatigue and bewilderment in their three faces, nor in the way their shining bodies sagged a little more with each state name. I told them, "What you need is a map. We could bring you one tomorrow, easy."

But their expressions did not change. The man said, "We cannot read."

"Not now," the woman said wistfully. "There was a time when our folk were taught the Greek in colthood, every one, and some learned the Latin as well, when it became necessary. But that was in another world that is no more . . . and learning unused fades with long years. Now only a few of our elders know letters enough to read such things as maps in your tongue—the rest of us journey by old memory and starlight. Like the birds."

Her own eyes were different from her husband's honey-colored eyes: more like dark water, with deep-green wonder turning and glinting far down. Phil never could get them right, and he tried for a long time.

He said quietly now, "I could draw you a picture."

I can't say exactly how the centaurs reacted, or how they looked at him. I was too busy gawking at him myself. Phil said, "Of your route, your road. I could draw you something that'll get you to Mexico."

The man started to speak, but Phil anticipated him. "Not a map. I said a *picture*. No words." I remember that he was sitting cross-legged on the Rock, like our idea of a swami or a yogi; and I remember him leaning intensely forward, toward the centaurs, so that he seemed almost to be joined to the Rock, growing out of it, as they were joined to their horse bodies. He was already drawing invisible pictures with his right forefinger on the palm of his left hand, but I don't think he knew it.

I opened *my* mouth then, but he cut me off too. "It'll take me all day tomorrow, and most likely all night too. You'll be okay till the day after tomorrow?"

The woman said to Phil, "You can do this?"

He grinned at her with what seemed to me outrageous confidence. "I'm an artist. Artists are always drawing people's journeys."

I said, "You could wait right here, if you like. We hardly ever see anybody but us in this part of the park. I mean, if it would suit you," for it occurred to me that I had no idea what they ate, or indeed how they survived in the twentieth century. "I guess we could bring you food."

The man's teeth showed white and large in his black beard. "The forage here is most excellent, even this late in the year."

"There are lots of acorns," the boy said eagerly. "I love acorns."

His mother turned her dark gaze to me. "Can you also make such pictures?"

"Never," I said. "But I could maybe write you a poem." I wrote a lot of poems for girls when I was thirteen. She seemed pleased.

Phil was gathering his equipment and scrambling off the Rock, imperiously beckoning me to follow. "Quit fooling around, Beagle. We got work to do." Standing among them, the size and sheer presence of all three centaurs was, if not intimidating, definitely daunting. Even the boy looked down at us, and we barely came up to the shoulders of his parents' horse-bodies. I've always enjoyed the smell of horses—in those days, they were among the very few animals I wasn't allergic to—but centaurs in groups smell like thunder, like an approaching storm, and it left me dizzy and a bit disoriented. Phil repeated briskly, "Day after tomorrow, right here."

We were halfway up the slope when he snapped his fingers, said, "Ah, *shit!*", dropped his equipment and went running back toward the centaurs. I waited, watching as he moved swiftly between the three of them; but I couldn't, for the life of me, make out what he was doing. He came back almost as quickly, and I noticed then that he was tucking something into his shirt pocket. When I asked what it was, he told me it was nothing I needed to trouble my pretty little head about. You couldn't do anything with him in those tempers, so I left it alone.

He didn't say much else on the walk home, and I managed to keep my curiosity in check until we were parting at my apartment building. Then I burst out with it: "Okay, you're going to draw them a picture that's going to get a family of migrating centaurs all the way to Mexico. This, excuse me, I want to hear." His being on the hook meant, as always, *us* being on the hook, so I felt entitled to my snottiness.

"I can do it. It's been done." His jaw was tight, and his face had the ferocious pallor that I associated entirely with street fights, usually with fat Stewie Hauser and Miltie Mellinger, who never tired of baiting him. "Back in the Middle Ages, I read about it—Roger Bacon did it, somebody like that. But you have to get me some maps, as many as you can. A *ton* of maps, a *shitload* of maps, covering every piece of ground between here—right here, your house—and the Texas border. You got that? *Maps.* Also, you should stop by Bernardo's and see can you borrow that candle of his mother's. He says she got it from a *bruja*, back in San Juan, what could it hurt?"

"But if they can't read maps—"

"Beagle, I have been extraordinarily lenient about that two bucks—"

"Maps. Right. Maps. You think they came down from Canada? Summer up north, winter in Mexico? I bet that's what they do."

"*Maps*, Beagle."

The next day was Saturday, and he actually called me around seven in the morning, demanding that I get my lazy ass on the road and start finding some maps for him. I said certain useful things that I had picked up from Angel Salazar, my Berlitz in such affairs, and was at the gas station up the block by 7:30. By 10:00, I'd hit every other station I could reach on my bike, copped my parents' big Rand McNally road atlas, and triumphantly dumped them all—Bernardo's mother's witch-candle included—on Phil's bed, demanding, "*Now* what, fearless leader?"

"Now you take Dusty for her morning walk." He had his favorite easel set up, and was rummaging through his paper supplies. "Then you go away and write your poem, and you come back when it's time to take Dusty for her evening walk. Then you go away again. All well within your capacities."

Dusty was his aged cocker spaniel, and the nearest thing I had to the longed-for dog of my own. I went home after tending to her, and sat down at the desk in my bedroom to write the poem I'd promised to the centaur mother. I still remember the first lines:

> If I were a hawk,
> I would write you letters—

featherheaded jokes,
scribbled on the air.
If I were a dog
I would do your shopping.
If I were a cat
I would brush your hair.
If I were a bear,
I would build your fires,
bringing in the wood,
breaking logs in two.
If I were a camel
I'd take out the garbage.
If I were a fox
I would talk to you . . .

There was more and sillier, but never mind. I was very romantic at thirteen, on very short notice, and I had never seen beauty like hers.

Okay, a little bit extra, because I do like the way it ended:

If I were a tiger,
I would dance for you.
If I were a mouse,
I would dance for you.
If I were a whale,
I would dance for you . . .

When I came back in the evening to walk Dusty again, Phil was working in his bedroom with the door closed, and an unattended dinner plate cooling on the sill. His parents were more or less inured to his habits by now, but it fretted at them constantly, just as my unsociability worried my mother, who would literally bribe Phil and Jake to get me out of the house. I reassured them, as I always did, that he was working on a really demanding, really challenging project, then grabbed

57

up dog and leash and was gone. It was dark when I brought her back, but Phil's door was still shut.

As it was the next morning, and remained until mid-afternoon, when he called me to say, "Done. Get over here."

He sounded awful.

He looked worse. His eyes were smudgy red pits in a face so white that his own small freckles stood out, and he moved like an old man, as though no part of his body could be trusted not to hurt. He said, "Let's go."

"You're kidding. You wouldn't make it to Lapin's." That was the candy-and-newspaper store across the street. "Take a nap, for God's sake, we'll go when you wake up."

"*Now.*" When he cleared his throat, it sounded exactly like my father's car trying to start on a cold morning.

He was holding a metal tube that I recognized as a tennis-ball can. I reached for it, but he snatched it away. "You'll see it when *they* see it." Just then, he didn't look like anyone I'd ever known.

So we trudged to Van Cortlandt Park, which seemed to take the rest of the afternoon, as slowly as Phil was walking. He had clearly been sitting in more or less the same position for hours and hours on end, and the cramps weren't turning loose without a fight. Now and then he paused to shake his arms and legs violently, and by the time we reached the Park, he was moving a little less stiffly. But he still hardly spoke, and he clung to that tennis-ball can as though it were a cherished trophy, or a life raft.

The centaurs were waiting at the Rock. The boy, a little way up the forest slope from his parents, saw us first, and called out, "They're here!" as he galloped to meet us. But he turned shy midway, as children will, and ran back to the others as we approached. I remember that the man had his arms folded across his chest, and that there were a couple of dew-damp patches on the *centauride's* coat, the weather having turned cloudy. They said nothing.

Phil said, "I brought it. What I promised. Here, I'll show you."

They moved close, plainly careful not to crowd him with their bodies, as he opened the air-tight can and took out a roll of light, flexible drawing paper. He handed the free end to the man, saying, "See? There you are, all three of you. And there's your road to Mexico."

Craning my neck, I could see a perfectly rendered watercolor of the oak forest, so detailed that I saw not only our Rock with its long groove along the top surface, but also such things as the bird's nest in the upper branches of the tallest sycamore and its family of occupants. I couldn't tell what sort of birds they were, but I knew past doubt that Phil knew. The centaurs in the painting, on the other hand, were not done in any detail beyond the generic, except for relative size, the boy being obviously smaller than the other two. They might have been pieces in a board game.

The man said slowly, not trying to conceal his puzzlement, "This is very pretty, I can see that it is pretty. But it is not our road."

"No, you don't understand," Phil answered him. "Look, take both ends, so." He handed the whole roll to the centaur. "Now . . . hold it up so you can watch it, and walk straight ahead. Just walk."

The man moved slowly forward, his eyes fixed on the image of the very place where he stood. He had not gone more than a few paces when he cried out, "But it moves! It moves!"

His wife and son—and I—pressed close now, and never mind who stepped on whose feet. The watercolor had changed, though not by much; only a few paces' worth. Now it showed a distinctly marked path in front of the centaur's feet: the path we ourselves took, coming and going in the oak forest. He said again, this time in a near-whisper, "It moves . . ."

"And we too," the woman said. "The little figures—as we move, so do they."

"Not always." Phil's voice was sounding distinctly fuller and stronger. "Go left now, walk off the path—see what happens."

The man did as directed—but the figures remained motionless in the watercolor, reproving him with their stillness. When he returned to the path and stepped along it, they moved with him again, sliding like the magnet-based toys we had then. I noticed for the first time that each one's painted tail had a long, coarse hair embedded in the pigment: chestnut, gray, dark-bay.

Almost speechless, the man turned to Phil, holding up the roll to stare at it. "And all our journey is in this picture, truly? And all we need do is follow these . . . poppets of ourselves?"

Phil nodded. "Just pay attention, and they won't let you go wrong. I fixed it so they'll guide you all the way to Nogales, Texas—that's right on the Mexican border. You'll know the way from there." He looked up with weary seriousness at the proud, bearded face above him. "It's a very long way—almost two thousand miles. I'm sorry."

"We have made longer journeys, and with no such guide." The man was still moving forward and back, watching in fascination as the little images mimicked his pacing. "Nothing to compare," he murmured, "not in all my life . . ." He halted and faced Phil again. "One with the wisdom to create this for us is also wise enough to know that there is no point in even trying to show our gratitude properly. Thank you."

Phil reached up to take the proffered hand. "Just go carefully, that's all. Stay off the main roads—the way I drew it, you shouldn't ever have to set foot on a highway. And don't ever let that picture out of your sight. Definitely a one-shot deal."

He climbed up onto the Rock and instantly fell asleep. The man seemed to doze on his feet, as horses do, while the boy embarked on one last roundup of every last acorn in the area. For myself, I spent the time saying my poem over and over to the *centauride*, until she had it perfectly memorized, and could repeat it back to me, line for line. "Now I will never forget it," she told me. "The last time anyone wrote a poem for me, it was in the Greek, the oldest Greek that none speak today." She recited it to me, and while I understood not one word, I would know it if I heard it again.

Phil was still asleep when the centaurs left at twilight. I did try to wake him to bid them farewell, but he only blinked and mumbled, and was gone again. I watched them out of sight among the oaks: the man in the lead, intently following the little moving images on Phil's painting; the boy trotting close behind, exuberant with adventure, for good or ill. The woman turned once to look back at us, and then went on.

I don't remember how I finally got Phil on his feet and home; only that it was late, and that both sets of parents were mad at us. The next day was school, and after that I had a doctor's appointment, and Phil had flute lessons, and what with one family thing or another, we had almost no time together until close to the end of the week. We didn't go to the Rock—the weather had turned too grim even for us—rather we sat shivering on the front stoop of my apartment building, like winter birds on a telephone line, and didn't say much of anything. I asked if Phil thought they'd make it all the way to Mexico, and he shrugged and answered, "We'll never know." After a moment, he added, "All I know, I got a roomful of stupid maps, and my whole body hurts. Never again, boy. You and your damn hallucinations."

I said, "I didn't know you could do stuff like that. Like what you made for them."

He turned to stare intently into my face. "You saw those hairs in those little figures? I saw you seeing them." I nodded. "Well, each was from one of their tails—Mom, Pop or the Kid. And I plucked a few more hairs, wove those into my brushes. That was the magic part: centaurs may have a lousy sense of direction, but they're still magic. Wouldn't have worked for a minute without that." I stared, and he sighed. "I keep telling you, the artist isn't the magic. The artist is the *sight*, the artist is someone who knows magic when he sees it. The magic doesn't care whether it's seen or not—that's the artist's business. My business."

I tried earnestly, stumblingly, to absorb what he was telling me. "So all that—I mean, the painting moving and guiding them, and all . . ."

Phil gave me that crooked, deceptively candid grin he'd had since we were five years old. "I'm a good artist. I'm really good. But I ain't *that* good."

We sat in silence for a while, while the leaves blew and tumbled past us, and a few sharp, tiny raindrops stung our faces. By and by Phil spoke again, quietly enough that I had to lean closer to hear him. "But we were magic too, in our way. You rounding up every single map between here and Yonkers, and me . . ." He hunched over, arms folded on his knees, the way he still does without realizing it. "Me at that damn easel, brush in one hand, gas-station map in the other, trying to make art out of the New Jersey Turnpike. Trying to make all those highways and freeways and interstates and Tennessee and Georgia come alive for a family of mythological, nonexistent . . . hour after goddam miserable, backbreaking, cockamamie hour, and that San Juan candle dropping wax everywhere . . ."

His voice trailed off into the familiar disgusted mumble. "I don't *know* how I did it, Beagle. Don't ask me. All I knew for sure was, you can't let centaurs wander around lost in the Bronx—you can't, it's all wrong—and there I was."

"It'll get them to Mexico," I said. "I know it will."

"Yeah, well." The grin became a slow, rueful smile, less usual. "The weird thing, it's made me . . . I don't know *better*, but just *different*, some way. I'm never going to have to do anything like that again, thank God—and I bet I couldn't. But there's other stuff, things I never thought about trying before, and now it's all I'm doing in my head, right now—my head's full of stuff I have to do, even if I can't ever get it right. Even *though*." The smile faded, and he shrugged and looked away. "That's them. They did that."

I turned my coat collar up around my face. I said, "I read a story about a boy who draws cats so well that they come to life and fight off demons for him."

"Japanese," Phil said. "Good story. Listen, don't tell anybody, not even Jake and Marty. It gets out, they'll want me to do all kinds of stuff, all the time. And magic's not an all-the-time thing, you're not ever *entitled* to magic—not ever, no matter how good you are. Best you can do—all you can do—is make sure you're ready when it happens. If."

His voice had grown somber again, his eyes distant, focusing on nothing that I could recognize. Then he brightened abruptly, saying, "Still got the brushes, anyway. There's that. Whatever comes next, there's the brushes."

THE RABBI'S HOBBY

I was never *bar mitzvah* (which, for those of you who are not Jewish or don't happen to know, is a specific religious coming-of-age ceremony for thirteen-year-old Jewish boys, and literally means "son of the commandments"). My brother was *bar mitzvah*, though—our parents left the choice up to us—as were most of my male childhood friends. So I'm more or less familiar with the ceremony, and I know something of my narrator's struggle with Hebrew and with his fearful attitude toward the whole ritual in general. I have also met more than one rabbi as wise and patient and sensitive as lucky Joseph's Rabbi Tuvim, and know the world is better for them. Beyond that, I can only say with certainty that like "The Rock in the Park," and several other favorite stories of mine, "The Rabbi's Hobby" was born out of my old neighborhood, and out of a time and a culture grown more intensely real and clear to me today than perhaps it was then. Back then I was mostly reading science-fiction, and listening to baseball games on the Crosley radio in the kitchen . . .

I T TOOK ME A WHILE to get to like Rabbi Tuvim. He was a big, slow-moving man with a heavy-boned face framed by a thick brown beard; and although he had spent much of his life in the Bronx, he had never quite lost the accent, nor the syntax, of his native Czechoslovakia. He seemed stony and forbidding to me at first, even though he had a warm, surprising laugh. He just didn't look like someone who would laugh a lot.

What gradually won me over was that Rabbi Tuvim collected odd, unlikely things. He was the only person I knew who collected, not baseball cards, the way all my friends and I did, but boxers. There was one gum company who put those out, complete with the fighters' records and a few lines about their lives, and the rabbi had all the heavyweights, going back to John L. Sullivan, and most of the lighter champions too. I learned everything I know about Stanley Ketchel, Jimmy McLarnin, Benny Leonard, Philadelphia Jack O'Brien, Tommy Loughran, Henry Armstrong and Tony Canzoneri—to name just those few—from Rabbi Tuvim's cards.

He kept boxes of paper matchbooks too, and those little bags of sugar that you get when you order coffee in restaurants. My favorites were a set from Europe that had tiny copies of paintings on them.

And then there were the keys. The Rabbi had an old tin box, like my school lunch box, but bigger, and it was filled with dozens and dozens of keys of every shape and size you could imagine that a key might be. Some of them were tiny, smaller even than our mailbox key, but some were huge and heavy and rusty; they looked like the keys jailers or housekeepers always carried at their belts in movies about the Middle Ages. Rabbi Tuvim had no idea what locks they might have been for— he never locked up anything, anyway, no matter how people warned him—he just picked them up wherever he found them lying loose and plopped them into his key box. To which, by the way, he'd lost the key long ago.

When I finally got up the nerve to ask him why he collected something as completely useless as keys without locks, the rabbi didn't answer right away, but leaned on his elbow and thought about his answer. That was something else I liked about him, that he seemed to take everybody's questions seriously, even ones that were really, really stupid. He finally said, "Well, you know, Joseph, those keys aren't useless just because I don't have the locks they fit. Whenever I find a lock that's lost its key, I try a few of mine on it, on the chance that one of them might be the right one. God is like that for me—a lock none of my keys fit, and probably never will. But I keep at it, I keep picking up different keys and trying them out, because you never know. Could happen."

I asked, "Do you think God wants you to find the key?"

Rabbi Tuvim ruffled my hair. "Leben uff der keppele. Leave it to the children to ask the big ones. I would like to think he does, Yossele, but I don't know that either. That's what being Jewish is, going ahead without answers. Get out of here, already."

The rabbi had bookshelves stacked with old crumbly magazines, too, all kinds of them. Magazines I knew, like *Life* and *Look* and *Colliers* and the *Saturday Evening Post*; magazines I'd never heard of—like *Scribners*, the *Delineator*, the *Illustrated London News*, and even one called *Pearson's Magazine*, from 1911, with Christy Mathewson on the cover. Mrs. Eisen, who cleaned for him every other week, wouldn't ever go into the room where he kept them, because she said those old dusty, flappy things aggravated her asthma. My father said that some of them were collector's items, and that people who liked that sort of stuff would pay a lot of money for them. But Rabbi Tuvim just liked having them, liked sitting and turning their yellow pages late at night, thinking about what people were thinking so long ago. "It's very peaceful," he told me. "So much worry about so much—so much certainty about how things were going to turn out—and here we are now, and it didn't turn out like that, after all. Don't ever be too sure of anything, Joseph."

I was at his house regularly that spring, because we were studying for my Bar Mitzvah. The negotiations had been extensive and complicated: I was willing to go along with local custom, tradition and my parents' social concerns, but I balked at going straight from my regular classes to the neighborhood Hebrew school. I called my unobservant family hypocrites, which they were; they called me lazy and ungrateful, which was also true. But both sides knew that I'd need extensive private tutoring to cope with the haftarah reading alone, never mind the inevitable speech. I'd picked up Yiddish early and easily, as had all my cousins, since our families spoke it when they didn't want the kindelech to understand what they were talking about. But Hebrew was another matter entirely. I knew this or that word, this or that phrase— even a few songs for Chanukah and Pesach—but the language itself sat like a stone on my tongue, guttural and harsh, and completely alien. I not only couldn't learn Hebrew, I truly didn't like Hebrew. And if a proper Jew was supposed to go on studying it even after the liberating Bar Mitzvah, I might just as well give up and turn Catholic, spending my Sunday mornings at Mass with the Geohegans down the block. Either way, I was clearly doomed.

Rabbi Tuvim took me on either as a challenge or as a penance, I was never quite sure which. He was inhumanly patient and inventive, constantly coming up with word games, sports references and any number of catchy mnemonics to help me remember this foreign, senseless, elusive, boring system of communication. But when even he wiped his forehead and said sadly, "Ai, gornisht helfen," which means nothing will help you, I finally felt able to ask him whether he thought I would ever be a good Jew; and, if not, whether we should just cancel the Bar Mitzvah. I thought hopefully of the expense this would save my father, and felt positively virtuous for once.

The rabbi, looking at me, managed to sigh and half-smile at the same time, taking off his glasses and blinking at them. "Nobody in this entire congregation has the least notion of what Bar Mitzvah is," he said wearily. "It's not a graduation from anything, it is just an acknowledgment that at thirteen you're old enough to be called up in temple to read from the Torah. Which God help you if you actually are, but never mind. The point is that you are still Bar Mitzvah even if you never go through the preparation, the ritual." He smiled at me and put his glasses back on. "No way out of it, Joseph. If you never manage to memorize another word of Hebrew, you're still as good a Jew as anybody. Whatever the Orthodox think."

One Thursday afternoon I found the rabbi so engrossed in one of his old magazines that he didn't notice when I walked in, or even when I peered over his shoulder. It was an issue of a magazine called *Evening*, from 1921, which made it close to thirty years old. There were girls on the cover, posing on a beach, but they were a long way from the bathing beauties—we still called them that then—that I was accustomed to seeing in magazines and on calendars. These could have walked into my mother's PTA or Hadassah meetings: they showed no skin above the shin, wore bathing caps and little wraps over their shoulders, and in general appeared about as seductive as any of my mother's friends, only younger. Paradoxically, the severe costumes made them look much more youthful than they probably were, innocently graceful.

Rabbi Tuvim, suddenly aware of me, looked up, startled but not embarrassed. "This is what your mother would have been wearing to the beach back then," he said. "Mine, too. It looks so strange, doesn't it? Compared to Betty Grable, I mean."

He was teasing me, as though I were still going through my Betty Grable/Alice Faye phase. As though I weren't twelve now, and on the edge of manhood; if not, why were we laboring over the utterly bewildering haftarah twice a week? As though Lauren Bacall, Lena Horne and Lizabeth Scott hadn't lately written their names all over my imagination, introducing me to the sorrows of adults? I drew myself up in visible—I hoped—indignation, but the rabbi said only, "Sit down, Joseph, look at this girl. The one in the left corner."

She was bareheaded, so that her whole face was visible.

Even I could tell that she couldn't possibly be over eighteen. She wasn't beautiful—the others were beautiful, and so what?—but there was a playfulness about her expression, a humor not far removed from wisdom. Looking at her, I felt that I could tell that face everything I was ashamed of, and that she would not only reassure me that I wasn't the vile mess I firmly believed I was, but that I might even be attractive one day to someone besides my family. Someone like her.

I looked sideways at Rabbi Tuvim, and saw him smiling. "Yes," he said. "She does have that effect, doesn't she?"

"Who is she?" I blurted out. "Is she a movie star or something?" Someone I should be expected to know, in other words. But I didn't think so, and I was right. Rabbi Tuvim shook his head.

"I have no idea. I just bought this magazine yesterday, at a collectors' shop downtown where I go sometimes, and I feel as though I have been staring at her ever since. I don't think she's anybody famous—probably just a model who happened to be around when they were shooting that cover. But I can't take my eyes off her, for some reason. It's a little embarrassing."

The rabbi's unmarried state was of particular concern in the neighborhood. Rabbis aren't priests: it's not only that they're allowed to marry, it's very nearly demanded of them by their congregations. Rabbi Tuvim wasn't a handsome man, but he had a strong face, and his eyes were kind. I said, "Maybe you could look her up, some way."

The rabbi blinked at me. "Joseph, I am curious. That's all."

"Sure," I said. "Me too."

"I would just like to know a little about her," the rabbi said.

"Me too," I said again. I was all for keeping the conversation going, to stall off my lesson as long as possible, but no luck. The rabbi just said, "There is something about her," and we plunged once more into the cold mysteries of Mishnaic Hebrew. Rabbi Tuvim didn't look at the *Evening* cover again, but I kept stealing side glances at that girl until he finally got up and put the magazine back on the bookshelf, without saying a word. I think I was an even worse student than usual that afternoon, to judge by his sigh when we finished.

Every Monday and Thursday, when I came for my lessons, the magazine would always be somewhere in sight—on a chair, perhaps, or down at the end of the table where we studied. We never exactly agreed, not in so many words, that the girl on the cover haunted us both, but we talked about her a lot. For me the attraction lay in the simple and absolute aliveness of her face, as present to me as that of any of my schoolmates, while the other figures in the photograph felt as antique as any of the Greek and Roman statues we were always being taken to see at museums. For Rabbi Tuvim . . . for the rabbi, perhaps, what fascinated him was the fact that he was fascinated: that a thirty-year-old image out of another time somehow had the power to distract him from his studies, his students, and his rabbinical duties. No other woman had ever done that to him. Twelve years old or not, I was sure of that.

The rabbi made inquiries. He told me about them—I don't think there was anyone else he could have told about such a strange obsession.

Evening was long out of business by then, but his copy had credited the cover photograph only to "Winsor & Co., Ltd., Newark, New Jersey." Rabbi Tuvim—obviously figuring that if he could teach me even a few scraps of Hebrew he ought to be able to track down a fashion photographer's byline—found address and phone number, called, was told sourly that he was welcome to go through their files himself, but that employees had better things to do. Whereupon, he promptly took a day off and made a pilgrimage to Winsor & Co., Ltd., which was still in business, but plainly subsisting on industrial photography and the odd bowling-team picture. A clerk led him to the company archive, which was a room like a walk-in closet, walled around with oaken filing cabinets; he said it smelled of fixatives and moldering newsprint, and of cigars smoked very long ago. But he sat down and went to work, and in only three hours, or at most four, he had his man.

"His name is Abel Bagaybagayan," he told me when I came the next day. I giggled, and the rabbi cuffed the side of my head lightly. "Don't laugh at people's names, Joseph. How is that any stranger than Rosenwasser? Or Turteltaub, or Kockenfuss, or Tuvim, or your own name? It took me a long time to find that name, and I'm very proud that I did find it, and you can either stop laughing right now, or go home." He was really angry with me. I'd never before seen him angry. I stopped laughing.

"Abel Bagaybagayan," Rabbi Tuvim said again. "He was what's called a freelance—that means he wasn't on anyone's staff—but he did a lot of work for Winsor through the 1920s. Portraits, fashion spreads, architectural layouts, you name it. Then, after 1935 or so . . . nothing. Nothing at all. Most likely he died, but I couldn't find any information, one way or the other." The rabbi spread his hands and lifted his eyebrows. "I only met a couple of people who even remembered him vaguely, and nobody has anything like an address, a phone number—not so much as a cousin in Bensonhurst. Nothing. A dead end."

"So what are you going to do?" I asked. The old magazine lay between us, and I marveled once again at the way the mystery-girl's bright face made everyone else on the cover look like depthless paper-doll cutouts, with little square tabs holding their flat clothes on their flat bodies. The rabbi waggled a warning finger at me, and my heart sank. Without another word, I opened my Hebrew text.

When we were at last done for the day—approximately a hundred and twenty years later—Rabbi Tuvim went on as though I had just asked the question. "My father used to tell me that back in Lvov, his family had a saying: *A Tuvim never surrenders; he just says he does.* I'm going to find Abel Bagaybagayan's family."

"Maybe he married that girl on the cover," I said hopefully. "Maybe they had a family together."

"Very romantic," the rabbi said. "I like it. But then he'd probably have had mouths to feed, so if he didn't die, why did he quit working as a photographer? If he did quit, mind you—I don't know anything for sure."

"Well, maybe she was very rich. Then he wouldn't *have* to work." I didn't really think that was at all likely, but lately I'd come to enjoy teasing the rabbi the way he sometimes teased me. I said, "Maybe they moved to California, and she got into the movies. That could have happened."

"You know, that actually could," Rabbi Tuvim said slowly. "California, anyway, everybody's going to California. And Bagaybagayan's an Armenian name—much easier to look for. I have an Armenian friend in Fresno, and Armenians always know where there are other Armenians . . . thank you, Detective Yossele. I'll see you on Monday."

As I left, feeling absurdly pleased with myself, he was already reaching for the old *Evening*, sliding it toward him on the table.

In the following weeks, the rabbi grew steadily more involved with that face from 1921, and with the cold trail of Abel Bagaybagayan, who wasn't from Fresno. But there were plenty of people there with that name; and while none of them knew the man we were looking for, they had cousins in Visalia and Delano and Firebaugh who might. To my disappointment, Rabbi Tuvim remained very conscientious about keeping his obsession from getting in the way of his teaching; at that point, the Fresno phone book would have held more interest for me than halakha or the Babylonian Talmud. On the other hand, he had no hesitation about involving me in his dogged search for either photographer or model, or both of them. I was a great Sherlock Holmes fan back then, and I felt just like Doctor Watson, only smarter.

This was all before the Internet, mind you; all before personal computers, area codes, digital dialing . . . that time when places were farther from each other, when phone calls went through operators, and a long-distance call was as much of an event as a telegram. Even so, it was I, assigned to the prairie states, who found Sheila Bagaybagayan, only child of Abel, in Grand Forks, North Dakota, where she was teaching library science at the university. I handed the phone to Rabbi Tuvim and went off into a corner to hug myself and jump up and down just a bit. I might not know the Midrash Hashkem from "Mairzy Doats" but, by God, I was Detective Yossele.

Watching the rabbi's face as he spoke to Sheila Bagaybagayan on the phone was more fun than a Saturday matinee at Loew's Tuxedo, with a double feature, a newsreel, eighteen cartoons, Coming Attractions and a *Nyoka the Jungle Girl* serial. He smiled—he laughed outright—he frowned in puzzlement—he spoke rapidly, raising a finger, as though making a point in a sermon—he scratched his beard—he looked suddenly sad enough to weep—he said, "Yes . . . yes . . . yes . . ." several times, and then "Of course—and thank you," and hung up. He stood motionless by the phone for a few minutes, absently rubbing his lower lip, until the phone started to buzz because he hadn't got it properly back on the hook. Then he turned to me and grinned, and said, "Well. That was our Sheila."

"Was she really the right one? Mr. Baba . . . uh, Abel's daughter?" The passing of weeks hadn't made me any more comfortable around the photographer's name.

Rabbi Tuvim nodded. "Yes, but her married name is Olsen. Her mother died when she was practically a baby, and Abel never remarried, but raised her alone. She says he stopped working as a photographer during the Depression, when she was in her teens, because he just couldn't make a living at it anymore. So he became a salesman for a camera equipment company, and then he worked for Western Union, and he died just after the war." He smacked his fist into his palm. "*Rats!*"—which was his strongest expletive, at least around me. "We could have met him, we could have asked him . . . *Ach, rats!*" I used to giggle in shul sometimes, suddenly imagining him saying that at the fall of Solomon's Temple, or at the news that Sabbatai Zevi, the false Messiah, had turned Muslim.

"The girl," I asked. "Did she remember that girl?"

The rabbi shook his head. "Her father worked with so many models over the years. She's going to look through his records and call me back. One thing she did say, he preferred using amateurs when he could, and she knows that he sneaked a lot of them into the *Evening* assignments, even though they ordered him not to. She thinks he was likely to have kept closer track of the amateurs than the professionals, in case he got a chance to use them again, so who knows?" He shrugged slightly. "As the Arabs say, inshallah—if God wills it. Fair enough, I guess."

For quite some time I cherished a persistent hopeful vision of our cover girl turning out to be Sheila Olsen's long-gone mother. But Abel Bagaybagayan had never employed his wife professionally, Sheila told us; there were plenty of photographs around the Grand Forks house, but none of the young woman Rabbi Tuvim described. And no magazine covers. Abel Bagaybagayan never saved the covers.

All the same, Sheila Olsen plainly got drawn into the rabbi's fixation—or, as he always called it—his hobby. They spoke on the phone frequently, considering every possibility of identifying the *Evening* girl; and my romantic imagination started marrying them off, exactly like the movies. I knew that she had been divorced—which was not only rare in our neighborhood then, but somehow exotic—and I figured that she had to be Rabbi Tuvim's age, or even younger, so there we were. Their conversations, from my end, sounded less formal as time went on; and a twelve-year-old romantic who can't convert "less formal" into "affectionate" at short notice just isn't trying.

No, of course it never happened, not like that. She wasn't Jewish, for one thing, and she really liked living in North Dakota. But her curiosity, growing to enthusiasm, at last gave the rabbi someone besides me to discuss his hobby with, and fired up his intensity all over again. I wasn't jealous; on the contrary, I felt as though we were a secret alliance of superheroes, like the Justice Society of America, on the trail of Nazi spies, or some international warlord or other. The addition of Sheila Olsen, our Grand Forks operative, made it all that much more exciting.

I spoke to her a couple of times. The first occasion was when a call from old Mrs. Shimkus interrupted my Monday Hebrew lesson. I was always grateful when that happened, but especially so in this case, since we were doing vowels, and had gotten to shva. That is all you're going to hear from me about shva. Mrs. Shimkus was always calling, always dying, and always contributing large sums for the maintenance of the temple and scholarships for deserving high-school students. This entitled her, as the rabbi said with a touch of grimness, to her personal celestial attorney, on call at all times to file suit against the Angel of Death. "Answer the phone, if it rings. Go back to page twenty-nine, and start over from there. I'll be back sooner than you hope, so get to it."

I did try. Shva and all. But I also grabbed up the telephone on the first ring, saying importantly, "Rabbi Tuvim's residence, to whom am I speaking?"

The connection was stuttery and staticky, but I heard a woman's warm laughter clearly. "Oh, this has simply got to be Joseph. The rabbi's told me all about you. *Is* this Joseph?"

"All about me?" I was seriously alarmed at first; and then I asked, "Sheila? Olsen? Is this you?"

She laughed again. "Yes, I'm sure it is. Is Rabbi Tuvim available?"

"He's visiting Mrs. Shimkus right now," I said. "She's dying again. But he ought to be back pretty soon."

"Very efficient," Sheila Olsen said. "Well, just tell him I called back, so now it's his turn." She paused for a moment. "And Joseph?" I waited. "Tell him I've looked all through my father's files, all of them, and come up empty every time. I'm not giving up—there are a couple of other possibilities—but just tell him it doesn't look too good right now. Can you please do that?"

"As soon as he gets back," I said. "Of course I'll tell him." I hesitated myself, and then blurted, "And don't worry—I'm sure you'll find out about her. He just needs to find the lock she fits." I explained about the rabbi's key collection, and expected her to laugh for a third time, whether in amusement or disbelief. But instead she was silent long enough that I thought she might have hung up. Then she said quietly, "My dad would have liked your rabbi, I think."

Rabbi Tuvim, as he had predicted, returned sooner than I could have wished—Mrs. Shimkus having only wanted tea and sympathy—and I relayed Sheila Olsen's message promptly. I hoped he'd call her right away, but his sense of duty took us straight back to study; and at the end of our session we were both as pale, disheveled and sweating as Hebrew vowels always left us. Before I went home, he said to me, "You know, it's a funny thing, Joseph. Somehow I have connected that *Evening* model with you, in my head. I keep thinking that if I can actually teach you Hebrew, I will be allowed to find out who that girl was. Or maybe it's the other way around, I'm not sure. But I know there's a connection, one way or the other. There is a connection."

A week later the rabbi actually called me at home to tell me that Sheila Olsen had come across a second *Evening* with what—she was almost certain—must be the same model on the cover. "She's already sent it, airmail special delivery, so it ought to be here day after tomorrow." The rabbi was so excited that he was practically chattering like someone my age. "I'm sure it's her—I took a photo of my copy and sent it to her, and she clearly thinks it's the same girl." He slowed down, laughing in some embarrassment at his own enthusiasm. "Listen, when you come tomorrow, if you spot me hanging around the mailbox like

Valentine's Day, just collar me and drag me inside. A rabbi should never be caught hanging around the mailbox."

The magazine did arrive two days later. I used my lucky nickel to call Rabbi Tuvim from school for the news. Then I ran all the way to his house, not even bothering to drop my books off at home. The rabbi was in his little kitchen, snatching an absent-minded meal of hot dogs and baked beans, which was his idea of a dish suitable for any occasion.

The *Evening* was on a chair, across from him. I grabbed it up and stared at the cover, which was an outdoor scene, showing well-dressed people dining under a striped awning on a summer evening. It was a particularly busy photograph—a lot of tables, a lot of diners, a lot of natty waiters coming and going—and you had to look closely and attentively to find the one person we were looking for. She was off to the right, near the edge of the awning, her bright face looking straight into the camera, her eyes somehow catching and holding the twilight, even as it faded. There were others seated at her table; but, just as with the first cover photo, her presence dimmed them, as though the shot had always been a single portrait of her, with everyone else added in afterward.

But it was just this that was, in a vague, indeterminate way, perturbing the rabbi, making him look far less triumphant and vindicated than I had expected. I was the one who kept saying, "That's her, that's her! We were right—we found her!"

"Right about what, Joseph?" Rabbi Tuvim said softly. "And what have we found?"

I stared at him. He said, "There's something very strange about all this. Think—Abel Bagaybagayan kept very precise records of every model he used, no matter if he only photographed him or her once. Sheila's told me. For each one, name, address, telephone number, and his own special filing system, listing the date, the magazine, the occasion, and a snapshot of that person, always. But not *this* one." He put his finger on the face we had sought for so long. "Not this one girl, out of all those photographs. Two magazine covers, but no record, no picture— *nothing*. Why is that, Detective Yossele? Why on earth would that be?"

His tone was as playful as when he asked me some Talmudic riddle, or invited me to work a noun suffix out for myself, but his face was serious, and his blue eyes looked heavy and sad. I really wanted to help him. I said, "She was special to him, some way. You can see that in the photos." Rabbi Tuvim nodded, though neither he nor I could ever have explained what we meant by *seeing*. "So maybe he wanted to keep her separate, you know? Sort of to keep her for himself, that could be it. I mean, he'd always know where she was, and what she looked like—he'd never have to go look her up in his files, right? That could be it, couldn't it?" I tried to read his face for a reaction to my reasoning. I said, "Kind of makes sense to me, anyway."

"Yes," the rabbi said slowly. "Yes, of course it makes sense, it's very good thinking, Joseph. But it is *human* thinking, it is *human* sense, and I'm just not sure . . ." His voice trailed away into a mumble as he leaned his chin into his fist. I reached to move the plate of baked beans out of range, but I was a little late.

"What?" I asked. "You mean she could be some kind of Martian, an alien in disguise?" I was joking, but these were the last days of the pulp science-fiction magazines (*and* the pulp Westerns, *and* romances, *and* detective stories), and I read them all, as the rabbi knew. He laughed then, which made me feel better.

"No, I didn't mean that." He sighed. "I don't know what I meant, forget it. Let's go into the living room and work on your speech."

"I came to see the magazine," I protested. "I wasn't coming for a lesson."

"Well, how lucky for you that I'm free just now," the rabbi said. "Get in there." And, trapped and outraged, I went.

So now we had two photographs featuring our mystery model, and were no closer than we'd ever been to identifying her. Sheila Olsen, as completely caught up in the quest as we two by now, contacted every one of her father's colleagues, employers, and old studio buddies that she could reach, and set them all to rummaging through their own files, on the off-chance that one or another of them might have worked with

Abel Bagaybagayan's girl twenty or thirty years before. (We were all three calling her that by now, though more in our minds than aloud, I think: "Abel's girl.") Rabbi Tuvim didn't hold much hope for that course, though. "She didn't work with anyone else," he said. "Just him. I know this." And for all anyone could prove otherwise, she never had.

My birthday and my Bar Mitzvah were coming on together like a freight train in the old movies, where you see the smoke first, rising away around the bend, and then you hear the wheels and the whistle, and finally you see the train barreling along. Rabbi Tuvim and I were both tied to the track, and I don't know whether he had nightmares about it all, but I surely did. There was no rescue in sight, either, no cowboy hero racing the train on the great horse Silver or Trigger or Champion, leaping from the saddle to cut us free at the last split-second. My parents had shot the works on the hall, the catering, the invitations, the newspaper notice, and the party afterward (the music to be provided by Herbie Kaufman and his Bel-Air Combo). We'd already had the rehearsal—a complete disaster, but at least the photographs got taken—and there was no more chance even of postponing than there would have been of that train stopping on a dime. Remembering it now, my nightmares were always much more about the rabbi's embarrassment than my own. He had tried so hard to reconcile Hebrew and me to one another; it wasn't his fault that we loathed each other on sight. I felt terrible for him.

A week before the Bar Mitzvah, Sheila Olsen called. We were in full panic mode by now, with me coming to the rabbi's house every day after school, and he himself dropping most of his normal duties to concentrate less on teaching me the passage of Torah that I would read and comment on, but on keeping me from running away to sea and calling home from Pago Pago, where nobody gets Bar Mitzvahed. When the phone rang, Rabbi Tuvim picked it up, signed to me to keep working from the text, and walked away with it to the end of the cord. Entirely pointless, since the cord only went a few feet, it was still a request for privacy, and I tried to respect it. I did try.

"What?" the rabbi said loudly. "You found *what?* Slow down, Sheila, I'm having trouble . . . . When? You're coming . . . Sheila, slow *down!* . . . So how come you can't just tell me on the phone? Wait a minute, I'm not understanding—you're *sure?*" And after that he was silent for a long time, just listening. When he saw that that was all I was doing too, he waved me sternly back to my studies. I bent my head earnestly over the book, pretending to be working, while he tried to squeeze a few more inches out of that phone cord. Both of us failed.

Finally the rabbi said wearily, "I do not have a car, I can't pick you up. You'll have to . . . oh, okay, if you don't mind taking a cab. Okay, then, I will see you tomorrow. . . . What? Yes, yes, Joseph will be here . . . yes—goodbye, Sheila. Goodbye."

He hung up, looked at me, and said "Oy."

It was a profound *oy*, an *oy* of stature and dignity, an *oy* from the heart. I waited. Rabbi Tuvim said, "She's coming here tomorrow. Sheila Olsen."

"Wow," I said. "*Wow.*" Then I said, "Why?"

"She's found another picture. Abel's girl. Only this one she says she can't send us—she can't even tell me about it. She just has to get on a plane and come straight here to show us." The rabbi sat down and sighed. "It's not exactly the best time."

I said, "Wow," for a third time. "That's *wonderful.*" Then I remembered I was Detective Yossele, and tried to act the part. I asked, "How did she sound?"

"It's hard to say. She was talking so fast." The rabbi thought for a while. "As though she *wanted* to tell me what she had discovered, really wanted to—maybe to share it, maybe just to get rid of it, *I* don't know. But she couldn't do it. Every time she tried, the words seemed to stick in her throat, like Macbeth's *amen.*" He read my blank expression and sighed again. "Maybe they'll have you reading Shakespeare next year. You'll like Shakespeare."

In spite of that freight train of a Bar Mitzvah bearing down on us, neither the rabbi nor I were worth much for the rest of the day. We never exactly quit on the Torah, but we kept drifting to a halt in the middle of work, speculating more or less silently on what could possibly set a woman we'd never met flying from Grand Forks, North Dakota, to tell us in person what she had learned about her father and his mysterious model. Rabbi Tuvim finally said, "Well, I don't know about you, but I'm going to have to drink a gallon of chamomile tea if I'm to get any sleep tonight. What do you do when you can't sleep, Joseph?"

He always asked me questions as though we were the same age. I said, "I guess I listen to the radio. Baseball games."

"Too exciting for me," the rabbi said. "I'll stick with the tea. Go home. She won't be here until your school lets out." I was at the door when he called after me, "And bring both of your notebooks, I made up a test for you." He never gave up, that man. Not on Abel Bagaybagayan, not on me.

Sheila Olsen and I arrived at Rabbi Tuvim's house almost together. I had just rung the doorbell when her cab pulled around the corner, and the rabbi opened the door as she was getting out. She was a pleasant-faced blonde woman, a little plump, running more to the Alice Faye side than Lauren Bacall, and I sighed inwardly to think that only a year before she would have been my ideal. The rabbi—dressed, I noticed, in his second-best suit, the one he wore for all other occasions than the High Holidays—opened the door and said, "Sheila Olsen, I presume?"

"Rabbi Sidney Tuvim," she answered as they shook hands. To me, standing awkwardly one step above her, she said, "And you could only be Joseph Makovsky." The rabbi stepped back to usher us in ahead of him.

Sheila—somehow, after our phone conversations, it was impossible to think of her as Mrs. Olsen—was carrying a large purse and a small overnight bag, which she set down near the kitchen door. "Don't panic, I'm not moving in. I've got a hotel reservation right at the airport, and I'll fly home day after tomorrow. But at the moment I require—no, I request—a glass of wine. Jews are like Armenians, bless them, they've always got wine in the house." She wrinkled her nose and added, "Unlike Lutherans."

The rabbi smiled. "You wouldn't like our wine. We just drink it on Shabbos. Once a week, believe me, that's enough. I can do better."

He went into the kitchen and I stared after him, vaguely jealous, never having seen him quite like this. Not flirtatious, I don't mean that; he wouldn't have known how to be flirtatious on purpose. But he wasn't my age now. Suddenly he was an adult, a grownup, with that elusive but familiar tone in his voice that marked grownups talking to other grownups in the presence of children. Sheila Olsen regarded me with a certain shrewd friendliness in her small, wide-set brown eyes.

"You're going to be thirteen in a week," she said. "The rabbi told me." I nodded stiffly. "You'll hate it, everybody does. Boy or girl, it doesn't make any difference—everybody hates thirteen. I remember."

"It's supposed to be like a borderline for us," I said. "Between being a kid and being a man. Or a woman, I guess."

"But that's just the time when you don't know *what* the hell you are, excuse my French," Sheila Olsen said harshly. "Or *who* you are, or even *if* you are. You couldn't pay me to be thirteen again, I'll tell you. You could not pay me."

She laughed then, and patted my hand. "I'm sorry, Joseph, don't listen to me. I just have . . . associations with thirteen." Rabbi Tuvim was coming back into the room, holding a small tray bearing three drinks in cocktail glasses I didn't know he had. Sheila Olsen raised her voice slightly. "I was just telling Joseph not to worry—once he makes it through thirteen, it's all downhill from there. Wasn't it that way for you?"

The rabbi raised his eyebrows. "I don't know. Sometimes I feel as though I never did get through thirteen myself." He handed her her drink, and gave me a glass of cocoa cream, which is a soft drink you can't get anymore. I was crazy about cocoa cream that year. I liked to mix it with milk.

The third glass, by its color, unmistakably contained Concord grape wine, and Sheila Olsen's eyebrows went up further than his. "I thought you couldn't stand Jewish wine."

"I can't," the rabbi answered gravely. "L'chaim."

Sheila Olsen lifted her glass and said something that must have been the Armenian counterpart of "To life." They both looked at me, and I blurted out the first toast that came into my head. *"Past the teeth, over the gums / Look out, gizzard—here she comes!"* My father always said that, late in the evening, with friends over.

We drank. Sheila Olsen said to the rabbi, clearly in some surprise, "You make a mean G-and-T."

"And you are stalling," Rabbi Tuvim said. "You come all this way from Grand Forks because you have found something connecting your father and that cover girl we're all obsessed with—and now you're here, you'll talk about anything but her." He smiled at her again, but this time it was like the way he smiled at me when I'd try in every way I knew to divert him from haftarah and get him talking about the Dodgers' chances of overtaking the St. Louis Cardinals. For just that moment, then, we were all the same age, motionless in time.

I wasn't any more perceptive than any average twelve-year-old, but I saw a kind of grudging sadness in Sheila Olsen's eyes that had nothing in common with the dryly cheerful voice on the phone from North Dakota. Sheila Olsen said, "You're perfectly right. Of course I'm stalling." She reached into her purse and took out a large manila envelope. It had a red string on the flap that you wound around a dime-sized red anchor to hold it closed. "Okay," she said. "Look what I found in my father's safety-deposit box yesterday."

It was a black-and-white photograph, clipped to a large rectangle of cardboard, like the kind that comes back from the laundry with your folded shirt. The photo had the sepia tint and scalloped edges that I knew meant that it was likely to be older than I was. And it was a picture of a dead baby.

I didn't know it was dead at first. I hadn't seen death then, ever, and I thought the baby was sleeping, dressed in a kind of nightgown with feet, like Swee'Pea, and tucked into a little bed that could almost have fitted into a dollhouse. I don't know how or when I realized the truth. Sheila Olsen said, "My sister."

Rabbi Tuvim had no more to say than I did. We just stared at her. Sheila Olsen went on, "I never knew about her until yesterday. She was stillborn."

I was the one who mumbled, "I'm sorry." The rabbi didn't bother with words, but came over to Sheila Olsen and put his arm around her. She didn't cry; if there is one sound I know to this day, it's the sound people make who are not going to cry, *not going to cry*. She put her head on the rabbi's shoulder and closed her eyes, but she didn't cry. I'm her witness.

When she could talk, she said in a different voice, "Turn it over."

There was a card clipped to the back of the mounting board, and there was very neat, dark handwriting on it that looked almost like printing. Rabbi Tuvim read it aloud.

> *"Eleanor Araxia Bagaybagayan.*
> *Born: 24 February 1907*
> *Died: 24 February 1907*
> *Length: 13½ inches*
> *Weight: 5 lbs, 9 oz.*
> *We planned to call her Anoush."*

Below that, there was a space, and then the precise writing gave way to a strange scrawl: clearly the same hand, but looking somehow shrunken and warped, as though the words had been left out in the rain. The rabbi squinted at it over his glasses, and went on reading:

> *"She has been dead for years—she never lived—how can she be invading my pictures? I take a shot of men coming to work at a factory—when I develop it, there she is, a little girl eating an apple, watching the men go by. I photograph a train—she has her nose against a window in the sleeping car. It is her, I know her, how could I not know her? When I take pictures of young women at outdoor dinner parties—"*

"That's your magazine cover!" I interrupted. My voice sounded so loud in the hushed room that I was suddenly embarrassed, and shrank back into the couch where I was sitting with Sheila Olsen. She patted my arm, and the rabbi said patiently, "Yes, Joseph." He continued:

> "—I see her sitting among them, grown now, as she was never given the chance to be. Child or adult, she always knows me, and she knows that I know her, She is never the focal point of the shot; she prefers to place herself at the edge, in the background, to watch me at my work, to be some small part of it, nothing more. She will not speak to me, nor can I ever get close to her; she fades when I try. I would think of her as a hallucination, but since when can you photograph a hallucination?"

The rabbi stopped reading again, and he and Sheila Olsen looked at each other without speaking. Then he looked at me and said, somewhat hesitantly, "This next part is a little terrible, Joseph. I don't know whether your parents would want you to hear it."

"If I'm old enough to be Bar Mitzvah," I said, "I'm old enough to hear about a baby who died. I'm staying."

Sheila Olsen chuckled hoarsely. "One for the kid, Rabbi." She gestured with her open hand. "Go on."

Rabbi Tuvim nodded. He took a deep breath.

> "She was born with her eyes open. Such blue eyes, almost lavender. I closed them before my wife had a chance to see. But I saw her eyes. I would know her eyes anywhere . . . is it her ghost haunting my photographs? Can one be a ghost if one never drew breath in this world? I do not know—but it is her, it is her. Somehow, it is our Anoush."

Nobody said anything for a long time after he had finished reading.

The rabbi blew his nose and polished his glasses, and Sheila Olsen opened her mouth and then closed it again. I had all kinds of things I wanted to say, but they all sounded so stupid in my head that I just let them go and stared at the photo of Sheila Olsen's stillborn baby sister. I thought about the word *still* . . . quiet, motionless, silent, tranquil, at rest. I hadn't known it meant *dead*.

Sheila Olsen asked at length, "What do Jews believe about ghosts? Do you even *have* ghosts?"

Rabbi Tuvim scratched his head. "Well, the Torah doesn't really talk about supernatural beings at all. The Talmud, yes—the Talmud is up to here in demons, but ghosts, as we would think of them . . . no, not so much." He leaned forward, resting his elbows on his knees and tenting his fingers, the way he did when he was coaxing me to think beyond my schooling. "We call them *spirits*, when we call them anything, and we imagine some of them to be malevolent, dangerous— demonic, if you like. But there are benign ones as well, and those are usually here for a specific reason. To help someone, to bring a message. To comfort."

"Comfort," Sheila Olsen said softly. Her face had gone very pale; but as she spoke color began to come back to it, too much color. "My dad needed that, for sure, and from Day One I couldn't give it to him. He never stopped missing my mother—this person I never even knew, and couldn't be—and now I find out that he missed someone else, too. My perfect, magical, *lost* baby sister, who didn't have to bother to get herself born to become legendary. Oh, Christ, it explains so much!" She had gone pale again. "And you're telling me she came back to comfort him? That's the message?"

"Well, I don't know that," the rabbi said reasonably. "But it would be nice, wouldn't it, if that turned out to be true? If there really were two worlds, and certain creatures—call them spirits, call them demons, angels, anything you like—could come and go between those worlds, and offer advice, and tell the rest of us not to be so scared of it all. I'd like that, wouldn't you?"

"But do you believe it? Do you believe my stillborn sister came back to tell my father that it wasn't his fault? Sneaking into his photographs just to wave to him, so he could see she was really okay somewhere? Because it sure didn't comfort him much, I'll tell you that."

"Didn't it?" the rabbi asked gently. "Are you sure?"

Sheila Olsen was fighting for control, doggedly refusing to let her voice escape into the place where it just as determinedly wanted to go. The effort made her sound as though she had something caught in her throat that she could neither swallow nor spit up. She said, "The earliest memory I have is of my father crying in the night. I don't know how old I was—three, three and a half. Not four. It's like a dream now—I get out of my bed, and I go to him, and I pat him, pat his back, the way someone . . . someone used to do for me when I had a nightmare. He doesn't reject me, but he doesn't turn around to me, either. He just lies there and cries and cries." The voice almost got away from her there, but she caught it, and half-laughed. "Well, I guess that *is* rejection, actually."

"Excuse me, but that's nonsense," Rabbi Tuvim said sharply. "You were a baby, trying to ease an adult's pain. That only happens in movies. Give me your glass."

He went back into the kitchen, while Sheila Olsen and I sat staring at each other. She cleared her throat and finally said, "I guess you didn't exactly bargain for such a big dramatic scene, huh, Joseph?"

"It beats writing a speech in Hebrew," I answered from the heart. Sheila Olsen did laugh then, which emboldened me enough to say, "Do you think your father ever saw her again, your sister, after he stopped being a photographer?"

"Oh, he never stopped taking pictures," Sheila Olsen said. "He just quit trying to make a living at it." She was trying to fix her makeup, but her hands were shaking too much. She said, "He couldn't go through a day without taking a dozen shots of everything around him, and then he'd spend the evening in his closet darkroom, developing them all. But if he had any more photos of . . . *her*, I never saw them. There weren't any others in the safe-deposit box." She paused, and then added, more to herself than to me, "He was always taking pictures of me, I used to get annoyed sometimes. Had them up all over the place."

Rabbi Tuvim came back with a fresh drink for her. I was hoping for more cocoa cream soda, but I didn't get it. Sheila Olsen practically grabbed the gin-and-tonic, then looked embarrassed. "I'm not a drunk, really—I'm just a little shaky right now. So you honestly think that's her, my sister . . . my sister Anoush in those old photographs?"

"Don't you?" the rabbi asked quietly. "I'd say that's what matters most."

Sheila Olsen took half her drink in one swallow and looked him boldly in the face. "Oh, I do, but I haven't trusted my own opinion on anything for . . . oh, for years, since my husband walked out. And I'm very tired, and I know I'm halfway nutsy when it comes to anything to do with my father. He was kind and good, and he was a terrific photographer, and he lost his baby and his wife, one right after the other, so I'm not blaming him that there wasn't much left for me. I'm *not!*"— loudly and defiantly, though the rabbi had said nothing. "But I just wish . . . I just wish . . . ."

And now, finally, she did begin to cry.

I didn't know what to do. I hadn't seen many adults crying in my life. I knew aunts and uncles undoubtedly *did* cry—my cousins told me so—but not ever in front of us children, except for Aunt Frieda, who smelled funny, and always cried late in the evening, whatever the occasion. My mother went into the bathroom to cry, my father into his basement office. I can't be sure he actually cried, but he did put his head down on his desk. He never made a sound, and neither did Sheila Olsen. She just sat there on the couch with the tears sliding down her face, and she kept on trying to talk, as though nothing were happening. But nothing came out—not words, not sobs; nothing but hoarse breathing that sounded terribly painful. I wanted to run away.

I didn't, but only because Rabbi Tuvim did know what to do. First he handed Sheila Olsen a box of tissues to wipe her eyes with, which she did, although the tears kept coming. Next, he went to his desk by the window and took from the lowest drawer the battered tin box which I knew contained his collection of lost keys, Then he went back to Sheila Olsen and crouched down in front of her, holding the tin box out. When she didn't respond, he opened the box and put it on her lap. He said, "Pick one."

Sheila Olsen sniffled, "What? Pick *what?*"

"A key," Rabbi Tuvim said. "Pick two, three, if you like. Just take your time, and be careful."

Sheila Olsen stared down into the box, so crowded with keys that by now Rabbi Tuvim couldn't close it so it clicked. Then she looked back at the rabbi, and she said, "You really *are* crazy. I was worried about that."

"Indulge me," the rabbi said. "Crazy people have to be indulged."

Sheila Olsen brushed her hand warily across the keys. "You mean, you want me to just *take* a couple? For keeps?" She sounded like a little girl.

"For keeps." The rabbi smiled at her. "Just remember, each of those keys represents a lock you can't find, a problem you can't solve. As you can see. . . ." He gestured grandly toward the tin box without finishing the sentence.

I thought Sheila Olsen would grab any old key off the top layer, to humor him; but in fact she did take her time, sifting through a dozen or more, before she finally settled on a very small, silvery one, mailbox-key size. Then she looked straight at Rabbi Tuvim and said, "That's to represent *my* trouble. I know it's a little bitty sort of trouble, not worth talking about after a war where millions and millions of people died. Not even worth thinking about by myself—nothing but a middle-aged woman wishing her father could have loved her . . . could have *seen* her, the way he saw that strange girl who turned out to be my sister, for God's sake." Her voice came slowly and heavily now, and I realized how tired she must be. She said, "You know, Rabbi, sometimes when I was a child, I used to wish *I* were dead, just so my father would miss me, the way I knew he missed my mother. I did—I really used to wish that."

89

The rabbi called a taxi to take her to her airport hotel. He walked her to the cab—I noticed that she put the little key carefully into her bag—and I saw them talking earnestly until the driver started looking impatient, and she got in. Then he came back into the house, and, to my horrified amazement, promptly gave me the Torah test he'd written up for me. Nor could I divert him by getting him to talk about Sheila Olsen's photographs, and her father's notes, and the other things she had told us. To all of my efforts in that direction, he replied only by pointing to the test paper and leaning back in his chair with his eyes closed. I mumbled a theatrically evil Yiddish curse that I'd learned from my Uncle Shmul, who was both an authority and a specialist, and bent bitterly to my work. I did not do well.

I didn't imagine that I would ever see Sheila Olsen again. She had a job, a home and a life waiting for her, back in Grand Forks, North Dakota. But in fact I saw her that Saturday afternoon, in the audience gathered at the Reform synagogue to witness my Bar Mitzvah. Rabbi Tuvim's other students had all scheduled their individual ceremonies a year or more in advance, and I didn't know whether to be terrified at the notion of being the entire center of attention, or grateful that at least I wouldn't be shown up for the pathetic schlemiel I was by contrast with those three. We had a nearly full house in the main gathering room of the synagogue, my schoolmates drawn by the lure of the after-party, the adults either by family loyalty or my mother's blackmail, or some combination of both. My mother was the Seurat of blackmail: a dot here, a dot there. . . .

The rabbi—coaching me under his breath to the very last minute—was helping me tie the tefillin around my head and my left arm when I messed up the whole process by pulling away to point out Sheila Olsen. He yanked me back, saying, "Yes, I know she's here. Stand still."

"I thought she went home," I said. "She said goodbye to me."

"Hold your head up," Rabbi Tuvim ordered. "She decided she wanted to stay for your Bar Mitzvah—said she'd never seen one. Now, remember, you stand there after your speech, while I sing. With, please God, your grandfather's tallis around your shoulders, *if* your mother remembers to bring it. If not, I guess you must use mine."

I had never seen him nervous before. I said, "When this is over, can I still come and look at your old magazines?"

The rabbi stopped fussing with the tefillin and looked at me for a long moment. Then he said very seriously, "Thank you, Detective Yossele. Thank you for putting things back into proportion for me. You have something of a gift that way. Yes, of course you can look at the magazines, you can visit for any reason you like, or for no reason at all. And don't worry—we will get through this thing today just fine." He gave the little leather phylactery a last tweak, and added, "Or we will leave town on the same cattle boat for Argentina. Oh, thank God, there's your mother. Stay right where you are."

He hurried off—I had never seen him hurry before, either—and I stayed where I was, turning in little circles to look at the guests, and at the hard candies ranged in bowls all around the room. These were there specifically for my friends and family to hurl at me by way of congratulations, the instant the ceremony was over. I don't know whether any other Jewish community in the world does this. I don't think so.

Sheila Olsen came up to me, almost shyly, once Rabbi Tuvim was gone. She gave me a quick hug, and then stepped back, asking anxiously, "Is that all right? I mean, are you not supposed to be touched or anything until it's over? I should have asked first, I'm sorry."

"It's all right," I said. "Really. I'm so scared right now . . ." and I stopped there, ashamed to admit my growing panic to a stranger. But Sheila Olsen seemed to understand, for she hugged me a second time, and it was notably comforting.

"Your rabbi will take care of you," she said. "He'll get you through it, I know he will. He's a good man." She hesitated then, looking away. "I'm a little embarrassed around both of you now, after yesterday. I didn't mean to carry on like that." I had no idea what to say. I just smiled stupidly. Sheila Olsen said, "I'll have to leave for the airport right after this is over, so I wanted to say goodbye now. I guess it was all foolishness, but I'm glad I came. I'm glad I met you, Joseph."

"Me, too," I said. We saw Rabbi Tuvim returning, waving to us over the heads of the milling guests. Sheila Olsen, shy again, patted my shoulder, whispered "*Courage*," and began to slip away. The rabbi intercepted her deftly, however, and they talked for a few minutes, at the end of which Sheila Olsen nodded firmly, pointed to her big purse, and went to find a seat. Rabbi Tuvim joined me and went quietly over my Torah portion with me again. He seemed distinctly calmer, or possibly I mean resigned.

"All right, Joseph," the rabbi said at last. "All right, time to get this show on the road. Here we go."

I'm not going to talk about the Bar Mitzvah, not *as* a Bar Mitzvah, except to say that it wasn't nearly the catastrophe I'd been envisioning for months. It couldn't have been. I stumbled on the prayers, Lord knows how many times, but Rabbi Tuvim had his back to the onlookers, and he fed me the lines I'd forgotten, and we got through. Oddly enough, the speech itself—I had chosen to discuss a passage in Numbers 1–9, showing how the Israelites first consolidated themselves as a community at Sinai—flowed much more smoothly, and I found myself practically enjoying the taste of Hebrew in my mouth. If the rabbi could teach me nothing else, somehow I'd come to understand the sound. Not the words, not the grammar, and certainly not the true meaning . . . just the *sound*. Nearing the grand finale, I wasn't thinking at all about the gift table in the farthest corner of the room. I was already beginning to regret that the speech wasn't longer.

That was when I saw her.

Anoush.

Small and dark, olive-skinned, she was no magazine cover girl now, but a woman of Sheila Olsen's age. She stood near the back of the room, away on the margins, as always. Sheila Olsen didn't see her, but I did, and she saw that I did, and I believe she saw also that I knew who and *how* she was. She didn't react, except to move further into shadow—she cast none of her own—but I could still see her eyes. No one else seemed to notice her at all; yet now and then someone would bump into her, or step on her foot, and immediately say, "Oh, sorry, excuse me," just as though she were living flesh. I tried to catch Sheila Olsen's eye, and then Rabbi Tuvim's, to indicate with my chin and my own eyes where they should look, but they never once turned their heads. It was very nearly as frustrating as learning Hebrew.

I finished the speech any old how, and when I was done, my mother came out and put her father's tallis on my shoulders, and everybody cheered except me. All I wanted to do was to draw Sheila Olsen's attention to the shy, ghostly presence of her sister, but I lost track of both of them when the hard round candies began showering down on me. It was going to make for an uncertain dance floor—Herbie Kaufman's Bel-Air Combo were busily setting up—but a number of my schoolmates were crowding onto it, followed by a few wary older couples. I was down from the little stage and weaving through the crush, tallis and all, pushing past congratulatory shoulder punches and butt slaps, not to mention the flash cameras—forbidden during the ceremony itself—going off in my face as I hunted for Sheila Olsen, frantic that she might already have left. She had a plane to catch, after all, and things to decide to remember or forget.

I was slowing down, beginning to give up, when I spotted her heading for the door, but slowed down by the press of bodies, so that she heard when I called her name. She turned, and I waved wildly, not at her, but toward the shadowless figure motionlessly watching her leave. And for the first time, Sheila Olsen and Eleanor Araxia Bagaybagayan saw each other.

Neither moved at first. Neither spoke—Sheila Olsen plainly didn't dare, and I don't think Anoush could. Then, very slowly, as though she were trying to slip up on some wild thing, Sheila Olsen began to ease toward her sister, holding out her open hands. She was facing me, and I saw her lips moving, but I couldn't hear the words.

But for every step Sheila Olsen took, Anoush took one step back from her, remaining as unreachable—*there, not there*—as her father Abel had found her, so many years before. Strangely, for me, since I had never seen her as beautiful on the magazine covers—only hypnotically *alive*—now, as a middle-aged woman, she almost stopped my newly-manly heart. There was gray in her hair, a heaviness to her face and midsection, and in the way she moved . . . but my heart wanted to stop, all the same.

I was afraid that Sheila Olsen might snap, out of too much wishing, and make some kind of dive or grab for Anoush, but she did something else. She stopped moving forward, and just stood very still for a moment, and then she reached into her purse and brought out the lacy little key that she had taken from Rabbi Tuvim's collection. She stared at it for a moment, and then she kissed it, very quickly, and she tossed it underhand toward Anoush. It spun so slowly, turning in the light like a butterfly, that I wouldn't have been surprised if it never came down.

Anoush caught it. Ghost or no ghost, ethereal or not, she picked Sheila Olsen's key out of the air as daintily as though she were selecting exactly the right apple on a tree, the perfect note on a musical instrument. She looked back at Sheila Olsen, and she smiled a little—I *know* she smiled, I *saw* her—and she touched the key to her lips . . .

. . . and I don't know what she did with it, or where she put it—maybe she *ate* it, for all I could ever tell. All I can say for certain is that Sheila Olsen's eyes got very big, and she touched her own mouth again, and then she turned and hurried out of the synagogue, never looking back, I was going to follow her, but Rabbi Tuvim came up and put his hand gently on my shoulder. He said, "She has a plane to catch. You have a special party. Each to his own."

"You saw," I said. "Did you see her?"

"It is more important that you saw her," the rabbi answered. "And that you made Sheila Olsen see her, you brought them together. That was the mitzvah—the rest is unimportant, a handful of candy." He patted my shoulder. "You did well."

Anoush was gone, of course, when we looked for her. So was the rabbi's key, though I actually got down on my knees to feel around where she had stood, half-afraid that it had simply fallen through her shade to the floor. But there was no sign of it; and the rabbi, watching, said quietly, "One lock opened. So many more." We went back to the party then.

Film took longer to develop in those days, unless you did it yourself. As I remember, it was more than a week before friends and family started bringing us shots taken at my Bar Mitzvah party. I hated almost all of them—somehow I always seemed to get caught with my mouth open and a goofy startled look on my face—but my mother cherished them all, and pored over them at the kitchen table for hours at a time. "There you are again, dancing with your cousin Marilyn, what was Sarah ever *thinking*, letting her wear that to a Bar Mitzvah?" "There you are in your grandpa's tallis, looking so grownup, except I was so afraid your yarmulke was going to fall off." "Oh, there's that one I love, with you and your father, I *told* him not to wear that tie, and your friend what's-his-name, he should lose some weight. And there's Rabbi Tuvim, what's that in his beard, dandruff?" Actually, it was cream cheese. The rabbi loved cream cheese.

Then she turned over a photo she'd missed before, and said in a different tone, "Who's that woman? Joseph, do you know that woman?"

It was Anoush, off to one side beyond the dancers I'd been shoving my way through to reach Sheila Olsen. She had her arms folded across her breast, and she looked immensely alone as she watched the party; but she didn't look lonely at all, or even wistful—just alone. As long as it's been, I remember a certain mischievousness around her mouth and eyes, as though she had deliberately slipped into this photograph of my celebration, just as she had slipped comfortably into her father's work—yes, to wave to him, as Sheila Olsen had said mockingly then. To wave to her sister now . . . and maybe, a little, to me.

I practically snatched the picture our of my mother's hand—making up some cockamamie story about an old friend of Rabbi Tuvim's—and brought it to him immediately. We both looked at it in silence for a long while. Then the rabbi put it carefully into a sturdy envelope, and addressed it to Sheila Olsen in Grand Forks, North Dakota. I took it to the post office myself, and paid importantly, out of my allowance, to send it Airmail Special Delivery. The rabbi promised to tell me as soon as Sheila Olsen wrote back.

It took longer than I expected: a good two weeks, probably more. After the first week, I was badgering the rabbi almost every day; sometimes twice, because they still had two postal deliveries back then. How he kept from strangling me, or anyway hanging up in my ear, I have no idea—perhaps he sympathized with my impatience because he was anxious himself. At all events, when Sheila Olsen's letter did arrive, he called me immediately. He offered to read it to me over the phone, but I wanted to see it, so I ran over. Rabbi Tuvim gave me a glass of cocoa cream soda, insisted maddeningly on waiting until I could breathe and speak normally, and then showed me the letter.

It was short, and there was no salutation; it simply began:

> "She sits on my bedside table, in a little silver frame. I say goodnight and good morning to her every day. I have tried several times to make copies for you, but they never come out. I'm sorry.
> Thank you for the key, Rabbi.
> And Joseph, Joseph—thank you."

I still have the letter. The rabbi gave it to me. It sits in its own wooden frame, and people ask me about it, because it's smudged and grubby from many readings, and frayed along the folding, and it looks as though a three-year-old has been at it, which did happen, many years later. But I keep it close, because before that letter I had no understanding of beauty, and no idea of what love is, or what can be born out of love. And after it I knew enough at least to recognize these things when they came to me.

THE WAY IT WORKS OUT
AND ALL

Okay, it's my fault. I'm largely the one who spread the rumor, so I'm responsible to put it to rest. Avram Davidson did *not* know everything in the world.
Almost . . . but not quite. I have a distinct memory of doing a reading at U. C.
Irvine, where Avram was teaching at the time, to find him sitting in a front
row, holding a frisky helium balloon in one hand, and a pretty young student's
hand in the other. After I finished my gig (somewhat distracted by performing in front of one of my major heroes, old friend or no), Avram came
up to give me a hug and to inquire, quite seriously, "What do you know about
feral camels?" As it happened, I *did* know something about a tentative attempt by the American Army, in the days after the Civil War, to introduce
a small force of camels into the deserts of the Southwest. The attempt was
soon abandoned; but for many years afterward, soldiers and nineteenth-cen-
tury tourists alike would report having seen impossible ghostlike creatures
materializing out of a sandstorm, and vanishing again just as swiftly. I still
find it unlikely that Avram really didn't know something that I, with my
ragbag, hit-or-miss education, actually knew. More than likely, he was just
being kind to my ego.

However, it would certainly have been Avram who discovered the
Overneath. He would.

In the ancient, battered, altogether sinister filing cabinet where I
stash stuff I know I'll lose if I keep it anywhere less carnivorous,
there is a manila folder crammed with certain special postcards—
postcards where every last scintilla of space not taken by an image or
an address block has been filled with tiny, idiosyncratic, yet perfectly
legible handwriting, the work of a man whose only real faith lay in the

written word (emphasis on the written). These cards are organized
by their postmarked dates, and there are long gaps between most of
them, but not all: thirteen from March of 1992 were mailed on con-
secutive days.

A printed credit in the margin on the first card in this set identifies
it as coming from the W. G. Reisterman Co. of Duluth, Minnesota.
The picture on the front shows three adorable snuggling kittens. Avram
Davidson's message, written in his astonishing hand, fills the still-legible
portion of the reverse:

> MARCH 4, 1992
>
> Estimado Dom Pedro del Bronx y Las Lineas sub-
> terraneos D, A, y F, Grand High Collector of Revenues
> both Internal and External for the State of North Da-
> kota and Points Beyond:

He always addressed me as "Dom Pedro."

> Maestro!
>
> I write you from the historic precincts of Darkest
> Albany, where the Erie Canal turns wearily around and
> trudges back to even Darker Buffalo. I am at present
> engaged in combing out the utterly disheveled files of
> the New York State Bureau of Plumbing Designs, De-
> vices, Patterns, and Sinks, all with the devious aim of
> rummaging through New York City's dirty socks and
> underwear, in hope of discovering the source of the

There is more—much more—but somewhere between his hand and
my mailbox it had been rendered illegible by large splashes of something unknown, perhaps rain, perhaps melting snow, perhaps spilled
Stolichnaya, which had caused the ink of the postcard to run and smear.
Within the blotched and streaky blurs I could only detect part of a

word which might equally have read *phlox* or *physic*, or neither. In any case, on the day the card arrived even that characteristic little was good for a chuckle, and a resolve to write Avram more frequently, if his address would just stay still.

But then there came the second card, one day later.

> March 5, 1992
>
> Intended solely for the Hands of the Highly Esteemed and Estimated Dom Pedro of the Just As Highly Esteemed North Bronx, and for such further Hands as he may Deem Worthy, though his taste in Comrades and Associates was Always Rotten, as witness:
>
> Your Absolute Altitude, with or without mice . . .
>
> I am presently occupying the top of a large, hairy quadruped, guaranteed by a rather shifty-eyed person to be of the horse persuasion, but there is no persuading it to do anything but attempt to scrape me off against trees, bushes, motor vehicles, and other horses. We are proceeding irregularly across the trackless wastes of the appropriately-named <u>Jornada del Muerto</u>, in the southwestern quadrant of New Mexico, where I have been advised that a limestone cave entrance makes it possibly possible to address

Here again, the remainder is obliterated, this time by what appears to be either horse or cow manure, though feral camel is also a slight, though unlikely, option. At all events, this postcard too is partially, crucially—and maddeningly—illegible. But that's really not the point.

The next postcard showed up the following day.

> March 6, 1992
>
> To Dom Pedro, Lord of the Riverbanks and Midnight Hayfields, Dottore of Mystical Calligraphy,

Lieutenant-Harrier of the Queen's Coven—greetings!

This epistle comes to you from the Bellybutton of the World—to be a bit more precise, the North Pole—where, if you will credit me, the New York State Civic Drain comes to a complete halt, apparently having given up on ever finding the Northwest Passage. I am currently endeavoring, with the aid of certain Instruments of my own Devising, to ascertain the truth—if any such exists—of the hollow-Earth legend. Tarzan says he's been there, and if you can't take the word of an ape-man, I should like to know whose word you can take, huh? In any case, the entrance to Pellucidar is not my primary goal (though it would certainly be nice finally to have a place to litter, pollute, and despoil in good conscience). What I seek, you—faithful Companion of the Bath and Poet Laureate of the High Silly—shall be the first to know when/if I discover it. Betimes, bethink your good self of your bedraggled, besmirched, beshrewed, belabored, and generally verklempt old friend, at this writing attempting to roust a polar bear out of his sleeping bag, while inviting a comely Inuk (or, alternatively, Inuit, I'm easy) in. Yours in Mithras, Avram, the A. K.

Three postcards in three days, dated one after the other. Each with a different (and genuine—I checked) postmark from three locations spaced so far apart, both geographically and circumstantially, that even the Flash would have had trouble hitting them all within three days, let alone a short, stout, arthritic, asthmatic gentleman of nearly seventy years' duration. I'm as absent-minded and unobservant as they come, but even I had noticed that improbability before the fourth postcard arrived.

THE WAY IT WORKS OUT AND ALL

March 7, 1992

Sent by fast manatee up the Japanese Current and down the Humboldt, there at last to encounter the Gulf Stream in its mighty course, and so to the hands of a certain Dom Pedro, Pearl of the Orient, Sweetheart of Sigma Chi, and Master of Hounds and Carburetors to She Who Must Not Be Aggravated.

So how's by you?

By me, here in East Wimoweh-on-the-Orinoco, alles ist maddeningly almost. I feel myself on the cusp (precisely the region where we were severely discouraged from feeling ourselves, back in Boys' Town) of at last discovering—wait for it—*the secret plumbing of the world!* No, this has nothing to do with Freemasons, Illuminati, the darkest files and codexes of Mother Church, nor—*ptui, ptui*—the Protocols of the Learned Elders of Zion. Of conspiracies and secret societies, there is no end or accounting; but the only one of any account has ever been the Universal International Brotherhood of Sewer Men (in recent years corrected to Sewer Personnel) and Plumbing Contractors. This organization numbers, not merely the people who come to unstop your sink and hack the tree roots out of your septic tank, but the nameless giants who laid the true underpinnings of what we think of as civilization, society, culture. Pipes far down under pipes, tunnels beyond tunnels, vast valves and connections, profound couplings and joints and elbows—all members of the UIBSPPC are sworn to secrecy by the most dreadful oaths and the threat of the most awful penalties for revealing . . . well, the usual, you get the idea. Real treehouse boys' club stuff. Yoursley yours, Avram

I couldn't read the postmark clearly for all the other stamps and post-marks laid over it—though my guess would be Brazil—but you see my point. There was simply no way in the world for him to have sent me those cards from those four places in that length of time. Either he had widely scattered friends, participants in the hoax, mailing them out for him, or . . . but there wasn't any *or*, there couldn't be, for that idea made no sense. Avram told jokes—some of them unquestionably translated from the Middle Sumerian, and losing something along the way—but he didn't *play* jokes, and he wasn't a natural jokester.

Nine more serially dated postcards followed, not arriving every day, but near enough. By postmark and internal description they had been launched to me from, in order:

> Equatorial Guinea
> Turkmenistan
> Dayton, Ohio
> Lviv in Ukraine
> The Isle of Eigg
> Pinar del Río (in Cuba, where Americans weren't
> permitted to travel!)
> Hobart, capital of the Australian territory of Tasmania
> Shigatse, Tibet

And finally, tantalizingly, from Davis, California. Where I actually lived at the time, though nothing in the card's text indicated any attempt to visit.

After that the flurry of messages stopped, though not my thoughts about them. Trying to unpuzzle the mystery had me at my wits' rope (a favorite phrase of Avram's), until the lazy summer day I came around a corner in the Chelsea district of New York City . . .

. . . and literally ran into a short, stout, bearded, flat-footed person who seemed almost to have been running, though that was as unlikely a prospect as his determining on a career in professional basketball. It

was Avram. He was formally dressed, the only man I knew who habitually wore a tie, vest, and jacket that all matched; and if he looked a trifle disheveled, that was equally normal for him. He blinked at me briefly, looked around him in all directions, then said thoughtfully, "A bit close, that was." To me he said, as though we had dined the night before, or even that morning, "I did warn you the crab salad smelled a bit off, didn't I?"

It took me a moment of gaping to remember that the last time we had been together was at a somewhat questionable dive in San Francisco's Mission District, and I'd been showing signs of ptomaine poisoning by the time I dropped him off at home. I said meekly, "So you did, but did I listen? What on earth are you doing here?" He had been born in Yonkers, but felt more at home almost anyplace else, and I couldn't recall ever being east of the Mississippi with him, if you don't count a lost weekend in Minneapolis.

"Research," he said briskly: an atypical adverb to apply to his usual rambling, digressive style of speaking. "Can't talk. Tomorrow, two-twenty-two, Victor's." And he was gone, practically scurrying away down the street—an unlikely verb, this time: Avram surely had never scurried in his life. I followed, at an abnormally rapid pace myself, calling to him; but when I rounded the corner, he was nowhere in sight. I stood still, scratching my head, while people bumped into me and said irritated things.

The "two-twenty-two" part I understood perfectly well: it was a running joke between us, out of an ancient burlesque routine. That was when we always scheduled our lunch meetings, neither of us ever managing to show up on time. It was an approximation, a deliberate mockery of precision and exactitude. As for Victor's Café, that was a Cuban restaurant on West 52nd Street, where they did—and still do—remarkable things with unremarkable ingredients. I had no idea that Avram knew of it.

I slept poorly that night, on the cousin's couch where I always crash in New York. It wasn't that Avram had looked frightened—I had never seen him afraid, not even of a bad review—but perturbed, yes . . . you could have said that he had looked *perturbed*, even perhaps just a touch *flustered*. It was distinctly out of character, and Avram out of character worried me. Like a cat, I prefer that people remain where I leave them—not only physically, but psychically as well. But Avram was clearly not where he had been.

I wound up rising early on a blue and already hot morning, made break-fast for my cousin and myself, then killed time as best I could until I gave up and got to Victor's at a little after 1 P.M. There I sat at the bar, nursing a couple of Cuban beers, until Avram arrived. The time was exactly two-twenty-two, both on my wrist, and on the clock over the big mirror, and when I saw that, I knew for certain that Avram was in trouble.

Not that he showed it in any obvious way. He seemed notably more relaxed than he had been at our street encounter, chatting easily, while we waited for a table, about our last California vodka-deepened con-versation, in which he had explained to me the real reason why garlic is traditionally regarded as a specific against vampires, and the rather shocking historical misunderstandings that this myth had occasionally led to. Which led to his own translation of Vlad Tepes's private diaries (I never did learn just how many languages Avram actually knew) and thence to Dracula's personal comments regarding the original Mina Harker . . . but then the waiter arrived to show us to our table; and by the time we sat down, we were into the whole issue of why certain Nilotic tribes habitually rest standing on one foot. All that was before the *Bartolito* was even ordered.

It wasn't until the entrée had arrived that Avram squinted across the table and pronounced, through a mouthful of sweet plantain and black bean sauce, "Perhaps you are wondering why I have called you all here today." He was doing his mad-scientist voice, which always sounded like Peter Lorre on nitrous oxide.

"Us all were indeed wondering, Big Bwana, sir," I answered him, making a show of looking left and right at the crowded restaurant. "Not a single dissenting voice."

"Good. Can't abide dissension in the ranks." Avram sipped his wine and focused on me with an absolute intensity that was undiluted by his wild beard and his slightly bemused manner. "You are aware, of course, that I could not possibly have been writing to you from all the destinations that my recent missives indicated."

I nodded.

Avram said, "And yet I was. I did."

"Um." I had to say something, so I mumbled, "Anything's possible. You know, the French rabbi Rashi—tenth, eleventh century—he was supposed—"

"To be able to walk between the raindrops," Avram interrupted impatiently. "Yes, well, maybe he did the same thing I've done. Maybe he found his way into the Overneath, like me."

We looked at each other: him waiting calmly for my reaction, me too bewildered to react at all. Finally I said, "The Overneath. Where's that?" Don't tell *me* I can't come up with a swift zinger when I need to.

"It's all around us." Avram made a sweeping semicircle with his right arm, almost knocking over the next table's excellent Pinot Grigio—Victor's does tend to pack them in—and inflicting a minor flesh wound on the nearer diner, since Avram was still holding his fork. Apologies were offered and accepted, along with a somewhat lower-end bottle of wine, which I had sent over. Only then did Avram continue. "In this particular location, it's about forty-five degrees to your left, and a bit up—I could take you there this minute."

I said *um* again. I said, "You are aware that this does sound, as directions go, just a bit like 'Second star to the right, and straight on till morning.' No dissent intended."

"No stars involved." Avram was waving his fork again. "More like turning left at this or that manhole cover—climbing this stair in this old building—peeing in one particular urinal in Grand Central Station." He chuckled suddenly, one corner of his mouth twitching sharply upward. "Funny . . . if I hadn't taken a piss in Grand Central . . . hah! Try some of the vaca frita, it's really good."

"Stick to pissing, and watch it with that fork. What happened in Grand Central?"

"Well. I shouldn't have been there, to begin with." Avram, it could have been said of him, lived to digress, both as artist and companion. "But I had to go—you know how it is—and the toilet in the diner upstairs was broken. So I went on down, into the kishkas of the beast, you could say . . ." His eyes had turned thoughtful and distant, looking past me. "That's really an astonishing place, Grand Central, you know? You ought to think about setting a novel there—you set one in a graveyard, after all—"

"So you were in the Grand Central men's room—*and?*" I may have raised my voice a little; people were glancing over at us, but with tolerant amusement, which has not always been the case. "And, *maître?*"

"Yes. And." The eyes were suddenly intent again, completely present and focused, his own voice lower, even, deliberate. "And I walked out of that men's room through that same door where in I went—" he could quote the Rubáiyát in the damnedest contexts—"and walked into another place. I wasn't in Grand Central Station at all."

I'd seen a little too much, and known him far too long, not to know when he was serious. I said simply, "Where were you?"

"Another country," Avram repeated. "I call it *the Overneath*, because it's above us and around us and below us, all at the same time. I wrote you about it."

I stared at him.

"*I did*. Remember the Universal International Brotherhood of Sewer Persons and Plumbing Contractors? The sub-basement of reality—all those pipes and valves and tunnels and couplings, sewers and tubes . . . the everything other than everything? That's the Overneath, only I wasn't calling it that then—I was just finding my way around, I didn't know *what* to call it. *Got* to make a map . . ." He paused, my bafflement and increasing anxiety obviously having become obvious. "No, no, stop that. I'm testy and peremptory, and sometimes I can be downright fussy—I'll go that far—but I'm no crazier than I ever was. The Overneath is real, and by gadfrey, I *will* take you there when we're done here. You having dessert?"

I didn't have dessert. We settled up, complimented the chef, tipped the waiter, and strolled outside into an afternoon turned strangely . . . not foggy, exactly, but *indefinite*, as though all outlines had become just a trifle uncertain, willing to debate their own existence. I stopped where I was, shaking my head, taking off my glasses to blow on them and put them back on. Beside me, Avram gripped my arm hard. He said, quietly but intensely, "Now. Take two steps to the right, and turn around."

I looked at him. His fingers bit into my arm hard enough to hurt. "Do it!"

I did as he asked, and when I turned around, the restaurant was gone.

I never learned where we were then. Avram would never tell me. My vision had cleared, but my eyes stung from the cold, dust-laden twilight wind blowing down an empty dirt road. All of New York—sounds, smells, voices, texture—had vanished with Victor's Café. I didn't know where we were, nor how we'd gotten there; but I suppose it's a good thing to have that depth of terror over with, because I have never been that frightened, not before and not since. There wasn't a living thing in sight, nor any suggestion that there ever had been. I can't even tell you to this day how I managed to speak, to make sounds, to whisper a dry-throated *"Where are we?"* to Avram. Just writing about it brings it all back—I'm honestly trembling as I set these words down.

Avram said mildly, "Shit. Must have been *three* steps right. Namporte," which was always his all-purpose reassurance in uneasy moments. "Just walk *exactly* in my footsteps and do me after me." He started on along the road—which, as far as I could see, led nowhere but to more road and more wind—and I, terrified of doing something wrong and being left behind in this dreadful place, mimicked every step, every abrupt turn of the head or arthritic leap to the side, like a child playing hopscotch. At one point, Avram even tucked up his right leg behind him and made the hop on one foot; so did I.

I don't recall how long we kept this up. What I *do* recall, and wish I didn't, was the moment when Avram suddenly stood very still—as, of course, did I—and we both heard, very faintly, a kind of soft, scratchy padding behind us. Every now and then, the padding was broken by a clicking sound, as though claws had crossed a patch of stone.

Avram said, "Shit" again. He didn't move any faster—indeed, he put a hand out to check me when I came almost even with him—but he kept looking more and more urgently to the left, and I could see the anxiety in his eyes. I remember distracting myself by trying to discern, from the rhythm of the sound, whether our pursuer was following on two legs or four. I've no idea today why it seemed to matter so much, but it did then.

"Keep moving," Avram said. He was already stepping out ahead of me, walking more slowly now, so that I, constantly looking back—as he never did—kept stepping on the backs of his shoes. He held his elbows tightly against his body and reached out ahead of him with hands and forearms alone, like a recently blinded man. I did what he did.

Even now . . . even now, when I dream about that terrible dirt road, it's never the part about stumbling over things that I somehow knew not to look at too closely, nor the unvarying soft *clicking* just out of sight behind us . . . no, it's always Avram marching ahead of me, making funny movements with his head and shoulders, his arms prodding and twisting the air ahead of him like bread dough. And it's always me tailing along, doing my best to keep up, while monitoring every slightest gesture, or what even *looks* like a gesture, intentional or not. In the dream, we go on and on, apparently without any goal, without any future.

Suddenly Avram cried out, strangely shrilly, in a language I didn't know—which I imitated as best I could—then did a complete hopscotch spin-around, and actually flung himself down on the hard ground to the left. I did the same, jarring the breath out of myself and closing my eyes for an instant. When I opened them again, he was already up, standing on tiptoe—I remember thinking, *Oh, that's got to hurt, with his gout*—and reaching up as high as he could with his left hand. I did the same . . . felt something hard and rough under my fingers . . . pulled myself up, as he did . . .

. . . and found myself in a different place, my left hand still gripping what turned out to be a projecting brick in a tall pillar. We were standing in what felt like a huge railway station, its ceiling arched beyond my sight, its walls dark and blank, with no advertisements, nor even the name of the station. Not that the name would have meant much, because there were no railroad tracks to be seen. All I knew was that we were off the dirt road; dazed with relief, I giggled absurdly—even a little crazily, most likely. I said, "Well, I don't remember *that* being part of the Universal Studios tour."

Avram drew a deep breath, and seemed to let out more air than he took in. He said, "All right. That's more like it."

"More like *what?*" I have spent a goodly part of my life being bewildered, but this remains the gold standard. "Are we still in the Overneath?"

"We are in the *hub* of the Overneath," Avram said proudly. "The heart, if you will. That place where we just were, it's like a local stop in a bad part of town. *This* . . . from here you can get anywhere at all. Anywhere. All you have to do is—" he hesitated, finding an image—"point yourself properly, and the Overneath will take you there. It helps if you happen to know the exact geographical coordinates of where you want to go—" I never doubted for a moment that he himself did—"but what matters most is to focus, to feel the complete and unique reality of that particular place, and then just . . . *be* there." He shrugged and smiled, looking a trifle embarrassed. "Sorry to sound so cosmic and one-with-everything. I was a long while myself getting the knack of it all. I'd aim for Machu Picchu and come out in Capetown, or try for the Galapagos and hit Reykjavik, time after time. Okay, tovarich, where in the world would you like to—"

"Home," I said before he'd even finished the question. "New York City, West Seventy-ninth Street. Drop me off at Central Park, I'll walk from there." I hesitated, framing my question. "But will we just pop out of the ground there, or shimmer into existence, or what? And will it be the real Seventy-ninth Street, or . . . or not? Mon capitaine, there does seem to be a bit of dissension in the ranks. Talk to me, Big Bwana, sir."

"When you met me in Chelsea," Avram began; but I had turned away from him, looking down to the far end of the station—as I still think of it—where, as I hadn't before, I saw human figures moving. Wildly excited, I waved to them, and was about to call out when Avram clapped his hand over my mouth, pulling me down, shaking his head fiercely, but speaking just above a whisper. "You don't want to do that. You don't ever want to do that."

"Why not?" I demanded angrily. "They're the first damn *people* we've seen—"

"They aren't exactly people." Avram's voice remained low, but he was clearly ready to silence me again, if need be. "You can't ever be sure in the Overneath."

The figures didn't seem to be moving any closer, but I couldn't see them any better, either. "Do they live here? Or are they just making connections, like us? Catching the red-eye to Portland?"

Avram said slowly, "A lot of people use the Overneath, Dom Pedro. Most are transients, passing through, getting from one place to another without buying gas. But . . . yes, there *are* things that live here, and they don't like us. Maybe for them it's 'there goes the neighborhood,' I don't know—there's so much I'm still learning. But I'm quite clear on the part about the distaste . . . and I think I could wish that you hadn't waved quite so."

There *was* movement toward us now—measured, but definitely concerted. Avram was already moving himself, more quickly than I could recall having seen him. "This way!" he snapped over his shoulder, leading me, not back to the pillar which had received us into this nexus of the Overneath, but away, back into blind dark that closed in all around, until I felt as if we were running down and down a subway tunnel with a train roaring close behind us, except that in this case the train was a string of creatures whose faces I'd made the mistake of glimpsing just before Avram and I fled. He was right about them not being people.

We can't have run very far, I think now. Apart from the fact that we were already exhausted, Avram had flat feet and gout, and I had no wind worth mentioning. But our pursuers seemed to fall away fairly early, for reasons I can't begin to guess—fatigue? boredom? the satisfaction of having routed intruders in their world?—and we had ample excuse for slowing down, which our bodies had already done on their own. I wheezed to Avram, "Is there another place like that one?"

Even shaking his head in answer seemed an effort. "Not that I've yet discovered. Namporte—we'll just get home on the local. *All will be well, and all manner of things shall be well.*" Avram hated T. S. Eliot, and had permanently assigned the quotation to Shakespeare, though he knew better.

I didn't know what he meant by "the local," until he suddenly veered left, walked a kind of rhomboid pattern—with me on his heels—and we were again on a genuine sidewalk on a warm late-spring afternoon. There were little round tables and beach umbrellas on the street, bright pennants twitching languidly in a soft breeze that smelled faintly of nutmeg and ripening citrus, and of the distant sea. And there were *people*: perfectly ordinary men and women, wearing slacks and sport coats and sundresses, sitting at the little tables, drinking coffee and wine, talking, smiling at each other, never seeming to take any notice of us. Dazed and drained, swimming in the scent and the wonder of sunlight, I said feebly, "Paris? Malaga?"

"Croatia," Avram replied. "Hvar Island—big tourist spot, since the Romans. Nice place." Hands in his pockets, rocking on his heels, he glanced somewhat wistfully at the holidaymakers. "Don't suppose you'd be interested in staying on awhile?" But he was starting away before I'd even shaken my head, and he wasn't the one who looked back.

Traveling in darkness, we zigzagged and hedge-hopped between one location and the next, our route totally erratic, bouncing us from Croatia to bob up in a music store in Lapland . . . a wedding in Sri Lanka . . . the middle of a street riot in Lagos . . . an elementary-school classroom in Bahia. Avram was flying blind; we both knew it, and he never denied it. "Could have gotten us home in one jump from the hub—I'm a little shaky on the local stops; really *need* to work up a proper map. Namporte, not to worry."

And, strangely, I didn't. I was beginning—just beginning—to gain his sense of landmarks: of the Overneath junctures, the crossroads, detours, and spur lines where one would naturally turn left or right to head *here*, spin around to veer off *there*, or trust one's feet to an invisible stairway, up or down, finally emerging in *that* completely unexpected landscape. Caroming across the world as we were, it was difficult not to feel like a marble in a pinball machine, but in general we did appear to be working our way more or less toward the east coast of North America. We celebrated with a break in a Liverpool dockside pub, where the barmaid didn't look twice at Avram's purchase of two pints of porter, and didn't look at me at all. I was beginning to get used to that, but it still puzzled me, and I said so.

"The Overneath's grown used to me," Avram explained. "That's one thing I've learned about the Overneath—it grows, it adapts, same as the body can adapt to a foreign presence. If you keep using it, it'll adapt to you the same way."

"So right now the people here see you, but can't see me."

Avram nodded. I said, "Are they real? Are all these places we've hit— these local stops of yours—are they real? Do they go on existing when nobody from—what? *outside,* I guess—is passing through? Is this an alternate universe, with everybody having his counterpart here, or just a little something the Overneath runs up for tourists?" The porter was quite real, anyway, if warm, and my deep swig almost emptied my glass. "I need to know, mon maître."

Avram sipped his own beer and coughed slightly; and I realized with a pang how much older than I he was, and that he had absolutely no business being a pinball—nor the only true adventurer I'd ever known. No business at all. He said, "The alternate universe thing, that's bullshit. Or if it isn't, doesn't matter—you can't get there from here." He leaned forward. "You know about Plato's Cave, Dom Pedro?"

"The people chained to the wall in the cave, just watching shadows all their lives? What about it?"

"Well, the shadows are cast by things and people coming and going outside the cave, which those poor prisoners never get to see. The shadows are their only notion of reality—they live and die never seeing anything but those shadows, trying to understand the world through shadows. The philosopher's the one who stands outside the cave and reports back. You want another beer?"

"No." Suddenly I didn't even want to finish the glass in my hand. "So our world, what we call our world . . . it might be nothing but the shadow of the Overneath?"

"Or the other way around. I'm still working on it. If you're finished, let's go."

We went outside, and Avram stood thoughtfully staring at seven and a half miles of docks and warehouses, seeming to sniff the gray air. I said, "My mother's family set off for America from here. I think it took them three weeks."

"We'll do better." He was standing with his arms folded, mumbling to himself: "No way to get close to the harbor, damn it . . . too bad we didn't fetch up on the other side of the Mersey . . . best thing would be . . . best thing . . . no . . . I wonder . . ."

Abruptly he turned and marched us straight back into the pub, where he asked politely for the loo. Directed, he headed down a narrow flight of stairs; but, to my surprise, passed by the lavatory door and kept following the stairway, telling me over his shoulder, "Most of these old pubs were built over water, for obvious reasons. And don't ask me why, not yet, but the Overneath likes water . . ." I was smelling damp earth now, earth that had never been quite dry, perhaps for hundreds of years. I heard a throb nearby that might have been a sump pump of some sort, and caught a whiff of sewage that was definitely not centuries old. I got a glimpse of hollow darkness ahead and thought wildly, *Christ, it's a drain! That's it, we're finally going right down the drain . . .*

Avram hesitated at the bottom of the stair, cocking his head back like a gun hammer. Then it snapped forward, and he grunted in triumph and led me, not into my supposed drain, but to the side of it, into an apparent wall through which we passed with no impediment, except a slither of stones under our feet. The muck sucked at my shoes—long since too far gone for my concern—as I plodded forward in Avram's wake. Having to stop and cram them back on scared me, because he just kept slogging on, never looking back. Twice I tripped and almost fell over things that I thought were rocks or branches; both times they turned out to be large, recognizable, disturbingly splintered bones. I somehow kept myself from calling Avram's attention to them, because I knew he'd want to stop and study them, and pronounce on their origin and function, and I didn't need that. I already knew what they were.

In time the surface became more solid under my feet, and the going got easier. I asked, half-afraid to know, "Are we under the harbor?"

"If we are, we're in trouble," Avram growled. "It'd mean I missed the . . . no, *no*, we're all right, we're fine, it's just—" His voice broke off abruptly, and I could feel rather than see him turning, as he peered back down the way we had come. He said, very quietly, "Well, *damn* . . ."

"What? *What?*" Then I didn't need to ask anymore, because I heard the sound of a foot being pulled out of the same mud I'd squelched through. Avram said, "All this way. They *never* follow that far . . . could have sworn we'd lost it in Lagos . . ." Then we heard the sound again, and Avram grabbed my arm, and we ran.

The darkness ran uphill, which didn't help at all. I remember my breath like stones in my lungs and chest, and I remember a desperate desire to stop and bend over and throw up. I remember Avram never letting go of my arm, literally dragging me with him . . . and the panting that I thought was mine, but that wasn't coming from either of us . . .

"Here!" Avram gasped. *"Here!"* and he let go and vanished between two boulders—or whatever they really were—so close together that I couldn't see how there could be room for his stout figure. I actually had to give him a push from behind, like Rabbit trying to get Pooh Bear out of his burrow; then I got stuck myself, and he grabbed me and pulled . . . and then we were both stuck there, and I couldn't breathe, and something had hold of my left shoe. Then Avram was saying, with a calmness that was more frightening than any other sound, even the sound behind me, "Point yourself. You know where we're going—point and *jump* . . ."

And I did. All I can remember is thinking about the doorman under the awning at my cousin's place . . . the elevator . . . the color of the couch where I would sleep when I visited . . . a kind of hissing howl

somewhere behind . . . a *shiver*, as though I were dissolving . . . or perhaps it was the crevice we were jammed into dissolving . . .

. . . and then my head was practically in the lap of Alice on her
mushroom: my cheek on smooth granite, my feet somewhere far away,
as though they were still back in the Overneath. I opened my eyes
in darkness—but a warm, different darkness, smelling of night grass
and engine exhaust—and saw Avram sprawled intimately across the
Mad Hatter. I slid groggily to the ground, helped to disentangle him
from Wonderland, and we stood silently together for a few moments,
watching the headlights on Madison Avenue. Some bird was whoop-
ing softly but steadily in a nearby tree, and a plane was slanting down
into JFK.

"Seventy-fifth," Avram said presently. "Only off by four blocks. Not
bad."

"Four blocks and a whole park." My left shoe was still on—muck and
all—but the heel was missing, and there were deep gouges in the sole.
I said, "You know, I used to be scared to go into Central Park at night."

We didn't see anyone as we trudged across the park to the West
Side, and we didn't say much. Avram wondered aloud whether it was
tonight or tomorrow night. "Time's a trifle hiccupy in the Overneath, I
never know how long . . ." I said we'd get a paper and find out, but I don't
recall that we did.

We parted on Seventy-ninth Street: me continuing west to my
cousin's building, and Avram evasive about his own plans, his own New
York destination. I said, "You're not going back there." It was not a question, and I may have been a little loud. "You're *not*."

He reassured me instantly—"No, no, I just want to walk for a while,
just walk and think. Look, I'll call you tomorrow, at your cousin's, give
me the number. I promise, I'll call."

He did, too, from a pay phone, telling me that he was staying with
old family friends in Yonkers, and that we'd be getting together in the
Bay Area when we both got back. But we never did; we spoke on the
phone a few times, but I never saw him again. I was on the road, in

Houston, when I heard about his death.

I couldn't get home for the funeral, but I did attend the memorial. There were a lot of obituaries—some in the most remarkable places— and a long period of old friends meeting, formally and informally, to tell stories about Avram and drink to his memory. That still goes on to- day; it never did take more than two of us to get started, and sometimes I hold one all by myself.

And no, I've never made any attempt to return to the Overneath. I try not to think about it very much. It's easier than you might imag- ine: I tell myself that our adventure never really happened, and by the time I'm decently senile, I'll believe it. When I'm in New York and pass Grand Central Station, I never go in, on principle. Whatever the need, it can wait.

But *he* went back into the Overneath, I'm sure—to work on his map, I suppose, and other things I can't begin to guess at. As to how I know . . .

Avram died on May 8th, 1993, just fifteen days after his seventieth birthday, in his tiny dank apartment in Bremerton, Washington. He closed his eyes and never opened them again. There was a body, and a coroner's report, and official papers and everything: books closed, doors locked, last period dotted in the file.

Except that a month later, when the hangover I valiantly earned during and after the memorial was beginning to seem merely colorful in memory rather than willfully obtuse, I got a battered postcard in the mail. It's in the file with the others. A printed credit in the margin identifies it as coming from the Westermark Press of Stone Heights, Pennsylvania. The picture on the front shows an unfrosted angel food cake decorated with a single red candle. The postmark includes the flag of Cameroon. And on the back, written in that astonishing, unmistak- able hand, is an impossible message.

May 9, 1993
To the Illustrissimo Dom Pedro, Compañero de

Todos mis Tonterias and Skittles Champion of Pacific
Grove (Senior Division), Greetings!

It's a funny thing about that Cave parable of Plato's.
The way it works out and all. Someday I'll come show
you.

Years have passed with nothing further . . . but I still take corners
slowly, just in case.

All corners.

Anywhere.

THE BEST WORST MONSTER

I like monsters. My children liked monsters (they often asked for monster stories at bedtime). I also like dogs, and poets—one day I'll set that poem of Beppo the Beggar's to music—and of course I was raised on mad scientists at Saturday matinees. So here they are, the lot of them, an all-star assemblage recalled for one last farewell performance, as though I were still leaning against a bunk bed in a room cluttered with picture-books and stuffed animals . . .

FROM THE TIPS of his twisted, spiky horns all the way down to his jagged claws, the monster was without any doubt the biggest, ugliest, most horrible creature ever made. Since his master had put him together out of spare parts lying around the house, some bits of him were power tools and old television sets, while other bits were made of plastic and wood and stone. His fiery eyes were streaked red and yellow, like the autumn moon, and even his ears and his hair had claws.

"There!" his master said proudly. "Aren't you a fine fellow?"

"Am I?" the monster asked. He had just seen himself in a mirror, and wasn't sure.

"You certainly are," said his master. Then he sent the monster off to stamp the post office flat, because the mailman never delivered any nice letters. This was a real pleasure for the monster, with all the mail flying in every direction, and boxed packages crunching like toast under his feet. It was even better the next day, when his master ordered him to use his great claws to pull the town's dance pavilion to pieces, just because no girl ever asked his master to dance with her. That was as much fun as a birthday party. He tore down the strings of bright colored lights, and chased the musicians away, and jumped up and down on the bandstand until all that remained was a lot of tiny splinters and a few small shreds of sheet music. The monster was sorry when there was nothing left to smash, because he would have loved to do it all over again.

That night though, while his master slept, the monster sat outside in the cold, clear air and noticed something that troubled him. He could see quite as well at night as in day, so it was easy for him to look down the rocky slope of his master's home and study the town curled up in the valley below. He could count every leaf and tile, every window and chimney. And he could see the small dark gaps where the post office and dance pavilion had stood. They were like two hollow eyes in a mask, staring back at him.

The monster didn't know much, being only two days old, but he knew that he didn't like how he was feeling. He wondered if there was something wrong with him.

Monsters are afraid of wondering, so when morning came he went to his master and said, "Something is happening to me. I don't know what it is, but it frightens me. Maybe you ought to order me to build something today—just for the change, just until this feeling goes away. I'm sure it will go away."

His master was horrified, and very angry too. "I can't *believe* this!" he screamed at the monster. "Are you growing a soul in that unspeakable patchwork body of yours? Well I'll take care of *that*, and right now!"

Whereupon he sprayed the monster from horns to claws to antenna-tipped tail with a nasty-smelling mixture called "SoulAway," which he had invented himself for just such occasions. After that he opened up the monster's intake valves and poured in gallons of another potion called "SoulBegone." Then he fed the monster an enormous pill that didn't have a name, and which stuck in the monster's throat. He had to climb up on a tall ladder and pound the monster on his back until it went down.

"There!" he said, "*That* should do it. A soul's no trouble to get rid of, if you catch it early."

120

"I still feel all funny," the monster mumbled.

But his master told him not to be a fool, and ordered him to go out and pull up the train tracks, because the whistle of the train was half a note sharp. "And while you're at it, smash up the bakery—I practically broke a tooth on a walnut in a cupcake yesterday. Go!"

From that morning on, no matter how hard the monster tried to please his master, things kept going wrong. Sometimes he actually found himself being kind, in a monsterish sort of way—like not trampling a home all the way flat, or making a lot of noise before he arrived, so people would have time to run away. Once he even ran away himself, to keep from being sent to squash a whole school where his master was never asked to come speak at graduation. But he couldn't stay away, because he got lonely. And that worried him even more, because he knew that wicked, soulless monsters were never ever supposed to feel lonely.

Then one evening, while the monster was watching the stars and wishing he were someone else, his master called for him. After giving him an extra-large dose of "SoulAway," his master smiled and ordered him to go into town and find a poet named Beppo the Beggar. When he found him, the monster was supposed to step on him, just as though he were a bakery or a post office.

"Why?"

"Because he made up a song about me, and I don't like it. Go and get him. Not his house, mind. *Him.*"

So the monster trudged unhappily away to trample a poet.

He found Beppo the Beggar lying on the riverbank with his hands behind his head, watching the sky and making up a poem. Beppo's little dog, who was called Pumpernickel, was fast asleep by his side, covered by Beppo's ragged old coat.

Beppo's poem began like this:

> "We fish together every night,
> My Uncle Moon and I.
> We bait our hooks with dreams,

And throw them in the sky . . . "

He looked over at Pumpernickel to see what his best friend thought of the poem so far, but the dog did not even open his eyes. Beppo sighed and chuckled. He tucked the coat closer around his pet, and continued:

> "My Uncle Moon, he catches stars,
> All burning white and blue.
> But I keep angling for your heart—
> No other fish will do . . . "

It was only then that he looked up and saw the monster's foot poised high over him, hiding the night sky and all the stars.

Beppo did not leap up, screaming and begging for his life. Instead he turned to Pumpernickel and shook him gently awake, telling him, "Run away now, little one. Take care of yourself, and remember me."

The monster stood on one foot, not moving, not saying a word.

Pumpernickel got to his feet, looked at Beppo with his head tilted to one side, and then trotted off into the darkness. Beppo the Beggar lay down again, smiling cheerfully up at that huge foot ready to squash him like a bug. He asked politely, "Would you mind very much letting me finish my poem? I *think* there's only one more verse."

The monster nodded. Beppo closed his eyes and considered, tracing words in the air with his right forefinger. After a moment he went on:

> "But if I caught you on my line,
> Or in my net below,
> No matter you're my one desire,
> I'd always let you go."

He looked straight at the monster again, and said, "Not great for a last poem, but then I'm not exactly a great poet." He spread his arms out wide, beckoning the foot down. "It's a great riverbank, anyway," he said, and he laughed.

The monster's foot came down . . .

. . . not on Beppo the Beggar, but very slowly and gently on the ground next to him.

Neither of them said a word. But after a moment the monster turned and started back the way he had come, along the road and up the stony hill to his master's house. He stamped along as noisily as he could, and for the first time in his life he sang, making up his own music, louder and louder and louder, like a marching song:

> "I don't know if I have a soul,
> I don't know if I WANT a soul—
> But whatever Beppo the Beggar has,
> I want one of those!"

He was a really terrible singer.

His master heard him coming from a long way off, and he knew exactly what all that racket meant. He stayed just long enough to grab up some monster-making tools and his one good suit, and then he ran out the back door of his house before his monster even got there. And whatever became of him, nobody knows . . .

But everybody in town can tell you what became of his monster.

That very day the monster set about rebuilding everything he had ever smashed to pieces. When he was done with that, he built a house in town for himself, a very big house, with a back garden and a birdbath. After a time people began to ask him to come to dinner: he always went, and was careful not to eat too much or stay too long. He even learned to dance in the new pavilion . . . in a monsterish sort of way.

From time to time, though, he still felt lonely. On those nights he would sit on the hilltop where his master's house lay abandoned, and ask himself questions with no answers. "Do I have a soul? Do I only *think* I have a soul? Does it matter?"

And then—after waiting just the right amount of time, because that's what friends do—Beppo the Beggar would call up to him with a cheery hello. And Beppo's little dog, Pumpernickel, would jump up on his huge lap to lick his frightful face. And the monster would smile, with his fangs and his forked tongue and his puzzled, happy heart, and he'd pick Beppo and Pumpernickel up and carry them back down into town on his shoulders, singing dreadfully all the way.

LA LUNE T'ATTEND

I've always had a soft spot for shape-shifters in general, and the *loup-garou* legend in particular, yet my only two werewolf stories—"Lila the Werewolf" and this one—are more than forty years apart in age. A good deal has changed in that time. It's worth mentioning that "Lila," written on simple impulse in 1967, originally couldn't find any other publisher than an obscure UC Santa Cruz literary magazine; while "La Lune T'Attend" was specifically commissioned for an anthology of urban werewolf tales from a major publishing house, and hit bookstores in a world where such creatures have become a pop culture staple.

I've never yet been to Louisiana, but I've known many Creoles and Cajuns over time, listened to a lot of family stories, and have read and studied and questioned all I could into *voudun*, *Santeria*, and other rich and flourishing transplants from West African soil. (Arceneaux's prayers to the Yoruba god Damballa, by the way, were originally notated during late-night conversations that took place very long ago.) That said, "La Lune T'Attend" isn't a cultural treatise or an academic dissertation of any sort. It's a family story.

E VEN ONCE A MONTH, Arceneaux hated driving his daughter Noelle's car. There was no way to be comfortable: he was a big old man, and the stick-shift hatchback cramped his legs and elbows, playing Baptist hell with the bad knee. Garrigue was dozing peacefully beside him in the passenger seat, as he had done for the whole journey; but then, Garrigue always adapted more easily than he to changes in his circumstances. *All these years up north in the city, Damballa, and I still don't fit nowhere, never did.*

Paved road giving way to gravel, pinging off the car's undercarriage . . . then to a dirt track and the shaky wooden bridge across the stream;

then to little more than untamed underbrush, springing back as he plowed through to the log cabin. *Got to check them shutters—meant to do it last time. Damn raccoons been back. I can smell it.*

Garrigue didn't wake, even with all the jouncing and rattling, until Arceneaux cut the engine. Then his eyes came open immediately, and he turned his head and smiled like a sleepy baby. He was a few months the elder, but he had always looked distinctly younger, in spite of being white, which more often shows the wear. He said, "I was dreaming, me."

Arceneaux grunted. "Same damn dream, I ain't want to hear about it."

"No, wasn't that one. Was you and me really gone fishing, just like folks. You and me in the shade, couple of trotlines out, couple of Dixie beers, nice dream. A *real* dream."

Arceneaux got out of the car and stood stretching himself, trying to forestall a back spasm. Garrigue joined him, still describing his dream in detail. Arceneaux had been taciturn almost from birth, while Garrigue, it was said in Joyelle Parish, bounced out of his mother chattering like a squirrel. Regarding the friendship—unusual, in those days, between a black Creole and a blanc—Arceneaux's father had growled to Garrigue's, "Mine cain't talk, l't'en cain't shut up. Might do."

And the closeness had lasted for very nearly seventy years (they quarreled mildly at times over the exact number), through schooling, work, marriages, family struggles, and even their final, grudging relocation. They had briefly considered sharing a place after Garrigue moved up north, but then agreed that each was too old and cranky, too stubbornly set in his ways, to risk the relationship over the window being open or shut at night. They met once a week, sometimes at Arceneaux's apartment, but more usually at the home of Garrigue's son Claude, where Garrigue lived; and they both fell asleep, each on his own side of the great park that divided the city, listening to the music of Clifton Chenier, Dennis McGee and Amédé Ardoin.

Garrigue glanced up at the darkening overcast sky. "Cut it close again, moon coming on so fast these nights. I keep telling you, Jean-Marc—"

Arceneaux was already limping away from the rear of the car, having opened the trunk and taken out most of the grocery bags. Still scolding him, Garrigue took the rest and followed, leaving one hand free to open the cabin door for Arceneaux and then switch on the single bare light in the room. It was right above the entrance, and the shadows, as though startled themselves to be suddenly awakened, danced briefly over the room when Garrigue stepped inside, swung the door to, and double-locked it behind them.

Arceneaux tipped the bags he carried, and let a dozen bloody steaks and roasts fall to the floor.

The single room was small but tidy, even homely, with two Indian-patterned rag rugs, two cane-bottomed rockers, and a card table with two folding chairs drawn up around it. There was a fireplace, and a refrigerator in one corner, but no beds or cots. The two windows were double-barred on the inside, and the shutters closing them were not wooden, but steel.

Another grocery bag held a bottle of Calvados, which Arceneaux set on the table, next to the two glasses, deck of cards and cribbage board waiting there. In a curiously military fashion, they padlocked and dropbolted the door, carefully checked the security of the windows, and even blocked the fireplace with a heavy steel screen. Then, finally, they sat down at the table, and Arceneaux opened the Calvados and said, "Cut."

Garrigue cut. Arceneaux dealt. Garrigue said, "My littlest grandbaby, Manette, she going to First Communion a week Saturday. You be there?" Arceneaux nodded wordlessly, jabbing pegs into the cribbage board. Garrigue started to say "She so excited, she been asking me, did I ever do First Communion, what did it feel like and all . . ." but then his words dissolved into a hoarse growl as he slipped from the chair. Garrigue was almost always the first, neither understood why.

Werewolves—loups-garoux in Louisiana—are notably bigger than ordinary wolves, running to larger skulls with bolder, more marked bones, deeper-set eyes, broader chests, and paws, front and rear, whose dewclaw serves very nearly as an opposable thumb. Even so, for a small, chattery white man Garrigue stood up as a huge wolf, black from nose to tail-tip, with eyes unchanged from his normal snow-gray, shocking in their humanity. He was at the food before Arceneaux's front feet hit the floor, and there was the customary snarling between them as they snapped up the meat within minutes. The table went over, cards and brandy and all, and both of them hurled themselves at walls and barred windows until the entire cabin shook with their frenzied fury. The wolf that was Arceneaux stood on its hind legs and tried to reach the window latches with uncannily dextrous paws, while the wolf that was Garrigue broke a front claw tearing at the door. They never howled.

First madness spent, they circled the room restlessly, their eyes glowing as dogs' and wolves' eyes do not glow. In time they settled into a light, reluctant sleep—Garrigue under a chair, Arceneaux in the ruins of the rug he had torn to pieces. Even in sleep they whined softly and eagerly, lips constantly twitching back from the fangs they never quite covered.

Towards dawn, with the moon gray and small, looking almost triangular because of the moisture in the air, something brought Arceneaux to the barred window nearest the door, rearing once again with his paws on the sill. There was nothing to see through the closed metal shutters, but the deep, nearly inaudible sound that constantly pulsed through his body in this form grew louder as he stared, threatening to break its banks and swell into a full-throated howl. Once again he clawed at the bars, but Garrigue had screwed down the bolts holding them in place too tightly even for a loup-garou's deftness, and Arceneaux's snarl bared his fangs to the black gums. Garrigue joined him, puzzled but curious, and the two of them stood side by side, panting rapidly, ears flattened against their skulls. And still there was no hint of movement anywhere outside.

Then the howl came, surging up from somewhere very near, soaring over the trees like some skeletal ancient bird, almost visible in its dreadful ardency. The werewolves went mad, howling their own possessed challenges, even snapping furiously at each other. Arceneaux sprang at the barred windows until they shivered. He was crouching to leap again when he heard the familiar whimper behind him, and simultaneously felt the brief but overwhelming pain, unlike any other, of distorted molecules regaining their natural shape. Coming back always took longer, and hurt worse.

As always afterward, he collapsed to the floor and lay there, quickly human enough to curse the weakness that always overtook a returning loup-garou, old or young, He heard Garrigue gasping, "Duplessis . . . Duplessis . . ." but could not yet respond. A face began to form in his mind: dark, clever, handsome in a way that meant no good to anyone who responded to it. . . . Still unable to speak, Arceneaux shook his head against the worn, stained floorboards. He had better reason than most to know why that sound, that cold wail of triumph, could not have been uttered by Alexandre Duplessis of Pointe Coupee Parish.

They climbed slowly to their feet, two stiff-jointed old men, looking around them at the usual wreckage of the cabin. Over the years that they had been renting it together, Garrigue and Arceneaux had made it proof, as best they could, against the rage of what would be trapped there every month. Even so, the rugs were in shreds, the refrigerator was on its side, there were deep claw-marks on the log walls to match the ones already there, and they would definitely need a new card table. Arceneaux pointed at the overturned Calvados bottle and said, "Shame, that. Wish I'd got the cap back on."

"Yeah, yeah." Garrigue shivered violently—common for most after the return. He said, "Jean-Marc, it was Duplessis, you know and I know. Duplessis *back.*"

"Not in this world." Arceneaux's voice was bleak and slow. "Maybe in some other world he back, but ain't in this one." He turned from the window to face Garrigue. "I killed Duplessis, man. Ain't none of us come back from what I done, Duplessis or nobody. You was there, Rene Garrigue! You saw how I done!"

Garrigue was hugging himself to stop the shivering, closing his eyes against the seeing. Abruptly he said in a strangely quiet tone, "He outside right now. He *there*, Jean-Marc."

"Naw, man," Arceneaux said. "Naw, Rene. He gone, Rene, my word. You got my word on it." But Garrigue was lunging past him to fumble with the locks and throw the door wide. The freezing dawn air rushed in over the body spilled across the path, so near the door that Garrigue almost tripped over it. It was a woman—a vagrant, clearly, wearing what looked like five or six coats, sweaters and undergarments. Her throat had been ripped out, and what remained of her intestines were draped neatly over a tree branch. Even in the cold, there were already flies.

Arceneaux breathed the name of his god, his loa, Damballa Wedo, the serpent. Garrigue whispered, "Women. Always the women, always the belly. Duplessis."

"He carry her here." Arceneaux was calming himself, as well as Garrigue. "Killed her somewhere back there, maybe in the city, carry her here, leave her like a business card. You right, Rene. Can't *be*, but you right."

"Business card." Garrigue's voice was still tranquil, almost dreamy. "He know this place, Jean-Marc. If he know this place, he know everything. *Everything.*"

"Hush you, man, hush now, mind me." Arceneaux might have been talking to a child wakened out of a nightmare. "Shovel out back, under the crabapple, saw it last time. We got to take her off and bury her, first thing. You go get me that shovel, Rene."

Garrigue stared at him. Arceneaux said it again, more gently. "Go on, Rene. Find me that shovel, compe'."

Alone, he felt every hair on his own body standing up; his big dark hands were trembling so that he could not even cover the woman's face or close her eyes. *Alexandre Duplessis, c'est vraiment li, vraiment, vraiment*; but the knowledge frightened the old man far less than the terrible lure of the crumpled thing at his feet, torn open and emptied out, gutted and drained and abandoned, the reek of her terror dominating the hot, musky scent of the beast that had hunted her down in the hours before dawn. *The fear, Damballa, the fear—you once get that smell in you head, you throat, you gut, you never get it out. Better than the meat, the blood even, you smell the fear.* He was shaking badly now, and he knew that he needed to get out of there with Garrigue before he hurled himself upon the pitiful remains, to roll and wallow in them like the beast he was. *Hold me, Damballa. Hide me, hold me.*

Garrigue returned with the rusty shovel and together they carried the dead woman deeper into the woods. Then he stood by, rubbing his mouth compulsively as he watched Arceneaux hack at the hard earth. In the same small voice as before, he said, "I scare, me, Ti-Jean," calling Arceneaux by his childhood nickname. "What we do to him."

"What he did to us." Arceneaux's own voice was cold and steady. "What he did to ma Sophie."

As he had known it would, the mention of Arceneaux's sister immediately brought Garrigue back from wherever terror and guilt together had taken him. "I ain't forget Sophie." His gray eyes had closed down like the steel shutters whose color they matched. "I ain't forget nothing."

"I know, man," Arceneaux said gently. He finished his work, patted the new grave as flat as he could make it—*one good rain, two, grass cover it all*—and said, "We come back before next moon, clean up a little. Right now, we going home." Garrigue nodded eagerly.

In the car, approaching the freeway, Garrigue could not keep from talking about Sophie Arceneaux, as he had not done in a very long while. "So pretty, that girl, that sister of yours. So pretty, so kind, who wouldn't want to marry such a fine woman like her?" Then he hurriedly added, "Of course, my Elizabeth, Elizabeth was a fine woman too, I don't say a word against Elizabeth. But Sophie . . . la Sophie . . ." He fell silent for a time, and then said in a different voice, "I ain't blame Duplessis for wanting her. Can't do that, Jean-Marc."

"She didn't want him," Arceneaux said. There was no expression at all in his voice now. "Didn't want nothing to do with him, no mind what he gave her, where he took her, never mind what he promised. So he killed her." After a pause, he went on, "You know how he killed her."

Garrigue folded his hands in his lap and looked at them.

So low he could barely be heard, he answered, "In the wolf . . . in the wolf shape. Hadn't seen it, I wouldn't have believed."

"Ripped her throat out," Arceneaux said. "Ma colombe, ma pauv' p'ti, she never had no chance—no more than him with her." He looked off down the freeway, seeing, not a thousand cars nor a distant city skyline, but his entire Louisiana family, wolves all, demanding that as oldest male he take immediate vengeance on Duplessis. For once—and it was a rare enough occurrence—he found himself in complete agreement with his blood kin and their ancient notions of honor and retribution. In company with Garrigue, one of Sophie's more tongue-tied admirers, he had set off on the track of his sister's murderer.

"Duplessis kill ma Sophie, she never done nothing but good for anyone. Well, I done what I done, and I ain't sorry for it." His voice rose as he grew angry all over again, more than he usually allowed himself these days. He said, "Ain't a bit sorry."

Garrigue shivered, remembering the hunt. Even with an entire werewolf clan sworn to avenge Sophie Arceneaux, Duplessis had made no attempt to hide himself, or to flee the region, so great was his city man's contempt for thick-witted backwoods bumpkins. Arceneaux had run him to earth in a single day, and it had been almost too easy for Garrigue to lure him into a moonshiner's riverside shebeen: empty for the occasion and abandoned forever after, haunted by the stories of what was done there to Alexandre Duplessis.

It had taken them all night, and Garrigue was a different man in the morning.

After the first scream, Garrigue had never heard the others; he could not have done otherwise and held onto his sanity. Sometimes it seemed to him that he had indeed gone mad that night, and that all the rest of his life—the flight north, the jobs, the marriage, the beloved children and grandchildren, the home—had never been anything but a lunatic's hopeless dream of forgetfulness. More than forty years later he still shuddered and moaned in his sleep, and at times still whimpered himself awake. *All the blood, all the shit . . . the . . . the . . . sound when Ti-Jean took that old cleaver thing . . . and that man wouldn't die, wouldn't die . . . wasn't nothing left of him but open mouth, awful open mouth, and he wouldn't die. . . .*

"Don't make *no* sense," Arceneaux said beside him. "Days burying . . . four, five county lines—"

"Five," Garrigue whispered. "Evangeline. Joyelle. St. Landry. Acadia. Rapides. Too close together, I *told* you . . . ."

Arceneaux shook his head. "Conjure. Conjure in it somewhere, got to be. Guillory, maybe, he evil enough . . . old Fontenot, over in St. Landry. Got to be conjure."

They drove the rest of the way in near silence, Arceneaux biting down hard on his own lower lip, Garrigue taking refuge in memories of his wife Elizabeth, and of Arceneaux's long-gone Pauline. Both women, non-Creoles, raised and encountered in the city, believed neither in werewolves nor in conjure men; neither one had ever known the truth about their husbands. Loups-garoux run in families: Arceneaux and Garrigue, marrying out of their clans, out of their deep back-country world, had both produced children who would go through their lives completely unaware of that part of their ancestry. The choice had been a deliberate one, and Garrigue, for his part, had never regretted it. He doubted very much that Arceneaux had either, but it was always hard to tell with Arceneaux.

Pulling to the curb in front of the frame house where Garrigue lived with Claude and his family, Arceneaux cut the engine, and they sat looking at each other. Garrigue said finally, "Forgot to fish. Grandbabies always wanting to know did we catch anything."

"Tell them fish wasn't biting today. We done that before."

Garrigue smiled for the first time. "Claude, he think we don't do no fishing, we goes up there to drink, get away from family, get a little wild. Say he might just come with us one time." Arceneaux grunted without replying. Garrigue said, "I keeps ducking and dodging, you know? Ducking and dodging." His voice was growing shaky again, but he never took his eyes from Arceneaux's eyes. He said, "What we going to do, Ti-Jean?"

"Get you some sleep," Arceneaux said. "Get you a good breakfast, tell Claude you likely be late. We go find Duplessis tomorrow, you and me."

Garrigue looked, for a moment, more puzzled than frightened. "Why we bothering that? He know right where we live, where the chirrens lives—"

Arceneaux cut him off harshly. "We find him fast, maybe we throw him just that little bit off-balance, could help sometime." He patted Garrigue's shoulder lightly. "We use what we got, Rene, and all we got is us. You go on now—my knee biting on me a little bit."

In fact—as Garrigue understood from the fact that Arceneaux mentioned it at all—the bad knee was hurting him a good deal; he could only pray that it wouldn't have locked up on him by morning. He brought the car back to Noelle, who took one look at his gait and insisted on driving him home, lecturing him all the way about his need for immediate surgery. She was his oldest child, his companion from her birth, and the only one who would ever have challenged him, as she did now.

"Dadda, whatever you and Compe' Rene are up to, I will find it out—you know I always do. Simpler tell me now, *oui?*"

"Ain't up to one thing," Arceneaux grumbled. "Ain't up to nothing, you turning such a suspicious woman. You mamere, she just exactly the same way."

"Because you're such a bad liar," his daughter replied tenderly. She caressed the back of his neck with a warm, work-hardened hand. "Ma'dear and me, we used to laugh so, nights you'd be slipping out to drink, play cards with Compe' Rene and your old zydeco friends. Make some crazy little-boy story—*whoo,* out the door, gone till morning, come home looking like someone dragged you through a keyhole backwards. Lord, didn't we *laugh!*"

There had been a few moments through the years when pure loneliness had made him seriously consider turning around on her and telling her to sit herself down and listen to a story. This moment was one of them; but he only muttered something he forgot as soon as he'd said it, and nothing more until she dropped him off at his apartment building. Then she kissed his cheek and told him, "Come by for dinner tomorrow. Antoine will be home early, for a change, and Patrice just got to show his gam'pair something he drew in school."

"Day after," Arceneaux said. "Busy tomorrow." He could feel her eyes following him as he limped through the lobby doors.

The knee was still painful the next morning, but it remained functionally flexible. He could manage. He caught the crosstown bus to meet Garrigue in front of Claude's house, and they set forth together to search for a single man in a large city. Their only advantage lay in possessing, even in human form, a wolf's sense of smell; that, and a bleak awareness that their quarry shared the very same gift, and undoubtedly already knew where they lived, and—far more frightening— whom they loved. *We ain't suppose to care, Damballa. Bon Dieu made the loup-garou, he ain't mean us to care about nothing. The kill only. The blood only . . . the fear only. Maybe Bon Dieu mad at us, me and Rene, disobeying him like we done. Too late now.*

Garrigue had always been the better tracker, since their childhood, so Arceneaux simply stayed just behind his left shoulder and went where he led. Picking up the werewolf scent at the start was a grimly easy matter: knowing Duplessis as they did, neither was surprised to cross his trail not far from the house where Garrigue's younger son Fernand lived with his own wife and children. Garrigue caught his breath audibly then, but said no word. He plunged along, drawn by the strange, unmistakable aroma as it circled, doubled back on itself, veered off in this direction or that, then inevitably returned to patrolling the streets most dear to two weary old men. Frightened and enraged, stubborn and haunted and lame, they followed. Arceneaux never took his eyes from Garrigue, which was good, because Garrigue was not using his eyes at all, and would have walked into traffic a dozen times over, if not for Arceneaux. People yelled at him.

They found Duplessis in the park, the great Park that essentially divided the two worlds of the city. He wore a long red-leather coat over a gray suit of the Edwardian cut he always favored—*just like the one we tear off him that night, Damballa, just like that suit*—and he was standing under a young willow tree, leaning on a dainty, foppish walking stick, smiling slightly as he watched children playing in a sandbox. When Arceneaux and Garrigue came up with him, one on each side, he did not speak to them immediately, but stood looking calmly from one face to the other, as his smile broadened. He was as handsome as ever, velvet-dark and whip-lean, unscarred in any way that they could see; and he appeared no older than he had on the night they had spent whittling him down to screaming blood, screaming shit, *Damballa* . . . .

Duplessis said softly, "My friends."

Arceneaux did not answer him. Garrigue said inanely, "You looking well, Compe' Alexandre."

"Ah, I have my friends to thank for that." Duplessis spoke, not in Creole, but in the Parisian French he had always affected. "There's this to say for hell and death—they do keep a person in trim." He patted Garrigue's arm, an old remembered habit of his. "Yes, I am quite well, Compe' Rene. There were some bad times, as you know, but these days I feel as young and vigorous as . . . oh, say, as any of your grandchildren." And he named them then, clearly tasting them, as though to eat the name was to have eaten the child. "Sandrine . . . Honore . . . your adorable little Manette . . . ." He named them all, grinning at Garrigue around the names.

Arceneaux said, "Sophie."

Duplessis did not turn his head, but stopped speaking.

Arceneaux said it again. "Sophie, you son of a bitch—pere de personne, fils de cent mille. Sophie."

When Duplessis did turn, he was not smiling, nor was there any bombast or mockery in his voice. He said, "I think you will agree with me, Jean-Marc, that being slashed slowly to pieces alive pays for all.

Like it or not, I own your poor dear Sophie just as much as you do now. I'd call that fair and square, wouldn't you?"

Arceneaux hit him then. Duplessis hadn't been expecting the blow, and he went over on his back, shattering the fragile walking stick beneath him. The children in the sandbox looked up with some interest, but the passersby only walked faster.

Duplessis got up slowly, running his tongue-tip over a bloody upper lip. He said, "Well, I guess I don't learn much, do I? That's exactly how one of you—or was it both?—knocked me unconscious in that filthy little place by the river. And when I came to . . . ." He shrugged lightly and actually winked at Arceneaux. He said softly, "But you haven't got any rope with you this time, have you Jean-Marc? And none of your little—ah—sculptor's tools?" He tasted his bloody mouth again. "A grandfather should be more careful, I'd think."

The contemptuous lilt in the last words momentarily cost Garrigue his sanity. Only Arceneaux's swift reaction and strong clutch kept him from knocking Duplessis down a second time. His voice half-muffled against Arceneaux's chest, Garrigue heard himself raging, "You touch my chirren, you—you touch the *doorknob* on my grandbabies' house—I cut you up all over again, cut you like Friday morning's bacon, you hear me?" And he heard Duplessis laughing.

Then the laughter stopped, almost with a machine's mechanical click, and Duplessis said, "No. You hear *me* now." Garrigue shook himself free of Arceneaux's preventive embrace, nodded a silent promise, and turned to see Duplessis facing them both, his mouth still bleeding, and his eyes as freezingly distant as his voice. He said, "I am Alexandre Duplessis. You sent me to hell, you tortured me as no devils could have done—no devils would have conceived of what you did. But in so doing, you have set me free, you have lost all power over me. I will do what I choose to you and yours, and there will be nothing you can do about it, nothing you can threaten me with. Would you like to hear what I choose to do?"

He told them.

He went into detail.

"It will take me some little while, obviously. That suits me—I want it to take a while. I want to watch you go mad as I strip away everything you love and cannot protect, just as you stripped away my fingers, my face, my organs, piece by piece by piece." The voice never grew any louder, but remained slow and thoughtful, even genial. The soulful eyes—still a curious reddish-brown—seemed to have withdrawn deep under the telltale single brow and contracted to the size of cranberries. Arceneaux could feel their heat on his skin.

"This is where I live at present," Duplessis said, and told them his address. He said, "I would be delighted if you should follow me there, and anywhere else—it would make things much more amusing. I would even invite you to hunt with me, but you were always too cowardly for that, and by the looks of you I can see you've not changed. Wolves— God's own *wolves* caging themselves come the moon, not even surviving on dogs and cats, mice and squirrels and rabbits, as you did in Joyelle Parish. Lamisere a deux . . . Misere et Compagnie—no wonder you have both grown so old, it's almost pitiful. Now *I*"—a light inward flick of his two hands invited the comparison—"I dine only on the diet that le Bon Dieu meant for me, and it will keep me hunting when you two are long-buried with the humans you love so much." He clucked his tongue, mimicking a distressed old woman, and repeated, "Pitiful. Truly pitiful. A très—très—tot . . . my friends."

He bowed gracefully to them then, and turned to stroll away through the trees. Arceneaux said, "Conjure." Duplessis turned slowly again at the word, waiting. Arceneaux said, "You ain't come back all by yourself, we took care. You got brought back—take a conjure man to do that. Which one—Guillory? I got to figure Guillory."

Duplessis smiled, a little smugly, and shook his head. "I'd never trust Guillory out of my sight—let alone after my death. No, Fontenot was the only sensible choice. Entirely mad, but that's always a plus in a conjure man, isn't it? And he hated you with all his wicked old heart, Jean-Marc, as I'm sure you know. What on earth did you *do* to that man—rape his black pig? Only thing in the world he loved, that pig."

"Stopped him feeding a lil boy to it," Arceneaux grunted. "What he do for you, and what it cost you? Fontenot, he come high."

"They all come high. But you can bargain with Fontenot. Remember, Jean-Marc?" Duplessis held out his hands, palms down. The two little fingers were missing, and Arceneaux shivered with sudden memory of that moment when he'd wondered who had already taken them, and why, even as he had prepared to cut into the bound man's flesh . . . .

Duplessis laughed harshly, repeating, "My insurance policy, you could say. Really, you should have thought a bit about those, old friend. There's mighty conjuring to be done with the fingers of a loup-garou. It was definitely worth Fontenot's while to witch me home, time-consuming as it turned out to be. I'm sure he never regretted our covenant for a moment."

Something in his use of the past tense raised Arceneaux's own single brow, his daughters' onetime plaything. Duplessis caught the look and grinned with the flash of genuine mischief that had charmed even Arceneaux long ago, *though not ma Sophie, never*—she knew. "Well, let's be honest, you couldn't have a man with that kind of power and knowledge running around loose—not a bad, bad man like Hipolyte Fontenot. I was merely doing my duty as a citizen. Au 'voir again, mon ami. Mon assassin."

Watching him walk away, Arceneaux was praying so hard for counsel and comfort to Damballa Wedo, and to Damballa's gentle wife, the rainbow Ayida, that he started when Garrigue said beside him, "Let's go, come *on*. We don't let that man out of our sight, here on in."

Arceneaux did not look at him. "No point in it. He *want* us to follow him—he want us going crazy, no sleep, no time to think straight, just wondering *when*. . . . I ain't go play it his way, me, unh-uh."

"You know another way? You got a better idea?" Garrigue was very nearly crying with impatience and anxiety, all but dancing on his toes, straining to follow Alexandre Duplessis. Arceneaux put his hands on the white man's arms, trying to take the trembling into himself.

"I don't know it's a better idea. I just know he still think we nothing but a couple back-country fools, like he always did, and we got to keep him thinking that thing—*got* to. Because we gone kill him, Rene, you hearing me? We done it before—this time we gone kill him *right*, so he stay dead. Yeah, there's only two of us, but there's only one of him, and he ain't God, man, he just one damn old loup-garou in a fancy suit, talking fancy French. You hear what I'm saying to you?"

Garrigue did not answer. Arceneaux shook him slightly. "Right now, we going on home, both of us. He ain't go do nothing tonight, he want us to spend it thinking on all that shit he just laid on us. Home, Rene."

Still no response. Arceneaux looked into Garrigue's eyes, and could not find Garrigue there, but only frozen, helpless terror. "Listen, Rene, I tell you something my daddy use to say. Daddy, he say to me always, '*Di moin qui vous lamein, ma di cous qui vous ye.*' You tell me who you love, I tell you who you are." Garrigue began returning slowly to his own eyes, looking back at him: expressionless, but present. Arceneaux said, "You think just maybe we know who we are, Compe' Rene?"

Garrigue smiled a little, shakily. "Duplessis . . . Duplessis, he don't love nobody. Never did."

"So Duplessis ain't nobody. Duplessis don't exist. You gone be scared of somebody don't exist?" Arceneaux slapped his old friend's shoulder, hard. "Home now. Ti-Jean say." They did go to their homes then, and they slept well, or at least they told each other so in the morning. Arceneaux judged that Garrigue might actually have slept through the night; for himself, he came and went, turning over a new half-dream of putting an end to Alexandre Duplessis each time he turned in his bed. Much of the waking time he spent simply calling into darkness inside himself, calling on his loa, as he had been taught to do when young, crying out, *Damballa Wedo, great serpent, you got to help us, this on you . . . . Bon Dieu can't be no use here, ain't his country, he don't speak the patois. . . . Got to be you, Damballa . . . .* When he did sleep, he dreamed of his dead wife, Pauline, and asked her for help too, as he had always done.

A revitalized Garrigue was most concerned the next morning with the problem of destroying a werewolf who had already survived being sliced into pieces, themselves buried in five different counties. "We never going to get another chance like that, not in this city. City, you got to *explain* why you do somebody in—and you definitely better not say it's cause he turn into a wolf some nights. Be way simpler if we could just shoot him next full moon, tell them we hunters. Bring him home strap right across the hood, hey Ti-Jean?" He chuckled, thinking about it.

"Except we be changing too," Arceneaux pointed out. "We all prisoners of the moon, one way another."

Garrigue nodded. "Yeah, you'd think that'd make us—I don't know—hold together some way, look out for each other. But it don't happen, do it? I mean, here I am, and I'm thinking, I ever do get the chance, I'd kill him wolf to wolf, just like he done Sophie. I would, I just don't give a damn no more."

"Come to that, it come to that. Last night I been trying to work out how we could pour some cement, make him part of a bridge, an underpass—you know, way the Mafia do. Couldn't figure it."

Garrigue said, "You right about one thing, anyway. We can't be waiting on the moon, cause he sure as hell won't be. Next full moon gone be short one loup-garou for certain."

"Maybe two," Arceneaux said quietly. "Maybe three, even. Man ain't going quietly no second time."

"Be worth it." Garrigue put out his hand and Arceneaux took it, roughness meeting familiar lifelong roughness. Garrigue said, "Just so it ain't the little ones. Just so he don't ever get past us to the little ones." Arceneaux nodded, but did not answer him.

For the next few days they pointedly paid no attention to Duplessis's presence in the city—though they caught his scent in both neighborhoods, as he plainly made himself familiar with family routines—but spent the time with their children and grandchildren, delighting the latter and relieving the men of babysitting duties. Garrigue, having only sons, got away without suspicions; but neither Noelle nor Arceneaux's daughter-in-law Athalie were entirely deceived. As Athalie put it, "Women, we are so used to men's stupid lies, we're out of practice for a good one, Papajean," which was her one-word nickname for him. "I *know* you're lying, some way, but this one's really good."

On Saturday Arceneaux, along with most of his own family, accompanied Garrigue's family to the Church of Saints Philip and James for Manette Garrigue's First Communion. The day was unseasonably warm, the group returning for the party large, and at first no one but Arceneaux and Garrigue took any notice of the handsome, well-dressed man walking inconspicuously between them. Alexandre Duplessis said thoughtfully, "What a charming little girl. You must be very proud, Rene."

Garrigue had been coached half the night, or he would have gone for Duplessis's throat on the instant. Instead he answered, mildly enough, "I'm real proud of her, you got that right. You lay a hand on her, all Fontenot's gris-gris be for nothing next time."

Duplessis seemed not to have heard him. "Should she be the first—not Jean-Marc's Patrice or Zelime? It's so hard to decide—"

The strong old arms that blocked Garrigue away also neatly framed Duplessis's throat. Arceneaux said quietly, "You never going to make it to next moon, Compe' Alexandre. You know that, don't you?"

Duplessis looked calmly back at him, the red-brown eyes implacable far beyond human understanding. He said, "Compe' Jean-Marc, I died at your hands forty and more years ago, and by the time you got through with me I was very, very old. You cannot kill such a man twice, not so it matters." He smiled at Arceneaux. "Besides, the moon is perhaps not everything, even for a loup-garou. I'd give that a little thought, if I were you." His canine teeth glittered wetly in the late-autumn sunlight as he turned and walked away.

After a while Noelle dropped back to take her father's arm. She rubbed her cheek lightly against Arceneaux's shoulder and said, "Your knee all right? You're looking tired."

"Been a long morning." Arceneaux hugged her arm under his own. "Don't you worry about the old man."

"I do, though. Gotten so I worry about you a whole lot. Antoine does too." She looked up at him, and he thought, *Her mama's eyes, her mama's mouth, but my complexion—thank God that's all she got from me.* . . . She said, "How about you spend the night, hey? I make gumbo, you play with the grandbabies, talk sports with Antoine. Sound fair?"

It sounded more than fair; it sounded such a respite from the futile plans and dreaded memories with which he and Garrigue had been living that he could have wept. "I'm gone need take care some business first. Nothing big, just a few bits of business. Then I come back, stay the night." She prompted him with a silent, quizzical tilt of her head, and he added, "Promise." It was an old ritual between them, dating from her childhood: he rarely used the word at all, but once he did he could be absolutely relied on to keep it. His grandchildren had all caught onto this somewhat earlier than she had.

He slipped away from the party group without even signaling to Garrigue: a deliberately suspicious maneuver that had the waiting Duplessis behind him before he had gone more than a block from the house. It was difficult to pretend not to notice that he was being followed—this being one of the wolf senses that finds an echo in the human body—but Arceneaux was good at it, and took a certain pleasure in leading Duplessis all over the area, as the latter had done to him and Garrigue. But the motive was not primarily spite. He was actually bound for a certain neighborhood botanica run by an old Cuban couple who had befriended him years before, when he first came to the city. They were kind and brown, and spoke almost no English, and he had always suspected that they knew exactly what he was, had known others like him in Cuba, and simply didn't care.

He spent some forty-five minutes in the crowded little shop, and left with his arms full of brightly colored packages. Most amounted to herbal and homeopathic remedies of one sort and another; a very few were gifts for Damballa Wedo, whose needs are very simple; and one—the only one with an aroma that would have alerted any loup-garou in the world—was a largish packet of wolfbane.

Still sensing Duplessis on his track, he walked back to Noelle's house, asked to borrow her car briefly, claiming to have heard an ominous sound from the transmission, and took off northeast, in the direction of the old cabin where he and Garrigue imprisoned themselves one night in every month. The car was as cramped as ever, and the drive as tedious, but he managed it as efficiently as he could. Arriving alone, for the first time ever, he spent some while tidying the cabin, and the yet-raw grave in the woods as well; then carefully measured out all the wolfbane in a circle around the little building, and headed straight back to the city. He bent all his senses, wolf and human alike, to discovering whether or not Duplessis had trailed him the entire way, but the results were inconclusive.

"Way I been figuring it over," he said to Garrigue the next day, drinking bitter chicory coffee at the only Creole restaurant whose cook understood the importance of a proper roux, "we lured him into that blind pig back on the river, all them years ago, and he just know he way too smart for us to get him like that no second time. So we gone do just exactly what we done before, cause we ain't but pure-D country, and that the onliest trick we know." His sigh turned to a weary grunt as he shook his head. "Which ain't no lie, far as I'm concerned. But we go on paying him no mind, we keep sneaking up there, no moon, no need . . . he smell the wolfbane, he keep on following us, we got to be planning *something*. . . . All I'm hoping, Compe' Rene, I'm counting on a fool staying a fool. The smart ones, they do sometimes."

Garrigue rubbed the back of his neck and folded his arms. "So what you saying, same thing, except with the cabin? Man, *I* wouldn't fall for that, and you *know* I'm a fool."

"Yeah, but see, see, we know we fools—we used to it, we live with it like everybody, do the best we can. But Duplessis. . . ." He smiled, although it felt as though he were lifting a great cold weight with his mouth. "Duplessis *scary*. Duplessis got knowledge you and me couldn't even spell, never mind understand. He just as smart as he think he is, and we just about what we were back when we never seen a city man before, we so proud to be running with a city man." He rubbed the bad knee, remembering Sophie's warnings, not at all comforted by the thought that no one else in the clan had seen through the laughter, the effortless charm, the *newness* of the young loup-garou who came so persistently courting her. He said, "There's things Duplessis never going to understand."

He missed Garrigue's question, because it was mumbled in so low a tone. He said, "Say what?"

Garrigue asked, "It going to be like that time?" Arceneaux did not answer. Garrigue said, "Cause I don't think I can do that again, Ti-Jean. I don't think I can watch, even." His face and voice were embarrassed, but there was no mistaking the set of his eyes, not after seventy years.

"I don't know, me." Arceneaux himself had never once been pursued by dreams of what they had done to Alexandre Duplessis in Sophie's name; but in forty years he had gently shaken Garrigue out of them more than once, and held him afterward. "We get him there—just you, me and him, like before—I know then. All I can tell you now, Rene."

Garrigue made no reply, and they separated shortly afterward. Arceneaux went home, iced his knee, turned on his radio (he had a television set, but rarely watched it), and learned of the discovery of a second homeless woman, eviscerated and partly devoured, her head almost severed from her body by the violence of the attack. The corpse had been found under the Viaduct, barely two blocks from Arceneaux's apartment, and the police announced that they were taking seriously the disappearance of the woman Arceneaux had buried. Arceneaux sat staring at the radio long after it had switched to broadcasting a college football game.

He called Garrigue, got a busy signal, and waited until his friend called him back a moment later. When he picked up the phone, he said simply, "I know."

Garrigue was fighting hysteria; Arceneaux could feel it before he spoke the first word. "Can't be, Ti-Jean. Not full moon. Can't *be*."

"Well," Arceneaux said. "Gone have to ask old Duplessis what else he sold that Fontenot." He had not expected Garrigue to laugh, and was not surprised. He said, "Don't be panicking, you hear me, Rene? Not now. Ain't the time."

"Don't know what else to do." But Garrigue's voice was slightly steadier. "If he really be changing any damn time he like—"

"Got to be rules. Le Bon Dieu, he wouldn't let there not be rules—"

"Then we got to tell them, you hear me? They got to know what out there, what we dealing with—what coming *after* them—"

"And what we are? What they come from, what they part of? You think your little Manette, my Patrice, you think they ready for that?"

"Not the grandbabies, when I ever said the grandbabies? I'm talking the chirren—yours, mine, they husbands, wives, all them. They old enough, they got a right to know." There was a pause on the other end, and then Garrigue said flatly, "You don't tell them, I will. I swear."

It was Arceneaux's turn to be silent, listening to Garrigue's anxious breathing on the phone. He said finally, "Noelle. Noelle got a head on her. We tell her, no one else."

"She got a husband, too. What about him?"

"Noelle," Arceneaux said firmly. "Antoine ain't got no werewolf for a daddy."

"Okay." Garrigue drew the two syllables out with obvious dubiousness. "Noelle." The voice quavered again, sounding old for the first time in Arceneaux's memory. "Ti-Jean, he could be anywhere right now, we wouldn't know. Could be *at* them, be tearing them apart, like that woman—"

Arceneaux stopped him like a traffic cop, literally—and absurdly—with a hand held up. "No, he couldn't. Think about it, Rene. Back in Louzianne—back *then*—what we do after that big a kill? What *anybody* do?"

"Go off . . . go off somewhere, go to sleep." Garrigue said it grudgingly, but he said it.

"How long for? How long you ever sleep, you and that full belly?"

"A day, anyway. Slept out two whole days, one time. And old Albert

Vaugine . . . ." Garrigue was chuckling a bit, in spite of himself. He said, "Okay, so we maybe got a couple of days—*maybe*. What then?"

"Then we get ourselves on up to the cabin. You and me and him." Arceneaux hung up.

It had long been the centerpiece of Arceneaux's private understanding of the world that nothing was ever as good as you expected it to be, or as bad. His confession of her ancestry to Noelle fell into the latter category. He had expected her reaction to be one of horrified revulsion, followed by absolute denial and tearful outrage. Instead, after withdrawing into silent thought for a time, and then saying slow, mysterious things like, "So *that's* why I can never do anything with my hair," she told him, "You do know there's no way in the world you're going without me?"

His response never got much beyond, "The hell you preach, girl!" Noelle set her right forefinger somewhere between his Adam's apple and his collarbones, and said, "Dadda, this is my fight too. As long as that man's running around loose"—the irony of her using the words that Alexandre Duplessis had used to justify his murder of the conjure man Fontenot was not lost on Arceneaux—"my children aren't safe. You know the way I get about the children."

"This won't be no PTA meeting. You don't know."

"I know you and Uncle Rene, you may both be werewolves, but you're *old* werewolves, and you're not exactly in the best shape. Oh, you're going to need me, cause right now the both of you couldn't tackle Patrice, never mind Zelime." He was in no state to tackle her, either; he made do with a mental reservation: *Look away for even five minutes and we're out of here, me and Rene. You got to know how to handle daughters, that's all. Specially the pushy ones.*

But on the second day, it didn't matter, because it was Noelle who was gone. And Patrice with her. And her car.

After Antoine had called the police, and the house had begun to fill with terrified family, but before the reporters had arrived, and before Zelime had stopped crying for her mother and little brother, Arceneaux borrowed his son Celestin's car. It was quite a bit like renting it, not because Celestin charged him anything, but because answering all his questions about why the loan was necessary almost amounted to filling out a form. Arceneaux finally roared at him, in a voice Celestin had not heard since his childhood, "Cause I'm your father, me, and I just about to snatch you balder than you already are, you don't hand me them keys." He was on the road five minutes later.

He did not stop to pick up Garrigue. His explanation to himself was that there wasn't time, that every minute was too precious to be taken up with a detour; but even as he made it, he knew better. The truth lay in his pity for Garrigue's endless nightmares, for his lonesome question, "It gone be like that time?" and for his own sense that this was finally between him and the man whom he had carved to obscene fragments alive. *I let him do it all back to me, he lets them two go. Please, Damballa, you hear? Please.*

But he was never certain—and less now than ever before—whether Damballa heard prayers addressed to him in English. So for the entire length of the drive, which seemed to take the rest of his life, he chanted, over and over, a prayer-song that little Ti-Jean Arceneaux, who spoke another language, had learned young, never forgotten, and, until this moment, never needed.

> *"Baba yehge, amiwa saba yehge,*
> *De Damballa e a miwa,*
> *Danou sewa yehge o, djevo de.*
> *De Damballa Wedo, Bade miwa . . . ."*

Rather than bursting into the cabin like the avenging angel he had planned to be, he hardly had the strength or the energy to open the car door, once he arrived. The afternoon was cold, and he could smell snow an hour or two away; he noticed a few flakes on the roof of Noelle's car. There was flickering light in the cabin, and smoke curling from the chimney, which he and Garrigue mistrusted enough that they almost never lighted a fire. He moved closer, noticing two sets of footprints leading to the door, *Yeah, she'd have been carrying Patrice, boy'd have been too scared to walk.* The vision of his terrified four-year-old grandson made him grind his teeth, and Duplessis promptly called from within, "No need to bite the door down, Jean-Marc. Half a minute, I'll be right there."

Waiting, Arceneaux moved to the side of the house and ripped down the single power line. The electric light went out inside, and he heard Duplessis laugh. Standing on the doorstep as Arceneaux walked back, he said, "I thought you might do that, so I built a handsome fire for us all—even lit a few candles. But if you imagine that's going to preclude the use of power tools, I feel I should remind you that they all run on batteries these days. Nice *big* batteries. Come in, Jean-Marc, I bid you welcome."

It was not the shock of seeing Noelle tied in a chair that almost caused Arceneaux to lose what control he had and charge the smiling man standing beside her. It was the sight of Patrice, unbound on her lap, lighting up at the sight of him to call "Gam'pair!" He had been crying, but his face made it clear that everything would be all right now. Duplessis said pleasantly, "I wouldn't give it a second thought, old friend. I'm sure you know why."

"Fontenot," Arceneaux said. "Never knowed the old man had *that* much power."

"Oh, it cost me an arm and a leg . . . so to speak." Duplessis laughed softly. "Another reason he had to go. I mean, suppose everyone could change whenever he chose, things might become a bit . . . chaotic, don't you agree? But it certainly does come in handy, those nights when you're suddenly peckish, just like that, and everything's closed."

Noelle's eyes were terrified, but her voice was surprisingly steady. She said, "He broke in in the night, I don't know how. I couldn't fight him, because he had Patrice, and he said if I screamed . . . ."

"Yeah, honey," Arceneaux said. "Yeah, baby."

"He made me drive him up here. Poor Patrice was so frightened."

Patrice nodded proudly. "I was *scared*, Gam'pair."

"He tried to rape me," Noelle said evenly. "He couldn't."

Duplessis looked only mildly abashed. "Everything costs. And it did seem appropriate—you and little Rene working so hard to entice me up here. I thought I'd just take you up on it a bit early."

Arceneaux took a step, then another; not toward Duplessis, but toward Noelle in the chair. Duplessis said, "I really wouldn't, Jean-Marc."

Noelle said, "Dadda, get out of here! It's you he wants!"

Arceneaux said, "He got me. He ain't getting you."

Duplessis nodded. "I'll let them go, you have my word. But they have to watch first. That's fair. Her and the little one, watching and remembering . . . you know, that might even make up for what you did to me." His smile brightened even more. "Then we'll be quits at last, just think, after all the years. I might even leave some of the others alive— lagniappe, don't you know, our greatest Louzianne tradition. As your folks say down in the swamp, lagniappe c'est bitin qui bon—lagniappe is lawful treasure."

Arceneaux ignored him. To Patrice he said, "Boy, you get off your mama's lap now, I got to get those ropes off her. Then we all go get some ice cream, you like that?"

Patrice scrambled down eagerly. Noelle said, "Dadda, *no*. Take Patrice and get *out*—" just as Duplessis's voice sharpened and tightened, good cheer gone. "Jean-Marc, I'm warning you—"

The ropes were tight for stiff old fingers, and Noelle's struggling against them didn't help. Behind him, Arceneaux heard Patrice scream in terror. A moment later, looking past him, Noelle went absolutely rigid, her mouth open but no smallest sound emerging. He turned himself then, knowing better than they what he would see.

Petrifying as the sight of a werewolf obviously is, it is the transformation itself that is the smothering fabric of nightmare. On the average, it lasts no more than ten or fifteen seconds: but to the observing eyes and mind the process is endless, going on and on and on in everlasting slow-motion, as the grinning mouth twists and lengthens into a fanged snarl, while the body convulses, falls forward, catches itself on long gray legs that were arms a lifetime ago, and the eyes lengthen, literally reseat themselves in the head at a new angle, and take on the beautiful insane glow that particularly distinguishes the loup-garou. Alexandre Duplessis—cotton-white, except for the dark-shaded neck-ruff and the jagged black slash across the chest—uttered a shattering half-human roar and sprang straight at Arceneaux.

Whether it was caused by the adrenaline of terror or of rage he couldn't guess, but suddenly the ropes fell loose from the chair and his fingers, and Noelle, in one motion, swept up the wailing Patrice and was through the door before the wolf that had been Duplessis even reached her father. The bad knee predictably locked up, and Arceneaux went down, with the wolf Duplessis on him, worrying at his throat. He warded the wide-stretched jaws off with his forearm, bringing the good knee up into the loup-garou's belly, the huge white-and-black body that had become all his sky and all his night. Duplessis threw back his head and bayed in triumph.

Arceneaux made a last desperate attempt to heave Duplessis away and get to his feet. But he was near to suffocation from the weight on his chest—*Saba yehge, amiwa saba yehge, de Damballa e a miwa*—and then the werewolf's jaws were past his guard, the great fangs sank into his shoulder, and he heard himself scream in pain—*Danou sewa yehge o, djevo de, Damballa come to us, they are hurting us, Damballa come quickly . . .*

. . . and heard the scream become a howl of fury in the same moment, as he lunged upward, his changing jaws closing on Duplessis's head, taking out an eye with the first snap. Wolf to wolf—the greatest sin of all—they rose on their hind legs, locked together, fangs clashing, each streaked and blotched with the other's blood. Arceneaux had lost not only who he was, but *what*—he had no grandchildren now, no children either, no lifelong down-home friend, no memories of affection . . . there had never been anything else but this murderous twin, and no joy but in hurting it, killing it, tearing it back once again to shreds, where it belonged. He had never been so happy in his life.

In the wolf form, loups-garoux do not mate; lovemaking is a gift for ordinary animals, ordinary humans. Yet this terrible, transcendent meshing was like nothing Arceneaux had ever known, even as he was aware that his left front leg was broken and one side of his throat laid open. Duplessis was down now . . . or was that some other wolf bleeding and panting under him, breath ragged, weakened claws finding no purchase in his fur? It made no difference. There was nothing but battle now, nothing but hunger for someone's blood.

Most of the lighted candles had been knocked over—some by Noelle's flight to the door, some during the battle. The rag rugs that he and Garrigue had devastated and not yet replaced were catching fire, and spreading the flames to dry furniture and loose paper and kindling. Arceneaux watched the fire with a curious detachment, as intense, in its way, as the ecstasy with which he had he had closed his wolf jaws on Duplessis's wolf flesh. He was aware, with the same disinterest, that he was bleeding badly from a dozen wounds; still, he was on his feet, and Duplessis was sprawled before him, alive but barely breathing, lacking the strength and will to regain the human shape. Arceneaux was in the same condition, which was a pity, for he would have liked to give his thanks to Damballa in words. He considered the helpless Duplessis for a moment longer, as the fire began to find its own tongue, and then he pushed the door open with his head and limped outside.

Noelle cried out at first as he stumbled toward her; but then she knew him, as she would always have known him, and knelt down before him, hugging his torn neck—Duplessis had come very near the throat—and getting blood all over the pajamas in which she had been kidnapped. She had no words either, except for *Dadda*, but she got plenty of mileage out of that one, even so.

The cabin was just reaching full blaze, and Patrice had worked up the courage to let the strange big dog lick his face, when the police car came barreling up the overgrown little path, very nearly losing an axle to the pothole Garrigue had been warning them about for the last couple of miles. Antoine was with them too, and Garrigue's son Claude, and a police paramedic as well. There was a good deal of embracing among one group, and an equal amount of headscratching, chinrubbing and cell-phone calling by the other.

And Jean-Marc Arceneaux—"Ti-Jean" to a very few old friends— nuzzled his grandson one last time, and then turned and walked back into the blazing cabin and threw himself over the body of the wolf Alexandre Duplessis. Noelle's cry of grief was still echoing when the roof came down.

When Garrigue could talk—when anyone could talk, after the fire engine came—he told Noelle, "The ashes. He done it because of the ashes."

Noelle shook her head weakly. "I don't understand."

Garrigue said, "Duplessis come back once, maybe do it again, even from ashes. But not all mixed up together with old Ti-Jean, no, not with their jaws locked on each other in the other world and the loa watching. Not even a really good conjure man out of Sabine, Vernon Parish, pull off that trick. You follow me?"

"No," she said. "No, Rene. I don't, I'm trying."

Garrigue was admirably patient, exhausted as he was. "He just making sure you, the grandbabies, the rest of us, we never going to be bothered by Compe' Alexandre no more." His gray eyes were shining with prideful tears. "He thought on things like that, Ti-Jean did. Knew him all my life, that man. All my life."

Patrice slept between her and Antoine that night: the police psychologist who had examined him said that just because he was showing no sign of trauma didn't mean that he might not be affected in some fashion that wouldn't manifest itself for years. For his part, Patrice had talked about the incident in the surprisingly matter-of-fact way of a four-year-old for the rest of the day; but after dinner he spent the evening playing one of Zelime's mysterious games that seemed, as far as adults could tell, to have no rules whatsoever. It was only when he scrambled into bed beside his mother that he asked seriously, "That man? Not coming back?"

Noelle hugged him. "No, sweetheart. Not coming back. Not ever. You scared him away."

"Gam'pair come back." It was not a question.

You're not supposed to lie to children about anything. Bad, bad, bad. Noelle said, "He had to go away, Patrice. He had to make sure that man wouldn't come here again."

Patrice nodded solemnly. He wrapped his arms around himself and said, "I hold Gam'pair right here. Gam'pair not going anywhere," and went to sleep.

THE STORY OF KAO YU

World folklore traditions basically present three varieties of unicorn: the classic Western version (immortal, unspeakably beautiful, vulnerable to deceitful virgins), the Asian unicorn (one of the Four Significant Animals, along with the Phoenix, the Tortoise, and the Dragon), and the Karkadann of the Arabian desert (powerful, pitilessly aggressive, and ugly as fried sin, according to Marco Polo). I've written at least one tale about each species; and while I can't choose a favorite, I have a special feeling for this one—perhaps because of the manner in which, to my own surprise, the story stubbornly insisted on telling itself. Standing out of the way and leaving the narrative to its own business doesn't always work, but when it does, it makes the author look so good, so professional . . .

THERE WAS A JUDGE once in south China, a long time ago—during the reign of the Emperor Yao, it was—named Kao Yu. He was stern in his rulings, but fair and patient, and all but legendary for his honesty; it would have been a foolish criminal—or, yes, even a misguided Emperor—who attempted to bribe or coerce Kao Yu. Of early middle years, he was stocky and wide-shouldered, if a little plump, and the features of his face were strong and striking, even if his hairline was retreating just a trifle. He was respected by all, and feared by those who should have feared him—what more can one ask from a judge even now? But this is a story about a case in which he came to feel—rightly or no—that *he* was the one on trial.

Kao Yu's own wisdom and long experience generally governed his considerations in court, and his eventual rulings. But he was unique among all other judges in all of China in that when a problem came down to a matter of good versus evil—in a murder case, most often, or

155

arson, or rape (which Kao Yu particularly despised)—he would often submit that problem to the judgment of a unicorn.

Now the chi-lin, the Chinese unicorn, is not only an altogether different species from the white European variety and the menacing Persian karkadann; it is also a different *matter* in its essence from either one. Apart from its singular physical appearance—indeed, there are scholars who claim that the chi-lin is no unicorn at all, but some sort of mystical dragon-horse, given its multicolored coat and the curious configuration of its head and body—this marvelous being is considered one of the Four Superior Animals of good omen, the others being the phoenix, the turtle, and the dragon itself. It is the rarest of the unicorns, appearing as a rule only during the reign of a benign Emperor enjoying the Mandate of Heaven. As a result, China has often gone generation after weary generation without so much as a glimpse of a chi-lin. This has contributed greatly to making the Chinese the patient, enduring people they are. It has also toppled thrones.

THE STORY OF KAO YU

But in the days of Judge Kao Yu, at least one chi-lin was so far from being invisible as to appear in his court from time to time, to aid him in arriving at certain decisions. Why he should have been chosen— and at the very beginning of his career—he could never understand, for he was a deeply humble person, and would have regarded himself as blessed far beyond his deservings merely to have seen a chi-lin at a great distance. Yet so it was; and, further, the enchanted creature always seemed to know when he was facing a distinctly troublesome problem. It is well-known that the chi-lin, while wondrously gentle, will suffer no least dishonesty in its presence, and will instantly gore to death anyone whom it knows to be guilty. Judge Kao Yu, it must be said, always found himself a little nervous when the sudden smell of a golden summer meadow announced unmistakably the approach of the unicorn. As righteous a man as he was, even he had a certain difficulty in looking directly into the clear dark eyes of the chi-lin.

More than once—and the memories often returned to him on sleep-less nights—he had pleaded with the criminal slouching before him, "If you have any hope of surviving this moment, do not lie to me. If you have some smallest vision of yet changing your life—even if you have lied with every breath from your first—tell the truth *now*." But few there—tragically few—were able to break the habit of a lifetime; and Judge Kao Yu would once again see the dragonlike horned head go down, and would lower his own head and close his eyes, praying this time not to hear the soft-footed rush across the courtroom, and the terrible scream of despair that followed. But he always did.

China being as huge and remarkably varied a land as it is, the judge who could afford to spend all his time in one town and one court was in those days very nearly as rare as a unicorn himself. Like every jurist of his acquaintance, Kao Yu traveled the country round a good half of the year: his usual route, beginning every spring, taking him through every village of any size from Guangzhou to Yinchuan. He traveled always with a retinue of three: his burly lieutenant, whose name was Wang Da; his secretary, Chou Qingshan; and Hu Longwei, who was both cook and porter—and, as such, treated with even more courtesy by Kao Yu than were his two other assistants. For he believed, judge or no, that the more lowly-placed the person, the more respect he or she deserved. This made him much-beloved in rather odd places, but not nearly as wealthy as he should have been.

The chi-lin, naturally, did not accompany him on his judicial rounds; rather, it appeared when it chose, most often when his puzzlement over a case was at its height, and his need of wisdom greatest. Nor did it ever stay long in the courtroom, but simply delivered its silent judgment and was gone. Chou Qingshan commented—Kao Yu's other two assistants, having more than once seen that judgment executed, were too frightened of the unicorn ever to speak of it at all—that its presence did frequently shorten the time spent on a hearing, since many criminals tended to be even more frightened than they, and often blurted out the truth at first sight. On the other hand, the judge just as often went months without a visit from the chi-lin, and was forced to depend entirely on his own wit and his own sensibilities. Which, as he told his assistants, was a very good thing indeed.

"Because if it were my choice," he said to them, "I would leave as many decisions as I was permitted at the feet of this creature out of Heaven, this being so much wiser than I. I would then be no sort of judge, but a mindless, unreasoning acolyte, and I would not like that in the least." After a thoughtful moment, he added, "Nor would the chi-lin like it either, I believe."

Now it happened that in a certain town, where he had been asked on very short notice to come miles out of his way to substitute for a judge who had fallen ill, Kao Yu was asked to pass judgment on an imprisoned pickpocket. The matter was so far below his rank—it would have been more suited for a novice in training—that even such an unusually egalitarian person as Kao Yu bridled at the effrontery of the request. But the judge he was replacing, one Fang An, happened to be an esteemed former teacher of his, so there was really nothing for it but that he take the case. Kao Yu shrugged in his robes, bowed, assented, arranged to

THE STORY OF KAO YU

remain another night at the wagoners' inn—the only lodging the town could offer—and made the best of things.

The pickpocket, as it turned out, was a young woman of surpassing, almost shocking beauty: small and slender, with eyes and hair and skin to match that of any court lady Kao Yu had ever seen, all belying her undeniable peasant origins. She moved with a gracious air that set him marveling, "What is she doing before me, in this grubby little court-room? She ought to be on a tapestry in some noble's palace, and I . . . I should be in that tapestry as well, kneeling before *her*, rather than this other way around." And no such thought had ever passed through the mind of Judge Kao Yu in his entirely honorable and blameless life.

To the criminal in the dock he said, with remarkable gentleness that did not go unnoticed by either his lieutenant or his secretary, "Well, what have you to say for yourself, young woman? What is your name, and how have you managed to place yourself into such a disgraceful situation?" Wang Da thought he sounded much more like the girl's fa-ther than her judge.

With a shy bow—and a smile that set even the chill blood of the secretary Chou Qingshan racing—the pickpocket replied humbly, "Oh, most honorable lord, I am most often called Snow Ermine by the evil companions who lured me into this shameful life—but my true name is Lanying." She offered no family surname, and when Kao Yu requested it, she replied, "Lord, I have vowed never to speak that name again in this life, so low have I brought it by my contemptible actions." A single delicate tear spilled from the corner of her left eye and left its track down the side of her equally delicate nose.

Kao Yu, known for leaving his own courtroom in favor of another judge, if he suspected that he was being in some way charmed or coz-ened by a prisoner, was deeply touched by her manner and her obvious repentance. He cleared his suddenly hoarse throat and addressed her thus: "Lanying . . . ah, young woman . . . this being your first offense, I am of a mind to be lenient with you. I therefore sentence you, first, to return every single liang that you have been convicted of stealing from the following citizens—" and he nodded to Chou Qingshan to read off the list of the young pickpocket's victims. "In addition, you are hereby condemned"—he saw Lanying's graceful body stiffen—"to spend a full fortnight working with the nightsoil collectors of this community, so that those pretty hands may remember always that even the lowest, filthiest civic occupation is preferable to the dishonorable use in which they have hitherto been employed. Take her away."

To himself he sounded like a prating, pompous old man, but everyone else seemed suitably impressed. This included the girl Lanying, who bowed deeply in submission and turned to be led off by two sturdy officers of the court. She seemed so small and fragile between them that Kao Yu could not help ordering Chou Qingshan, in a louder voice than was strictly necessary, "Make that a week—a week, not a whole fortnight. Do you hear me?"

Chou Qingshan nodded and obeyed, his expression unchanged, his thoughts his own. But Lanying, walking between the two men, turned her head and responded to this commutation of her sentence with a smile that flew so straight to Judge Kao Yu's heart that he could only cough and look away, and be grateful to see her gone when he raised his eyes again.

To his assistants he said, "That is the last of my master Fang An's cases, so let us dine and go to rest early, that we may be on our way at sunrise." And both Wang Da and Chou Qingshan agreed heartily with him, for each had seen how stricken he had been by a thief's beauty and charm; and each felt that the sooner he was away from this wretched little town, the better for all of them. Indeed, neither Kao Yu's lieutenant nor his secretary slept well that night, for each had the same thought: "He is a man who has been much alone—he will dream of her tonight, and there will be nothing we can do about that." And in this they were entirely correct.

For Kao Yu did indeed dream of Lanying the pickpocket, not only that night, but for many nights thereafter, to the point where, even to his cook Hu Longwei, who was old enough to notice only what he was ordered to notice, he appeared like one whom a lamia or succubus is visiting in his sleep, being increasingly pale, gaunt, and exhausted, as well as notably short-tempered and—for the first time in his career—impatient and erratic in his legal decisions. He snapped at Wang Da, rudely corrected Chou Qingshan's records and transcriptions of his trials, rejected even his longtime favorites of Hu Longwei's dishes, and regularly warned them all that they could easily be replaced by more accomplished and respectful servants, which was a term he had never employed in reference to any of them. Then, plainly distraught with chagrin, he would apologize to each man in turn, and try once again to evict that maddening young body and captivating smile from his nights. He was never successful at this.

During all this time, the chi-lin made not a single appearance in his various courtrooms, which even his retinue, as much as they feared it, found highly unusual, and probably a very bad omen. Having none but each other to discuss the matter with, often clustered together in one more inn, one more drovers' hostel, quite frequently within earshot of Kao Yu tossing and mumbling in his bed, Chou Qingshan would say, "Our master has certainly lost the favor of Heaven, due to his obsession with that thieving slut. For the life of me, I cannot understand it—she was pretty enough, in a coarse way, but hardly one to cost *me* so much as an hour of sleep."

To which Wang Da would invariably respond, "Well, nothing in this world would do *that* but searching under your bed for a lost coin." They were old friends, and, like many such, not particularly fond of each other.

But Hu Longwei—in many ways the wisest of the three, when off duty—would quiet the other two by saying, "If you both spent a little more time considering our master's troubles, and a little less on your own grievances, we might be of some actual use to him in this crisis. He is not the first man to spend less than an hour in some woman's company and then be ridden sleepless by an unresolved fantasy, however absurd. Do not interrupt me, Wang. I am older than both of you, and I know a few things. The way to rid Kao Yu of these dreams of his is to return to that same town—I cannot even remember what it was called—and arrange for him to spend a single night with that little pickpocket. Believe me, there is nothing that clears away such a dream faster than its fulfillment. Think on it—and keep out of my cooking wine, Chou, or I may find another use for my cleaver."

The lieutenant and the secretary took these words more to heart than Hu Longwei might have expected, the result being that somehow, on the return leg of their regular route, Wang Da developed a relative in poor health living in a village within easy walking distance of the town where Lanying the pickpocket resided—employed now, all hoped, in some more respectable profession. Kao Yu's servants never mentioned her name when they went together to the judge to implore a single night's detour on the long way home. Nor, when he agreed to this, did Kao Yu.

It cannot be said that his mental or emotional condition improved greatly with the knowledge that he was soon to see Lanying once again. He seemed to sleep no better, nor was he any less gruff with Wang, Chou, and Hu, even when they were at last bound on the homeward journey. The one significant difference in his behavior was that he regained his calm, unhurried courtroom demeanor, as firmly decisive as always, but paying the strictest attention to the merits of the cases he dealt with, whether in a town, a mere village, or even a scattering of huts and fields that could barely be called a hamlet. It was as though he was in some way preparing himself for the next time the beautiful pickpocket was brought before him, knowing that there *would* be a next time, as surely as sunrise. But what he was actually thinking on the road to that sunrise . . . that no one could have said, except perhaps the chi-lin. And there is no account anywhere of any chi-lin ever speaking in words to a human being.

The town fathers were greatly startled to see them again, since there had been no request for their return, and no messages to announce it. But they welcomed the judge and his entourage all the same, and put them up without charge at the wagoners' inn a second time. And that evening, without notifying his master, Wang Da slipped away quietly and eventually located Lanying the pickpocket in the muddy alley where she lived with a number of the people who called her "Snow Ermine." When he informed her that he came from Judge Kao Yu, who would be pleased to honor her with an invitation to dinner, Lanying favored him with the same magically rapturous smile, and vanished into the hovel to put on her most respectable robe, perfectly suitable for dining with a man who had sentenced her to collect and dispose of her neighbors' nightsoil. Wang Da waited outside for her, giving earnest thanks for his own long marriage, his five children, and his truly imposing ugliness.

On their way to the inn, Lanying—for all that she skipped along beside him like a child on her way to a puppet show or a party—shrewdly asked Wang Da, not why Kao Yu had sent for her, but what Wang Da could tell her about the man himself. Wang Da, normally a taciturn man, except when taunting Chou Qingshan, replied cautiously, wary of her cleverness, saying as little as he could in courtesy. But he did let her know that there had never been a woman of any sort in Kao Yu's life, not as long as he had worked for him—and he did disclose the truth of the judge's chi-lin. It is perhaps the heart of this tale that Lanying chose to believe one of these truths, and to disdain the other.

Kao Yu had, naturally, been given the finest room at the inn, which was no great improvement over any other room, but did have facilities for the judge to entertain a guest in privacy. Lanying fell to her knees and kowtowed—knocked head—the moment she entered, Wang Da having simply left her at the door. But Kao Yu raised her to her feet and served her Dragon In The Clouds tea, and after that huangjiu wine, which is made from wheat. By the time these beverages had been consumed— time spent largely in silence and smiles—the dinner had been prepared and brought to them by Hu Longwei himself, who had pronounced the inn's cook "a northern barbarian who should be permitted to serve none but monkeys and foreigners." He set the trays down carefully on the low table, peered long and rudely into Lanying's face, and departed.

"Your servants do not like me," Lanying said with a small, unhappy sigh. "Why should they, after all?"

Kao Yu answered, bluntly but kindly, "They have no way of knowing whether you have changed your life. Nor did I make you promise to do so when I pronounced sentence." Without further word, he fed her a bit of their roast pork appetizer, and then asked quietly, "Have you done so? Or are you still Lanying the Pickpocket?"

Lanying sighed again and smiled wryly at him. "No, my lord, these days I am Lanying the Seamstress. I am not very good at it, in truth, but I work cheaply. Sometimes I am Lanying the Cowherd—Lanying the Pig Girl—Lanying the Sweeper at the market." She nibbled daintily at her dish, plainly trying to conceal her hunger. "But the pickpocket, no, nor the thief, nor . . ." And here she looked directly into Kao Yu's eyes, and he noticed with something of a shock that her own were not brown, as he had remembered them, but closer to a kind of dark hazel, with flecks of green coming and going. "Nor have I yet been Lanying the Girl on the Market, though it has been a close run once or twice. But I have kept the word I never gave you"—she lowered her eyes then—"perhaps out of pride, perhaps out of gratitude—perhaps . . ." She let the words trail away unfinished, and they dined without speaking for some while, until Lanying was able to regard Kao Yu again without blushing.

Then it was Kao Yu's turn to feel his cheeks grow hot, as he said, "Lanying, you must understand that I have not been much in the society of women. At home, I dine alone in my rooms, always; when I am traveling, I am more or less constantly in the company of my assistants Wang, Chou, and Hu, whom I have known for many years. But since we met, however unfortunately, I have not been able to stop thinking of you, and imagining such an evening as we are enjoying. I am certain that this is wrong, unquestionably wrong for a judge, but when I look at you, I cannot breathe, and I cannot feel my heart beating at all. I am too old for you, and you are too beautiful for me, and I think you should probably leave after we finish our meal. I do."

Lanying began to speak, but Kao Yu took her wrists in his hands, and she—who had some experience in these matters—felt his grip like manacles. He said, "Because, if you never make away with another purse in your life, Lanying the Pickpocket is still there in the back of those lovely eyes. I see her there even now, because although I am surely a great fool, I am also a judge."

He released his hold on her then, and they sat staring at one another—for how long, Kao Yu could never say or remember. Lanying finally whispered, "Your man Wang told me that a unicorn, a chi-lin, sometimes helps you to arrive at your decisions. What do you think it would advise you if it were here now?"

Nor was Kao Yu ever sure how many minutes or hours went by before he was finally able to say, "The chi-lin is not here." And outside the door, Chou Qingshan held out his open palm and Wang Da and Hu Longwei each grudgingly slapped a coin into it as the three of them tiptoed away.

Lanying was gone when Kao Yu woke in the morning, which was, as it turned out, rather a fortunate thing. He was almost finished tidying up the remains of their meal—several items had been crushed and somewhat scattered, and one plate was actually broken—when Wang Da entered to tell him that his dinner guest had stopped long enough while departing the inn in the deep night to empty the landlord's money box, leaving an impudent note of thanks before vanishing. And vanish she certainly had: the search that Kao Yu organized and led himself turned up no trace of her, neither in her usual haunts nor in areas where she claimed to have worked, or was known to have friends. Snow Ermine had disappeared as completely as though she had never been. Which, in a sense, she never had.

Kao Yu, being who he was, compensated the landlord in full—over the advice of all three of his assistants—and they continued on the road home. No one spoke for the first three days.

Finally, in a town in Hunan province, where the four of them were having their evening meal together, Kao Yu broke his silence, saying, "Every one of you is at complete liberty to call me a stupid, ridiculous old fool. You will only be understating the case. I beg pardon of you all." And he actually kowtowed—knocked head—in front of his own servants.

Naturally, Chou, Wang, and Hu were properly horrified at this, and upset their own dishes rushing to raise Kao Yu to his feet. They assured him over and over that the robbery at the inn could not in any way be blamed on him, even though he *had* invited the thief to dinner there, and she *had* spent the night in his bed, taking fullest advantage of his favor . . . the more they attempted to excuse him of the responsibility, the more guilty he felt, and the angrier at himself for, even now, dreaming every night of the embraces of that same thief. He let his three true friends comfort him, but all he could think of was that he would never again be able to return the gaze of the unicorn in his courtroom with the same pride and honesty. The chi-lin would know the truth, even of his dreams. The chi-lin always knew.

When they returned without further incident to the large southern city that was home to all four of them, Kao Yu allowed himself only two days to rest, and then flung himself back into his occupation with a savage vengeance aimed at himself and no one else. He remained as patient as ever with his assistants—and, for the most part, with the accused brought to him for judgment. Indeed, as culpable as his dreams kept telling him he was, he sympathized more with these petty, illiterate, drink-sodden, hopeless, useless offscourings of decent society than he ever had in his career—in his life. Whether the useless offscourings themselves ever recognized this is not known.

Wang Da, Chou Qingshan, and Hu Longwei all hoped that time and work would gradually free his mind of Snow Ermine—which was the only way they spoke of her from then on—and at first, because they wanted it so much to be true, they believed that it must be. And while they were at home in the city, living the life of a busy city judge and his aides, dining with other officials, advising on various legal matters, speaking publicly to certain conferences, and generally filling their days with lawyers and the law, this did indeed seem to be so. Further, to their vast relief, Kao Yu's unicorn paid him no visits during that time; in fact, it had not been seen for more than a year. In private, he himself regarded this as a judgment in its own right, but he said nothing about that, considering it his own harsh concern. So all appeared to be going along in a proper and tranquil manner, as had been the case before the mischance that called him to an all-but-nameless town to deal with the insignificant matter of that wretched—and nameless—pickpocket.

Consequently, when it came the season for them to take to the long road once more, the judge's assistants each had every reason to hope that he would show himself completely recovered from his entanglement with that same wretched pickpocket. Particularly since this time, they would have no reason to pass anywhere near that town where she plied her trade, and where Kao Yu might just conceivably be called upon again to pass sentence upon her. It was noted as they set out, not only that the weather was superb, but that their master was singing to himself: very quietly, true—almost wordlessly, almost in a whisper—but even so. The three looked at each other and dared to smile; and if smiles made any sound, that one would have been a whisper, too.

At first the journey went well, barring the condition of the spring roads, which were muddy, as always, and sucked tiresomely at the feet of their horses. But there were fewer criminal cases than usual for Kao Yu to deal with, and most of those were run-of-the-mill affairs: a donkey or a few chickens stolen *here*, a dispute over fishing rights or a right of way *there*, a wife assaulting her husband—for excellent reasons—over *there*. Such dull daily issues might be uninteresting to any but the participants, but they had the distinct advantage of taking up comparatively little time; as a rule, Kao Yu and his retinue never needed to spend more than a day and a night in any given town. On the rare occasions when they stayed longer, it was always to rest the horses, never themselves. But that suited all four of them, especially Wang Da, who, for all his familial responsibilities, remained as passionately devoted to his wife as any new bridegroom, and was beginning to allow himself sweet visions of returning home earlier than expected. The others teased him rudely that he might well surprise the greengrocer or the fishmonger in his bed, but Kao Yu reproved them sharply, saying, "True happiness is as delicate as a dragonfly's wing, and it is not to be made sport of." And he patted Wang Da's shoulder, as he had never done before, and rode on, still singing to himself, a very little.

But once they reached the province where the girl called Snow Ermine lived—even though, as has been said, their route had been planned to take them as far as possible from her home—then the singing stopped, and Kao Yu grew day by day more silent and morose. He drew apart from his companions, both in traveling and in their various lodgings; and while he continued to take his cases, even the most trifling, as seriously as ever, his entire courtroom manner had become as dry and sour as that of a much older judge. This impressed very favorably most of the local officials he dealt with, but his assistants knew what unhappiness it covered, and pitied him greatly.

Chou Qingshan predicted that Kao Yu would return to his old self once they were clear of the province that had brought him to such shame and confusion; and to some degree that was true as they rode on from town to village, village to town. But the soft singing never did come again, which in time caused the cook Hu Longwei to say, "He is like a vase or a pot that has been shattered into small bits, and then restored, glued back together, fragment by fragment. It will look as good as new, if the work is done right, but you have to be careful with it. *We* will have to be careful."

Nevertheless, their progress was so remarkable that they were almost two weeks ahead of schedule when they reached Yinchuan, where they were accustomed to rest and resupply themselves for a few days before starting home. But within a day of their arrival, Kao Yu had been approached by both the mayor of the town and the provincial governor, each asking him if he would be kind enough to preside over a particular case for them tomorrow. A Yinchuan judge had already been chosen, of course, and would doubtless do an excellent job; but, like every judge available, he had no experience handling such a matter as murder, and it was well-known that Kao Yu—

Kao Yu said, "Murder? This is truly a murder case you are asking me to deal with?"

The mayor nodded miserably. "We know that you have come a long journey, and have a long journey yet before you . . . but the victim was an important man, a merchant all the way from Harbin, and his family is applying a great deal of pressure on the entire city administration, not me alone. A judge of your stature agreeing to take over . . . it might calm them somewhat, reassure them that something is being done . . ."

"Tell me about the case," Kao Yu interrupted brusquely. Hu Longwei groaned quietly, but Chou and Wang were immediately excited, though they properly made every effort not to seem so. An illegally-established tollgate—a neighbor poaching rabbits on a neighbor's land—what was that to a real murder? With Kao Yu, they learned that the merchant— young, handsome, vigorous, and with, as even his family admitted, far more money than sense—had wandered into the wrong part of town and struck up several unwise friendships, most particularly one with a young woman—

"A pickpocket?" Kao Yu's voice had suddenly grown tight and rasping.

No, apparently not a pickpocket. Apparently her talents lay else-where—

"Was she called . . . Snow Ermine?"

"That name has not been mentioned. When she was taken into custody, she gave the name 'Spring Lamb.' Undoubtedly an alias, or a nickname—"

"Undoubtedly. Describe her." But then Kao Yu seemed to change his mind, saying, "No . . . no, do not describe her to me. Have all the evidence in the matter promptly delivered to our inn, and let me decide then whether or not I will agree to sit on the case. You will have my an-swer tonight, if the evidence reaches the inn before we do."

It did, as Kao Yu's assistants knew it would; but all three of them agreed that they had never seen their master so reluctant even to handle the evidence pertaining to a legal matter. There was plenty of it, certainly, from the sworn statements of half a dozen citizens swearing to having seen the victim in the company of the accused; to the proprietor of a particularly disreputable wine shop, who had sold the pair enough liquor, jar on jar, to float a river barge; let alone the silent witness of the young merchant's slit-open purse, and of the slim silver knife still buried to the hilt in his side when he was discovered in a trash-strewn alley with dogs sniffing at his body. There was even—when his rigor-stiffened left hand was pried open, a crushed rag of a white flower. Judge Kao Yu's lamp burned all night in his room at the inn.

But in the morning, when Wang Da came to fetch him, he was awake and clear-eyed and had already breakfasted, though only on green tea and sweetened congee. He was silent as they walked to the building set aside for trials of all sorts, where Hu Longwei and Chou Qingshan awaited them, except to remark that they would be starting home on the day after tomorrow, distinctly earlier than their usual practice. He said nothing further until they reached the courtroom.

There were two minor cases to be disposed of before the matter of the young merchant's murder: one a suit over a breach of contract, the other having to do with a long-unpaid family debt. Kao Yu settled these swiftly, and then—a little pale, his words a bit slower, but his voice quiet and steady—signaled for the accused murderer to be brought into court.

It was Lanying, as he had known in his heart that it would be, from the very first mention of the case. Alone in his room, he had not even bothered to hope that the evidence would prove her innocent, or, at the very least, raise some small doubt as to her guilt. He had gone through it all quickly enough, and spent the rest of the night sitting very still, with his hands clasped in his lap, looking toward the door, as though expecting her to come to him then and there, of her own will, instead of waiting until morning for her trial. From time to time, in the silence of the room, he spoke her name.

Now, as the two constables who had led her to his high bench stepped away, he looked into her calmly defiant eyes and said only, "We meet again."

"So we do," Lanying replied equably. She was dressed rakishly, having been seized before she had time to change into garments suitable for a court appearance; but, as ever, she carried herself with the pride and poise of a great lady. She said to Kao Yu, "I hoped you might be the one."

"Why is that? Because I let you off lightly the first time? Because I . . . because it was so easy for you to make a fool of me the next time?" Kao Yu was almost whispering. "Do you imagine that I will be quite as much of a mark today?"

"No. But I did wish to apologize."

"Apologize?" Kao Yu stared at her. "*Apologize?*"

Lanying bowed her head, but she looked up at him from under her long dark eyelashes. "Lord, I am a thief. I have been a thief all my life. A thief steals. I knew the prestige of your invitation to dine would give me a chance at the inn's money box, and I accepted it accordingly, because that is what a thief does. It had nothing to do with you, with my . . . liking for you. I am what I am."

Kao Yu's voice was thick in his throat. "You are what you have become, which is something more than a mere thief and pickpocket. Now you are a murderer."

The word had not been at all hard to get out when he was discussing it with the mayor, and with his three assistants, but now it felt like a thornbush in his throat. Lanying's eyes grew wide with fear and protest. "*I?* Never! I had *nothing* to do with that poor man's death!"

"The knife is yours," Kao Yu said tonelessly. "It is the same one I noticed at your waist when you dined with me. Nor have I ever seen you without a white flower in your hair. Do not bother lying to me any further, Lanying."

"But I am not lying!" she cried out. "I took his money, yes—he was stupid with wine, and that is what I do, but killing is no part of it. The knife was stolen from me, I swear it! Think as little of me as you like—I have given you reason enough—but I am no killer, you *must* know that!" She lowered her voice, to keep the words that followed from the constables. "Our bodies tell the truth, if our mouths do not. My lord, my judge, you know as much truth of me as anyone does. Can you tell me again that I am a murderer?"

Kao Yu did not answer her. They looked at each other for a long time, the judge and the lifelong thief, and it seemed to Chou Qing-shan that there had come a vast weariness on Kao Yu, and that he might never speak again to anyone. But then Kao Yu lifted his head in wonder and fear as the scent of a summer meadow drifted into the room, filling it with the warm, slow presence of wild ginger, hibis-cus, lilacs, and lilies—and the chi-lin. The two constables fell to their knees and pressed their faces to the floor, as did his three assistants, none of them daring even to look up. The unicorn stood motionless at the back of the courtroom, and Kao Yu could no more read its eyes than he ever could. But in that moment, he knew Lanying's terrible danger for his own.

Very quietly he said to her, "Snow Ermine, Spring Lamb, thief of my foolish, foolish old heart . . . nameless queen born a criminal . . . and, yes, murderer—I am begging you now for both our lives. Speak the truth, if you never do so again, because otherwise you die here, and so do I. Do you hear me, Lanying?"

Just for an instant, looking into Lanying's beautiful eyes, he knew that she understood exactly what he was telling her, and, further, that neither he nor the chi-lin was in any doubt that she had slain the mer-chant she robbed. But she was, as she had told him, what she was; and even with full knowledge of the justice waiting, she repeated, spacing the words carefully, and giving precise value to each, "Believe what you will. I am no killer."

Then the judge Kao Yu rose from his bench and placed himself between Lanying and the unicorn, and he said in a clear, strong voice, "You are not to harm her. Everything she says is a lie, and always will be, and still you are not to harm her." In the silence that followed, his voice shook a little as he added, "Please."

The chi-lin took a step forward—then another—and Lanying closed her eyes. But it did not charge; rather, it paced across the courtroom to face Kao Yu, until they were standing closer than ever they had before, in all the years of their strange and wordless partnership. And what passed between them then will never be known, save to say that the chi-lin turned away and was swiftly gone—never having once glanced at Lanying—and that Kao Yu sat down again and began to weep, without ever making a sound.

When he could speak, he directed the trembling constables to take Lanying away, saying that he would pass sentence the next day. She went, this time without a backward glance, as proudly as ever, and Kao Yu did not look after her, but walked away alone. Wang Da and Chou Qingshan would have followed him, but Hu Longwei took them both by the arms and shook his head.

Kao Yu spent the night alone in his room, where he could be heard pacing constantly, sometimes talking to himself in ragged, incomprehensible tatters of language. Whatever it signified, it eliminated him as a suspect in Lanying's escape from custody that same evening. She was never recaptured, reported, or heard of again—at least, not under that name, nor in that region of China—and if each of Kao Yu's three friends regarded the other two skeptically for a long time thereafter, no one accused anyone of anything, even in private. Indeed, none of them ever spoke of Lanying, the pickpocket, thief, and murderer for whom their master had given up what they knew he had given up. They had no words for it, but they knew.

For the chi-lin never came again, and Kao Yu never spoke of that separation either. The one exception came on their silent road home, when darkness caught them between towns, obliging them to make camp in a forest, as they were not unaccustomed to doing. They gathered wood together, and Hu Longwei improvised an excellent dinner over their fire, after which they chatted and bantered as well as they could to cheer their master, so silent now for so many days. It was then that Kao Yu announced his decision to retire from the bench, which shocked and dismayed them all, and set each man entreating him to change his mind. In this they were unsuccessful, though they argued and pleaded with him most of the night. It was nearer to dawn than to midnight, and the flames were dwindling because everyone had forgotten to feed them, when Chou Qingshan remarked bitterly, "So much for justice, then. With you gone, so much for justice between Guangzhou and Yinchuan."

But Kao Yu shook his head and responded, "You misunderstand, old friend. I am only a judge, and judges can always be found. The chi-lin . . . the chi-lin is justice. There is a great difference."

He did indeed retire, as he had said, and little is known of the rest of his life, except that he traveled no more, but stayed in his house, writing learned commentaries on curious aspects of common law, and, on rare occasions, lecturing to small audiences at the local university. His three assistants, of necessity, attached themselves to other circuit-riding judges, and saw less of one another than they did of Kao Yu, whom they never failed to visit on returning from their journeys. But there was less and less to say each time, and each admitted—though only to himself—a kind of guilt-stricken relief when he died quietly at home, from what his doctors termed a sorrow of the soul. China is one of the few countries where sadness has always been medically recognized.

There is a legend that after the handful of mourners at his funeral had gone home, a chi-lin kept silent watch at his grave all that night. But that is all it is, of course, a legend.

TRINITY COUNTY, CA:
YOU'LL WANT TO COME AGAIN AND WE'LL BE GLAD TO SEE YOU!

My late friend Pat Derby (with whom I wrote my one as-told-to book, *The Lady and Her Tiger*) was forever rescuing half-starved wolves, bears, and mountain lions, kept as guardians of their compounds by drug dealers all over hidden wilderness camps in northern California, mostly to ward off, not so much the police and the FBI, as their fellow dealers. I lived in the Santa Cruz area for twenty-two years, during which time it became one of the major sources of marijuana and—far worse—crystal methedrine, which, by the time you read this, may have been officially recognized as the leading cash crop of the state. I knew Trinity County in those days less well than I knew Santa Cruz, Alpine, El Dorado, and Monterey, but the underground economy was the same, and everyone from Sacramento officialdom to boardwalk hippies knew it. This story merely takes the hidden world that Pat Derby showed me a notch further: what if drug dealers employed dragons, instead of lions. . . ?

"**T**HIS STUFF *STINKS*," Connie Laminack complained. She and Gruber were dressing for work in the yard's cramped and makeshift locker room, which, thanks to budget cuts, was also the building's only functional toilet. To get to the dingy aluminum sink, she had to step around the urinal, then dodge under Gruber's left arm as he forced it up into the sleeve of his bright yellow outer coverall.

"You get used to it."

"No, I won't. They let me use my Lancôme in school. *That* smells human."

"And has an FPF rating that's totally bogus," Gruber said. "Anything you can buy retail is for posers and pet-shop owners. Won't cut it out here."

Laminack unscrewed the top from the plain white plastic jar on the shelf below the mirror, and squinted in disgust at the gray gloop inside. "I'm just saying. Gack."

Gruber smiled. Stuck with a newbie, you could still get some fun out of it. Sometimes. "Make sure you get it every damn place you can reach. Really rub it in. State only pays quarter disability if you come home Extra Crispy."

"Nice try, but some of us actually do read the HR paperwork we sign."

"Oh, right," Gruber said. "College grad." She gave him a hard look in the mirror, but dutifully started rubbing the D-schmear on her hands and arms anyway, then rolled up her pants legs to get at her calves.

"Face, too. Especially your face, and an inch or two into the hairline. Helps with the helmet seal."

"Just saving the worst for last."

Gruber laughed wryly. "It's all the worst."

"You'd be the one to know, wouldn't you?"

"Got *that* right, trainee."

By the time they headed out to the Heap, he was throwing questions at her, as per the standard training drill, but not enjoying it the way he usually did. For one thing, she'd actually done a good job with the D-schmear, even getting it up into her nostrils, which first-timers almost never did. For another, she seemed to truly know her shit. Book shit, to be sure, not the real-world shit she was here to start learning . . . but Gruber was used to catching new kids in some tiny mistake, then pile-driving in to widen the gap, until they were panicked and stammering. Only Laminack wasn't tripping up.

It had begun to bug him. That, and the fact that she bounced. Like he needed *perky* to deal with, on top of everything else.

He waved back to Manny Portola, the shift dispatcher, who always

176

stood in the doorway to see the different county crews off. It was one of Manny's pet superstitions, and in time it had become Gruber's as well, though he told himself he was just keeping the old guy happy.

Laminack waved to the dispatcher as well, which irritated Gruber, even though he knew it shouldn't. He slapped the day-log clipboard against his leg.

"Next! Name the three worst invasives in Trinity."

"Trick question."

"Maybe, maybe not."

"No," she insisted. "Definitely. You didn't define your terms." Her bland smile didn't change, but Gruber thought he heard a tiny flicker of anger. Maybe he was finally getting to her. "Are we talking plants or animals here? 'Cause Yellow Star Thistle and Dalmatian Toadflax and Kamathweed are hella invasive, even if the tourists do like the pretty yellow flowers. And if we are talking animals, not plants, do you want me to stick to the Ds, or do you want me to rattle off the three worst things that have ever crawled or flown or swum in here from somewhere they shouldn't? Which I could. And what do you mean by 'worst,' anyway? Because for my money, jet slugs are about as yucky as it gets, and there are a lot more of them up here now than there are China longs. So yeah, I call trick question."

Gruber definitely wasn't ready for two weeks of this. "Nobody likes a show-off, Laminack."

"No, sir."

"We're not County Animal Control, and we're damn well not the State Department of Food and Agriculture or the California Invasive Plant Council. So what do you think I wanted to hear when I asked that question?"

Reaching the Heap, Laminack opened the driver's-side door for him and stepped back. She didn't exactly stand at attention, but near enough.

"I think you wanted me to tell you that last year's baseline survey put quetzals, China longs, and Welsh reds at the top of the list in Trinity, but winter was rough, so it's too early to know yet what we'll be dealing with this season. Especially with the pot growers and meth labs upping their black-market firepower."

"Hunh." Without meaning to, he found himself nodding. "Not bad, Laminack."

"Call me Connie, okay? My last name sounds like a duck call."

Great, Gruber thought. *She even bounces standing still.*

First scheduled stop of the day was more than thirty miles out of Weaverville, up 299 into the deep woods of Trinity National Forest, almost all the way to Burnt Ranch. Despite everything eating at him, Gruber always found the views in this corner of the county restful, an ease to the soul, and he enjoyed watching Connie begin to get clear on just how big the place was, even in this first tiny taste: 3,200 square miles by outline, same size as Vermont on the map—or all of Texas, if ever God came along and stomped the Trinity Alps out flat—and only 13,000 people to get in the way, the majority of whom lived in Weaverville and Lewiston and Hayfork. The rest were so spread out that words like "sparse" and "isolated" didn't do the situation justice. Gruber had been on the job for sixteen years, and he knew there were people living in corners of these woods so deep he still hadn't been there yet.

They turned off onto a tributary road that wasn't shown on the state-supplied map, and wound uphill for five snaky miles before Gruber stopped the Heap and killed the engine.

"Welcome to your first block party. Another mile or so up, we're going to do a little Easter egg hunt. You want to guess what kind?"

For the first time this morning, Connie hesitated. Then she caught herself and said, firmly, "Belgian wyverns. I thought maybe double-backs, for a minute, but that would have been a couple of weeks ago at this latitude. Right?"

Gruber nodded. "Almost all the other Ds are late-summer, early-autumn layers, but wyverns and doublebacks—and Nicaraguan charlies, only we don't have those up here, not yet, thank God—they lay their eggs in the spring, so they'll hatch and be ready in time to eat the other Ds' eggs. Just this side of parasites, you ask me. But some elements of the Asian community think ground-up prepubescent wyvern bones are an aphrodisiac, so there's always some idiot in the woods willing to try and raise the little bastards. We got an anonymous tip on this place a week ago."

"So let's go. I'm ready."

Gruber shook his head. "Ground rules, first. And fair warning: say anything but yes—and I do mean anything—and we're home in Weaverville before lunch, with your ass planted firmly on the next bus back to UC Davis. This is not a joke up here. This isn't the classroom. Mostly we don't run into trouble, but that's *mostly*, and you can't let that get in the way of being ready for everything else."

Connie didn't say a word. She looked at Gruber for a moment, and then nodded.

"First rule," Gruber continued. "What I tell you to do, you do. If I say 'run,' you damn well *sprint*, and you don't look back. If I shout, 'Get back in the Heap!' you jump in here and hit the autolock, even if I'm still outside."

"Yes," Connie said.

"Second rule. If you're in here and I'm in trouble, you hit the screechers."

"Yes."

"Third rule. If that doesn't help, then you drive the hell out of sight as fast as you can, and you keep calling in to the sheriff's office for backup until you finally reach a live zone and get through. Then you *sit and wait for somebody to show up.* This is not—I repeat *not*—some reality TV show. There are reasons Manny's got that NO HEROES sign on his desk."

"Got it." She blinked and corrected herself. "Yes."

"Fourth rule, you see even a hint of a gun, you don't wait for me to yell. You get your butt back in the Heap and duck down. The plate on this thing can handle pretty much anything one of the locals is likely to be carrying." He didn't wait for her to respond before he went on. "And finally, fifth rule, today you don't say anything to anybody without checking with me first. Walk straight, stand tall, and make like you're Clint Eastwood with laryngitis. Got that?"

She nodded once.

Not so bouncy now. Good.

"Helmet and gloves on, then. Let's go."

The road wound on a while longer, then turned left over a ridge and started down. As it did, the landscape changed, the usual Trinity mix of tall oak, pine, and fir trees giving way to high pasture and orchards, green and peaceful as a children's book.

The farmhouse wasn't out of a picture book, but a new coat of paint masked its aged and fraying condition. An old woman in a sun hat was down on both knees, pruning roses and humming to herself, not even looking at the Heap as it pulled in. There was a one-gallon lawn and garden sprayer sitting next to her.

"Deaf or on guard," Gruber said. "And you know how I vote. Keep your tapper handy, but stay behind me."

The old woman only looked up when Gruber opened the Heap's door and stepped out, his coverall a bright yellow blotch in the middle of a bright blue day. He checked her out. Pure Grandma. Straw hat, pink cheeks, worn old flannel shirt, muddy-kneed jeans . . . no jury would convict her of stealing cookies, let alone raising Ds.

"Can I help you?" she asked.

Gruber turned on the big bland smile that came packaged with the uniform and started forward, nice and easy. He heard Connie fall into line.

"Ma'am, good morning. My name is Mike Gruber, and this is my partner, Connie Laminack. We're D Patrol for the county." He pointed at the big agency patch on the front of his coverall, the one just below the California state seal, then made a show of checking his clipboard. "Are you Mrs. Johanna Watkins?"

The woman leaned back on her haunches, shading her eyes with one hand, even though the sun was behind her.

"That's me. Beautiful day, isn't it?"

"Yes, ma'am. Surely is."

"Nice to be outside. Have to spray these roses every day, you know, or else the deer eat them. What can I do for you?"

"Well . . ." Gruber paused. "The thing of it is, Mrs. Watkins, Johanna, we have reliable information that you and Mr. Watkins have been breeding wyverns—Belgian wyverns, to be precise—and selling the younglings to a crew down in Douglas City. Now, as I'm sure you know, there are both state and federal statutes against wyvern trafficking of any kind: live or dead, eggs, skins, organs, you name it. It's illegal."

The Watkins woman was good: Gruber had to give her that. She flashed a crinkly smile straight out of a biscuit-mix commercial and said, "Oh, but everyone does it, surely—that's just one of those laws, you know, like they say, more honored in the breach than the observance—"

Gruber interrupted her. "Well, actually no, ma'am, everybody *doesn't* do it, whatever you've been told. And the laws *are* enforced, as I'm afraid you're about to find out. Now I'm going to need to speak to your husband—and then, if you two could give us a brief walking tour of your operation—"

Johanna Watkins was on her feet, periwinkle-blue eyes wide, moving smoothly into Plan B: shocked and trembling innocence. "Officer, we really didn't . . . I mean, Eddie, my husband, Eddie and I, we're just two old people living on a fixed income, and it seemed . . . I mean, nobody really told us, and we were just trying . . . we didn't want to be a burden on our son—"

Gruber stopped her as courteously as he could, keeping one eye on the garden shears dangling in her left hand. He had once been attacked by an old man swinging a fan belt studded with bits of broken glass, and the event had left him with a certain wariness regarding senior citizens. "Well, ma'am, all I'm required to do is write you up a citation, like a traffic ticket—the rest'll be up to Sheriff Trager's discretion. So if Mr. Watkins is home . . ." He had always found it better—and often safer—to leave commands implied.

"Yes," Mrs. Watkins stammered, letting her voice tremble affectingly.

"Yes, yes, of course. If you'll just wait here, I'll be, I'll get . . ." She too left the sentence unfinished, dropping the shears and wandering toward the house in a seeming daze.

Behind him, Connie murmured, "Permission to speak, sir?"

"Only 'til Sweetie Bat gets back." He took a few steps and craned his neck to observe the surprisingly large stretch of tightly-fenced paddock that was located south and downslope from the house. Several rough-hewn wooden poles sporting a makeshift power line ran between the two. Beyond the paddock, the woods began.

Connie said, "I know it's silly—I guess—but she does look like my grandmother. She really does."

Gruber shrugged. "She's *somebody's* grandmother. Retirement, kids gone, a little problem with cash flow . . . we see a lot of that. Sometimes they're just bored, you'd be surprised."

"She looked so scared," Connie sighed. "I just wanted to tell her, *'It's okay, it'll be all right'*—"

She was interrupted by the sound of a slamming door at the back of the house, followed immediately by a stumbling clatter and scraps of a shrill and breathless quarrel—then the unmistakable growl of a two-stroke engine. Gruber said mildly, "Well, *shit.*" Loping around the corner of the old farmhouse, he saw Johanna Watkins and a lanky old man wearing checked pants and a yellow sweater racing toward the tree line on a metallic green minibike. Gruber halted, scratching his head, and began to laugh.

Connie came up beside him, staring after the sputtering little bike as it vanished into the trees. "Shouldn't we go after them, or something?"

"Not our job, I'm happy to inform you. We're contraband, not perps. Trager's boys can track them later, or maybe nab them when they sneak back to the house, likely tonight. They weren't carrying anything, and it gets cold up here after sunset."

He flipped his tapper to trank and started toward the paddock, saying over his shoulder, "Stay back 'til I call you." The gate was clearly meant to be opened by a remote switch—*probably in the kitchen, right next to the cookie jar*—but the lock was cheap, and Gruber forced it easily. The two wyverns came out of hiding as soon as he opened the gate, bounding toward him like little kangaroos on their powerful hind legs. Red, with dark-gold chests and bellies, they stood just under three feet high; three-foot-six was a King Kong among wyverns. "Geese with teeth," Manny called them, but for all that they could do damage. The wings—a much deeper red, almost black—were useless for flying, but tipped with sharp, curving claws. Gruber had always considered them more dangerous than the fangs, which were just as sharp, and more numerous, but easier to keep track of.

He let the wyverns get close, having no illusions regarding his own ability with hand-held weapons, but then he dropped them with one dart apiece. They were out before they hit the ground, and would stay that way for ten, maybe twelve hours: the current generation of tranquilizers was a lot more reliable than what he'd started the job with, and good for a wider range of Ds, no matter how many hearts they had, or whether their blood was acid or base. Gruber had no nostalgia for the old days, except as they involved long-gone movies and breweries.

"Easter Bunny time," he called over his shoulder. Connie approached the paddock slowly, casting a wary eye toward the sedated wyverns. Watching her, Gruber said, "No, I take it back, it's May. Time to go gathering nuts."

"They actually do look like nuts, don't they?" Connie frowned, remembering. "We had a whole extra series on protective coloration just in eggs."

"Yeah, they look like coconuts," Gruber said. "Except for the ones that don't. Belgian wyverns can be weird. So you watch where you're putting your feet." Remembering altogether too well how long it had taken him to get the knack, he kept a close eye on Connie as they worked through the paddock together, never letting her get too far from him. What worried him more, as they loaded the eggs into the standard McNaughton keeper—clumsier to carry than the old Dorchester, but it could hold twice as many eggs as their thirty-seven in perfect thermal stasis as long as its battery pack held out—was feeling their rising warmth in his palms, and realizing just how close they had been to hatching.

When a third pass didn't turn up anything new, he had Connie drive the Heap down to the paddock while he tagged and chipped the wyverns, then bound their wings and legs with Thermo-Kevlar banding. It took a shared effort to get the sleeping creatures locked away in the back, him lifting and her pushing. The male was particularly troublesome: its head and neck kept flopping in the wrong direction as they tried to angle it into the Heap's fireproofed main containment module. After they finally managed the trick, Gruber took Connie with him to the farmhouse. He showed her how to fill out the official citation form, and had her tape it to the front door with four strips of bright orange waterproof tape, one strip per side.

Back in the Heap, he took the wheel while Connie stored the McNaughton under her seat. Gruber would have sworn that he saw her pat it once, quickly and shyly.

As they headed out, Connie asked, "Where do you suppose the proud parents went?"

"Hiding out with family, maybe. Calling lawyers. Not a lot of options when it gets to this point. When we hit a place where my cell works, I'll call Manny. Trager's people will make things plain to them, one way or another." The Watkins farm disappeared from the rearview mirror as he spoke. "How you liking it so far?"

"Is that another trick question?" Her voice was quiet and subdued, all the early-morning attitude gone. She said, "They were little, but they were scary. The way they went straight for you . . ."

"They can hurt you," Gruber said. He glanced sideways at her. "Not like class, huh? Not like field trips, even."

Connie was silent for some time. In this stretch, the narrow old road was rough, all pebbles and potholes. They passed a couple of abandoned trailers, and a lean, ugly dog chased along after the Heap for a while, until it got bored. She said finally, "What are they like . . . the big ones? What does it *feel* like?"

Gruber shrugged. "Not that different, you been doing it long enough. Sure, you wet your pants, first time it's a quetzal coming at you, first time you look right into the eyes of a China long. But there aren't as many in the county as people think—I went two years one time, never saw anything bigger than a doubleback—and as long as you stay cool, long as you treat each and every damn D as though it was twelve feet tall, you're pretty much okay. Usually."

"Usually," Connie said. "Right."

"I'm forty-seven years old," Gruber said, smiling at her before he could stop himself. "Forty-eight in three weeks. Believe me, *usually* is as good as it gets. Ds, anything else. I'll settle for *usually* any time."

He turned his head away quickly to watch the road; you could break an axle as easily as an ankle in this country. Connie had her back to him, looking out, one elbow braced on the window frame. She said, half to herself, "Looks just like eastern Mendocino."

"Spent some time there?"

"Visited my cousins, growing up. They're over in Ukiah."

"Mendocino's got the same troubles we have. The farms mostly don't pay worth a damn anymore, so a lot of folks either sell out to the pot growers and meth makers or go into the business themselves."

"Will—my older cousin—he told me stories." She shook her head. "But I never saw anything. No Ds, for sure, though I heard they were there. Sheltered life, I guess."

"Pot farms aren't on your typical family-outing list."

She laughed, a bit shakily, and replied, "I liked the trees and the space okay, but I was a city kid. I just wanted a Barbie. A Barbie and a utility belt, like Batman's." Gruber looked at her. "I had to know how he got all that *stuff* into all those little compartments. And what about the gadgets and things we never saw? I had to *know*, that's all."

"Permission to speak revoked," Gruber said. "Forever."

❧

The rest of the morning went smoothly, standard drill-and-drop-in for every live report like the Watkins' place: drive the neighboring roads, watch for burn marks or D scat, stop every few miles to let the pheromone detectors take a sniff, and knock on whatever doors they could find. In that fashion, they checked out half a dozen farms and isolated cabins, the Heap toiling up one barely-visible dirt track to break into briefly-dazzling alpine blue, and then plunging straight down another into a hemlock valley dense with a heavy, motionless dark green. Only one place was harboring a D, a pitiful little half-starved sniggerbit that might actually have been a family pet, like the kids clinging to their silent father's legs claimed. The man himself said nothing. He just looked at Gruber and Connie and the filled-out citation as though they were all different kinds of snakes, then led his kids inside so they wouldn't have to see the sniggerbit tranked and taken away.

In the ordinary manner, Gruber reported back to Manny in Weaverville as soon as he got up high enough on some hill to see a bar or two on his cell. Life would have been easier with a sat phone, but the county wouldn't spring for the service plan.

Manny's voice sounded like he was on the other side of the moon, or maybe trapped in a room full of rabid washing machines.

"... ob's guys say they need ... back at the Watkins' ..."

"Say again, please, Manny. This connection sucks."

"Who's 'ob'?" asked Connie.

"Sheriff Trager," he told her. Then back into the cell: "Say again, please. I'm not getting this."

"... burned down. Whole house gone. Big ... tracks, fire score, maybe some tail marks. Bob wants you there for a walkaround. Meet ... 299 south of—"

That was it. Gruber looked at the cell phone in his hand. No bars, just a lot of crackling noise. No point in even trying to call back. Briefly he considered going higher, trying to get back in touch, but to do that he'd have to get out and climb for who knows how long, or else head downhill in the Heap and hope he could find the forest service road that tracked the facing ridge.

"Was that about the Watkins' place? *It's burned down?*"

"You heard what I heard," he said. Then: "County map. Glove compartment." She fumbled for it even as he kept speaking. "Sheriff Trager is not exactly a patient man, so let's see if we can find a shortcut."

They were still several miles away, by the map, headed downhill on a road that didn't deserve the name, when a yellow light started blinking on the dashboard. Gruber slammed on the brakes. The Heap skidded to a halt, and he and Connie were jolted against their shoulder belts so hard Gruber knew they'd be feeling it the next day.

Connie shot him a look. "What's wrong?"

"Stay here. I'll be right back." He threw the Heap into park but left it running. With one hand, he unstrapped himself as fast as he could; with the other, he pushed the door open wide.

"Gruber?"

"Just *stay here.*"

He shut the door behind him as gently as he could, but the *clatch* sound still seemed like a gunshot in the quiet under the trees. Gruber held his breath and listened. He heard the Heap's low idling and some distant bird sounds, but nothing else. He looked down the rough road in the direction they were going, then back the way they'd come, and off to either side. All the time, he kept his eyes vague and unfocused, paying attention mainly to his peripheral vision, trying to tease some hint of motion out of the tangle of trees and leaves and brush. Nothing that way, either. He did get detailed then, leaving the side of the Heap to explore a little way into the woods, peering low on the tree trunks and high into the branches, looking for firesign or fresh breaks.

After five minutes, he came back to the Heap, opened the driver's-side door, and stood there without getting in, frowning at the still-blinking yellow light.

"You are seriously freaking me out," Connie said, not even trying to hide the worry in her voice. "What's going on? Why'd you stop?"

"That," Gruber said, pointing at the light.

"What, do we have engine trouble?"

"No," he said, getting back in the Heap. He pulled the door shut normally and started to belt himself back in. "That's the emergency telltale for the passive pheromone traps. Manny calls it the 'oh shit' light."

"You mean—"

"Oh yeah," he nodded. "I can't find any sign of it out there, but we just crossed serious D trail. That or the damn sensor is showing a false positive, which could be, given the jouncing it's gotten today."

"What do we do?"

"We check it out. Burnt house in the neighborhood, that might have been Grandma and Grandpa coming back to get rid of evidence. But Manny said Trager spotted fire score . . . so we check it out. Cautiously."

She shook her head. "My folks are going to call me at the motel tonight and ask me how my first day went, and I'm so going to have to lie to them. They never wanted me doing this."

"That's not your big problem," Gruber said.

"It isn't?"

"Nope." His lips pulled back in a flat grin as he put the Heap back into drive, then eased down on the gas. "Didn't I tell you? Newbies have to write the first drafts of the incident reports. You're going to be up to your eyebrows in paperwork 'til midnight."

"Thanks."

When he saw her expression, he wanted to laugh, but the light that was still blinking on the dash wouldn't let him.

Connie spotted them before he did—a scattering of trees, all firs, all fairly close together, bearing the unmistakable fingerprint of fire: scorch marks like whip weals, ten or twelve feet off the ground. On the ground next to the trees was what would have looked like an abandoned turnoff, except for the fresh tire tracks vanishing into it. Gruber shifted to four-wheel drive and turned the Heap to follow, doggedly pushing it through clinging, scraping underbrush that grabbed at the tires and fenders and menacingly low boughs that actually blocked the way. He coaxed and cajoled the truck over logs that had obviously been hauled into position. Finally, around a hundred yards in, things eased off, and he found himself driving on a well-tended trail, flat and easy and wide enough for a commercial trailer.

Without turning his head, Gruber said, "Name the seven major Ds that actually breathe fire."

Connie welcomed the distraction. "Uh . . . Welsh reds, quetzals, China longs—the North China subgenus, *not* the southern longs."

"Keep going."

"Himalayans, the San Ysidro group, the Yilbegan . . . and the Chuvash. Right?"

"Right. So what do we have here? Consider the evidence."

Gruber swung the Heap past a couple of trees burnt charcoal-black, as though they had been through a forest fire. Connie said quickly, "Anything could have done those: they burned from the ground up. But the fire marks back there, those were pretty high. A *humungous* Welsh red could do it, maybe, but more likely a quetzal or a China long. I'm betting on a long."

Gruber nodded. "Agreed. But why *not* a quetzal? Why not any of the others?"

"Well . . ." She swallowed hard. Her voice sounded dry and rough to him, like it hurt to speak. "They've never been reported up here, not even once. And longs outnumber quetzals and reds six to one in the reclamation stats. The longs have been invasive up here since '82, they're a lot easier to get hold of . . . no, it's got to be a long."

A rambling, ranch-style house was coming into view through the trees, and Gruber braked the Heap to an easy stop at the first sight of it. "Guess we're going to find out."

He put on his helmet and gloves and opened the driver's-side door. Keeping his voice low, he said, "Rules still apply. You lock up after me, stay right where you are, and if I get into trouble, you are solid *gone*, yelling for help all the way."

She said, "I thought we were contraband, not perps."

"All I'm going to do is look around a little bit, size up the operation—then we're out of here. Just keep your eyes open and the engine running."

"All right." Her voice was almost inaudible, a child's mumble. She said, "I wish you didn't have to do this."

Gruber said, "It's not the D I'm worried about, not so much—it's the people. People are always scarier than Ds, that's the first rule of the job. I'll be fine. You sit *tight*, you got that? You got it, Connie?" It was the first time he had actually called her by her name.

"I said all right, didn't I?" She frowned at him.

"Back in a flash." He popped a rack of Winged Monkeys out of the holder in the door and stuffed all six into different pockets of his coverall. The little handball-sized spheres were a cross between an insect fogger and a grenade, only with a payload of burst-release broad-spectrum tranquilizers. Gruber hated them, fully trusting neither their accuracy nor their cargo, but at least this way he could go in without looking aggressively armed, while still carrying something useful at longer range than the standard tapper.

Walking alone toward the house, he knew from just tasting the air that one of the big Ds was nearby, though he couldn't yet make out which breed. *They always smell like garbage-dump fires, just different kinds.* Part of him wanted to bolt back inside the Heap and head straight for Weaverville, but he knew the grief he'd catch from Trager's boys if something like *that* ever got around. So he turned, with the Heap already barely visible among the dark trees, and gave Connie a jaunty little wave.

That's when he saw the green minibike parked off to one side, near the bushes. He'd walked right by it, but hadn't noticed because the angle had been wrong.

Well, he thought. *That answers that.*

He turned without letting his face show anything, then walked the rest of the way to the ranch house. When he got there, he climbed the three steps to the low veranda, knocked on the front door, and stood quickly to one side, just in case.

He was not especially surprised when the door was answered fairly promptly, but the wispy, pallid creature who opened it did catch him off-guard. Not quite an albino, having watery blue eyes and watery red hair, the man was still pale as the liquid that pours off yogurt or tofu when the container is first opened. Clearly in his early twenties, he already had the ruined mouth and teeth of a scrofulous old man. But his voice was guilelessly friendly as he inquired, "Yes? What can I do for you?" He stepped over the threshold toward Gruber, pulling the door almost shut behind him.

"D Control, sir," Gruber said. "Not here for you, just trying to trace a couple of elderly persons, last seen heading in this direction on a motorbike." He gestured vaguely behind him. "Kind of like that one out there, actually. We have some reason to believe that they were running a breeding operation out of their farm. Belgian wyverns, to be precise. Would they be here with you presently, by any chance?"

"Elderly persons." The young man wrinkled his genuine alabaster brow and uttered a light, soft chuckle. "Well, I suppose that could be Mr. and Mrs. Edward J. Watkins, my grandparents—I'm Larry Watkins—but breeding Ds? *Please*—those two couldn't cross the street on a red light. Can't help you, I'm afraid. That's my minibike, and I haven't seen the grandsters for at least a month, not a close family, sorry." He turned back toward the house, saying apologetically, "I'd invite you in, but I've got company just now. Old friends getting together, you know how it is. Please do say hello to my supposedly felonious grandparents for me, should you ever find 'em." He vanished through the door, still chuckling.

Gruber knew he'd already pushed his luck as far as it was going to stretch. The sane thing to do was leave, consult with Trager, and not return until he had proper support. But the snotty little shit had put his back up, so instead of hightailing it straight for the Heap, he found himself moving around the side of the house as carefully and quietly as he could.

Just a quick little look-see . . .

There were two buildings up the overgrown rise to the rear: Quonset-type huts, like man-sized culverts closed at both ends. One sniff told him what they were making there, and how they were making it. Nobody was ever going to confuse the rotting-fish smell of phosphine gas with anything else.

He had just enough time to feel really stupid before the first shot rang out. It didn't come anywhere close to him—tweakers didn't tend to be Olympic marksmen—but it was definitely large-caliber, and the next one whanged off a rock and ricocheted by his left ear. He bellowed, "D Control! Not after you!" but he might as well have yelled, "Hey, who ordered the Extra-Large with sausage and mushrooms?" for all the good it did him. People were spilling out of the nearest Quonset now: a couple of large guys with muscle shirts and walrus mustaches, followed by a slighter Latino. Gruber counted two automatic rifles and a shotgun between them, before he spun and ran, praying not to turn an ankle on the tangly, pebbly slope.

He skidded around the house and came face to face with a nightmare.

As many years as Gruber had been with D Control, he had never seen anything like it, not in real life—just in YouTube videos, which definitely didn't do the beast justice. It was deep, deep ebony all the way, even the wings, at least nine feet tall at its breastbone, easily thirty feet long from head to tail-tip, and spiked *everywhere*, with a flattened viperine head that looked too big for its body, and yellow-orange eyes that blazed in the twilight like amber stars. The fire dancing in its open mouth seemed redder than any other flame in the world, and different as well, as though it was the D's real tongue, ready to lick and caress and savor.

Gruber froze. *How in hell had they gotten a full-grown San Ysidro Black up here without anyone knowing? And how in hell had they trained it?* He'd only ever heard of three San Ysidros getting past Homeland Security, all eggs, for Christ's sake, all in Florida, and every one of the animals was recovered when the hatchlings ripped up the fools who'd bought them.

It wasn't possible. But here it was, planted firmly between him and the Heap—dammit, couldn't Connie see the thing? Why wasn't she gone already?—while assorted bad people with large guns converged on his aging tail. Gruber was suddenly less concerned about them, at the moment. They'd most likely just watch while the San Ysidro did its job and gave Connie her very first experience of watching a partner vanish in fire.

But he couldn't worry about Connie just now. *Or the meth-lab commandos.* Not if he wanted to live more than a few seconds.

"Hey, Big D," Gruber said casually, stepping backward, slipping both hands into his pockets. The San Ysidro ran out its blazing red tongue and seemed to grin at him.

He threw the first Flying Monkey at it left-handed, then turned without waiting to see what happened and fired the second one straight at the front window of the house. It shattered the glass, and as it did, he beat feet for the door. Fore and aft, he heard two loud *whumps*—the internal CO_2 cartridges going off—and the hissing spray of the tranquilizer release. He saw thick white tendrils of it coming through the broken window, and for a moment he thought his crazy improvisation might actually work. He didn't expect one half-assed throw to take down the San Ysidro, and the drug mist wouldn't knock out people, just make them cough a lot and tear up badly. But they had to have guns in the house, and obviously the beast was trained to leave the occupants alone. If he could just get inside while the Watkins clan was distracted, grab himself a real weapon—

As a rule, firebreathers weren't big on accuracy; they didn't have to be, not when they could burn down a whole forest to get at the one thing they were after. The San Ysidro's first blast missed Gruber, but took out a sizable chunk of the veranda, and he had to duck away to keep splashes of the clinging, fiery fluid from lighting him up, too. His straight path to the door vanished behind a wall of heat and smoke.

"Crap!" he shouted, then ran uphill in the only clear direction left to him. He could feel the D turn slowly to follow. The guys with guns didn't. In the quick glimpse he allowed himself, he saw them shouting at Larry Watkins, who was out on the veranda with a halon fire extinguisher, spinning like a dervish as he tried to quench the flames.

Gruber jumped over a couple of fallen trees and kept moving. The San Ysidro glided slowly in pursuit, quick and graceful for its size, coming at an angle. Gruber realized that the thing was *trying* to drive him into the undergrowth, where he'd be surrounded on all sides by easily flammable material. "What, you had to be smart as well as big?" he muttered to himself. Meanwhile it came on without making a sound, though he could hear the fire building in its throat and chest, rustling like terrible wings.

Gruber knew his tapper was useless against something this large, even if it let him get close enough to try it. The four Winged Monkeys were all he had. He got another one ready, turning it over and over again in his right hand as he watched the D come on, banging its way through the trees as if it barely knew they were there.

When the San Ysidro had a clear path, it sped up, closing fast as it prepared to let loose another blast. Gruber got a proper two-seam cut fastball grip on the Winged Monkey and reared back, hurling it dead-center straight into the flames and fangs of the thing's open mouth. He didn't wait to see it go down the San Ysidro's gullet, being far too busy hurling himself to one side. Flames shot over him as he tumbled backward down the hillside, trying to spot some cover somewhere as he rolled. He fetched up hard against a tree and sat up slowly, struggling to catch his breath. He'd lost his helmet, and one of his overall sleeves was on fire. He rubbed the yellow fabric in the dirt until it was out, barely noticing what he was doing. Other things had his attention.

The *whump*, when he heard it, was barely audible. He saw the San Ysidro stop still, not dead or disabled, by any means, but definitely looking puzzled. It hacked once, like a cat with a hairball, then bellowed in decided discontent. The trickle of fire that splashed out this time had a flickering green streak to it.

Gruber pushed himself to his feet and let the tree trunk keep him there. His shoulder hurt like hell. He whispered, "Hold *still*, you bastard," and threw two more Monkeys, one after the other, as fast and hard as the pain would let him. The first bounced off when the San Ysidro raised its head, and blew uselessly when it hit the ground; but the other one played crazy pinball in a nest of cranial spikes and burst right above the thing's left eye, surrounding its whole head and torso in a thick gray-white fog. The San Ysidro started to take a step, but didn't finish; instead, both hind legs jerked stiff and stopped moving, causing it to fall over on one side. The spikes on its right hip and shoulder plowed deep furrows in the soil, and it shook its head up and down, rumbling to itself. Gruber had seen horses in pain do the same thing.

For whatever reason, the Heap was still parked where he'd left it, so he began to circle back through the trees, hoping to get there without being spotted by any of the meth-heads standing around the wrecked and smoking veranda. No such luck; fifty yards short of his goal, he heard the jagged tear of a semiautomatic rifle firing, and sprays of dirt and splintering tree bark stitched a line between him and his goal. Gruber found himself pinned down behind a fallen sapling that wasn't nearly big enough to be good cover. Every time he moved, every time he showed so much as his bald spot, the chips flew; and that log couldn't afford to lose too many chips. He had one Winged Monkey left, but bitterly concluded that it was no help. He couldn't have reached the gunmen from here anyway, even if his shoulder wasn't screaming; and standing up to try would be suicide.

"Quit firing, already!" he shouted. "The sheriff knows I'm here! You want to get the needle for a murder charge, instead of six years on some punkass meth conviction?"

195

"Go to hell, asshole!" It was the Watkins kid shouting. "You wouldn't even be my first today!"

Gruber thought about meth paranoia and burned-down houses, abruptly certain that Johanna and Eddie Watkins were never going to see the inside of the Trinity County Courthouse. He shivered.

Then he heard the Heap's engine suddenly rev to a roar, and had his mouth open to yell to Connie not to try and pick him up, that they'd both be exposed the moment she opened the door for him. But in a moment, he realized that wasn't her plan.

The nerve-rending wail of screechers came on as she gunned the Heap straight for the house, picking up speed fast. The tweakers fired at it, of course, but the Heap had been built to withstand flames, claws, fangs, and pretty much anything short of an RPG. When the guys with the walrus mustaches realized the howling metal monster wasn't slowing down, not even a little bit, they threw away their guns and bailed, running for the trees. The Latino followed a moment later. Only Larry Watkins kept firing, his eyes wide and insane.

With nobody paying attention to him anymore, it was safe for Gruber to stick his head out: even at this distance, the screechers were so loud he had to put his hands over his ears. He watched the whole scene in disbelief, tensing at the inevitable collision. Then—not twenty feet from the house—Connie must have braked hard and spun the steering wheel all the way to the left, or nearly so, because the Heap suddenly went into a great skidding turn that almost tipped it over, trading back for front as the rear end came round and three tons of reinforced metal hammered what was left of the veranda into kindling. Watkins vanished somewhere in the debris.

The Heap came to a stop. So did the screechers.

Gruber jumped to his feet and ran full-tilt toward the house. He couldn't see Connie through the fissured, pockmarked glass of the Heap's front window, and for a moment he was certain that one of the bullets had gotten through, that she was lying dead on the floor of the cab and it was all his goddamn fault. But before he got there, the Heap lurched once, then again, and finally detached itself from whatever piece of the house it had gotten caught on, moving forward smoothly. In a dim, distant way, he realized he was shouting.

Connie slowed the Heap to a crawl when she spotted him. As Gruber pulled open the driver's-side door and jumped in, she moved over, making room for him to take the wheel. He stomped on the gas without bothering to belt himself in.

"You better be okay to drive, and not in shock or anything," she said. "I've got something to take care of here."

He turned to look at her and ask what, but a shadow at the corner of his eye made him pull his head back just in time to see the San Ysidro standing smack in the middle of the flattened dirt road they'd driven up, a century or so earlier. It looked profoundly pissed off, and if it didn't know that Gruber was the human being responsible for its pain and confusion, then he was in the wrong line of work.

Two seconds, three choices. He could jam on the brakes and pulp both of them against the windshield—Connie wasn't belted in, either— or he could ram the D and make it even angrier, or he could veer round

it one way or the other and pray not to front-end a tree before he managed to pull the Heap back onto the road. Connie had the McNaughton on her lap, messing with it, doing something he couldn't figure, but Gruber knew she hadn't seen the San Ysidro yet, and there was no time to shout an explanation. He picked Door Number Three, threw all his weight on cranking the wheel to the right, crashed into a blackberry bramble, and came out the other side just as a blast from the San Ysidro sent it up in flames. Gruber had the wheel to hold on to. Connie didn't. She screamed as inertia threw her against his aching right shoulder, and *he* yelled as she hit him, the pain causing him to white out for a moment. His foot slipped off the accelerator and the Heap slowed down, half on the road and half off.

When he could focus again, the Heap had stopped, and the San Ysidro had climbed on top of it. The D was hammering on the cab with everything it had—wings, spikes, tails, and claws—trying to get in. It brought its head down even with the side window, and Gruber found himself staring straight into one of its glaring yellow eyes from ten inches away.

It knew, all right. It knew who he was, why he was there, what he had done to it, how he had felt about doing it; and it knew he wasn't going to get away. Not this time.

It reared its head back, opened its jaws, and let loose hell.

The Heap was completely fireproof, of course, like every D-retrieval vehicle—flames couldn't even get under the door, normally—but the designers hadn't done any tests after shooting one all the hell up, slamming it into a house, and driving it through a bunch of scrub and fallen tree limbs. Gruber saw tiny fingers of flame squeezing through cracks in the windshield, and smelled insulation and wiring burning inside the dash. The air in the cab was so hot it hurt to breathe: Gruber couldn't guess what was going to kill them first, roasting to death or smoke inhalation. He turned the key in the ignition, but couldn't even hear the starter motor turning over. If the San Ysidro's fire had gotten through the engine compartment seals, it was all over.

For a single moment, he rested his head on the wheel and—only for a moment—closed his eyes.

A sudden raw blast of heat on his face made him aware that Connie had opened the window on her side. He looked and saw her leaning out through it, hurling wyvern eggs at the San Ysidro as fast as she could pull them out of the keeper. No, not eggs—blazing orange hatchlings, literally biting at her fingers as she scooped them up and threw them. Gruber screamed at her to get down, but she paid him no heed, not until the McNaughton was completely empty. Then she slumped back onto her seat and tried to roll the window up, but couldn't get a grip on the handle. Despite the D-schmear, her crabbed-up fingers were a mass of red and blistered burns, and both hands bled from a dozen bad nips and slices. He reached past and rolled the window up for her, certain that any second they were both going to be incinerated by the San Ysidro's fire.

Only that wasn't happening. Something else was.

The San Ysidro was howling. The cab shook hard as it lurched away, letting go. Gruber saw it rolling and thrashing on the ground, speckled with bright moving sparks, as if its own fire was leaking out from the inside.

Connie was laughing hysterically, her wounded hands curled in her lap. "How do *you* like being on the receiving end for once, hey? You like that?"

Gruber finally understood what she had done. Ds—all the Ds— were as fiercely territorial as different species of ants . . . and newborn wyverns had teeth that could puncture Kevlar, a mean body temperature hotter than boiling water, and a drive to eat that wouldn't stop until they'd consumed five or six times their own body weight. One of them, the San Ysidro could have handled. Seven or eight, even, with some permanent damage. But more than thirty, and every single tiny mouth eating its way straight in from wherever it started?

Gruber and Connie sat in the Heap's cab, saying nothing, and watched the San Ysidro die by inches. It took nearly an hour before it stopped moving. Somewhere in there Gruber got out the first-aid kit and did what he could for Connie's hands.

It was full night out by the time it was over. Connie was slumped beside him, almost bent double, her arms crossed palm-up in front of her chest. They both felt hollow, still half in shock and no longer amped on adrenaline.

She mumbled, "Nobody should be allowed to have them."

"Nobody is," Gruber said. "But they have them anyway." Connie did not seem to have heard him.

"You're a walking mess," he said with weary affection. Her dark-brown hair was scorched short on the right side, just as her right cheek and ear were singed, and all of her right arm had a first-degree burn inside her coverall sleeve. He didn't want to think about what was under the bandages on both her hands, but for now the kit's painkiller was keeping the nerves properly numb. That was good. "Thanks for saving my dumbass life. Twice, even."

Connie gave him a wary sideways glance. Most of her right eyebrow was gone too. "Trick compliment?"

"No trick. That was smart, cranking up the McNaughton so the wyverns would hatch out faster. I wouldn't have thought of that one." He rubbed his right shoulder, which was out-and-out killing him, now that it had regained his attention.

"I had to do *something* when the San Ysidro showed up. It was the only thing that occurred to me."

"You could have peeled out of there, like I told you to."

She shook her head. "I'm not actually so good about following orders. I was going to tell you that tomorrow."

He thought for a silent while. "Consider the message conveyed."

A minute later, he pushed the door open and stepped out. "Come on. The Heap's not going anywhere, and we've got a job to finish."

"What, we're going back?" She stiffened in the seat, leaning away from his extended hand.

"Not a chance. I think you must have creamed Junior pretty good, or else we'd have had company by now. But it's anybody's guess whether those other idiots came back or not." He made a brusque *hurry-up* gesture, and turned away once he saw she was finally starting to move. "So no, we're not going back. What we're going to do is hike down to 299. Somewhere around the turnoff, we're going to find Trager or one of his guys. They were expecting us hours ago, they'll be looking. After we tell them what went down, we can get you to Mountain Community Medical."

"You too," Connie said.

"Yeah, me too."

He stood where the San Ysidro had finally ceased thrashing, and looked down at the bloody, riddled corpse. Somehow it looked even bigger, splayed out dead in the darkness. Connie stopped a few feet behind him.

"Hey, trainee. How long before the baby wyverns wake up and start eating their way back out?"

"I have no idea," she said, looking a little worried.

"Good to learn there's *something* about Ds you don't know." Despite the pounding snarl in his shoulder, he realized he felt happier than he had in months. Maybe years. "The answer, for your information, is twelve to fifteen hours. Plenty of time for somebody else to come here and handle this mess, and good luck to them."

He started off the way they'd first come, hunching forward slightly as he walked to keep his torso from swinging too much. Connie caught up with him, matching his pace. The stars were out, and it wasn't hard to find their way.

Neither of them said anything for more than twenty minutes. Then Connie spoke up. "They had a *San Ysidro black.* Can you *believe* it?"

"There's a lot of people who'll be asking that one," Gruber nodded. "From the Feds on down. Get ready to star in one hell of an investigation."

Connie stopped walking. "Oh my god," she whispered. "Oh no. What are my parents going to say? I can't tell them about this! I mean—"

"Nice try," Gruber grinned at her. "Parents or no, hands or no, you're still writing up the report. If you can't type, you can dictate."

She tried to kick him in the shin, but he managed to get out of range. The first time, anyway.

MARTY AND THE MESSENGER

This tale is one of a group featuring the three friends I grew up with in the Bronx of the 1940s and 1950s: Robert Jacobs, Phil Sigunick—always the painter, as I was always the writer—and Marty Sandler, the foreigner from a couple of blocks down Gunhill Road. Marty, the shyest and least flamboyant of all of us, was also the brilliant one, trained as a physicist and fortunate enough to live into an age when men walked on the moon and the Hubble Telescope unfolded a universe whose magnificent vastness only people like Marty had ever imagined. I always believed that if beings from far across the dimensions ever wanted to contact humanity, they'd seek out Marty to carry their message to us Earthlings. I still do.

MARTY SANDLER was always the shy one. To begin with, he was a year younger than the rest of us, and lived two or three blocks further down Gunhill Road. He was further set apart by the fact of having been stricken by polio as a child, and dragging one leg just enough to be noticeable. Remember, my friends and I were growing up in a time before Salk and Sabin's vaccines, when polio was feared as greatly as AIDS is today, and each of us knew plenty of adults whose faces bore the unmistakable traces of smallpox survived. The universe, which is a spiteful place, had let Marty off lightly.

He was also the brilliant one. Jake was an excellent student—I did my foredoomed best—and Phil simply denied the very existence of school, even while attending it. Marty was a completely other matter: a nerd before there was such a word, a geek when that word meant someone who bit the heads off chickens in a carnival. He spoke math, for one thing, which made him a shaman in my eyes, since to me the simplest equation was—as it remains—a magical feat on the order of communicating with the spirits of the dead. He was equally and effortlessly skilled in science, which was the particular specialty of our high school, and in all branches of which—biology, chemistry, physics—I floundered like a mastodon in a tarpit. Watching him moving gracefully through this mysterious world, so hopelessly shut to me, I felt (to employ another animal simile) like a sloth looking up at a gibbon floating by between treetops and sky. Polio might have been weighing down his leg, but when it came to the forest of the mind, Marty danced and flew.

We were drawn together, I think, by our mutual lack of the usual social graces, and by the fact that we compensated as we could by living deeply in our imaginations. We knew perfectly well how out of place we were, but we found ways to make that dislocation into a place of its own, which was harder than it may seem now in the Bronx of 1953.

That January, everything shut down except school, which was manifestly unfair. Compared to Midwesterners, New Englanders, and citizens of the Great Plains states, New Yorkers have it easy in winter, but my bones still remember that one. The subways ran on schedule—as much as the subways ever did—but the buses largely vanished from Bronx streets, and Marty and I both needed to get to the High School of Science on 183rd Street, just off the Grand Concourse. That meant walking up a strangely still Gunhill Road, where the only traffic was little kids on their Flexible Flyer sleds, and all the way down Bainbridge Avenue to the IND line, trudging along in our overcoats, mufflers and galoshes (can you still even *buy* galoshes?), bending forward into the dirty wind that flailed at our faces from all directions, even with our earflaps tied under our chins. And then the slog home, in six hours or so, in even deeper snow and icier wind. Writing this, even now, my bones do remember.

Marty and I had no business in high school, both of us being far too young. But I was great on aptitude tests, where you didn't actually have to *know* anything, and thirteen-year-old Marty could already hold his own with the best, in a school that had produced seven Nobel Prize winners in science. So there we were, one January morning in the cafeteria: Marty already growing into his element, and me still the graceless stranger I'd always been. But I wrote stories and poems by the score, and I wisecracked in class to cover my fears, and I began slowly to learn to get by.

Jake often ate with us when our schedules coincided, but today it was just Marty and me, off by the window, darkly considering the falling snow steadily piling up on the sill, and debating the exact makeup of the Daily Special. This time it was Salisbury steak, which Marty pointed out was a deceptive misnomer on several fronts. "Okay, first, it's not steak—it's hamburger shaped to *look* like steak—and it's got nothing to do with Salisbury Plain or Salisbury Cathedral. It was invented by a doctor named Salisbury, right here in America." He looked suddenly embarrassed, the way Marty always did when he knew something you didn't, and added quickly, "I looked it up."

"And they only serve it in institutions," I said. "Schools, hospitals, prisons—captive consumers. Your mother ever cook it at home? You ever see it in a restaurant? Nobody who's got any choice at all would go near it."

"As for the gravy," Marty continued, excited now, warmer than the Salisbury steak itself. His eyes were sparkling and his cheeks genuinely rosy, as though he were pinning a math problem to the wall. "The gravy's a secret formula, an entirely chemical contrivance, known only to four people in Hoboken. They row it across the Hudson on the darkest nights, when there's no moon. Muffled oars, no running lights, people waiting onshore to take delivery. No names."

"The formula," I said. "Your best guess. You're the chemist around here." Marty had fallen in love with organic chemistry, which clearly returned his passion, to judge by his grades, and by the fact that he was constantly drawing diagrams of molecules on all of his textbook covers. For my part, I was still trying to memorize the periodic table; and each time I thought I finally understood valences, I didn't. Marty was already starting to scribble on the tablecloth, but I said, "Not the *formula* formula—I couldn't read it anyway. I mean the *stuff*."

"Oh," Marty said. "Well, I'm tasting acetone, but it's really more a sense than a taste. A *lot* of flour . . . a bit of bacon grease . . . chicken broth"—he grinned like a marvelously wicked child—"and a whole *bunch* of crayons. The Crayola Burnt Sienna would be my guess."

I nibbled at the ground meat for the sake of appearances, and then turned my attention to the lime Jell-O on both of our trays. "Yours has whipped cream, mine doesn't."

"What an outrage," Marty said. "Here, I don't like whipped cream anyway." I pushed my cup closer, and Marty scraped the topping off his dessert and onto mine as thoroughly as he could. "There. I like *my* Jell-O in the nude. No fruit, no cream, no way you can really mess up green gelatin." He raised his spoon over his own cup. They gave you real silverware and real glasses back then, not plastic.

I had my head turned away, staring sourly at the window, now half-obscured by a new snow flurry, so I didn't actually see the lime Jell-O speak, not that first time. But I heard the clear, chiming little voice, and I heard Marty's startled yelp, and the clank of his spoon against the cup. The lime Jell-O said, "Do not eat me. I am a messenger."

Marty and I looked at each other. I think that sentence about covers it.

Marty's face had gone absolutely colorless, looking brittle and transparent as glass. He managed to whisper, "*What?*" and nothing more.

"It's your Jell-O," I said.

The lime Jell-O's chirped, "Great Sandler, I am privileged to bring you an urgent message. I beg you to hear me out."

It *looked* like perfectly ordinary lime Jell-O: seasick green, with a couple of white flecks where Marty hadn't gotten all the whipped cream, and no obvious features, such as eyes or a mouth, though its surface sort of *rippled* when it spoke. Marty poked it gingerly with the spoon, and its tone took on a certain definite anxiety. It said, "Please, Great Sandler, hear my message before you choose to eat me. I have been sent to beg your assistance in a matter of vital significance. Only you—you alone—can aid my poor people now."

Marty gulped. He looked around the cafeteria, as though for assistance; but we were off in the farthest corner by ourselves, isolated by our youth even from fellow freaks. Bronx Science didn't have jocks in the usual sense—the swim team and the chess team were our athletic aristocrats—but there was a pecking order all the same, as there always is anywhere, and we didn't even have a place in it yet. All we had was a cup of lime Jell-O with a long-distance call for Marty. I looked at my own dessert and put it carefully aside.

"Sir," Marty began politely. "Mr. Jell-O, sir—"

"My name is—" the Jell-O cup interjected, and laid out a name studded with sharp-edged consonants like a Christmas orange with cloves. It went on long enough that I couldn't tell when it was over; but somehow Marty could, and he'd even memorized the first three syllables, which sounded something like *Daglktrlk*, He said he'd call the lime Jell-O that for short, and the lime Jell-O said it was an honor to have even part of his name—or hers, or its—in Marty's mouth. Marty had more trouble believing that than I did.

The lime Jell-O hadn't spoken to me at all, and plainly wasn't about to, as focused on Marty as it was; but I couldn't help asking, "How can you *look* like that? What *are* you?"

"I am," the lime Jell-O piped, "a citizen of—" and here came another rapid-fire burst of syllables with no more vowels than a Polish menu. "Your spaceships—when you develop spaceships in a few years—will not find us, because we do not exist on a planet, as you know planets, but in a dimension at a seventy-nine degree angle to your universe. As for this appearance, our scientists have studied humans extensively, and learned that you are easily frightened and highly mistrustful of strangers, of beings who do not look like you." It hesitated for a moment before it continued. "We do not look at all like you. This is clearly a highly dangerous thing in your world, and we are advised that you would be repelled by our true form. But all humans everywhere appear to love Jell-O, whatever the color or the cost—so . . ." And it almost seemed to shrug, even though it couldn't have. All it could do was that ripple thing.

Shy but practical as ever, Marty asked it, "Why are you looking for me? I'm thirteen years old—I don't know anything about any Great Sandler,"

If a cup of lime Jell-O could draw its breath in awe and reverence, this one would have. "In our universe you are renowned as the greatest of alien scientists. Schoolchildren yet know your name, and recite your accomplishments. Whom else should we seek in this, our greatest crisis?"

Marty blushed. It was lovely to see. He always blushed easily, but this was a little different. He said, "But why seek me now? I mean, I just entered high school—why not ask that . . . that *grown* me?" I can still see him, bashfully reminding a cup of lime Jell-O that after all, he was still a kid.

I will swear old Daglktrlk looked uncomfortable. Maybe I was just going by the tone of its voice, except that it didn't exactly *have* a tone. Anyway, there was another pause, longer, before it said, "In our universe, you . . . died. Long ago."

"Oh," Marty said. It's a lot to take in at thirteen, I don't care *what* your grades are. We'd actually talked a lot about infinite alternate universes, both of us being great science-fiction readers. We used to amuse ourselves carrying the notion out to its furthest theoretical point: what if there's a universe in which everything is exactly the same as it is here, now, except that one particular cockroach was never born. Hatched, or whatever. Would that count like an alternate universe? All of us debated questions like that, but only Marty would have tried to work out an equation proving—or disproving—the real existence of such phenomena. I forget how it came out. It's been a long time.

Across the cafeteria, a certain hush had fallen over the Chess Rats' habitual table, where team members lorded it over the wistful wannabes and played vicious challenge matches with each other, spotting pieces, mocking dithering tactical choices, and occasionally setting cooking timers on the table to speed up the game. Betty Koosman was passing by, and Betty Koosman was a walking hush that year, having developed breasts over the summer, along with a Veronica Lake hairstyle, a husky Lauren Bacall voice, and a new swaying gait that someone else was about to make famous. She must just have come in from outside, because there was snow sparkling in her dark hair and color in her normally sallow skin. On her it looked good.

I'm writing all this down because that moment when she sauntered past our table remains, for no good reason, one of those crystal instants that stays with you forever. She ignored me, but ruffled Marty's hair and kept going. I'm sure she never noticed that Marty didn't look up, being occupied in talking to a dish of lime Jell-O. He was saying earnestly, "Well, I'll try to help, only I don't know if I can be as much help as . . . well, as I was, or somebody . . . I guess I mean as I used to be. I mean, *that* me was, I guess, really exceptional, and I'm not sure . . ." He went on like that for some time before he finally asked, "Um . . . well, what *is* your crisis, exactly?"

The lime Jell-O chose its words carefully as it replied. "We—my people—we are considered to be as intelligent as we are, to others, repulsive. You have a method of measuring intellect that you call . . . the Intelligence Quotient test, is it not?"

"It isn't very accurate," Marty said quickly. "Pretty meaningless, actually." If his own IQ had been a sound, it would have made dogs howl.

Daglktrlk ignored his comment. "The average IQ of any member of my own folk would probably measure on your scale . . ." and he pronounced a number somewhat smaller than the population of Fort Wayne, Indiana, but greater than that of Jersey City, St. Petersburg and Lincoln, Nebraska. I can't speak for Marty, but the number was as unreal to me as that thing about angels dancing on the head of a pin. When you're in the habit of measuring IQs in terms of three digits, six just doesn't register.

Marty said quietly, "I really don't think I can help you."

I spoke up then, having mostly not felt at all equal to the intellectual pressure of talking to lime Jell-O about alternate universes and alternate Martys. I said to the cup, "Don't pay any attention to him. He's just modest—I bet your grownup version was the exact same way. Believe me, he can take care of whatever you need taken care of—just lay it out for him and let him go to work."

I wasn't bullshitting, either. I had great faith in Marty—more than ever since a genuine alien disguised as a cup of lime Jell-O with an unpronounceable name had chased him across time and space, and other dimensions, and God alone knew what else, all to cope with some extraterrestrial emergency that even creatures with six-figure IQs couldn't handle. I felt like his agent.

"In brief," the lime Jell-O said, "the fact is that our population's intelligence—legendary through a dozen galaxies—is fading drastically. Measured against previous generations, our memory capacity has shrunk, our communication skills are rapidly dwindling, and we are increasingly prey to menacing illusions and senseless patterns of behavior that make concentrating on the problem and dealing logically with it all but impossible. Meaning no disrespect, Great Sandler"—it added that part in a hurry—"we are becoming much as your own people become in their old age. But the fall . . . our fall is somewhat steeper."

In the silence I looked at the wall clock in its catcher's-mask cage. I said, "Bell's going to ring in ten minutes."

Marty didn't answer me—or, really, the lime Jell-O either. He said slowly, to no one in this galaxy, "Now *this* interests me . . ." Then I knew we were all right. I'd heard him say that a time or two before.

"Diet," he murmured. "Mom always says everything's diet, in the end. What do your people eat?"

"We do not *eat*," Daglktrlk replied, "not as your folk would comprehend it. But we do, of course, ingest, after our fashion." It went into a lot of detail, all of which sounded complicated, and fairly disgusting, but Marty kept after it for as much minutiae as it could give him. The cafeteria was beginning to empty out, and I reminded him again about time.

Suddenly he asked, "Salt. What do you do for salt?"

Cups of lime Jell-O can't blink, but if it could have . . . "I do not understand."

"*Salt,*" Marty repeated. "In our universe, as far as we know, nothing but plant life can survive without some form of salt. Sodium chloride? Potassium chloride?" Nothing. "Calcium? Magnesium? It's a major electrolyte—too much of it can be bad for humans, but too little can really affect our minds, as well as our bodies." He tried several other chlorides without getting a reaction. By then he was drawing rapidly on a sheet of three-hole notebook paper, mumbling aloud to himself. "I can't believe you wouldn't be getting *some* form of salt from *somewhere* . . . maybe it's the trace minerals you need . . ."

I warned him again, "Marty, you know how Miss Lipeles gets when someone's late to class—"

Marty ignored me. He said to the lime Jell-O, "If I give you these molecule diagrams, can you synthesize them? Can you even get them home?"

"It is a little awkward without pseudopods," Daglktrlk admitted. "Hold the information over me, if you would, and I will try to absorb it."

Marty had covered four sheets of paper on both sides; but as we watched, his precise diagrams simply ran off the page and vanished into the green gelatin, leaving the sheet as blank as ever. The lime Jell-O said, "We will begin to synthesize these great gifts on the instant, and begin a series of experiments—"

"Very carefully," Marty said, "Very, *very* carefully. Especially if in your normal form you look like slugs or snails."

"As you advise us, Great Sandler. And you must know that our redoubled gratitude, our endless—"

Marty, who never interrupted anyone, interrupted. "I'm not the Great Sandler. That one . . . that one's gone. I'm just *a* Sandler—a substitute, a backup. But I hope I've been some use to you, maybe the way *he* would have done. And get in touch if it doesn't seem to be helping"

"Farewell, then," the lime Jell-O said. "I will be gone from this dish in a moment, and you may eat it if you choose—"

The bell rang just as I broke in, unable to keep from asking, "Wait, before you go—you know Marty's name in the future, or wherever you really are. Any chance . . . would you happen to know mine?" Daglktrlk did not answer, and I feared that it might already have flown. I said, "My name's Peter Beagle. I'm going to be a writer, the way Marty's going to be a galactically famous scientist. I just thought you might . . . that's *Peter Beagle*. . . ?"

The lime Jell-O from another universe said slowly, "*You* are Peter Beagle?"

The blood tingled in my face. I whispered, "Yes."

After a moment, the lime Jell-O said, "Well, it can't be helped."

Then it was gone, and Marty and I hurried to class, over floors still wet with melted snow.

THE MANTICHORA

"The Mantichora" is one of two stories I've written featuring Avram David-son. I wish I'd written more of them. He was a kindly, cranky, generous, utterly impossible man, and an absolutely unique writer, which did him no favors at all. Nobody wrote like Avram, or ever will. And nobody in the world would have sought out the very last mantichora in the world, or have been brave enough or learned enough (Avram knew everything in the world; this is simply a given) to have initiated a conversation. Only Avram, ever.

*B*EING AN ENTIRELY TRUE ACCOUNT, *Appraised and Attested to by a Number of Serious Gentlemen, and Further Translated from the Barbaric Visigothic Tongue, All in Regard to a Certain Exploit of That Near-Magus and Semi-Sorcerer Known Variously throughout the Wilder Regions of the Turning Globe as the Captain-General, the Viceroy of the Lesser Indies, and the Very Big Bwana. For the Purposes of This Account, He Shall Continue to Be Named and Renowned Simply as "A.D."*

He was short and stout, and his feet were flat, and his beard fell to his chest in a barbed-wire tangle. He lived alone, and he drank too much, and children ran in and out of his dark little house.

He knew everything in the world.

He was, among many other things, the last person on Earth who spoke Mountain Mantichora. (At this remove, it is sometimes diffi-cult to recall a time when mantichoras were viewed as mindless eating machines with neither the ability nor the need for communication or self-expression.) The tongue of the lowland subgroup, who still main-tain a (barely) sustainable population in the islands of Indonesia and the Philippines, has been widely studied and analyzed, to the point where the language will, sadly and unquestionably, survive its native speakers. Tragic, certainly, but historically inevitable. In the words of its greatest expert, *Herr Doktorprofessor* Heinrich von Schnibble und Scheisskopf, "The vocabulary, the grammar, the regional syntax and pronunciation . . . these are indispensable to the scholar. The mantichora, alas, is not."

Mountain Mantichora—like the creature itself—is decidedly another story. A.D. was not the first person to study this unique, vastly complex, and dizzyingly intricate language, nor was he the only researcher to employ it in actual conversation. He was certainly, however, the only one to retire uneaten from such a chat—hence his "last speaker" status. The conversation in question was undertaken on the highest Andean peak of Mount Aconcagua, at the very entrance to the mantichora's lair, to which A.D. had attained by such laborious trudging, climbing, slogging, marching, and climbing again as would have had Odysseus calling a cab. As modest as he was learned, he generally explained the mantichora's lack of interest in his calorific potential by saying, "Well, it was accustomed to facing heroes, soldiers, warriors"—he was in the habit of referring to any given mantichora as *it*, no one but a mantichora being capable of determining another mantichora's gender—"and here was this short, fat, asthmatic, unarmed, utterly beat person right on its doorstep, wheezing its own language into that face . . . that magnificently horrible human face with its blue, blue eyes and its triple rows of shark teeth." He would shrug and smile, almost sheepishly. "Hung it up, I guess."

Always a passionately curious and fanciful man, A.D. remained prudent enough nevertheless to decline the mantichora's invitation to enter its den for a civilized conversation and a glass of tea. Having neither guides nor porters—no indigenes being willing, at any price, to venture within miles of such a haunt of nightmare—A.D. simply made camp in a nearby hollow somewhat less snow-filled than other locations, nourished himself on canned and powdered military rations, and daily interviewed the monster regarding its life, habits, tastes, and personal history. He noted its replies in a characteristically minuscule hand on an elaborately cross-referenced matrix of three-by-five-inch index cards.

In addition to its own language, the mantichora spoke ancient Greek, in the strange, typically fluting voice that contemporary historians describe as sounding somewhere between panpipes and a chilling battle trumpet, and it was also reasonably fluent in Latin, Etruscan, early Visigoth (A.D.'s major at university, and his habitual style for note-taking), the Neapolitan dialect, and, as it said, "enough Spanish and Quechua to get by." It told A.D. that it sustained itself in this remote and elevated fastness primarily on mountain sheep and the occasional hardy tourist. "There used to be rock climbers, great flocks of them, but I think they must have changed their migration patterns. I can't say I grieve their absence. Stringy."

A.D., in his own recounting, took a couple of steps back at this point, but retained his calm scientific detachment. He inquired of the mantichora, "That scorpion's tail—is it true that the scarlet spine at its tip secretes poison, and that you can hurl it free of your body like a deadly arrow or javelin? I am striving for accuracy, you understand, and not to substantiate old myths and legends."

"Nonsense!" the mantichora replied spiritedly. "Where *do* humans get these ideas? The tail serves merely to scratch those places on my back that I can never reach otherwise, and also, at certain seasons"—here, A.D. swore solemnly that the horrid parody of a human face blushed just a trifle—"to proclaim my puissant availability to any females in the vicinity. Which, sadly . . ." The creature's sigh was no less profound for being eerily musical. "One adapts. One becomes resigned."

"But, if I may point it out, you did not originate in this high, cold, isolated clime," A.D. offered hesitantly. "My studies into Pliny and Ctesias, Bartholomaeus Anglicus, and similar scholars suggest that all mantichoras derive from a far-wandering Persian stock, ranging to India and beyond to the central Caucasus in one direction and even to the British Isles in other. How does it happen that I find you here, alone in the Argentine Andes—"

"There are surely others scattered at somewhat lower levels," the mantichora objected. "I used to know of several inhabiting the slopes of Mount Chimborazo, in Ecuador, always a popular resort among my kind, and I believe there were a few more on Ojos del Salado, on the Chile-Argentina border. But. . . ." It sighed a second time, somewhat more heavily. "You are correct in this, we have been a hunted folk for a thousand years, more. Between the Romans and the Celts, the Scythians and the Sarmatians, the barbarians and the Britons and the Greeks, whose hand was not against us? We took to the mountains, moving steadily higher and higher—but even the Alps, those utmost peaks of Switzerland and Italy, proved still within range of the armored men, the crossbows, and, in time, the rifles. Some of us found shelter in the Himalayas, on the great frozen Tibetan plateau, while the rest. . . ." It shrugged, as well as a lion's body can manage the shoulder ripple, and added, after a moment's silence, "We make do as we can. Thank the gods for skiers."

A.D., finding himself grown curiously sympathetic, yet keeping his distance, inquired, with some slight trepidation, "If I may ask, how old are you?" The mantichora gave sign of considering this an impertinent question, and A.D. hastened to explain himself. "Pausanias, that Romanized Greek, and Philostratus in his *Life of Apollonius of Tyana* both put forth the claim that the mantichora is immortal, but clearly, by your own testimony, you are not invulnerable. Do you have—besides humankind—any natural enemies?"

The mantichora was silent for some while before it spoke again. A.D., for all his compassion—and even, to some degree, his identification with the creature—kept one wary eye on the scorpion tail (which was twitching like any cat's) and on its taloned hind legs, lest they begin crouching, storing impetus for a pounce. The mantichora said slowly, heavily, "Once, long ago, I would have answered you simply, saying no, we fear nothing but your arrows, your torches, your armored horses.

But that was in the flat country, on the plains and in the forests of Persia and India. We were masters there—even your masters, for a time—but as we were forced steadily upward, higher than even the snow leopard cares to hunt, we met the true Master of the Mountains, He whom your folk name *Meh-Teh, Kang Admi, JoBran.* . . ." The strange, scratchy, musing voice trailed away.

"The Snowman?" A.D.'s own voice dried in his throat. "Yeti?" The word itself had him looking over his shoulder before he was even aware that he had turned his head. The mantichora smiled bitterly, an unnerving expression to watch crawling across the tusked mouth. A.D. said, "I had no idea."

"Nor did we, though we should have had." In a brief burst of antique fury and regret, the scorpion tail lashed the mantichora's sides, scoring them brutally. "Little enough game on these heights, why should any creature wish to share its hunting grounds? Let alone beasts with a hunger as great and constant as ours—and young bellies to fill, too, for they mate and breed and bear as we do but rarely. There is no peace between us—there could never even be truce. I cannot blame them for attacking us on sight, for seeking us out, hunting us down, and battering us to death against the stones of our own lairs. They might as well be human." The weary contempt in the mantichora's chiming voice dragged it almost to a mumble.

A.D. said quietly, dazedly, "We—my people—we like to imagine the Yeti as gentle, innocent . . . ourselves before the Fall, if you will. It does seem to be true that they smell rather strong—every report mentions this—"

"All carnivores smell bad," the mantichora interrupted bluntly. "The Yeti-folk are man-eaters, just as I am, though I do think that we have a shadow the better of it when it comes to olfactory matters." For the first time in their acquaintance, the creature chuckled; the sound scraped in A.D.'s ears like a matchhead on stone. "You may yet wish on your way from this place that I had been the one to devour you, swiftly and efficiently. The Yeti tend to play with their food."

"Ah," said A.D., and then, "Ah," again.

He had made a careful note of one other question to ask the mantichora that day, and would have asked it comparatively lightly, but for the unsettling effect of the creature's words. Now it came out with a peculiarly ominous ring to it: "How long has it been since you have seen others of your kind?" The mantichora, which had been scanning a distant peak in an almost dreamy manner, now turned its head slowly toward him, but did not respond. A.D. continued, "In all the time that we have been conducting our colloquies, I have seen no other tracks but yours, heard no other voice like yours, observed you sensing neither a rival nor a possible mate in this vicinity. Am I wrong to assume that there are no other mantichoras within your effective range?"

"Not at all," the mantichora replied with surprising graciousness, since it generally took poorly to queries of this nature. "We are a solitary folk, and value our privacy, here in our last redoubt. Beyond the rare siren call of desire, we truly have no need of any society but our own."

Later—and not all that much later, either—A.D. was to learn how foolish he had been to press the issue. But his scientific blood was up, and he felt that he was on the edge of a truly momentous discovery. "How long has it been?" The mantichora did not answer this time. "Do you ever consider the possibility that you might well be the last of your kind?"

The mantichora looked directly into A.D.'s eyes then, and it smiled for the second and last time in their acquaintance. "No, why should I? That would do me nothing but great evil." It yawned politely then, baring all three rows of shark teeth, and A.D. excused himself shortly afterward.

That night, for whatever reason—dark dreams, flurries of high winds, a sudden drop in temperature—A.D. slept only fitfully, and had almost decided to fire up his propane lamp and go over his most recent notes, when a sound a skin away from his own froze him as no blizzard could have done. Even before he heard the slow, eager breathing, before the first lion claw showed through the tent flap, he smelled the hunger.

He was up out of his bedroll faster than he ever imagined moving, stumpy legs gathered under him for a spring . . . to where? The tent was set skillfully into solid ground (he had been immensely vain of that accomplishment); even if a desperate lunge could open an escape, the whole thing would surely come down, trapping him in its folds with the mantichora. There was a gun, a shiny new just-in-case pistol . . . where was the gun? Had he ever loaded it—and could it conceivably stop what was glaring in at him through the shredded tent flap? The mantichora said, in its dreadfully musical bird voice, "You should not have asked that question."

"No one will ever know the answer," A.D. whispered. "You may not be . . . and in any case, I would never tell. . . ."

"No," replied the mantichora, "no, you never will." Yet it seemed oddly diffident, lingering at the entrance. It said, "If it is any comfort, I have never apologized to a human being before—"

It never finished the sentence. A growl like the first warning of a landslide shook the tent, and the mantichora vanished, snatched out of sight as abruptly as night falls in the high mountains. It made no sound itself; or if it did, the chiming, fluting voice was lost in the maniacal bellowing of whatever had hold of it. A.D. dropped back onto his bedroll, covering his ears with every pillow at hand, but the battle was raging so closely around the tent that he felt as though both monsters were inside, roaring and rending, tearing each other to pieces over his body. Never having been in the habit of prayer, he closed his eyes, turned himself over to the purposeless emptiness of the universe—and, remarkably, fell asleep.

It cannot have been for more than a very few minutes, of course, but it was restful while it lasted. When he woke, the noises had changed: they were lower, and more widely spaced, and there was clearly only one beast making them. The ugly, grunting contentment in their tone was more frightening to A.D. than all the previous uproar, and he dared not imagine what it could signify for his own safety. It went on all night, and by pale morning, A.D. was an older man.

He never saw the Yeti, then or ever. At one point, near dawn, something filled the torn entrance to the tent, but he lay very quietly against a far wall, consciously trying to breathe through his skin, like a frog, and by and by, the great something grumbled away and went back to whatever it had been so voraciously and wetly savoring. A.D. lay where he was, never moving, for a good hour or more after he finally heard the creature leaving. He would have waited longer, but he was so numb with fear as to be past fear; and besides, his bladder was bursting. The first thing he did, when he went outside at last, was to urinate in the red snow.

It was very red—deep maroon, really—almost to the horizon, or so it seemed to A.D. Trying to summon both his scientific training and his naturally dispassionate, analytical nature, he studied the incarnadined lumps for some while before realizing that they were lumps of snow, not gobbets of flesh, as he had first assumed. There was nothing identifiable left of the mantichora: not a barb from the scorpion tail, not a claw from one of the lion paws, not so much as a snapped-off shark tooth from the inhuman mouth. There was fur. There was a lot of blood-soaked fur. But the mantichora was gone, either devoured on the spot or dragged off along the horrid trail that led down the near slope and blessedly out of sight. A.D. built a fire.

It is a long walk down from the Andes, and even at the lower levels, he often sighted great humanlike tracks altogether too near his campground. But he was never attacked—though once his stores were ravaged in the night—and in time, he passed out of the range of the Yeti-folk, who are also named Kang Admi, JoBran, Meh-Teh, and Abominable Snowman, and so came presently to Yonkers, New York, where he kicked off his shoes, fixed himself a Black Russian, and sat down to write up his voluminous notes on the customs and habits of the last mountain mantichora. Unpublished yet, they remain in the possession of his cousin Sidney, a laundromat owner in Queens, despite an attempt by A.D.'s last landlord to seize them in lieu of a security deposit. There has been movie talk.

MR. McCaslin

Another one about Jake, Phil, Marty and me at the age of twelve or so, dealing with Death as a literal physical manifestation, and of the three of us helping a man we didn't even like to hold it off for a little time. Death has turned up a lot in my work over the years, beginning when I was in elementary school. I don't know what this says about me, and on the whole I'd as soon not know. Mr. McCaslin himself is based—very loosely—on an old Irishman in our neighborhood who used to pronounce the same toast to his family every New Year's Eve: "Well, boys, we're through with wan hell iv a bad year, and here goes for another just like it . . ." I say that one myself, to myself, altogether too often, these New Years' Eves.

O N Gunhill Road old people die in summer, not winter. At least that was so when I was a boy, in the middle of another century. New York winters could be bad enough—I remember the entire city shutting down for two days one time—but you could bundle up, turn the radiator on full-blast and go to bed. The apartment buildings of my neighborhood, most dating to the 1920s, were thick-walled and generally stayed warm, even in a blizzard. You could get by in winter back then.

Summer was another matter. Open your windows as wide as you wanted, the stagnant air was almost too hot to breathe, and didn't always cool down after dark. Air-conditioners were still new then, and prohibitively expensive—no one in our neighborhood had a unit—so folks made do with electric fans, which were little more help than a handheld one or a folded newspaper. They sat through double and triple features at the movies, just for the air-conditioning there, when it was working, and soaked bedsheets in cold water to be able to sleep.

Old people hung out of their windows with their mouths open, gasping like stranded fish, until one day they weren't there anymore. I usually dressed up for two or three funerals every summer.

Irish families were rare in our otherwise diverse *quartier* back then. I only remember two: the Geohegans in my building, two floors down, and old Mr. McCaslin, who lived alone in my friend Jake's apartment house across Gunhill Road, beyond the vacant lot where everyone had planted Victory Gardens during the war. I knew one of the numerous Geohegan sons well enough to be regularly invited for New Year's Eve, and I always went, just to hear Mr. Geohegan deliver his customary toast at midnight: "Well, boys, we're t'rough wid wan hell of a bad year, and here goes for anither just like it." I still keep up the tradition, whether I'm with my own family and friends, or in solitude. It brings more back than merely New Year's Eve.

Mr. McCaslin was a stubby, white-haired man with a narrow red face, a retired subway motorman living on a pension and Social Security. Even though he had lived in that same apartment, a floor below Jake and his family, since before Jake and Phil and I were born, I can't recall his first name, and I'm not sure we ever knew it. It's hard to explain why we three took the personal interest that we did in Mr. McCaslin, as little use as he had for us. He was sour and bad-tempered, given to yelling through his door at kids who made noise in the halls, short even when he was being polite; if he was drunk, he might even take a swing at you. I don't think he ever intended them to land—it was just another way of saying, *get away, get away from me.* We never took it seriously.

Why and how he became *our* crabby old man, I can't tell you. Maybe we were reacting to his loneliness, or to what we saw or sensed as his loneliness. Children are a cruel, utterly self-concerned lot, innocently heartless; but the three of us were all loners and misfits in our different ways, blessed with imagination, cursed with empathy. We took Mr. McCaslin in somehow, beyond logic, beyond behavior, whether he wanted us to or not.

The summer of 1950 was evilly hot, even for New York. The little gardens along Tryon all withered early, for all the watering their owners did, and I used to imagine that you could hear the trees panting for rain and cool air, just like the old people. The police came by now and again to open the fire hydrants down on Decatur Avenue, but Phil and Jake and I all felt too old this year to play in the water with the little kids. Instead, we talked our parents into letting us sleep on the roof, or even on our fire escapes, and we shot our allowances on bus rides to the public pool at Tibbetts Brook Park. And we moved very, very slowly.

Mr. McCaslin suffered. Apart from the heat itself, we knew that he had some sort of lung ailment, contracted in the subway tunnels, and we could hear him wheezing behind his door, and often even when he yelled at us—or tried to, for he couldn't always get the words out. Most of the time his face was redder than ever, the way my Uncle Leon's had gotten before his stroke; but now and then, when he shuffled past us in the hallway, he looked as bloodless as cheese, as gray-white as candlewax. Jake's mother, who worked at a local hospital that had its own health plan, tried to get him to come in for a checkup, but he told her he couldn't afford it, and it wouldn't do any good anyway. She was a plainspoken woman: she said, "You know you won't last out the summer like this," and Mr. McCaslin nodded agreement and closed his door.

In a macabre way that I'm embarrassed to write about, her verdict only increased our fascination with him. We were kids: we had all known people who had died, but never anyone actually in the process, sentence spoken, date of execution set. So we went out of our way, individually and together, to do things for him. Fruit was big—someone was sick, you gave them fruit, everybody knew that. We brought his newspaper up from the lobby; we carried his grocery bags if we saw him struggling with them on the stair. I even sneaked him some of my own rather expensive cough syrup, which made me feel much better during an asthma attack, and which got taken off the market a year later. Mr. McCaslin gave me a long look when he read the label, but he took it, and that time he said thanks.

It was kind of us, certainly, but there was more to it than kindness;

children have ulterior motives that adults never imagine for a moment. If Mr. McCaslin should open his door to us—often he didn't answer the bell, and we had to leave this or that gift on the mat—then we'd get to peer around him for a moment, just to see what a dying person's apartment looked like. I never glimpsed more than a worn sofa, a radio on a three-legged card table, and a few photographs tacked at random on the one wall I could see. It smelled a bit of old man alone, and a bit more of aging Chinese food; nothing else. I think we were all vaguely disappointed, but none of us ever said.

One August morning, early enough that it should have been still cool, but wasn't, I was sitting on the front stoop of Jake's house, waiting for him to get back from a piano lesson, when Mr. McCaslin came out of the front door, started down the steps, and then turned suddenly to look at me. He said, in his increasingly hoarse, rasping voice, "Where's the ithers? Never see the one of youse without the ithers?" He didn't have Mr. Geohegan's strong accent—he'd lived in America longer—but his own surfaced now and then on certain words, and in certain rhythms. I heard later that he'd been born in County Wicklow, but I've no idea whether that was true or not.

I told him where Jake was, and that Phil was probably sleeping in; even then, he often stayed up all night, to his parents' dismay, drawing and sketching. Mr. McCaslin took this in, nodded briefly, grunted, "Want to talk to the three of youse tonight," and shambled on his way without another word.

Phil's mother and mine were both nervous about Mr. McCaslin's illness possibly being contagious, but Jake's mother reassured them that if that were so, there would have been a lot more people than us coming down with it over the years he'd lived in the building. So at nine o'clock that night, after months—even years—of peeking into that apartment, the three of us were finally perched solemnly on his couch, which wobbled at my end, watching as he poured himself a full tumbler of whiskey without apologizing. The living room was sparsely furnished, disappointingly so to a curious child. The centerpiece was a handsome old armchair with a plastic cover on it; for the rest I remember only a couple of other chairs, a few books on shelves mostly filled with china animal figures. The few photographs, close to, were mostly of children, except for one of a young woman with her dark hair piled and knotted high on her head. Mr. McCaslin took a deep drink from his glass, and spoke for the first time then, saying flatly, "Youse all know I'm dyin'."

We didn't say anything. Maybe we nodded. Whatever our response, Mr. McCaslin brushed it aside, saying, "I got no time for bullshit, that's one good thing about dyin'. I don't mind, I'm tellin' youse that straight off. It'll be a rest, that's what it'll be, and that's all I want, is a rest." He took a second swallow of the whiskey, coughed, and went on. "Y'ain't such bad fellas, for little shits, so I'll be askin' a favor of youse. One favor."

I remember watching Phil studying that hollowed-out red and pale face, and thinking, *he wants to draw him. He's drawing him in his head right now.* Mr. McCaslin said again, "One favor. Youse got to keep the dog from me."

We stared. Phil's family had a cocker spaniel named Dusty, but she only got out of the house when Phil walked her, mornings and evenings. I wanted a dog in the worst way, but I was allergic to practically everything in those days, and asthmatic as well. Jake had fish. Mr. McCaslin said, "The Dark Terrier."

It looks odd in print—maybe even a bit funny—but it didn't sound like that, the way Mr. McCaslin said the words. He pronounced it like *tarrier*, I remember: *the dark tarrier.* "Back in Ireland, the Dark Terrier, he always comes when a McCaslin's dyin'. He'll be comin' tomorrow, day after. Youse boys got to keep him from m'door."

Jake was the first one to find words. He said hesitantly, "You mean, if we keep this ... the Dark Terrier away, you won't die?"

Mr. McCaslin laughed, which I couldn't remember ever seeing him do in all the years we'd known him. It was a kind of tearing, ratchety sound, but it was definitely a laugh. "Boyo, nobody keeps the Dark Terrier away, you have m'word on that. All I want, I just want three days."

225

We were back staring, completely bewildered, and increasingly frightened—anyway, *I* was. Not by the words so much, as by the utterly serious tone of Mr. McCaslin's rough, painful voice. "I got to write a letter," he said. "Before I go with him. It'll take me three days. I'll be ready in three days."

"Who's it to?" Neither Jake nor I would have dared to ask, but Phil always had to know.

Mr. McCaslin didn't take offense at the question; he hardly seemed to have heard it. He said, almost dreamily, "It's to m'girl, m'daughter. There's things to set right, things we didn't understand, neither on us . . ." His voice trailed off, and he was silent for a few moments before he added, "Her name's Daisy. M'wife named her."

The notion that Mr. McCaslin had once had a wife—let alone a daughter named Daisy—was as strange and disconcerting to us as any doomful tale he might have told. It was easier then, somehow, for me to ask about the Dark Terrier. Did his coming always mean death, and only for a McCaslin? It seemed an important question, if we were going to be getting in the thing's way.

Mr. McCaslin didn't brush it off. "I never heard of him comin' for none but the McCaslins. It's three hundred years and more we've passed that story down, all the way back to bloody Cromwell's time. M'own father, he saw *his* father go off with the Dark Terrier, he told me so himself. Always warned me, *have your house in order, boyo, for the dog won't never wait.* And I done that, I done that, except for the one thing." His faded, almost colorless eyes were glittering with tears. "I got to write to Daisy."

"It'll take you three days to write a letter?" *Oh, please God, that wasn't me! Yes, it was, and with Phil and Jake looking at me . . .* But Mr. Mc-Caslin only said, with some dignity, "I got a lot to say to her, boy, and no practice in saying it."

I didn't ask any more questions after that. Neither did any of us, really.

I don't think we ever formally agreed to hold the Dark Terrier at bay for three days, either to Mr. McCaslin or to each other; but when we left that apartment we knew it was a done deal, as people say now. We didn't talk much afterward, except to decide that we'd watch in shifts, with Jake taking the first, me the second, and Phil the long third, since he hardly slept anyway. Then we went home and had bad dreams. All of us. I know this, because I checked.

As edgy and keyed-up as we were, not in the least sure what to believe, or what we'd actually *do* if the story turned out true—how do you plan to waylay a phantom dog?—it's a good thing that the Dark Terrier appeared on only the second day after our meeting with Mr. McCaslin. It happened on my shift, around noon: I was sitting cross-legged on the floor, a few doors down from the apartment, working in my special secret poetry notebook—people were used to seeing me like that—when I heard the soft clicking of blunt claws on slate tile, and looked up to see the black head come around the stairwell. I dropped the notebook and scrambled to my feet, and we regarded each other, the Dark Terrier and I.

It wasn't ghostly or transparent, nor at all menacing, and it wasn't exactly black, either. *Dark* really is the best word, for it seemed to be made of darkness: a darkness as far beyond black as the darkness of space must be from our simple night. Otherwise it was an ordinary-looking smallish dog, something like a fox terrier (I knew all about dog breeds back then), with a mild-mannered style, and an endearing way of carrying one ear up and the other down. It considered me amiably enough, plainly dismissed me, and started directly for Mr. McCaslin's door.

"No," I said. "Oh, no," and I beat it to the door and scooped it up before I had time to be scared of being bitten. Then I ran down the stairs, still saying *no, no, no*—completely forgetting my poetry note-book—and I ran almost all the way home across the sweltering street, carrying the Dark Terrier tightly in my arms.

It didn't struggle at all, nor growl, nor ever once try to bite me, but only put its head back and looked at me in a rather puzzled sort of way, as though this were the last thing in the world it had expected, which it probably was. When I slowed down, breathless and sweating, I panted to it, "We have to keep you for three days, Mr. McCaslin isn't ready, he has to finish his letter. It's very important, he'll go with you in three days, when it's done." Unlike a real dog, the Dark Terrier felt achingly cold against my chest, and I couldn't feel any heartbeat. It hurt me to hold him.

My parents were at a teachers' union meeting. I've never been more grateful for anything in my life than I was for that as I ran into our apartment, slamming and locking the door behind me. I put the Dark Terrier down, and went from room to room, closing and locking every window, even though we lived on the fifth floor, and despite the fact that I was cutting off what little flow of air there was. The Dark Terrier followed me, still with the same slightly bewildered air, not trying to escape, watching me intently as I phoned Phil and gasped out the story. Nearly six decades later, I still remember that the first thing he asked was, "You okay?"

"Yeah," I said slowly, not having considered allergies or asthma until then. "Yeah, I don't think it's like a regular dog. But they'll never let me keep it, not even for three days. I know they won't."

"I might just get away with it," Phil pondered. "*Might*. Tell my folks I'm keeping it for a friend, it'll be a playmate for Dusty. Give me a couple of hours, I'll call you back."

I called Jake after that, and he came over immediately, easing cautiously around the door while I blocked the hallway, to keep the Dark Terrier from making a break for it. He'd already told Mr. McCaslin that we had the dog, and the old man had thanked him feverishly and hurried back to continue writing to his daughter. "Anyway, I hope that's what he was doing," Jake said. "He smelled pretty strong."

We regarded the Dark Terrier together, and it looked back at us with calm impatience, if there is such a thing. Jake said thoughtfully, "Ordinary sort of dog, you come right down to it. You think it's really the Angel of Death?"

I shook my head. "If it's an angel, it could just waltz right out of here and right *through* Mr. McCaslin's door, and that'd be that. I think it's just something they've got over in Ireland. Maybe it doesn't have the same powers here? I don't know—but it sure knew where he lived, just like he said. It's the McCaslin family dog, all right."

"Three days," Jake said to it. "You can wait three lousy days, can't you?" The Dark Terrier gave no sign of hearing, comprehending, or complying.

Phil called in an hour to say that he had talked his parents into letting him babysit his friend's sweet little black dog for the couple of days the friend would be away. Jake and I promptly brought the Dark Terrier over, still unresisting: sleekly muscular and shockingly cold in our arms, and so clearly *waiting*, just biding its time, that Phil said, "I wish they made dog handcuffs. Dog hobbles, dog shackles, dog ball-and-chain things. We're never going to hold this one for three days."

But we did manage it for two. Two and a half, really.

Phil's mother was a well-meaning, anxious woman, a deal more nervous than Jake's mother or mine. Surprisingly she took to the strange black dog (as did Dusty, the old cocker spaniel, which was even more surprising), and spent time petting it and playing with it, even assuring Phil that he didn't have to be watching it absolutely every *minute*; he could leave Sweetie—as she was calling the Dark Terrier—with her, and just go back to his room to draw or paint for a while. Phil held out until the morning of the third day; then he yielded, leaving her with instructions and warnings enough for the keeper of King Kong. His mother, rather uncharacteristically, obeyed every one of them. It didn't help.

The moment Phil's mother opened the door for the plumber who had come to install the new kitchen sink, the Dark Terrier shot between her legs and was gone, leaving hysteria in its wake, and Phil on the phone to Jake and me, telling us to get over to Mr. McCaslin's and keep that dog away from his door; he'd be right there as soon as he'd finished yelling at his mother. I could hear his father rumbling in the background, and thought it might be a little longer than that.

For all that Jake lived in the same house, and knew exactly where the Dark Terrier was bound, it was at Mr. McCaslin's door before Jake could get there to head it off. It was on its hind legs, scratching at the door like any family dog wanting in, and Jake could hear Mr. McCaslin inside crying, "Not yet, not yet, I ain't finished! Please, not yet!" But the dog would not wait.

When Jake tried to prod the Dark Terrier away from the door, it turned on him and growled for the first time, showing only its front teeth, which he said was scarier than if it had bared every fang in its head. He retreated and stood by helplessly until Phil and I got there; then, between the three of us, we did manage to make the dog back off at least a little way, where it sat on its haunches, still growling in its chest, while we lined up before the door, linking arms theatrically and chanting "*No pasaran!*"—they shall not pass—like Jake's Uncle Irv, who had been in the Spanish Civil War, and had a blind eye to show for it. I wondered if any McCaslins had died during that one, and if the Dark Terrier had come for them too, trotting briskly between the lines.

We stayed there well into the afternoon, facing down a thing none of us truly understood, hoping that we were really buying time for Mr. McCaslin to finish his last letter to his daughter Daisy. We were hot and weary—emotionally weary as much as physically so—and when I think back on that last day now I'm amazed at how three eleven-year-olds held together: even three very bright eleven-year-olds, even knowing whatever it was we maybe knew. I remember Jake saying, "We're never going to be able to talk about this to *anybody*," and Phil answering, "I don't ever want to talk about it to *us*." For myself, I kept wishing I'd brought a book.

When the door behind us opened, it opened suddenly, catching us all—and maybe the Dark Terrier too—by surprise. Mr. McCaslin stood there. looking not exactly taller in the ragged green bathrobe he must have been living in for days, but somehow straighter, *lighter*, as though a great old weight on him had turned to wings. He did not look at us, but said simply to the Dark Terrier, "I'm done now. Come in, if ye will."

The dog that had come for every McCaslin for three centuries paced past him into the apartment, after a last long stare at each one of us. Its eyes were as unearthly dark as the beast itself, and completely expressionless; but it seemed to see us, and know us, as no one ever had.

Mr. McCaslin said to us, "I thank youse all three. Don't forget to mail m'letter to Daisy. I put stamps on it." Then he turned and followed the Dark Terrier into his apartment, and closed the door.

Jake nipped in and grabbed the letter when the paramedics came for the body the next day. Mr. McCaslin had died in bed, with an untouched bottle and glass on a chair nearby. There was no sign, or any trace, of a dog ever having been there.

The letter was fat and heavy, addressed in a surprisingly neat hand to Daisy McCaslin at a box number in Toronto. We stuck on a few extra stamps, just in case, and dropped it in the mailbox at the corner of Gunhill and Wayne. I like to think she received it, but of course I don't know.

We never did talk much about Mr. McCaslin, not then. The questions the whole episode raised were simply too much for eleven-year-olds to deal with. Where had he gone with the Dark Terrier, and did its existence imply the reality of an afterlife? Could there be other such creatures—phantoms, apparitions, spirits—and did they only attach themselves to certain families, certain sorts of people? Could they be considered evil or benign, finally? We could neither find nor invent answers to any of these; so, whatever we thought as individuals, as a group we just let it all go.

These days, though, all of us being older than Mr. McCaslin probably was at that time, we do discuss it now and again, from our three corners of the continent. Jake and Phil both swear that they've actually seen it: turning a street corner just ahead, pattering down the front steps of some old building late at night. I can't say that, but I've sometimes thought I've heard its claws clicking behind me, even though it's never yet shown itself. But all three of us, I know, still see it in our minds, standing up and scratching at Mr. McCaslin's door to be let in at last. And when that vision comes back to me, I hurry home to write my own letters, to make my own amends, to get done that which no one else can ever do for me . . . before I hear the claws at my own door.

THE FIFTH SEASON

This is—I'm almost sure—the last story about Jake, Phil, Marty and me. We were fifteen at the time of the Great Water-Pistol Battle (well, Marty, the Kid, was about a year or so younger.) Bright, gifted, alarmingly literate Bronx Jewish kids, we were all very aware of The Future looming over us . . . anyway, as we imagined The Future, according to our several fantasies. We're all over seventy now, and we've known one another for most of our long lives; and I like to think that each of us might today see that last anarchic free-for-all in our neighborhood park as a kind of *vale*, a near-conscious farewell to our shared Gunhill Road childhood . . . but maybe not. Maybe that's just me being the Writer, simply grateful for my friends—to whom this book is dedicated—and for the time and place, the families and circumstances, that made it possible for us to be whom we were, when we were. There can't be many nine-year-olds today who aren't hipper and more knowledgeable than we four were then, in the pride of our adolescence—but I'll take us as we were, gladly.

THERE ARE WAY MORE than four seasons, of course. Everybody knows that. I've been in countries where *I* was never able to differentiate more than two seasons—mud and dust, or freezing and not-quite-freezing—but I didn't live there, and I hadn't been born there, so I'm sure that I missed many of the dainty distinctions between days that you don't talk about when you're not a stranger to a place.

In the North Bronx of my youth, we had a particular nameless season that fell as it chose between one day when it was still soft new spring and another when it was high hard summer. I remember it now as a kind of bridge from rollerskates to bicycles, school dances to double-dating, and abandoning that safe haven in turn for the wilderness of movies and the boardwalks of Orchard Beach, otherwise known as the Bronx Riviera. It didn't occur every year, this special season—not like stickball, or my allergies, or geraniums in the window boxes at P.S. 94—but everybody always knew, without ever saying, when it happened.

Jake, Phil, and I were all fifteen. Marty was fourteen, and reminded of it more often than he should have been. We still hung out in our odd way—often together, sometimes in any combination of two or three—and we conversed in the private language of jokes, references and not quite meaningless one-liners that any such group accumulates. It shut strangers out, just as it was supposed to do, and made us part of something that *we* knew was special and different. Words have power, and phrases define nations, even declarations as odd as "Yeah, well, I'll butter *your* head, see how *you* like it." The four members of the Gunhill Road Gang were a country unto ourselves, and we liked it that way.

That season, that year, the nights were balmier than usual, and we went for a lot of long late walks in a drowsily lingering twilight along Mosholu Parkway and the Grand Concourse. One night Jake and I walked all the way down the Concourse, past the Paradise Theatre, to the Bronx High School of Science—which by day we took a bus and a subway train to reach—speaking entirely in spoonerisms, switching the first syllables of alternate words. I couldn't have told anyone the next day why rendering *bus stop* into *stuss bop* reduced both of us to hysterics; nor why inverting the old cliché to proclaim, "A potched wot bever noils" still does it to me even now. I suppose you could have gotten mugged just as easily then as today, but somehow that never came up as a possibility, even when we weren't all together. Which we weren't always, as I've said: one of the paradoxical things we had in common was that each of us had learned young to be his own best company. We drew a certain sustenance that we found nowhere else from one another's presence on the planet—let alone within a range of five blocks—but we could go days and weeks without seeing or talking to each other, and never feel anxious or abandoned. For me, it was quite simply comforting to know that there were others of my odd species (and I was just beginning to realize how odd it was) close at hand.

What Jake and Marty had in common was not only a seemingly inborn understanding of How Stuff Works, from a blossoming nova to a misbehaving reel-to-reel tape recorder, but a particular joy in that understanding which was a joy to observe, when I wasn't envying it until my teeth ached. Phil, God knows, would Figure Stuff Out through sheer rock-bottom stubbornness; but my own attitude toward such matters hadn't varied a great deal since the days when I worried about exhausting the little people who lived in my wind-up phonograph and sang for me. On my night walks with Marty—as long as any with Jake or Phil, because he took no pity on his polio-hobbled left leg—he would explain the beauties of chemistry and physics and astronomy to me, and the wonder is that I actually understood parts of what he told me. Small parts—bits, okay?—and not likely to be recalled the next day, but it was very kind of him. He didn't do it to be kind, though, but to share his pure delight in those studies that school had taught me to find utterly undelightful.

In that year, on the last night of that unspoken season, the four of us went back to the Oval.

Williamsbridge Reservoir Oval really was a reservoir long ago: from 1890 through 1934 it had distributed water to the North Bronx. In 1954 we thought of it as the *domesticated* park, where you took little kids to play on the swings and the jungle gym, and in the sandboxes and the wading pool. There were tennis and basketball courts there too, and a running track, and a football field for high-school teams, all on the park's lower level; while on the upper level, where you entered, there were benches and grass and water fountains, and any amount of places for older people to sit and keep an eye on the grandchildren, or to doze with big red and white handkerchiefs over their faces. Phil and Jake and Marty and I had all been raised in Reservoir Oval, almost literally spending entire weekends there, as often alone as with our families. Jake and I had roller-skated on the upper level, round and round the park, pretending to be Greek deities—Apollo, Hermes, Poseidon, Hades. Phil and I had played hooky there from junior high school, hiding in the bushes and thickets between the levels that seemed suddenly far too thin to conceal us from the APB that must surely be circulating everywhere. And Marty and I had walked there at night, to look at the stars. Now that we were worldly-wise high school students we regarded it as a kids' park, and didn't go round much anymore.

I can't recall that we ever took a vote, or otherwise formally decided that we were going to take a turn at the Oval on this perfect evening. We just started drifting in that direction together. It was an early twilight—green, with streaks of purple—and birds were still settling onto their nests as the dogs trotted reluctantly home beside their people, and the local feral cats more or less gave up on birds for the night. The park keepers—"parkies," everyone called them—with their olive-drab uniforms and their spiked sticks (meant for picking up garbage, but kids had their own beliefs)—looked sharply but briefly at the four of us, warned us that the gates would shortly be locked (though even our grandmothers could have climbed that fence), and went on their sensible way home, like everyone else. Within a short time, we had the entire Oval to ourselves.

We'd shared the Monster-Size Pizza at Sal's, up past DeKalb Avenue (sausage, onions, tomatoes and two kinds of cheese), and we all got thirsty at the same time. The biggest fountain—the one with two faucets—stood just across from the broad stone stairs down to the lower level, and we made for it by silent common consent. That was when we saw Jake's father.

Jake's mother was a great friend of my own mother's, and always came over to change my typewriter ribbon—a technical challenge I still hadn't quite mastered at fifteen. But I really only knew two things about Mr. Jacobs: that he had played correspondence chess with people, constantly sending postcards back and forth, as chess buffs did in those benighted days before computers; and that he had been dead for several years.

Yet there he was. It *was* him, I *did* see him, we all did, though we said nothing, not even Jake, not in words. He made a soft sound that I can still summon up, even after so much time, and never will. He took a couple of steps forward, and then stopped, as though to acknowledge the reality of his father's ghost was to lose him a second time. Mr. Jacobs was kneeling right by the fountain, smiling at us and setting out four guns on the grass. One was a .45 automatic; two were identical cowboy six-shooters; the fourth was a Tommy, a chopper, a Chicago piano—a Thompson submachine gun, right out of Al Capone and Prohibition. They call it *film noir* now, but back then it was all just movies. From a million matinees, we knew about guns.

They looked real. We had to touch them, pick them up, before we realized that they were only plastic water-pistols. By that time Mr. Jacobs had faded and vanished, still smiling. None of us said anything about that, no more than we had about the sudden fact of his presence—I think we were waiting to take our cue from Jake, and it wasn't happening. You could actually watch him determining not to have seen what would have bewildered his heart more than he could possibly have dealt with at fifteen. So he only shivered once, and shook his head, and Phil mumbled, barely audibly, "Some *weird* shit . . ." as he turned the .45 in his hands, staring at the space where Jake's father had been standing. And nobody spoke, and we didn't look much at each other. We looked at those plastic guns.

When Jake did speak, his voice was distant, strangely dreamy. "Pete and I had a really epic shootout here—when was it? two, three years ago? Went on all afternoon, and we didn't have anything like this arsenal."

"Your dad broke it up," I said. "Came to get you for home for dinner, remember? Saved your ass, too—I had you as soggy as my Aunt Sarah's *rugelach*." Which was a base libel on my aunt's perfectly acceptable pastry, but I was clumsily trying to provoke a further acknowledgment of his father, and not doing it well. Jake didn't take the bait.

"You *are* kidding? Once I cut you off from your ammo supply, it was over."

"Please. It was the St. Valentine's Day Massacre, only with soap-bubbles." I had sneaked detergent into my water pistol that time.

Marty was holding the Thompson up in the remaining light, estimating its own ammunition capacity. "Wow, the tank on this one holds more water than the other three combined. It's a hydraulic breakthrough."

I snatched it from him and started filling it at the fountain. "Gimme. Children shouldn't be playing with big old grownup weapons."

The Thompson must have held at least a gallon of water; it seemed to take forever to fill. When I'd finally thumbed the little rubber stopper in place, Phil grabbed it from me as I had grabbed it from Marty. "First dibs. Seniority rules."

"What seniority? You're four months younger than I am!"

"Okay, not seniority—law of the jungle. You want it, come and get it." And he nailed me between the eyes with a blast that knocked my glasses off and left me gasping. That thing had *firepower*.

"Sneak attack!" Jake yelled. "Fifth-column sabotage!" He had quietly been filling one of the six-shooters, and now he opened on Phil, who whirled, crouching dramatically, and shot back from the hip, catching Jake square in the mouth. Battle was joined.

It was all against all, perfectly spontaneous and completely improvised; no alliances endured for more than five minutes. Phil held the high ground, so to speak, as long as the Thompson's ammunition lasted—Marty had been quite right about the volume of the thing's water tank. The three of us—me in the forsythia bushes with the other six-shooter, Jake behind a tree, Marty prone under a bench—kept trying to lure him into wasting shots, since he wasn't as accurate as Jake, who was already entering .22 rifle competitions. But the Thompson gave him notably better range than any of us, and he hit most of what he aimed at. The wild and savage Yiddish-inflected war whoops were more unnerving than you might imagine.

Jake, showing previously unrevealed guerrilla instincts, kept moving closer, slipping from tree to tree the moment Phil took his eyes off him. Marty, too near and visible to mount an attack, but shielded by the bench, kept up his short bursts of sniper fire with the .45, and probably stayed drier than any of us. I, for my part, having in the excitement forgotten my allergy to forsythia, can be said to have provided a diversion by sneezing like a shotgun every couple of minutes. Obviously I'd have fled the bushes at the first opportunity; but Phil had me pinned down, and took knowing, cackling delight in keeping me right where I was. At one point I even called for a truce, raising a white—if snotty—handkerchief. Phil promptly shot at it, and Jake did too.

Vengefulness made me inventive: I crawled backwards through the forsythia, sniffling all the way out of range and down to the lower level. Then I blew my nose—never mind where—and practically circled the park, coming back up by way of a smaller stair on the far side, behind the tennis courts. Twilight had faded just enough for me to slip up unnoticed on the utterly anarchic water fight that was still raging. Phil's Thompson hadn't run dry yet; Jake had clearly managed a foray to some fountain out of range, to reload; and if Marty, under the bench, hadn't been so lucky, he was carefully husbanding his shots, waiting calmly and patiently for his moment. And over all, ringing defiantly through the dusk, Phil's challenge to us all, and to the entire world beyond: "Geva-a-a-a-a-a-l-t!"

There is no exact translation for *gevalt*. Beware? Look out? An "expression of alarm, shock, or dismay," as my desktop dictionary has it? All as good as any, I suppose, but it could equally well be used to mean *timber!* or *Fore!* Howled properly by a fifteen-year-old boy facing down three antagonists with a water gun in his hands, it can raise the hair, chill the blood, and shiver the timbers. You have my word.

What happened next . . .

Okay. The moon was rising—not quite full, but near enough—and moonlight changes things, I know that. And I know that I sound like people defending their sightings of UFOs on cable networks . . . but what I saw, I saw.

All of them were firing at the same time. Phil . . . Marty . . . Jake . . . every one completely soaked, every one laughing, every one fully given over to the Gunfight At The Reservoir Oval. A fine rainbow spray hovered constantly over their heads, sparkling and dancing in the moonlight like a living creature. And there were pictures in that luminous mist, images that shifted, slipped, dissolved, merged, reformed; yet somehow remained ever clear, ever individual, even so . . .

Jake, heavy, bearded and bald . . . a stent in his heart, a hearing-aid in each ear . . .

Marty, no longer limping as he had in our youth; limping now from two artificial hips and a titanium pelvis . . .

Phil, his hair steel-gray, thin face slightly tilted, a souvenir of the automobile accident that broke his neck . . .

I tell you that I saw this in one sweeping flash, just as I saw them laughing uncontrollably, like the children they were . . . just as I heard the laughter and glimpsed the faces of other children, and of women we did not know, and the walls and gardens and bookshelves of houses none of us had ever yet seen . . . just as I know they saw me, too— *white-bearded and balding, desperately fighting off a gut, teeth like a train wreck, jowls packed to move in, eyes like somebody else's eyes, somebody so much more weary than I ever imagined being*—as I moved in fast behind Phil, clapped my six-shooter to the back of his neck and rasped, "Drop d'gat, Louie! Drop it, yeh dirty rat!"

And all three of them shot me. At once, as one. On target. All three of my closest friends, then and still and ever.

That seemed to end it: that, and perhaps a shared understanding that we had all seen our own visions in the moonlit spray—perhaps, also, that we would never see such visions again, not together, and that our fifth season, neither spring nor summer, was over and would never come again. Nobody said much, though I'd swear I remember Marty venturing, "I'm pretty sure that was fun," and Phil growling, "Let me know." We left the guns on the grass where Jake's father had laid them out at the future's unknowable bidding. (Did he come—or was he sent to us?—because he was the only one of our parents who had yet died? Fifty-five years, and even now I wonder about that in the night.) There was never a question about keeping them, and I've never touched a water pistol since that night, not even when I had children of my own.

Sodden as we were, it was harder than usual to get over the locked park gates, but we managed it, walking home in squelchy silence. It was a private silence, such as I had never known before then, and it remains so to this day, for all that we remain the Gunhill Road Geezer Gang. Jake—recently retired from teaching political science in the Washington Cascades—won't talk about that night at all; while Phil—painting more intensely than ever these days—says, "You never did know what the hell you were looking at. That's why you have me." And Marty . . .

Well, Marty—still frolicking in the computer world that might have been invented just for him—Marty said it best, before we parted on that night of the Great Reservoir Oval Gunfight. In his shy, soft, clear voice, always on the edge of stammering, he said, "We all know what we all saw. Whatever it really was, it'll always be with us, and no one else. So wherever we go from here, it'll always keep us together." And so it has. True vision or not, truly seen or not, so it has.

TARZAN SWINGS BY BARSOOM

Personally I've always despised Burroughs's *John Carter of Mars*, and his Lost Cause vision of the Confederacy. Phil (who had all the Tarzan books) and I knew beyond doubt that if it came down to it, Tarzan of the Apes would have John Carter in three rounds. On the other hand, why red-skinned Dejah Thoris (not to mention the entrancing La of Opar) couldn't have lured Tarzan away from his tree house with Jane Porter will always be one of the great wonders of adult life to me. Jake and Phil and I used to discuss the matter at some length.

T HE APE-MAN WAS RESTLESS. Even on a night as warmly tranquil as this in the West African jungle that was far more his heart's home than the House of Lords—where, as John Clayton, Viscount Greystoke, he was entitled to sit among its members any time he wanted to—he could find no sleep in any of his favorite tree crotches or hollows. Nor did the pleasure of exhuming a week-buried haunch of antelope or lesser kudu provide anything more than a satisfactory belch and a good scratch. For the very first time in a life constantly adventurous from his birth, Tarzan was bored.

Looking longingly up at Goro, the red, gibbous moon, he thought, "What a night this would be to dance the Dum-Dum with a few of the old gang!" But of the Mangani, the great apes who had raised him from his infancy, few yet survived; and their descendants tended to avoid him, wary of his smell—human, yet *not*-human. . . . Tarzan sighed and stretched his mighty arms—also his mighty thews and sinews—up toward the star-sown jungle sky . . . and especially toward the brilliant red dot low on the horizon, stubbornly refusing to be rendered invisible by the moonlight. *Mars, god of war—the Warrior Planet! Perhaps it has always drawn me because I was born a warrior and had to remain so to survive. Mars . . . Mars . . .*

In a strangely detached manner, he felt the soul being drawn out of his body, taking flight towards the glow above . . . *beyond* the glow. He clutched the knife that dangled on the rawhide cord at his throat, and felt it seemingly dissolve in his hands—he had a single moment of coherent thought, *going to miss dinner, Jane will be*—then there was only intense cold—then nothing. . . .

He came to consciousness sprawled naked on dry, hot sand: somewhat dazed and disoriented, but apparently entirely himself in his own body, and in no least doubt of where he had been transmigrated to. The sky overhead was of a pale, Earth-like blue, but with a curious transparency about it, as though one could almost see through it to the pure blackness of deepest space beyond. There were two moons in this sky, both near enough to be visible in daylight, and both moving, as he stared, distinctly more swiftly than the satellite he knew. Of all the lost worlds and colonies that Tarzan had discovered on—and even within—his own planet, none had ever made him feel so lonely as he felt now. *Jane's going to think I've sneaked off back to Opar. She's always had a thing about La.*

His wide reading in several languages had prepared the ape-man for the law of gravity and lighter air pressure on Mars; but all the same, the movement involved merely in rising to his feet almost took him off the ground, and his very first step caused him literally to bounce two or three feet into the air, and then to fall on his face with the second step. Practice, and a good deal of falling down, eventually allowed him to evolve a method of cautious, slogging progression, punctuated by sudden inadvertent kangaroo hops of as much as nine or ten feet straight up. It was at the zenith of one such hop that he discerned the curious glass-roofed structure over the low hills to his right. This being the only suggestion of habitation of any sort, Tarzan determined to make his way to it.

While the distance was not great, achieving his goal took him well over an hour, since the bounces he was only slowly learning to control frequently took him off in one undesired direction or another. Finally arriving at the building, he recognized it as a kind of giant incubator, containing, as best he could enumerate them, several hundred eggs, all between two and three feet across. Tarzan had seen—and eaten—ostrich eggs from time to time; these would have fed a family of Mangani for over a week.

Tarzan dropped onto his haunches and scratched his head. Forty million miles from Big Ben, his only clock was his stomach, and that organ was informing him that interplanetary travel—however long it had actually taken him—was a hungry business. Those eggs undoubtedly belonged to someone, but Tarzan's stomach belonged to him, and the moral issue was never really up for discussion. He pried open the entrance to the incubator—of glass, like the roof—selected the nearest egg, brought it back outside, and, with his mouth watering in anticipation, used the haft of his knife to crack it open.

With a yelp of "*Shakahachie!*"—which is the Mangani equivalent of "Oh, *ick!*"—he tumbled backward onto the yellow mosslike growth covering much of this dry surface area. The embryo curled inside the egg was far too developed—and infinitely too ugly—for even a ravenous ape-man to consider eating. It looked to him rather like a cross between an Earth vulture chick and a dinosaur out of Pal-ul-don or Pellucidar. Tarzan found it so revolting that he promptly buried it in the sand, as deeply as he could. His stomach was just going to have to wait for better times. Tarzan of the Apes had gone hungry before.

Sleep, now . . . sleep was another matter, easier to deal with. Without hesitation—and having some notion of how cold Martian nights must be—the ape-man dug down to bury himself as deeply as he had the ruined and disgusting egg. Food would be something to consider when he awakened. Snug in his burrow, the ape-man matter-of-factly closed his eyes and went to dreamless sleep. His last waking thought was of Jane . . . Jane, his mate . . . whom . . .

He awakened with a bound, sensing the presence of enemies, even down through the sands of Mars. He had clearly slept through the night, for the sun was just above the horizon, and there was still a morning chill in the air. He blinked his eyes, not to clear his vision—Tarzan of the Apes always woke with all his jungle-trained senses completely alert—but because he perceived himself surrounded by such beings as he had not seen since he encountered the Ant-Men of Minunia, who had briefly enslaved him and reduced him to their own size. But these creatures were the complete opposite of the Minunians, standing anywhere from twelve to fifteen feet high and very nearly as naked as he. Their skins were all various shades of dark green; each had an additional pair of arms, set approximately at waist level; and their red-eyed, expressionless faces were each furnished with a set of hoglike tusks jutting upward from the lower jaw. Their mounts were almost as formidable: some ten feet high themselves, they had four legs on each side, which gave them something of the air of carnivorous caterpillars, since their enormous mouths seemed to stretch all the way to the back of their heads. The great green riders' air of menace was distinctly heightened by the lances and projectile weapons of some sort that each carried—and that were all trained on him.

Only two figures stood out among the twenty or so of this outlandish crew, by virtue of their relatively small size and their human features. One, though clad like the gigantic Martians, was obviously an Earthman: tall, dark-haired, and gray-eyed, like Tarzan himself, with a certain arrogance of bearing that made the ape-man dislike and distrust him on sight. The second . . . the second, red-skinned or no, was the loveliest woman Tarzan had ever seen, and he had known beauties from the highest English society to American movie sets to the mines and palaces of Opar. He had never considered allegiance to any woman other than his Jane Porter, never broken faith even in his imagination. But this one, from her cloud of black hair to her delicate feet, with her expression a blend of pride and wonder, of serenity and innocence. . . .

Tarzan shook his head, conscious of his nakedness for the first time since his arrival in this strange world whose name he was more and more afraid he knew. The Earthman riding beside the red woman dismounted and strode towards Tarzan, plainly more at ease than he in the low Martian gravity. Halting some yards before the ape-man, he asked, speaking with an unmistakable Tidewater accent, "Do you speak English, sir?"

"I do," the ape-man replied evenly. "And French, and German, Arabic, and Swahili, and the tongues of the Mangani, and the pithecanthropi of Pal-ul-don. . . ." He was just starting to enumerate the several dialects of Pellucidar when the Earthman waved him impatiently to silence, saying, "English will do. I am John Carter, of the Virginia Carters. This—" he gestured toward the red-skinned woman—"is my wife, the Princess Dejah Thoris of Helium."

His wife . . . Tarzan drew himself erect and bowed formally to both of them. "I am Tarzan of the Mangani." As Dejah Thoris appeared puzzled by the appellation, he added, "Tarzan of the Apes." Although he kept his eyes resolutely cast down when he looked at her, he felt his jungle-trained senses leaving him, and his mighty thews and sinews quivered alike with the raw passion of the bull ape. Aloud, he added, a bit faintly, "I also speak some Russian, though with a rather coarse Siberian accent, I'm afraid—"

"You're English," John Carter said flatly. Tarzan bowed again, without answering. John Carter said, "You were supposed to come in on our side."

"We thought better of it." The ape-man kept his voice level, his manner courteous.

"We lost the War because of your treachery." John Carter's growl might have been that of Kerchak, king of the apes among which Tarzan had been raised, regarding a rash upstart—and, in time, Tarzan himself. The ape-man could feel the old red scar on his brow beginning to throb dangerously—*I killed Kerchak, broke his neck*—but he controlled himself still, answering only, "I was in Africa, myself, during that regrettable confrontation. Perhaps civilized people may agree to disagree on that point. As we do in the House of Lords."

"The House of Lords?" The unexpected phrase clearly brought John Carter up short, but he rallied quickly, with a dry chuckle. "Well, you're not in any House of Lords here, Mr. Tarzan of the Apes. You're facing a squad of Tharks—friends of mine, if they're friends of anyone, even each other—and they're very upset to see that you've broken into their nursery, since their newest generation are so near to hatching. I don't mind telling you that if you weren't a fellow Earthman, and if you weren't our guest, I'd as soon—"

"But he *is*!" Dejah Thoris's voice was as quiet and steady as her eyes. "He *is* our guest, my lord—and plainly your countryman." She continued to regard Tarzan as she spoke, and the ape-man bowed his head in acknowledgment of her courtesy. This time, when he raised his head, he stared back boldly, until it was she who looked away.

John Carter noticed none of this silent exchange. He was musing, "Remarkable, how after one person transmigrates, suddenly everyone starts doing it. Your body's up in a tree in Africa somewhere, I suppose? Mine's in a cave in Arizona, with a bunch of Indians outside, waiting for me to come out." His laugh was no more than a quick, short bark. "They'll be very old Indians by the time I do."

"I have no idea where my body is," Tarzan admitted candidly. "Is this not my real body? It certainly feels like my body."

"What you're standing up in—that's your *astral* body," John Carter informed him. "The astral body can go anywhere, once you know how to project it—to the outer planets, to the stars! Mine"—he placed a possessive arm around the slight shoulders of Dejah Thoris—"is staying right here on Barsoom, as we Martians call it." Turning briefly, he gestured toward the tusked riders ranged in a semicircle behind him. "The Princess and I were accompanying our green friends on a quick inspection of the hatchery before we start home to Helium. You'd best come along with us—I don't imagine you'd last long among the Tharks. They're fighters, not tree-climbers. And *they* keep their word."

The last words set the ape-man's scar burning once again; but Jane Porter had spent a long time sweetly and lovingly domesticating the wild creature he knew himself to be. With some trepidation—and the aid of a large boulder as a mounting block—he got up behind one of the Tharks ("When a thoat gets to know you, he'll kneel down for you to get on," John Carter told him), although straddling the beast's spine stretched his mighty quadriceps painfully. But the eight-legged stride, much like that of a pacer, was surprisingly comfortable—perhaps because the thoat's well-padded feet absorbed the jolt of the Martian desert surface easily—and Tarzan quickly grew accustomed to the rolling rhythm. *Like riding a camel, really. Or a very big centipede.*

John Carter, with Princess Dejah Thoris riding behind him, kept pace with the ape-man's mount, keeping up conversation with a tone that made Tarzan's mighty teeth hurt. "Odd, you fetching up at exactly the same place where I arrived. Might be some sort of harbor for trans-migrating astral bodies, eh?"

"Perhaps." Tarzan kept his own tone noncommittal. "I have seen stranger things."

"From up in your tree, chattering and scratching with your monkey friends?" John Carter chuckled again. "I'll tell you what would have been strange—seeing a few British warships sailing into Charleston Bay, Mobile Bay. Seeing the British standing up like men, instead of a flock of monkeys—*that* would have been strange, don't you think?" He slanted his glance sideways at Tarzan, his contemptuous chuckle continuing.

Tarzan of the Apes, Lord of the Jungle, would have flown at his throat well before now, merely for the look of his eyes, ignoring his words. John Clayton, Viscount Greystoke, alone, friendless, weapon-less, and naked on Mars, kept his temper, replying simply, "We desired your cotton, certainly, but the price was too high. England has done well enough without slave labor for some while now."

John Carter's Virginia accent grew more pronounced; his skin seemed to grow taut with anger. "Wasn't long ago that our cotton was good enough for you, no matter where it came from. Now suddenly you're all bleeding-heart hypocrites." He spat, narrowly missing Tarzan's bare foot.

"I was a slave myself once," the ape-man mused aloud. "Never liked it much."

"The War was never about slavery!" John Carter jabbed his forefinger at Tarzan as though it were a sword blade, or the barrel of a pistol. "The War was about states' rights to refuse to be told how to live, what to think, what to grow, how to grow it. . . ." His face was flushed, and he was literally spluttering with furious disgust. "It was a second American Revolution, is what it was, and our Cause was just as honorable as theirs! Deny *that*, Sir House-of-Lords, and—" He checked himself abruptly, and his voice slowed and quieted to a menacing drawl. "Deny that, and we might quarrel."

It was Dejah Thoris who hastily changed the subject, describing the magnificence of the old city to which the ape-man was being escorted, so that by the time the caravanserai arrived there, toward evening, he was well prepared for the long, low marble buildings, brilliantly illuminated by the two Martian moons—both shockingly near, from an Earthman's perspective—and for the wide streets, now filling with the tusked green natives who spilled out into them to welcome their countrymen (and especially the great John Carter) back from their expedition into the barren wasteland.

Tarzan's mighty lip curled slightly to watch the Virginian visibly swelling under their praise; but he had to admit that the Tharks' previous experience with one Earthman made it a good bit easier for him to move around freely among the Martians—though every so often, he was waylaid and, with gestures toward John Carter, requested to *sak*, like his compatriot. Once it finally penetrated his comprehension that *sakking* meant bouncing straight up to fully the height of a Thark, he complied vigorously, and was eventually left alone, free to wander the city: no prisoner, but merely a visiting diplomat of some sort. He was well aware that he owed this privilege to John Carter's intervention, which pleased him not at all; but it amused him greatly, all the same, to feel snug around his bare shoulders the fur cloak that Princess Dejah Thoris had tossed to him off her own back against the cold of the

Martian night—and to recall the look that John Carter had thrown him with it. Smiling to himself, he strolled toward the deserted-looking building that crouched at the end of the street in the brilliant shadows cast by the Martian moons.

For someone who habitually slept curled up in the fork of a jungle tree, or stretched out along a branch like a leopard, the ape-man took a serious interest in architecture. The structures he had seen so far looked so much beyond the conception of any of the Tharks he had met so far that he desired to prowl for clues to their original creators: perhaps the extinct race that had once dwelled therein, when the empty Martian seas were full and high and teeming with life. *They couldn't have built all this. They can't even build furniture. . . .*

He was halfway crouched, examining the unusual configuration of some broken steps plainly never made for Thark feet, when all his jungle-trained senses suddenly had him off his own feet and rolling to the side, so that the creature silently dropping on him from above missed him almost entirely. Coming instantly erect, Tarzan gaped in amazement at the creature facing him. It stood as tall as any Thark he had yet encountered, and seemed equally as firm on its hind legs—but it was an ape, beyond any possible doubt, for all that it looked more like a hairless gorilla than a Thark, and even more, to Tarzan's eyes, like a being from Earth, six arms or no. With a scream like that of a leopard that has just made a kill, the thing rushed upon the ape-man, hands reaching out to clutch and strangle and rend.

Tarzan met it with his ancient war cry of *"Kreegahh!"*—which, to his great surprise, momentarily stopped the creature in its tracks. Then it came on again, but with a certain air of puzzlement, which allowed the ape-man to sidestep the crushing sweep of its four upper arms, all muscled to shame Bolgani, the gorilla. The white ape wheeled and came at him again; but Tarzan, taking full advantage of his new Martian agility, leaped over its head and came down behind it, striving for the full-Nelson hold with which he had more than once conquered Numa the lion. He was still having difficulty in learning to land correctly, however, and when he slipped and fell on his back, the ape was at him with a roar, two hands closing on his throat, another pair of arms encircling his chest and squeezing far more powerfully than he himself could have done. Desperately, Tarzan struck out wildly with his mighty fists, but his hardest blow seemed to make no impression on the thick, bald hide or the gorilla features. The Martian moonlight was swimming before the ape-man's eyes, when the creature suddenly eased its grip on his throat, stared into his face, and growled, with a distinct questioning lilt at the end, "*Kreegahh?*"

Almost as bewildered as he was grateful to be alive, Tarzan indicated that he wanted to sit up, and the white ape—again to his amazement—released him and moved warily back from him. Struggling for both air and coherence, Tarzan inquired hoarsely in Mangani, "*Speak?*"

The white ape shook its head . . . but its reply, while hardly up to the linguistic standards of the tribe of Kerchak, was perfectly comprehensible to Tarzan: "*Speak not now. Lost.*"

"You used to speak Mangani," the ape-man whispered. "Here, on Mars . . . Barsoom. How can that be . . . ?" He repeated the question in the tongue he had first spoken himself, and the white ape blinked blankly, and then made a gesture that was almost a shrug, while pointing indiscriminately at the heavens—to the stars and the two moons—and the Earth, dim on a far corner of the horizon. . . .

Tarzan's own slow nod turned into a bow of wonder. "Why should transmigration just be one way?" he muttered aloud. "Why should it be limited to humans?" Abruptly, he pointed in turn to the building behind them, and to the other vast marble structures visible in the moonlight. In Mangani, he asked, forming the words carefully, "Made these? You?"

The white ape stared back at him for a long moment, and it seemed to Tarzan that he saw the shadow of an immense sorrow in the beast's black eyes. "Not us now. Us . . . ," and it made a sort of pushing gesture with both hands, as though rolling away time. Again it said, "Not us now. . . ."

"Your ancestors," the ape-man said softly. "Your distant ancestors . . . all this was their doing. . . ." He began to smile wryly, thinking back himself. "If Kerchak had been your size, with extra arms. . . ."

The white ape stared uncomprehendingly. Tarzan suddenly clapped his hands. "Dum-Dum! Under two moons, with these new cousins of mine? Of course!" Again speaking Mangani with extreme precision, he asked, "Dum-Dum? Dance Dum-Dum? You?"

It seemed to him that a certain look of vague remembrance flickered in the creature's eyes. "Dum-Dum," it repeated several times, but nothing further.

"Dum-Dum!" The ape-man was up now, beginning to shift his weight rhythmically from one bare foot to the other. "Dum-Dum!" leaping now, coming down hard enough to make a slapping sound in the street. "*Dum-Dum!*" with his head thrown back and his mouth open, as though he were drinking the moonlight. "*Dum-Dum!*"

When he looked over at the white ape, it too was on its feet, clumsily mimicking his side-to-side steps, its huge feet creating pounding echoes between the marble buildings. "*Dum-Dum! Dum-Dum!*" Other white figures were emerging from the shadows, joining in the dance of the Mangani . . . their ancestors' dance. "*Dum-Dum! Dum-Dum!*" In Tarzan's jungle, there would have been a hollow log to beat out the rhythm on, but here in this street, on a far-distant world, there was no need. "*Dum-Dum! Dum-Dum!*"

So intoxicated with the ancient dance to the moon was the ape-man that it took him a moment to focus his eyes on the small, slender figure standing apart, her hands clasped before her, and her own eyes wide with marveling. Then he stopped, on the instant, and went quickly to take the hands of the Princess Dejah Thoris and lead her away from the growing horde of the dancing white apes, so caught up in the Dum-Dum themselves that none noticed his leaving. "You should not be here," he told her, his voice harsher than he meant it to sound. "I have set something loose among them. I don't know what it is, or what it will come to, but it could be dangerous. I think it *is* dangerous."

"But it was wonderful!" Dejah Thoris whispered. "I never saw anything so wonderful. I wish my lord could have seen it!" Then she caught herself and shook her head. "No, I do not wish that. He views the white apes as the Tharks do—as evil, murderous vermin that must be hunted down and wiped out altogether. . . . Of course, the Tharks feel that way about almost all other peoples. . . ." Her voice trailed away as she gazed up at Tarzan in helpless perplexity. "You think this is not so?"

"All I know, Princess," the ape-man responded gravely, "is that they are not vermin. In some way, they are distantly related to my own people, the great apes of Africa, who raised me as one of their own. For good or ill, I could never raise a hand against them ever again."

Dejah Thoris stepped closer, peering up at him, as though into the highest branches of a great tree. "You are as tall as my lord," she mused, "and your eyes are as gray as his. But you are a very strange sort of Earthman, are you not, Tarzan of the Apes?"

"I believe I am an ape in my deepest heart," Tarzan replied, "nothing more than an ape of Kerchak's tribe. But when I look at you, Princess Dejah Thoris of Helium, I cannot but remember that I am also a man."

That was how Tarzan of the Apes learned that a Red Martian can indeed blush. One quick, shaky smile that the ape-man took with him to his grave, then Dejah Thoris, without speaking further, fled ahead of him toward the building where he and John Carter and she were to spend the night. Finding the quarters assigned to him, Tarzan dropped into the pile of furs and silks waiting there and fell asleep with Princess Dejah Thoris's cloak still around his shoulders.

In the morning, after an excellent breakfast of items that Tarzan was quite happy not to have identified, he helped John Carter, Dejah Thoris, and their several Red Martian servants pack their belongings onto borrowed thoats, and assumed that they would be setting out shortly for distant Helium. He was getting acquainted with his own thoat, practicing mounting and dismounting, when John Carter suddenly said, "Hear you had a tussle with a few maggots last night." Tarzan blinked in puzzlement. "The white apes," John Carter explained. "That's what I call them, because they're white like maggots, and because there's not a thing to be done with them except kill them. Until there aren't any more." He was toying with a Thark pistol, a cut-down version of one of the rifles Tarzan had learned were powered by radium. "Show me where the struggle took place, Sir House-of-Lords."

"You won't find them out in daylight," Tarzan warned him. "And the Princess is clearly anxious to start home." In fact, Dejah Thoris had hardly spoken all morning.

"Sir Englishman," John Carter said without expression, "don't you ever presume to tell me whether or not my wife is *anxious*. . . ." He broke open his weapon, casually inspected the load, and snapped it shut again. "I told you, I want to see last night's battlefield. No one's going anywhere until I do."

If it is not this place, it will be some other. Might as well have it over with. The ape-man stood up. He said, "I will show you, and then we will get on our way."

"Absolutely," John Carter agreed. "Just indulge an old Johnny Reb, if you would." Dejah Thoris said nothing, but the fear in her eyes angered Tarzan in a way that he had not thought possible. He strode ahead, and John Carter followed close on his heels.

Nearing the deserted building where he had been attacked, Tarzan pointed ahead, saying, "There. One of them ambushed me, but I fought him off and he ran away. There was nothing more to it than that."

"Really?" John Carter was still toying with his pistol—then, to Tarzan's alarm, he suddenly lifted it. "Would that be the fellow, do you suppose?"

A moment of whiteness—a flash of a great hunched body trying to pass an empty window without being seen. John Carter's finger was already squeezing the trigger when Tarzan struck his arm up, so that the bullet whined harmlessly off the wall of the building in a flurry of marble chips. And John Carter struck Tarzan in the face with the butt of the revolver, so that the ape-man reeled backward and sat down hard in the Martian street.

"Been wanting to do that from the first day," John Carter said flatly. "I don't like you, Sir House-of-Lords. You're no better than a damn Yankee—worse, in some ways. And I don't like the way you look at my wife. Not from the first day."

The ape-man was on his feet now, smiling blood. He said simply, "Thank you for doing that."

"You're the challenged party—the choice of weapons is up to you." John Carter was smiling genially himself. "I've got a couple of Thark swords, or we can make it pistols. Up to you."

Tarzan shook his head. He said nothing, but simply beckoned John Carter in toward him. For the first time, the Virginian looked slightly uneasy, but he tossed the pistol aside, said, "Come and get it, then," and contradicted himself by taking a fifteen-foot spring straight at the ape-man, knocking him down again. The battle was on.

As against the white ape, Tarzan realized that he was fighting for his life—and perhaps against a less reasonable opponent. John Carter was a peerlessly brave man, and he came at the ape-man with a fury that had only partly to do with Tarzan himself and more to do with a lost war in which Tarzan had taken no part. Forced onto the defensive from the start of the combat, the ape-man warded off blow after blow as best he could, enduring as much punishment as he had ever taken in his youth from Bolgani or Kerchak. Dazed, semiconscious, he kept John Carter's hands from closing forever on his throat only by butting his head desperately into the Virginian's face, or doubling his legs to push him away, like Sheeta the leopard eviscerating a foe. He was vaguely aware of a growing crowd of noisy Tharks, as always happy to see someone, anyone, being beaten. He could not see Dejah Thoris anywhere.

Slowly, however, the battle began to turn. John Carter was a splendid fighter under any circumstances, as he had proven on two planets; but most of his victories over Martians had been achieved with the aid of weapons, low gravity, and the fact that Tharks are less muscular than they appear, and far less quick than a reasonably fit human. Tarzan hit him from all sides and all angles, employing, besides his mighty, jungle-trained fists, his mighty elbows and knees, and the mighty top of his head. But for all the battering, for all the blood, John Carter would not go down, nor would he surrender, not even when the ape-man stood back, holding up his open hands, whispering as the Virginian ambled blindly toward him, "Please . . . please fall, please stop. . . ." John Carter was still coming on at the end, muttering to himself . . . sinking to one knee . . . rising again . . . surely about to fall face forward at last at Tarzan's feet. . . .

It was then that Dejah Thoris picked up the Martian pistol and hit Tarzan over the head with it.

The ape-man went down without a sound. Dejah Thoris looked at the two fallen men, glanced at the grinning, cheering Tharks with utter contempt, quickly bent and kissed the ape-man's cheek, and then turned her attention to her fallen husband. She did not look back at Tarzan again.

The Lord of the Jungle smelled Africa before he opened his eyes. He was draped, highly uncomfortably, over the crotch of a tree, like the remains of a leopard's meal, which was exactly the way he felt. His skull thundered, his lower lip was split, and his entire body felt as bewildered as his head. Yet he was grateful for the pain, because it proved everything that had happened to him was real, and he could not have borne to have dreamed Dejah Thoris. He smiled slightly at the memory, then winced as his lip started bleeding again.

Now, did she kill me to protect him? Am I dead on Mars—Barsoom—and alive on Earth? Is this my astral body, or is that one still . . . and does she think of me sometimes . . . and what will happen to my relatives up there, the white apes—can they ever be safe? And does she ever think of me?

At last he simply lay back again on the branch and looked up through the softly shivering leaves at the stars.

THE BRIDGE PARTNER

I don't play bridge, and I don't know anything more about the game than I needed to know for this story, which is not a fantasy in any classic sense of the word. All I can really say about it is that I'd been reading a lot of Patricia Highsmith's work at the time, and Highsmith is one of those people who will sometimes stir depths you'd generally prefer not to have stirred. Since writing it, I've always seen "The Bridge Partner" in my head as a *nouvelle vague* movie by Truffaut or Resnais, or perhaps Claude Chabrol. Black-and-white, of course. Definitely black-and-white.

I WILL KILL YOU.

The words were not spoken aloud, but silently mouthed across the card table at Mattie Whalen by her new partner, whose last name she had not quite caught when they were introduced. Olivia *Korhanen* or *Korhonen*, it was, something like that. She was blonde and fortyish—Mattie was bad with ages, but the woman had to be somewhere near her own—and had joined the Moss Harbor Bridge Group only a few weeks earlier. The members had chosen at the very beginning to call themselves a group, rather than a Club. As Eileen Berry, one of the two founders, along with Suzanne Grimes, had said at the time, "There's an exclusivity thing about a club—a snobby, elitish sort of taste, if you know what I mean. A group just *feels* more democratic." Everyone had agreed with Eileen, as people generally did.

Which accounted, Mattie thought, for the brisk acceptance of the woman now sitting across from her, despite her odd name and unclassifiably foreign air. Mattie could detect only the faintest accent in her voice, and if her clothes plainly did not come from the discount outlet in the local mall, neither were they so aggressively chic as to offend or threaten. She had clear, pleasant blue eyes, excellent teeth, the delicately tanned skin of a tennis player—as opposed to a leathery beach bunny or an orange-hued tanning-bed veteran—and was pleasant to everyone in a gently impersonal manner. Her playing style showed not only skill, but grace, which Mattie noticed perhaps more poignantly than any other member of the Bridge Group, since the best that could have been said for Mattie was that she mostly managed to keep track of the trumps and the tricks. Still, she knew grace when she saw it.

I will kill you.

It made no possible sense—she must surely have misread both the somewhat long, quizzical lips and the intention in the bright eyes. No one else seemed to have heard or noticed anything at all unusual, and she really hadn't played the last hand as badly as all that. Granted, doubling Rosemarie's bid could be considered a mistake, but people make mistakes, and she *could* have pulled it off if Olivia Korhonen, or whoever, had held more than the one single miserable trump to back her up. You don't *kill* somebody for doubling, or even threaten to kill them. Mattie smiled earnestly at her partner, and studied her cards.

The rubber ended in total disaster, and Mattie apologized at some length to Olivia Korhonen afterward. "I'm not really a good player, I know that, but I'm not usually that awful, I promise. And now you'll probably never want to play with me ever again, and I wouldn't blame you." Mattie had had a deal of practice at apologizing, over the years.

To her pleasant surprise, Olivia Korhonen patted her arm reassuringly and shook her head. "I enjoyed the game greatly, even though we lost. I have not played in a long time, and you will have to make allowances until I start to catch up. We'll beat them next time, in spite of me."

She patted Mattie again and turned elegantly away. But as she did so, the side of her mouth repeated, clearly but inaudibly—Mattie could not have been mistaken this time—"*I will kill you.*" Then the woman was gone, and Mattie sat down in the nearest folding chair.

Her friend Virginia Schlossberg hurried over with a cup of tea, asking anxiously, "Are you all right? What is it? You look absolutely *ashen!*" She touched Mattie's cheek, and almost recoiled. "And you're *freezing!* Go home and get into bed, and call a doctor! I *mean* it—you go home right now!" Virginia was a kind woman, but excitable. She had been the same when Mattie and she were in dancing school together.

"I'm all right," Mattie said. "I am, Ginny, honestly." But her voice was shaking as much as her hands, and she made her escape from the Group as soon as she could trust her legs to support her. She was grateful on two counts: first, that no one sat next to her on the bus; and, secondly, that Don would most likely not be home yet from the golf course. She did not look forward to Don just now.

Rather than taking to her bed, despite Virginia's advice, she made herself a healthy G&T and sat in the kitchen with the lights on, going over and over everything she knew of Olivia Korhonen. The woman was apparently single or widowed, like most of the members of the Moss Harbor Bridge Group, but judging by the reactions of the few men in the Group, she gave no indication of being on the prowl. Seemingly un-employed, and rather young for retirement, still she lived in one of the pricey new condos just two blocks from the harbor. No Bridge Group member had yet seen her apartment except for Suzanne and Eileen, who reported back that it was smart and trendy, "without being too off-puttingly posh." Eileen thought the paintings were originals, but Suzanne had her doubts.

What else, *what else?* She had looked up "Korhonen" on the Internet, and found that it was a common Finnish name—not Jewish, as she had supposed. To her knowledge, she had never met a Finnish person in her life. Were they like Swedes? Danes, even? She had a couple of Danish acquaintances, a husband and wife named Olsen . . . no, they were nothing at all like the Korhonen woman; one could never imag-ine either Olsen saying *I will kill you* to so much as a cockroach, which, of course, they wouldn't ever have in the house. But then, who *would* say such a thing to a near-stranger? And over a silly card game? It made no sense, none of it made any sense. She mixed another G&T and was surprised to find herself wanting Don home.

Don's day, it turned out, had been a bad one. Trounced on the course, beaten more badly in the rematch he had immediately demanded, he had consoled himself liberally in the clubhouse; and, as a consequence, was clearly not in any sort of mood to hear about a mumbled threat at a bridge game. On the whole, after sixteen years of marriage, Mattie liked Don more than she disliked him, but such distinctions were essentially meaningless at this stage of things. She rather appreciated his presence when she felt especially lonely and frightened, but a large, furry dog would have done as well; indeed, a dog would have been at once more comforting and more concerned for her comfort. Dogs wanted their masters to be happy—Don simply preferred her uncomplaining.

When she told him about Olivia Korhonen's behavior at the Bridge Group, he seemed hardly to hear her. In his usual style of picking up in the middle of the intended sentence, he mumbled, " . . . take that damn game so damn seriously. Bud and I don't go yelling we're going to kill each other"—Bud Gorko was his steady golf partner—"and believe you me, I've got reason sometimes." He snatched a beer out of the refrigerator and wandered into the living room to watch TV.

Mattie followed him in, the second G&T strengthening a rare resolve to make him take her seriously. She said, "She did it twice. You didn't see her face." She raised her voice to carry over the yammering of a commercial. "She *meant* it, Don. I'm telling you, she *meant* it."

Don smiled muzzily and patted the sofa seat beside him. "Hear you, I'm right on it. Tell you what—she goes ahead and does that, I'm going to take a really dim view. A dim view." He liked the phrase. "Really dim view."

"You're dim enough already," Mattie said. Don did not respond. She stood watching him for a few minutes without speaking, because she knew it made him uncomfortable. When he got to the stage of demanding, "What? What?" she walked out of the room and into the guest bedroom, where she lay down. She had been sleeping there frequently enough in recent months that it felt increasingly like her own.

She had thought she would surely dream of Olivia Korhonen, but it was only in the sweet spot between consciousness and sleep that the woman's face came to her: the long mouth curling almost affectionately, almost seductively, as though for a kiss, caressing the words that Mattie could not hear. It was an oddly tranquil, even soothing vision, and Mattie fell asleep like a child, and did not dream at all.

The next morning she felt curiously young and hopeful, though she could not imagine why. Don had gone off to work at the real-estate office with his normal Monday hangover, pitifully savage; but Mattie indulged herself with a long hot shower, a second toasted English muffin and a long telephone chat with a much-relieved Virginia Schlossberg before she went to the grocery store. There would be an overdue hair appointment after that, then home in time for Oprah. A *good* day.

The sense of serenity lasted through the morning shopping, through her favorite tea-and-brioche snack at *La Place*, and on to her date with Mr. Philip at the salon. It ended abruptly while she was more than half-drowsing under the dryer, trying to focus on *Vanity Fair*, as well as on the buttery jazz on the P.A. system, when Olivia Korhonen's equally pleasant voice separated itself from the music, saying, "Mrs. Whalen— Mattie? How nice to see you here, partner." The last word flicked across Mattie's skin like a brand.

Olivia Korhonen was standing directly in front of her, smiling in her familiar guileless manner. She had clearly just finished her appointment: the glinting warmth and shine of her blonde hair made that plain, and made Mattie absurdly envious, her own mouse-brown curls' only distinction being their comb-snapping thickness. Olivia Korhonen said, "Shall we play next week? I look forward so."

"Yes," Mattie said faintly; and then, "I mean, I'm not sure—I have things. To do. Maybe." Her voice squeaked and slipped. She couldn't stop it, and in that moment she hated her voice more than she had ever hated anything in the world.

"Oh, but you must be there! I do not know anyone else to play with."
Mattie noticed a small dimple to the left of Olivia Korhonen's mouth
when she smiled in a certain way. "I mean, no one else who will put up
with my bad playing, as you do. Please?"

Mattie found herself nodding, just to keep from having to speak
again—and also, to some degree, because of the genuine urgency in Olivia Korhonen's voice. *Maybe I imagined the whole business . . . maybe it's
me getting old and scared, the way people do.* She nodded a second time,
with somewhat more enthusiasm.

Olivia Korhonen patted her knee through the protective salon apron,
plainly relieved. "Oh, good. I already feel so much better." Then, without
changing her expression in the least, she whispered, *"I will kill you."*

Mattie thought later that she must have fainted in some way; at all
events, her next awareness was of Mr. Philip taking the curlers out of
her hair and brushing her off. Olivia Korhonen was gone. Mr. Philip
peered at her, asking, "Who's been keeping *you* up at night, darling? You
never fall asleep under these things." Then he saw her expression, and
asked "Are you okay?"

"I'm fine," Mattie said. "I'm fine."

After that, it seemed to her that she saw Olivia Korhonen everywhere, every day. She was coming out of the dry cleaner's as Mattie
brought an armload of Don's pants in; she hurried across the street
to direct Mattie as she was parking her car; she asked Mattie's advice
buying produce at the farmers' market, or broke off a conversation
with someone else to chat with Mattie on the street. And each time,
before they parted, would come the silent words, more menacing for
being inaudible, *"I will kill you."* The dimple beside the long smile always showed as she spoke.

Mattie had never felt so lonely in her life. Despite all the years
she and Don had lived in Moss Harbor, there was no one in her local
circle whom she could trust in any sort of intimate crisis, let alone
with something like a death threat. Suzanne or Eileen? Out of the
question—things like that simply did not happen to members of the

Bridge Group. There was Virginia, of course . . . Virginia might very well believe her, if anyone did, but would be bound to fall apart under the burden of such knowledge. That left only going further afield and contacting Patricia.

Pat Gallagher lived directly across the Bay, in a tiny incorporated area called Witness Point. Mattie had known her very nearly as long as she had known Virginia, but the relationships could not have been more different. Pat was gay, for one thing; and while Mattie voted for every same-sex-marriage and hate-crimes proposition that came up on any ballot, she was honest enough to know that she was ill at ease with homosexuals. She could never explain this, and was truly ashamed of it, especially around someone as intelligent and thoughtful as Pat Gallagher. She found balance in distance, only seeing Pat two or three times a year, at most, and sometimes no more than once. They did email a reasonable amount though, and they talked on the phone enough that Mattie still knew the number by heart. She called it now.

They arranged to meet at Pat's house for lunch on the weekend. She lived in a shingly, flowery, cluttery cottage, in company with a black woman named Babs, an administrator at the same hospital where Pat was a nurse. Mattie liked Babs immediately, and was therefore doubly nervous around her, and doubly shamed, especially when Babs offered in so many words to disappear graciously, so that she and Pat could talk in private. Mattie would have much preferred this, but the very sugges-tion made it impossible. "I'm sure there's nothing I have to say to Patricia that I couldn't say to you."

Babs laughed. "That you may come to regret, my dear." But she set out second glasses of Pinot Grigio, and second bowls of Pat's mine-strone, and sat down with them. Her dark-brown skin and soft curly hair contrasted so perfectly with Pat's freckled Irish pinkness, and they seemed so much at ease with one another that Mattie felt a quick, startling stitch of what could only have been envy.

"Okay," Pat said. "Talk. What's got you scared this time?"

Babs chuckled. "Cuts straight to the chase, doesn't she?"

265

Mattie bridled feebly. "You make it sound as though I'm a big fraidy-cat, always frightened about something. I'm not like that."

"Yes, you are." The affection in Pat's wide grin took some of the sting from the words. "You never call me unless something's really got you spooked, do you realize that? Might be a thing you saw on the news, a hooha with your husband, a pain somewhere there shouldn't be a pain. Maybe a lump you're worried about—maybe just a scary dream." She put her hand on Mattie's hand. "It's fine, it's you. Talk. Tell."

She and Babs remained absolutely silent while Mattie told them about the Bridge Group, and about Olivia Korhonen. She was aware that she was speaking faster as the account progressed, and that her voice was rising in pitch, but all she wanted was to get the words out as quickly as she could. The words seemed strangely reluctant to be spoken: more and more, they raked at her throat and palate as she struggled to rid herself of them. When she was done, the roof of her mouth felt almost burned, and she gratefully accepted a glass of cold apple juice from Babs.

"Well," Pat said finally. "I don't know what I expected to hear from you, but *that* was definitely not it. Not hardly."

Babs said grimly, "What you have there is a genuine, certified stalker. I'd call the cops on her in a hot minute."

"How can she do that?" Pat objected. "The woman hasn't *done* anything! No witnesses, not one other person who heard what she said—what she keeps on saying. They'd laugh in Mattie's face, if they didn't do worse."

"It does sound such a *silly* story," Mattie said wretchedly. "Like a paranoiac, somebody with a persecution complex. But it's true, I'm not making it up. That's just exactly the way it's been happening."

Pat nodded. "I believe you. And so would a jury, if it ever came to that. Anyone who spends ten minutes around you knows right away that you haven't the first clue about lying." She sighed, refilling Babs' glass and her own, but not Mattie's. "Not you—you have to drive. And we wouldn't want to frustrate little Ms. What's-her-face, now would we?"

"That's not funny," Babs interrupted sharply. "That's not a bit funny, Patricia."

Pat apologized promptly and profusely, but Mattie was absurdly delighted. "You call her Patricia, too! I thought *I* was the only one."

"Only way to get her attention sometimes." Babs continued to glower at an extremely penitent Pat. "But she's right about the one thing, anyway. Even if the cops happened to believe you, they couldn't do a damn thing about it. Couldn't slap a restraining order on the lady, couldn't order her to stay X-number of feet away from you. Not until . . ." She shrugged heavily, and did not finish the sentence.

"I know," Mattie said. "I wasn't expecting you two to . . . fix things. Be my bodyguards, or something. But I do feel a bit better, talking to you."

"Now, if you were in the hospital"—Babs grinned suddenly and wickedly—"we really *could* bodyguard you. Between old Patricia and me, nobody'd get near you, except for the surfers we'd be smuggling in to you at night. You ought to think about it, Mattie. Safe *and* fun, both."

Mattie was still giggling over this image, and a couple of others, when they walked her out to her car. As she buckled her seatbelt, Pat put a hand on her shoulder, saying quietly, "As long as this goes on every day, you call every day. Got that?"

"Yes, Mama," Mattie answered. "And I'll send my laundry home every week, I promise."

The hand on her shoulder tightened, and Pat shook her a little more than slightly. "I mean it. If we don't hear, we'll come down there."

"Big bad bulldykes on the rampage," Babs chimed in from behind Pat. "*Not* pretty."

It was true that she did feel better driving home: not at all drunk, just pleasantly askew, easier and more rested from the warmth of company than she had been in a long time. That lasted all the way to Moss Harbor, and almost to her front door. The *almost* part came when, parking the car at the curb, she heard a horn honk twice, and looked up in time to see an arm waving cheerfully back to her as Olivia Korhonen's bright little Prius rounded a corner. Mattie sat in her car for a long time before she turned off the engine and got out.

Is she watching my house? Was she waiting for me?

She did not call Pat and Babs that night, even though she lay awake until nearly morning. Then, with Don gone to work, she forced herself to eat breakfast, and called Suzanne for Olivia Korhonen's home telephone number. Once she had it in hand, she stalled over a third cup of coffee, and then a fourth, before she finally dialed the number and waited through several rings, consciously hoping to hear the answering machine click on. But nothing happened. She was about to break the connection, when she heard the receiver being picked up, and Ms. Korhonen's cool, unmistakable voice said, "Yes? Who is this, please?"

Mattie drew a breath. "It's Mattie Whalen. From the Bridge Group, you remember?"

If she has the gall to even hesitate, stalking me every single day . . . But the voice immediately lifted with delight. "Yes, Mattie, of course I remember, how not? How good to hear from you." There was nothing in words or tone to suggest anything but pleasure at the call.

"I was wondering," Mattie began—then hesitated, listening to Olivia Korhonen's breathing. She said, "I thought perhaps we might get together—maybe one day this week?"

"To practice our bridge game?" Somewhat to Mattie's surprise, Olivia Korhonen pounced on the suggestion. "Oh, yes. That would be an excellent idea. We could develop our own strategies—that is what the great players work on all the time, is it not? Excellent, excellent, Mattie!" They arranged to meet at noon, two days from that date, at Olivia Korhonen's condo apartment. She wanted to make cucumber sandwiches—"in the English style, I will cut the crusts off"—but Mattie talked her out of that, or thought she had. In her imagining of what she planned to say to Olivia Korhonen, there would be no room for food.

On the appointed day Mattie woke up in a cold sweat. She considered whether she might be providentially coming down with some sort of flu, but decided she wasn't; then made herself a hot toddy in case she was, ate Grape-Nuts and yogurt for breakfast, went back to bed in pursuit of another hour's nap, failed miserably, got up, showered, dressed, and watched Oprah until it was time to go. She made another hot toddy while she waited, on the off-chance that the flu might be waiting too.

The third-floor condo apartment turned out as tastefully dressy as Eileen and Suzanne had reported. Olivia Korhonen was at the door, smilingly eager to show her around. The rooms were high and airy, with indeed a good many paintings and prints, of which Mattie was no judge—they *looked* like originals—and a rather surprising paucity of furniture, as though Olivia Korhonen had not been planning for long-term residence. When Mattie commented on this, the blonde woman only twinkled at her, saying, "The motto of my family is that one should always sink deep roots wherever one lives. Because roots can always be sold, do you see?" Later on, considering this, Mattie was not entirely certain what bearing it had on her question; but it sounded both sensible and witty at the time, in Olivia Korhonen's musical voice.

Nevertheless, when Olivia Korhonen announced, "Now, strategy!" and brought out both the cards and the cucumber sandwiches, Mattie held firm. She said, "Olivia, I didn't come to talk about playing cards."

Olivia Korhonen was clearly on her guard in an instant, though her tone remained light. She set the tray of sandwiches down and said slowly, "Ah? Ulterior motives? Then you had probably better reveal them now, don't you think so?" She stood with her head tipped slightly sideways, like an inquisitive bird.

Mattie's heart was beating annoyingly fast, and she was very thirsty. She said, "You are stalking me, Olivia. I don't know why. You are following me everywhere . . . and that *thing* you say every single time we meet." Olivia Korhonen did not reply, nor change her expression. Mattie said, "Nobody else hears you, but I do. You whisper it—*I will kill you.* I hear you."

Sleepless, playing variations on the scene over and over in her head the night before, she had expected anything from outrage and accusation to utter bewilderment to tearful, fervent denial. What happened instead was nothing she could have conceived of: Olivia Korhonen clapped her hands and began to laugh.

Her laughter was like cold silver bells, chiming a fraction out of tune, their dainty discordance more jarring than any rusty clanking could have been. Olivia Korhonen said, "Oh, I did wonder if you would ever let yourself understand me. You are such a . . . such a *timorous* woman, you know, Mattie Whalen—frightened of so very much, it is a wonder that you can ever peep out of your house, your little hole in the baseboard. Eyes flicking everywhere, whiskers twitching so frantically . . ." She broke off into a bubbling fit of giggles, while Mattie stared and stared, remembering girls in school hallways who had snickered just so.

"Oh, yes," Olivia Korhonen said. "Yes, Mattie, I will kill you—be very sure of that. But not yet." She clasped her hands together at her breast and bowed her head slightly, smiling. "Not just yet."

"*Why?* Why do you want . . . what have I ever, *ever* done to you?"

The smile warmed and widened, but Olivia Korhonen was some time answering. When she did, the words came slowly, thoughtfully. "Mattie, where I come from we have a great many sheep, they are one of Finland's major products. And where you have sheep, of course, you must have dogs. Oh, we do have many wonderful dogs—you should see them handle and guide and work the sheep. You would be so fascinated, I know you would."

Her cheeks had actually turned a bit pink with what seemed like earnest enthusiasm. She said, "But Mattie, dear, it is a curious thing about sheep and dogs. Sometimes stray dogs break into a sheepfold, and then they begin to kill." She did not emphasize the word, but it struck Mattie like a physical blow under the heart. Olivia Korhonen went on. "They are not killing to eat, out of hunger—no, they are simply killing blindly, madly, they will wipe out a whole flock of sheep in a night, and then run on home to their masters and their dog biscuits. Do you understand me so far, Mattie?"

Mattie's body was so rigid that she could not even nod her head. Olivia's softly chiming voice continued, "It is as though these good family dogs have gone temporarily insane. Animal doctors, veterinarians, they think now that the pure *passivity*, the purebred *stupidity* of the sheep somehow triggers—is that the right word, Mattie? I mean it like *to set off*—somehow triggers something in the dog's brain, something very old. The sheep are blundering around in the pen, bleating in panic, too stupid to protect themselves, and it is all just too much for the dogs—even for sheepdogs sometimes. They simply go mad." She spread her hands now, leaning forward, graceful as ever. "Do you see now, Mattie? I do hope you begin to see."

"No." The one word was all Mattie could force out between freezing lips. "No."

"You are my sheep," Olivia Korhonen said. "And I am like the dogs. You are a born victim, like all sheep, and it is your mere presence that makes you irresistible to me. Of course, dogs are dogs—they cannot ever wait to kill. But I can. I like to wait."

Mattie could not move. Olivia Korhonen stepped back, looked at

271

her wristwatch and made a light gesture toward the door, as though freeing Mattie from a spell. "Now you had better run along home, dear, for I have company coming. We will practice our strategy for the Bridge Group another time."

Mattie sat in her car for a long time, hands trembling, before she felt able even to turn the key in the ignition. She had no memory of driving home, except a vague awareness of impatient honking behind her when she lingered at intersections after the traffic light had changed. When she arrived home she sat by the telephone with her fingers on the keypad, trying to make herself dial Pat Gallagher's number. After a time, she began to cry.

She did call that evening, by which time a curious calm, unlike any other she had ever felt, had settled over her. This may have been because by then she was extremely drunk, having entered the stage of slow but very precise speech, and a certain deliberate, unhurried rationality that she never seemed able to attain sober. Both Pat and Babs immediately offered to come and stay with her, but Mattie declined with thanks. "Not much point to it. She said she'd wait . . . said she *liked* waiting." Her voice sounded strange in her own ears, and oddly new. "You can't bodyguard me forever. I guess *I* have to bodyguard me. I guess I just have to."

When she hung up—only after her friends had renewed their insistence that she call daily, on pain of home invasion—she did not drink any more, but sat motionless by the phone, waiting for Don's return. It was his weekly staff-meeting night, and she knew he would be late, but she felt like sitting just where she was. *If I never moved again, she'd have to come over here to kill me. And the neighbors would see.* The phone rang once, but she did not answer.

Don came home in, for him, a cheerful mood, having been informed that his supervisor at the agency, whom he loathed, was being transferred to another branch. He had every expectation of a swift promotion. Mattie—or someone in Mattie's body, shaping words with her still-cold lips—congratulated him, and even opened a celebratory bottle of champagne, though she drank none of her glass. Don began calling his friends to spread the news, and Mattie went into the kitchen to start a pot roast. The steamed fish with greens and polenta revolution had passed Don quietly by.

The act of cooking soothed her nerves, as it had always done; but the coldness of her skin seemed to have spread to her mind—which was not, when considered, a bad thing at all. There was a peculiar clarity to her thoughts now: both her options and her fears seemed so sharply defined that she felt as though she were traveling on an airplane that had just broken out of clouds into sunlight. *I live in clouds. I always have.*

Fork in one of his hands, cordless in the other, Don devoured two helpings of the roast and praised it in between calls. Mattie, nibbling for appearances' sake, made no attempt to interrupt; but when he finally put the phone down for a moment she remarked, "That woman at the Bridge Group? The one who said she was going to kill me?"

Don looked up, the wariness in his eyes unmistakable. "Yeah?"

"She means it. She really means to kill me." Mattie had been saying the words over and over to herself all afternoon; by now they came out briskly, almost casually. She said, "We discussed it for some time."

Don uttered a cholesterol-saturated sigh. "Damn, ever since you started with that bridge club, feels like I'm running a daycare center. Look, this is middle-school bullshit, you know it and she knows it. Just tell her, enough with the bullshit, it's getting real old. Or find yourself another partner, probably the best thing." He had the cordless phone in his hand again.

The strange, distant Mattie said softly, "I'm just telling you."

"And I'm telling you, get another partner. Silly shit, she's not about to kill anybody." He wandered off into the living room, dialing.

Mattie stood in the kitchen doorway, looking after him. She said—clearly enough for him to have heard, if he hadn't already been talking on the phone—"No, she's not." She liked the sound of it, and said it again. "She's not." Then she went straight off to bed, read a bit of

Chicken Soup for the Soul, and fell quickly asleep. She dreamed that Olivia Korhonen was leaning over her in bed, smiling widely and eagerly. There were little teeth on her tongue and small, triangular teeth fringing her lips.

Mattie got to the Bridge Group early the next afternoon, and waited, with impatience that surprised her, for Olivia Korhonen to arrive. The Group met in a community building within sight of the Moss Harbor wharf, its windows fronting directly on the parking lot. Mattie was already holding the door open when Olivia Korhonen crossed the lot.

Did she look even a little startled—the least bit taken aback by her prey's eager welcome? Mattie hoped so. She said brightly, "I was afraid you might not be coming today."

"And I thought that perhaps *you* . . ." Olivia Korhonen very deliberately let the sentence trail away. If she had been at all puzzled, she gathered herself as smoothly as a cat landing on its feet. "I am glad to see you, Mattie. I had some foolish idea that you might be, perhaps, ill?"

"Not a bit—not when we need to work on our strategy." Mattie touched her elbow, easing her toward the table where Jeannie Atkinson and old Joe Booker were both beckoning. "You know we need to do that." It was a physical effort to make herself smile into Olivia Korhonen's blue eyes, but she managed.

Playing worse than even she ever had, with foolish bids, rash declarations of trumps, scoring errors, and complete mismanagement of her partner's hand when Olivia Korhonen was dummy, she worked with desperate concentration—manifesting as lightheaded carelessness—on upsetting the woman's balance, her judgment of the situation. How well she succeeded, and to what end, she could not have said; but when Olivia Korhonen mouthed *I will kill you* once again at her as she was dealing a final rubber, she fought down the icepick stab of terror and gaily said, "*Ah-ah*, we mustn't signal each other—against the rules, bad, bad." Jeannie and Joe raised their eyebrows, and Olivia Korhonen, very briefly, *almost* looked embarrassed.

She left hurriedly, directly after the game. Mattie followed her out, blithely apologizing left and right, as always, for her poor play. At the car, Olivia Korhonen turned to say, evenly and without expression, "You are not spoiling the game for me. This is childish, all this that you are playing at. It means nothing."

Mattie felt her mouth drying, and her heart beginning to pound. But she said, keeping her voice as calm as she could, "Not everybody gets to know how and when they're going to die. If you're really going to kill me, you don't get to tell me how to behave." Olivia Korhonen did not reply, but got into her car and drove away, and Mattie walked back to the Bridge Group for tea and cookies.

"One for the sheep," Pat said on the phone that night. "You crossed her up—she figured you'd be running around in the pen, all crazy with fear, bleating and blatting and wetting yourself. The fun part. And instead you came right to her and practically spit in her eye. I'll bet she's thinking about that one right now."

On the extension, Babs said flatly, "Yes, she sure as hell is. And *I'm* thinking that she won't make that mistake again. She's regrouping, is what it is—she'll be coming from another place next time, another angle. Don't take her lightly, the way she took you. Nothing's changed."

"I know that." Mattie's voice, like her hands, was unsteady. "I wish I could say *I've* changed, but I haven't, not at all. I'm the same fraidy-cat I always was, but maybe I'm covering it a little better, I don't know. All I know is I just want to hide under the bed and cover up my head."

Pat said slowly, "I was raised in the country. A sheep-killing dog doesn't go for it just once. This woman has killed before."

Babs said, "Get in close. You snuggle up to her, you tail her around like she's been tailing you. That's not part of the game, she won't like that at all. You keep *coming* at her."

Pat said, "And you keep calling us. Every day."

It took practice. All her instincts told her to turn and run the moment she recognized the elegant figure on the street corner ahead of her, or heard the too-friendly voice at her elbow. But gradually she learned not only to force herself to respond with equal affability, but to become the one accosting, waving, calling out—even issuing impromptu invitations to join her for tea or coffee. These were never accepted, and the act of proposing them always left her feeling dizzy and sick; but she continued doggedly to "snuggle up" to Olivia Korhonen at every opportunity. Frightened and alone, still she kept coming.

She had the first inkling that the change in her behavior might be having some effect when Eileen mentioned that Olivia Korhonen had diffidently sounded her out about being partnered with a more skilled player for the Group's upcoming tournament. Eileen had explained that the teams had already been registered, and that in any case none of them would have taken kindly to being broken up and reassigned. Olivia Korhonen hadn't raised the subject again, but Eileen had thought Mattie would want to know. Eileen always told people the things she thought they would want to know.

For her part, Mattie continued to make a point of chattering buoyantly at the bridge table as she misplayed one hand after another; then apologizing endlessly as she trampled through another rubber, leaving ruin in her wake. She announced, laughing, after one particularly disastrous no-trump contract, "I wouldn't blame Olivia if she wanted to strangle me right now. I'd have it coming!" Their opponents looked embarrassed, and Olivia Korhonen smiled and smoothed her hair.

But once, when they were in the ladies' room together, she met Mattie's eyes in the mirror and said, "I will still kill you. Could you hand me the tissues, please?" Mattie did so. Olivia Korhonen blotted her lipstick and went on, "You are not nearly so bad a player as you pretend, and you have not turned impudently fearless overnight. Little sheep, you are as just as much afraid of me as you ever were. Tell me this is not true."

She turned then, taking a single step toward Mattie, who recoiled in spite of her determination not to. Olivia Korhonen did not smile in triumph, but yawned daintily and deliberately, like a cat. "Never mind, dear Mattie. It is almost over." She started for the restroom door.

"You are not going to kill me," Mattie said, as she had said once before in her own kitchen. "You've killed before, but you are not going to kill me." Olivia Korhonen did not bother to look back or answer, and a sudden burst of white rage seared through Mattie like fever. She took hold of Olivia Korhonen's left arm and swung her around to face her, savoring the surprise and momentary confusion in the blue eyes. She said, "I will not let you kill me. Do you understand? I will not let you."

Olivia Korhonen did not move in her grip. Mattie finally let her go, actually stumbling back and having to catch herself. Olivia Korhonen said again, "It is almost over. Come, we will go and play that other game."

That night Mattie could not sleep. Even after midnight, she felt almost painfully wide awake, unable to imagine ever needing to sleep again. Don had been snoring for two hours when she dressed, went to her car, and drove to the condominium where Olivia Korhonen lived. A light was still on in the living-room window of her apartment, and Mattie, parked across the street, could clearly make out the figure of the blonde woman moving restlessly back and forth, as though she shared her observer's restlessness. The light went out presently, but Mattie did not drive home for some while.

She did the same thing the next night, and for several nights thereafter, establishing a pattern of leaving the house when Don was asleep and returning before he woke. On occasion it became a surprisingly close call, since whether the light stayed on late or was already out when she reached the condo, she often lost track of time for hours, staring at a dark, empty window. She continued to check in regularly with Pat and Babs in Witness Point; but she never told them about her new night-time routine, though she could not have said why, anymore than she could have explained the compulsion itself. There was a mindless peacefulness in her vigil over her would-be murderer that made no sense, and comforted her.

From time to time, Olivia Korhonen came to stand at her window and look out at the dark street. Mattie, deliberately parking in the same space every night, fully expected to be recognized and challenged; but the latter, at least, never happened.

She took as well to following Olivia Korhonen through Moss Harbor traffic, whenever she happened to spot the gleaming Prius on the road. In an elusive, nebulous way, she was perfectly aware that she was putting herself as much at the service of an obsession as Olivia Korhonen, but this seemed to have no connection with her own life or behavior. She could not have cared less where the Prius might be headed—most often up or down the coast, plainly to larger towns—or whether or not she was visible in the rear-view mirror. The whole point, if there was such a thing, was to bait her bridge partner into doing something foolish, even coming to kill her before she was quite ready. Mattie had no idea what Olivia Korhonen's schedule or program in these matters might be, nor what she would do about it; only that whatever was moving in her would be present when the time came.

When it did come, on a moonless midnight, she was parked in her usual spot, directly across the street from the condominium. She was in the process of leaving a message on Pat and Babs' answering machine—"Just letting you know I'm fine, haven't seen her today, I'm about to go to bed"—when Olivia Korhonen came out of the building, strode across the street directly toward her, and pulled the unlocked car door open. She said, not raising her voice, "Walk with me, Mattie Whalen."

Mattie said into the cell phone, as quietly as she, "I'll call you tomorrow. Don't worry about me." She hung up then, and got out of the car. She said, "The people I was talking with heard your voice."

Olivia Korhonen did not answer. She took light but firm hold of Mattie's arm and they walked silently together toward the beach, beyond which lay the dark sparkle of the ocean. The sky was pale and clear as glass. Mattie saw no one on the sand, nor on the short street, except for a lone dog trotting self-importantly past them. Olivia Korhonen was humming to herself, at the farthest rim of Mattie's hearing.

Reaching the shore, they both took their shoes off and left them neatly side by side. The sand was cold and hard packed under Mattie's feet, this far from the water, and she thought regretfully about how little time she had spent on the beach, for all the years of living half a mile away. Something splashed in the gentle surf, but all she saw was a small swirl of foam.

Olivia Korhonen said reflectively, as though talking to herself, "I must say, this is a pity—I will be a little sorry. You have been . . . entertaining."

"How nice of you to say so." Mattie's own odd calmness frightened her more than the woman who meant to kill her. She asked, "Weren't any of your other victims entertaining?"

"Not really, no. One can never expect that—human beings are not exactly sheep, after all, for all the similarities. Things become so *hasty* at the end, so hurried and awkward and tedious—it can be very dissatisfying, if you understand me." She was no longer holding Mattie's arm, but looking into her eyes with something in her own expression that might almost have been a plea.

"I think I do," Mattie said. "I wouldn't have once." They were walking unhurriedly toward the water, and she could see the small surges far out that meant the tide was beginning to turn. She said, "You're more or less human, although I've had a few nasty dreams about you." Olivia Korhonen chuckled very slightly. Mattie said, "You feed on the fear. No, that's not it, not the fear—the *knowledge*. Fear makes people run away, but *knowledge*—the sense that there's absolutely no escape, that you can come and *pick* them, like fruit, whenever you choose—that freezes them, isn't that it? The knowing? And you like that very much."

Olivia Korhonen stopped walking and regarded Mattie without speaking, her blue eyes wider and more intense than Mattie had ever noticed them. She said slowly, "You have changed. I changed you."

Mattie asked, "But what would you have done if I *had* run? That first time, at the Bridge Group, if I had taken you at your word and just packed a bag, jumped in my car and headed for the border? Would you have followed me?"

"It is a long way to the border, you know." The chuckle was deeper and clearer this time. "But it would all have been so messy, really. Ugly, unpleasant. Much better this way."

Mattie was standing very close to her, looking directly into her face. "And the killing? That would have been pleasant?" She found that she was holding her breath, waiting for the answer.

It did not come in words, but in the slow smile that spread from Olivia Korhonen's eyes to her mouth, instead of the other way around. It came in the slight parting of her lips, in the flick of her cat-pink tongue just behind the white, perfect teeth; most of all in the strange way in which her face seemed to change its shape, almost to fold in on itself: the cheekbones heightening, the forehead rounding, the round chin in turn becoming more pointed, as in Mattie's dreams.

. . . and Mattie, who had not struck another person since a recess fight in the third grade, hit Olivia Korhonen in the stomach as hard as she possibly could. The blonde woman coughed and doubled over, her eyes huge with surprise and a kind of reproach. Mattie hit her again—a glancing blow, distinctly weaker, to the neck—and jumped on her, clumsily and impulsively. They went down together, rolling in the sand, the grains raking their skins, clogging their nostrils, coating and filling their mouths. Olivia Korhonen got a near-stranglehold on a coughing, gasping Mattie and began dragging her toward the water's edge. Breathless and in pain, she was still the stronger of the two of them.

The cold water on her bare feet revived Mattie a moment before her head was forced under an incoming wave. Panic lent her strength, and she lunged upward, banging the back of her head into Olivia Korhonen's face, turning in the failing grip and pulling her down with both hands on the back of her neck. There was a moment when they were mouth to mouth, breathing one another's hoarse, choking breath, teeth banging teeth. Then she rolled on top in the surf, throwing all her weight into keeping the struggling woman's bloody face in the water. The little waves helped.

At some point Mattie finally realized that Olivia Korhonen had stopped fighting her; she had a feeling that she had been holding the woman under much longer than she needed to. She stood up, soaked and shivering with both cold and shock, swaying dizzily, looking down at the body that stirred in the light surf, bumping against her feet. There was a bit of seaweed caught in its hair.

In a while, in a vague sort of way, she recognized what it was. Something glinted at the edge of a pocket, and she bent down and withdrew a ring of keys. She walked away up the beach, stopping to slip on her shoes.

She did not go back to her car then, but went straight to the condo and walked up the stairs to the third floor, leaving a thinning trail of water behind her. Entry was easy: she had no difficulty finding the right key to open the doorknob lock, and Olivia Korhonen had been in too much of a hurry to throw the deadbolt. Mattie wiped her shoes carefully, nevertheless, before she went inside.

Walking slowly through the graciously-appointed apartment, she realized that it was larger than she recalled, and that there were rooms that Olivia Korhonen had not shown her. One took particular effort to open, for the door was heavy and somewhat out of alignment. Mattie put a bruised shoulder to it and forced it open.

The room seemed to be a catchall for odd gifts and odder souvenirs—"tourist *tchotchkes*," Virginia Schlossberg would have called them. There were no paintings on the walls, but countless candid snapshots, mostly of women, though they did include a handful of men. Their very number bewildered Mattie, making her eyes ache. She recognized no one at first, and then froze: a photo of herself held conspicuous pride of place on the wall facing her. It had obviously been taken by a cell phone. Below it, thumbtacked to the wall, was a gauzy red scarf that she had lost before Olivia Korhonen had even joined the Moss Harbor Bridge Group. Mattie pulled it free, along with the picture, and put them both in her pocket.

All of the photographs had mementos of some sort attached to them, ranging in size from a ticket stub to a pair of sunglasses or a paper plate with a telephone number scrawled on it in lipstick. None of the subjects appeared to be aware that their pictures were being taken; each had a tiny smiley-face drawn with a fine-tipped ballpoint pen in the lower right corner. An entire section of one wall was devoted to images of a single dark-eyed young woman, taken from closer and closer angles, as though from the viewpoint of a shark circling to strike. These prints were each framed, not in wood or metal, but by variously-colored hair ribbons, all held neatly in place by pushpins of matching hues. The central photo, the largest, was set facing the wall; there were two ribbons set around it, both blue. Mattie took this picture down, turned it around, and studied it for some while.

Hurt, still damp, bedraggled, she was no longer trembling; nor, somehow, was she in the least exhausted. Still cold, yes, but the coldness had come inside; while a curious fervor was warming her face and hands, as though the pictures on the walls were reaching out, welcoming her, knowing her, speaking her name. Still holding the shot of the dark-eyed girl she moved from one new image to the other, feeling with each a kind of fracturing, a growing separation from everything else, until the walls themselves had dimmed around her, and the photos were all mounted on the panelings of her mind. She was aware that there were somehow more there than she could see, more than she could yet take in.

The police will come. They will find the body and find this place. They'll call her the Smiley-Face Killer. The photographs were pressing in around her, each so anxious to be properly savored and understood. Mattie put the dark-eyed victim into her pocket next to her own picture, and reached out with both hands. She did not touch any of the pictures or the keepsakes, but let her fingers drift by them all, one after another, as in a kind of soul-Braille, and felt the myriad pinprick responses swarming her skin, as Olivia Korhonen's souvenirs and trophies joined her. It was not possession of any sort; she was always herself. Never for a moment did she fancy that she was the woman she had killed on the beach, nor did any of this room's hoarded memories overtake and evict her own. It was rather a fostering, a sheltering: a full awareness that there was more than enough room in her not for Olivia Korhonen's life, but for what had given that life its only true meaning. Aloud, alone in that room filled with triumph and pride, she said, "Yes, she's gone. Yes, I'm here. Yes."

She walked out of the room, leaving it open, and did the same with the apartment door rather than pull it shut behind her.

Outside the stars were thin, and there were lights on in some of the neighboring condos. Mattie got in her car, started the engine, and drove home.

As chilled as she still was, as battered and scratched, with her blouse ripped halfway off her shoulder, there was a lightness in her, a sense of invulnerability, that she had never felt in all her life. The car seemed to be flying. With the windows down her damp hair whipped around her face, and she sang all the way home.

Reaching her house, she ran up the steps like an exuberant child, opened the door, and stopped in the hallway. Don was facing her, his face flushed and contorted with a mixture of outrage and bewilderment. His pajama jacket was buttoned wrong, which made him look very young. He said, "Where the fuck? Damn it, where the *fuck?*"

Mattie smiled at him. She loved the feel of the smile; it was like slipping into a beautiful silk dress that she had never been able to afford until just now, this moment. Walking past him, she patted his cheek with more affection than she had felt in a long while. She whispered, hardly moving her lips, "*She killed me,*" and kept on to the bedroom.

VANISHING

With any luck, this is as close as I'll ever come to passing a kidney stone.

The first seeds of "Vanishing" appeared in a story I wrote about 97 times back in the very early '60s, and never managed to sell. Called "The Vanishing Germans," it was an attempt at topical political satire that had all the subtlety of a Demolition Derby. One morning American Lieutenant Ethan Frome, guarding a checkpoint on the Berlin Wall, notices that all of West Germany has been replaced by a vast empty hole in the ground. His Russian counterpart, Captain Boris Godunov, confirms that the very same thing has happened to *East* Germany as well, leaving the Wall itself (and both of them) floating magically in space above an immeasurably deep chasm. The rest of the story contained no explanation for this event, but plenty of speculations; Kennedy and Kruschev both made appearances; and every remaining country in the world wanted the H-Bomb, just in case. Ultimately peace broke out as a direct result of Germany's disappearance, but I couldn't leave well enough alone and slapped on a quasi-science-fictional O. Henry ending that made even less sense than all the words preceding it.

The story was a mess. I wasn't surprised that it didn't sell, even back then, and after I buried the carbons in my filing cabinet I managed to forget they had ever existed.

Forty years later Connor Cochran discovered "The Vanishing Germans" in my files and started bugging me about it. The central visual of the story had seized him and would not let go; so he seized *my* metaphorical lapels and every now and then he'd shake them. *Consider that image,* he'd say. *The floating Wall. What if you took it seriously?*

"Vanishing" went through at least eleven drafts and any number of dodged deadlines, and remains further out of my normal range and comfort zone than any other story in this collection, including "Dirae." It's a ghost story, yes, but it's a lot of other things as well, and I suspect that I'll be rediscovering and relearning it for a long time to come. In the end I'm happy with how it came out, but I'd be almost as happy never to spend another hour of my life studying photographs of Checkpoint Charlie, pouring over architectural diagrams of East German guard towers, or cross-comparing Berlin street maps from 1964 and 2009.

J ANSEN KNEW PERFECTLY WELL that when Arl asked him to drive her to the clinic for her regular prenatal checkup, it meant that every single one of his daughter's usual rides was unavailable. She had already told him that it wouldn't be necessary for him to wait; that Elly, her mother, would be off work by the time the examination was done, and could bring her home. They drove down to Klamath Falls in silence, except for his stiffly phrased questions about the health of the child she was carrying, and the state of her preparations for its arrival. Once he asked when she expected her husband back, but her reply was such a vague mumble that he missed the sense of it completely. Now and then he glanced sideways at her, but when she met his eyes with her own fierce, stubborn brown ones, he looked away.

When they parked at the clinic, he said, "I'll come in with you."

"You don't have to," Arl said. "I told you."

"Yeah, I know what you told me. But it's my grandson in there"—he pointed at her heavily rounded belly—"and I'm entitled to know how he's getting on. Let's go."

Arl did not move. "Dad, I really don't want you in there."

Jansen consciously kept his voice low and casual. "Tell you what, I don't care." He got out of the car, walked around to the passenger side, and opened the door. Arl sat where she was for a moment, giving him the *I just dare you* face he'd known since her childhood; but then she sighed abruptly and pushed herself to her feet, ignoring his offered hand, and plodded ahead of him to the clinic. Jansen followed closely, afraid that she might fall, the walkway being wet with recently melted snow. He would have taken her arm, but he knew better.

VANISHING

This one would rather die than forgive me. Gracie almost has, Elly might— someday—but Arl? Not ever.

In the clinic they sat one chair apart after she signed in. Jansen pretended to be browsing through *Sports Illustrated* until Arl disappeared with the OB/GYN nurse. He lowered the magazine to his lap then, and simply stared straight ahead at the gray world beyond the window. A sticky-faced child, running by, kicked his ankle and kept going, leaving its pursuing mother to apologize; a young couple sitting next to him argued in savagely controlled whispers over the exact responsibility for a sexually transmitted disease. Jansen froze it all out and asked himself for the hundredth useless time why he shouldn't sell the shop—or just close it and leave, the way people were walking away from their own homes these days. Walk away and put some daylight between himself and trouble. Hanging around sure as hell wasn't doing him any good, and alimony checks didn't care whether you mailed them from Dallas or down the block. Neither did Elly and the girls, not so you'd notice. At least in Dallas he could be warm while he was lonely. He let his eyelids drift shut as he tried to imagine being somewhere else, being *someone* else, and failed miserably in the attempt. Eyes closed, all the screwups and disappointments just seemed to press in closer than ever.

Shit, he thought. *All of it, all of it.* And then, *At least the little rugrat quit zooming around. That's something.*

The magazine slid from his relaxed fingers, but he didn't hear it hit the floor, and when he opened his eyes to reach down and pick it up he saw that he wasn't in the waiting room anymore.

He wasn't in Klamath Falls anymore, either. It was night, and he was on the Axel-Springer-Strasse. Instantly alert, he knew where he was, and never thought for a second that he was dreaming. Despite shock, beyond the uncertainties and anxieties of age, he knew that after more than forty-five years he was back at the Wall. The Wall that didn't exist anymore.

Kreuzberg district, West Berlin, between Checkpoint Charlie and the checkpoint at Heinrich-Heine-Strasse, just past where the Zimmerstrasse runs out and the barbed wire and barriers start zigzagging west . . .

There it was, directly before him, just *there*, lit by streetlamps—not the graffiti-covered reinforced concrete of the *Grenzmauer 75* that had been hammered to bits by the joyously triumphant "woodpeckers," East and West, when Germany was reunited, and the pieces sold off for souvenirs, but the crude first version he had patrolled in 1963, a gross lump haphazardly thrown together from iron supports, tangles of barbed wire, and dirty gray cement building blocks the East German workers had pasted in place with slaps of mortar no one bothered to smooth. Jansen said softly, "No." He put his fingers to his mouth, like a child, shaking his head hard enough that his neck hurt, hoping desperately to make the clinic waiting room materialize around him; but the Wall stayed where it was, and so did he.

He was sitting, he realized, in the doorway of a building he did not want to think about; had, in fact, refused to think about for many years. The old ironwork of the entrance was hard and cold against his shoulders as he pushed away from it and struggled to his feet.

Everything around him was familiar, his memory somehow fresher for so rarely having been examined. To his right the Wall angled sharply, blocking the road and continuing along the Kommandantenstrasse, while across from him he could see, just barely, the top of the eastern guard tower that looked down on the Death Strip, that deadly emptiness between the eastern inner fence and the Wall, where the VoPos and Russians would fire on anyone trying to make it across to West Berlin.

Jansen turned from the Wall and took a few hesitant paces along the street. Most of it had actually belonged to East Germany—the Wall had been built several meters inside the formal demarcation line between East and West, so in some places any West Berliner who stepped too close was in danger of being arrested by East German guards; but elsewhere, in the West Berlin suburbs and beyond, there had been small family gardens growing literally in the shadow of the Wall, and even a little fishing going on. Jansen had always admired the Germans' make-do adaptiveness.

Here in the city's urban heart, however, the buildings and shops and little businesses displayed a jumble of conditions, some still unrepaired nearly twenty years after the Allies had bombed and blasted their way into Berlin. Aside from the pooling glow of the streetlamps, Jansen could see no slightest sign of life. All the windows were dark, no smoke rose from any chimneys, and there was no one else in the street. The world was as hushed as though it had stopped between breaths. Beneath the unnaturally starless, cloudless black of the night sky there was not so much as a pigeon searching for crumbs, or a stray dog trotting freely.

Jansen moved on in the silence, confused and wary.

A few buildings past the Zimmerstrasse, he couldn't take it any more. Feeling overwhelmed in the empty quiet, he knocked at the next door he came to, and waited, struggling to bring back what little German he had ever had. *Sprechen Sie Englische?* of course. He'd used that one a lot, and found enough Germans who did to get by. But there was also *Wo bin ich?*—"Where am I?"—and *Was ist los?*—"What is happening?"—and *Bitte, ich bin verloren*—"Please, I'm lost." They all seemed entirely appropriate to his situation.

When no one responded, he knocked again, harder; then tried the next door, with the same result, and then the three doors after that, each one in turn. Nothing. Yet he had no sense of the city being abandoned, evacuated; even the front window of the little shop where he and Harding had taken turns buying sausages and cheese for lunch was still crowded with its mysterious, wondrous wares. He saw his dark reflection in the shop window, and recognized his daily grizzled self: lean-faced and thin-mouthed, with deep-set, distant eyes . . . *no change there*, he thought: an old man caught, somehow, in this younger Jansen's place.

He might have graduated from knocking to shouting, except for what he discovered at the next intersection.

Ernie Hamblin—one of the traffic section MPs quartered with Jansen in the Andrews Barracks—had gotten a big laugh out of Jansen getting turned around and lost, twice, in his first week on duty, all because the two streets that met here had four different names, one for each direction of the compass. Jansen looked to the right, up the Kochstrasse, and saw nothing unusual when compared with his memory. Straight ahead—as Axel-Springer-Strasse became the Lindenstrasse—looked wrong, but in the darkness he couldn't quite make out why. To the left though, down the Oranienstrasse, there was nothing.

Literally nothing. No street, no houses, no streetlamps . . . only the same endless black as the sky, extending both outward and downward without the slightest hint of change. He walked as close to the road's sharp edge as he dared, trying to make sense of what he wasn't seeing, but could not. It wasn't a cliff face or a pit: it was simply emptiness, darkness vast and implacable, an utter end to the world, as if God had shrugged, shaken His head and walked away in the middle of the Third Day. The ground that should have been there was gone. The city that should have been built on it was gone and worse than gone, carved away with absolute, unhuman precision. Looking out and away at that edge, where it floated rootless in the black sky, Jansen could see buildings that had been neatly sliced in half, as though by some cosmic guillotine, their truncated interiors looking pitifully like opened dollhouses.

After a while Jansen realized that the edge had a shape; and that it matched, block for receding block, the cartoon lightning jag that was the corresponding section of the Wall. In the face of that understanding, rational thought was impossible. He turned and ran, and didn't notice anything at all until he stopped, out of breath and shaking, in front of the same doorway where he'd come back to this place.

It was open.

❦

Jansen stood for a long time at the foot of the narrow stair, looking up into the shadows and becoming more aware with every passing moment that the last thing he wanted to do was go even one step further, because that would commit himself irrevocably to whatever reality lay in wait at the top. When he did finally begin to climb, his body felt like the body of someone heavier than he, someone older, and even more weary.

The second floor stairs creaked on the sixth and eleventh steps, exactly as he remembered. All the interior doors were closed, blocking out the light from the street, so by the time he reached the fourth landing he was feeling his way, palms and fingers rasping over the rough burned wood and ragged wallpaper. The Berlin Brigade may have sworn by spotless uniforms and occupied fancy officers' quarters, but they took their OPs—their observation posts—largely as they found them. Jansen counted right-hand doorframes, stopping when he got to the third. His hand found the familiar shape of the brass doorknob, turned it, and eased the door open, grateful to see light again, even if it wasn't very strong this high above the streetlamps.

The first thing his eyes registered was the neatly folded khaki sweater on the one old armchair in the room. *Just where I left it . . . transferred to Stuttgart on half an hour's notice, never did get back here.* Then he saw the folding chair placed carefully on its handmade wooden riser, in front of the open window, and the crude signatures and battalion numbers and obscenities scratched into the walls, including six-inch high letters that said T HE "40" HIRED gUNS. Next to that was a blocky '50s-vintage German wall telephone, its cord dangling above a beaten-up oil heater. On the cheap metal table in the corner were a couple of paperbacks—Mickey Spillane, Erle Stanley Gardner—and some torn candy bar wrappers. *Harding*, he thought. *Three crap mysteries from the PX every week, like clockwork, along with half their Baby Ruths and Mounds. Good as gold or cigarettes when it came to bartering with the street kids.*

Jansen picked up the Spillane book, opened it, and realized that it was completely blank inside its lurid cover. He frowned, then dropped the empty book and lifted the wall telephone's absurdly light-blue handset. He held it to his ear, and the result was exactly what he expected: no dial tone, no static sputter—nothing but the dark silence of a long-dead line. He jiggled the hook, which was pointless but irresistible, and then hung up, a little harder than he perhaps needed to do.

After that he moved to the window, easing gently down into the folding chair positioned before it, because the dream-prop wooden riser under its legs was obviously just as flimsy as the one he'd teetered on so many times back in the real West Berlin. All he needed were his old binoculars and some wet-eared, short-time first lieutenant bitching at him and it would be like he'd never left. Except, of course, that there had been a couple of Germanys then, and as he looked out across the street he could see that the world was just as gone on the GDR side of the Wall as on this one. Ahead of him lay the Death Strip he had looked down upon every day for almost two years, the pale gravel raked over the flat ground between the crude outer Wall, topped with Y-shaped iron trees supporting a cloud of barbed wire, and the even cruder inner wall on the other side of the ramshackle watchtower. But the VoPo barracks he knew from before, the decaying and abandoned pre-War buildings that should have been there, were not; and as he looked from right to left, as far as he could see, sharp-edged blackness traced a line that paralleled the Wall itself. Spotting one or two of the old Russian T-62 tanks would have been a strange but distinct comfort right now, but of course there weren't any.

The telephone rang.

Jansen spun in his chair and the riser gave way beneath his shifting weight with a sharp crack, spilling him heavily to the ground. His back twisted, muscles on the lower left side spasming, and his right knee flared red with pain. *Fuck. Real enough to hurt like a son of a bitch!*

The phone rang a second time, then a third ring, a fourth. It took him that long to struggle back to his feet and hitch straight-legged over to it, his right knee still not trustworthy.

He put his hand on the receiver. It seemed to buzz like a rattlesnake in his fingers, and he held onto it for a second before he could make himself pick it up and put it to his ear.

He said, "Who is this?"

An instant of silence; then a sudden burst of surprised laughter. "So who should it be, *bulvan?*" The accent was Russian, as was the gruff timbre of the voice. Even the laughter was Russian. "Come to the window, so I can see you again. I am wondering if you are the Rawhide or the Two-Gun Kid."

Jansen said, "For God's sake, who are you? *Where* are you?"

"Come look. I will turn on light."

Jansen moved stiffly back to the window, the receiver cord just long enough to stretch. Stepping over the fallen chair, he put his free hand on the windowsill and leaned down to look out. A hundred yards away, toward the far side of the Death Strip, the lights inside the East German guard tower were blinking on and off. As he watched, the pattern stopped and the lights stayed on, allowing him to see a bundled-up figure pointing one forefinger at him, sighting along it like a pistol.

Into the handset, Jansen said, "You?"

"*Garazhi*, Rawhide. Me. So good to see you again." The distant figure executed a clumsy bow.

"Why are you calling me that?" Jansen's mouth was so dry it pained him.

The chuckle came through the receiver again. "The glorious Soviet Army was not nearly as efficient as your leaders liked to believe. Knew only the names of your officers, no one else. But from first day we looked across at each other, I had to call you *something*. I was learning English from comic books—very big on black market, you see, the Westerns with horses and guns and silly hats, so I called you *Rawhide Kid* and that short man—"

"Roscoe Harding."

"Really? For us he was *Two-Gun Kid*, and your mostly night fellows, *Kid Colt* and *Tex Hopalong*. Very satisfying, very shoot-'em-up. We had many such jokes."

"You don't want to know what we called you."

Another laugh. "Possibly not. But what name should I give you now, Rawhide? We are both older, I see, and it does not suit."

"My name's Jansen. Henry Jansen. Listen, you, whatever your name is—"

"Leonid," said the voice in his ear. "Leonid Leonidovich Nikolai Gavrilenko."

"That's a mouthful."

"True. But we are such old acquaintances, you must call me *Lyonya*. Or not, as you prefer. I do not presume." He paused, then said, "Welcome back to the Wall, my friend Jansen. Henry."

"Look behind you." Jansen kept his voice deliberately flat, but he could feel himself struggling not to panic. "This place isn't real."

"*Da, temnyi.* The darkness. I have seen."

Jansen said, "What the hell is going on? I can't be here. I was in a clinic waiting room with my daughter. She's seven months pregnant, and her husband's run off somewhere. She'll need me." Even as he spoke the words, he tasted their untruth in the back of his mouth. Arl had never had a chance to need him, and wouldn't know how to begin now, even if he wasn't who he was. But the Russian was impressed, or sounded so.

"Lucky man, Henry. I congratulate you, to have someone needing you. A good life, then? Since we saw each other last?"

"No," Jansen said. "Not so good. But I have to get back to it right now. Arl—my daughter—she won't know where I am. Hell, I don't know where I am."

"That is, I think, what we should be finding out. We put our thinking caps on, you and I." A certain growling bemusement had entered the Russian's voice. "Do Americans still say that? It cannot be accident, this place. Something is happening to us, *something* has brought us here. Have looked, but seen no one but you. So I think now, yes, after all, we must meet in person, do you not agree? At last, meet. With thinking caps."

As absolutely as Jansen wanted to leave the room, the deep suspicion that had been born in him here—never to abate fully—had its own hold. "I'm not sure that's a good idea, *tovarich*."

"No one is using that word anymore." Gavrilenko's voice was flat, without rancor or any sort of nostalgia. "Except the comedians. A comedy word now. Listen, Jansen, we don't give it up so fast! It is not good to be in this place alone, surely, whatever it is. That is why I called you. Old place, old face from old place, old time—this cannot be coincidence."

Jansen frowned. "Maybe, maybe not. But that's another thing. How did you know this number? Nobody was supposed to have it but the commander and the NCOIC. They didn't even give it to us! Some kraut spy sneak it out to you? Was that another one of the *jokes*?"

"You are not thinking, Henry."

"Fuck you, Gavrilenko. Why should I trust a single goddamn thing you say? I want to go home!"

There was a long silence.

He threw the receiver down, grabbed the empty window frame with both hands and stuck his head out into the night. "Do you hear me, you fucking Russian asshole? I want to go home! *I have to go home!*"

He saw the woman then, entering the Death Strip from somewhere just beyond and to the right of the watchtower. She walked quickly, looking from side to side, shoulders tense, head forward. She wore a faded light-brown coat, a transparent kerchief over her hair, and flat, run-down shoes. In one hand she carried what looked like a small duffel bag.

Oh God, oh no, Jansen thought. *Not this, not this, not again.*

The Russian had seen her too. Even at this distance Jansen clearly heard him shouting in Russian, and then in German. But she kept coming on, and suddenly Jansen understood that she was a ghost. He had never seen one before, but there was no doubt in his mind.

As the woman came even with Gavrilenko's tower she began to run, racing toward the Wall. Halfway there a battery of searchlights came on, so bright they were blinding to Jansen's dark-adjusted eyes. *Automatic, self-activated, never did figure where the trip must be. Maybe they moved it around, be just like them . . .*

And then the firing started.

He couldn't tell where it was coming from: there were no snipers shooting from jeeps or gun-trucks, and in the guard tower there was only the Russian—yelling and screaming, yes, but without any weapon in his hands. Yet real bullets were somehow crackling and spitting all around the woman's churning legs, kicking up little spouts in the neatly-raked gravel like pettish children scuffling their feet. It wasn't happening exactly as it had happened, though. Back then there had been alarms, VoPos and West Berliners shouting—Harding too, right in Jansen's ear—dogs barking, engines revving, the mixed sounds of panic and hope and adrenaline-spiked fear. Here, after Gavrilenko stopped shouting, there was only the spattering echo of gunfire as the woman dodged left and right between the concrete obstacles. *I couldn't have done anything.*

I couldn't!

The two paired hooks of a ship's ladder sailed over the Wall between two of the iron Ys, under the barbed wire, catching among the irregular concrete blocks and mortar. On the other side, out of his sight, the ghost pulled the ladder taut—Jansen could see the hooks shift, almost coming loose before catching. The woman climbed rapidly: in another moment her head topped the Wall, and she pulled a pair of clippers from her waistband and swiftly opened a gap in the barbed wire barrier. Then she braced herself with her hands and looked directly into Jansen's eyes.

She was twenty-three, or so he'd been told, though at the time he had thought she looked older. Now she seemed incredibly young to him, younger than Arl, even, but her plain little face was as gray as the Wall, and her eyes were an inexpressive pale-blue. They were not in the least accusatory or reproachful, but once they had hold of Jansen, he could not look away. He wanted to speak, to explain, to apologize, but that was impossible. The nameless dead woman held him with eyes that neither glittered nor burned, nor even judged him, but would not let go. Jansen stood as motionless as she, squeezing the window frame so hard that he lost feeling in his fingers.

Then a single shot cracked his heart and the woman was suddenly slammed forward, her body twisting so that she fell across the top of the Wall, her left foot kicking one of the ladder hooks loose. She rolled partway onto her side, lifting her head for a moment, and again he saw her eyes. When they finally closed and freed him, he began to cry silently.

How long he stood weeping, he couldn't say. Gavrilenko did not call out to him across the gap, and there were no other sounds anywhere in the world. Jansen was still staring at the body on the Wall when—exactly as though a movie were being run in reverse—the dead woman sat up, crawled backwards to the ladder, reattached the dangling hook, and began descending as she had come. This time she did not look at him at all, and as her head dropped almost out of view the barbed wire knitted itself together.

He watched for a time, but she did not reappear.

The receiver felt as heavy as a barbell when he finally lifted the telephone. He could hear Gavrilenko breathing hoarsely on the line, waiting for him. "The Friedrichstrasse," Jansen said. "Checkpoint Charlie. I'll meet you there."

It had never taken Specialist 4 Henry Jansen—twenty years old, of the 385th Military Police Battalion, specially attached to the 287th Military Police Company—more than eight minutes to cover the four and a half blocks from the Axel-Springer-Strasse observation post to Checkpoint Charlie. The sixty-six-year-old Jansen, kidnapped by the past and all but completely disoriented, took longer, partly because of his knee, but mostly due to mounting fear and bewilderment. The guillotine dark was constantly visible over the Wall that flanked him on his right, and to his left it waited at the end of every side street. Passing the T-intersections he couldn't help but stop and stare.

He consciously attempted to hold his shoulders as straight and swaggering as those of that young MP from Wurtsboro, but despite the effort his head kept lowering between his shoulders, like a bull trying to catch up with the dancing *banderilleros*, jabbing their maddening darts into him from all sides. The further he went into this unreal slice of an empty Berlin, the deeper the *banderillas* seemed to drive into his weary spirit.

I couldn't have helped her. I couldn't have helped, I couldn't . . . She lay there two hours, she bled to death right in front of me, and there wasn't anything I could do. Harding wouldn't let me go to her, anyway, and he outranked me.

But that thought didn't ease him, no more than it ever had. Why should he expect it to help now, in this false place and timeless time, this cage of memories?

By the time he reached Checkpoint Charlie he was sweating coldly, though not from exertion.

The checkpoint was a long, low shack set in the middle of the Friedrichstrasse, with a barrier of stacked sandbags arrayed facing the "Worker and Farmer Paradise" gate on the East German side. Just past the shack he could see the *imbiss* stand where he and his buddies had grabbed coffee, sodas, and sandwiches while on duty, and also the familiar hulk of a massive apartment building, abandoned and empty both then and now.

Someone was standing at the checkpoint, thoughtfully studying the guard shack, but it was not Gavrilenko. Jansen could tell that even from a distance. This stranger was a tall man with thinning blonde hair—probably American, to judge by his neat but casual dress—who looked to be in his middle to late forties. When the man turned and caught sight of Jansen he looked first utterly astonished, and then profoundly grateful to see another human being. He hurried forward, actually laughing with relief. "Well, thank *God*. I'd just about come to believe I was the only living creature in Berlin! Glad to see there's two of us."

He had the faintest of German accents, hiding shyly under the broad, flat vowels of the Midwest. When he got to Jansen he put out a hand, which Jansen took somewhat cautiously.

"Hi," the tall man said. "My name's Ben. Ben Richter."

"I'm Henry Jansen." He let go of Richter's hand. "This isn't Berlin, though. It's not anywhere."

"No," the stranger agreed. "But it's not a dream, either. I know it's not a dream." He peered closely and anxiously into Jansen's face. "Do you have *any* idea what's happened to us?"

"Don't fall asleep in a Planned Parenthood clinic, I'll tell you that much," Jansen said. "That's where I was."

"I was trying *not* to fall asleep," Richter answered. "I was driving home from a business meeting, and my eyelids kept dropping shut. Just a few seconds at a time, but it's terrifying, the way your head suddenly snaps awake, and you know you're just about to crash into someone. Couldn't figure it out. I wasn't tired when I started out, got plenty of rest the night before. Weird." He seemed suddenly alarmed. "Do you think my car just went on, with no driver?"

Jansen felt his face grow cold, almost numb. "Couldn't tell you." After a pause, he added, "Ben, was it?"

"Actually, it's Bernd, but everyone's always called me Ben, since I started school. Kids just decide, don't they?"

Jansen said, "I knew somebody named Richter when I was in junior high. You got any relatives in Wurtsboro, New York?"

The tall man laughed slightly. "I don't know if I've got any relatives *anywhere*. Not in the States, for sure."

"Forget it. Guess I'm just looking for connections."

Richter grinned. "Not exactly surprising, given the circumstances."

"We're not alone," Jansen told him. "There's at least one more of us, anyway, a Russian. Name's Gavrilenko. We spotted each other across the Wall. He was supposed to meet me here—I don't know what's keeping him." After a moment, he added, "Don't know how *he* got here; I mean, if he was asleep or not."

Richter asked hesitantly, "Did you and your friend—uh, the Russian—did you have any luck figuring this out?"

Jansen thought of the running dead woman, and the barbed wire mending itself. Even now some things were too crazy for him to say straight out.

"It has to be something to do with the Wall. Right? Has to. I mean, it's what's *here*." He watched for a reaction, but saw none. "And Gavrilenko and me, we were both on the Wall a couple of years after it went up. Nineteen sixty-three, sixty-four—kids, both of us. He was a guard over there, I was an MP over here. Never got above Specialist 4, so I did some of everything. Pulled patrol, hauling drunk GIs out of bars, clubs, like that. A little checkpoint duty right here"—he gestured around him—"but mostly I was in an observation post over on the Axel-Springer-Strasse. That's how we knew each other back then, two strangers waving across the Wall in the mornings." He realized that he was now talking much too fast, and consciously slowed his speech. "Long ago, all that crap. You wouldn't be interested—you weren't even born then."

"Yes, I was," Richter said quietly. He said nothing more for a few moments, studying Jansen out of chestnut-brown eyes set in an angular, thoughtful face. "There's a Marriott there now, you know, at that corner. In the real world, I mean. Right where the Wall was."

"How do you know that?"

"I've stayed there. My wife's German, so we visit. And I've got a little business going." He looked around slowly, then shrugged. "Weird. Only seen it like this in pictures. Maybe you can tell me about it?"

Jansen blinked. "Tell you about *what?*"

"Berlin in those days. When you were a kid MP—probably a couple of years out of high school, right?" He did not wait for Jansen's answering nod. "See, I was born in Berlin, but I wasn't raised here. Didn't come back until the Wall fell in '89—just felt I had to, somehow—and that's how I met Annaliese." The smile was simultaneously proud and tender. "We live in St. Paul. Three boys, a girl, and an Irish setter. I mean, how bourgeois American can you get?"

"Wouldn't know," Jansen said. "Wish I knew what's keeping Gavrilenko."

"Listen, let's sit down somewhere, okay? While we wait for your Russian friend."

Richter walked around the guard shack and hoisted himself up onto the top row of sandbags. Jansen followed him, and he and Richter sat with their legs dangling, looking straight ahead, both of them unconsciously kicking their heels against the sandbags' brown canvas. The tall man was the first to speak. "Hard to believe these were for real. Not exactly a lot of protection."

"Better than nothing," Jansen said. "I wasn't in the Army then, but in October of '61, a few months after the Wall went up, there was an all-day standoff right here between our guys—40th Armor, 6th Infantry—and about thirty Russian tanks. See, we were set to show them that we could still drive anywhere we wanted in the GDR, and they were going to show us that those days were *over*. And you better believe there were dogfaces crouching behind these same sandbags, locked and loaded and ready to start World War Three, just say the word. I saw the pictures in the Wurtsboro paper."

Richter shrugged. "I've read about the standoff. Seems a little ridiculous, frankly. Awful lot of chestbeating for something that didn't even last a day."

"True. But it *could* have been worse. Ask me, the Russkies came out on top, any way you slice it—from that point on they handed out a lot of shit here, every crossing, and it may have been small shit, but we couldn't give it back since we had orders to play nice. Well . . . not all of them. That's not fair. Mainly it was the generals who were trouble, the big ones who gave the orders and made asses of themselves when they'd come into West Berlin. The men were okay. Russkies, Krauts, they were okay. Even some of the VoPos."

"Ah. The *Volkspolizei*."

"Just like us MPs, only with more training and a *lot* more firepower." Jansen chuckled in his throat. "We had a big snowball fight with a bunch of VoPos one time." He paused, reflecting. "Couldn't make a decent snowball for shit, most of them. Always wondered about that."

Richter cocked his head slightly to the side, considering Jansen meditatively. "So you actually had fun, too. It wasn't all confrontations with tanks and going into bars after drunken soldiers."

"Trick was to keep from staying *in* the bars *with* the drunken soldiers," Jansen told him. "The city was booming with bars, with clubs, a couple new ones opening every week. Some you'd go to for the beer, some for the great music—one time I heard Nat King Cole and Les Paul and Mary Ford on the same night. Two-buck tickets! Some places, you'd take a young lady, some others you'd go to *find* a young lady. Yeah, we had a lot of fun in Berlin. Nineteen-, twenty-year-old kids with guns and money, never been away from home before, never drunk anything stronger than Pabst? We had fun."

Jansen studied Richter. The man's expression was an odd mixture of wistfulness and something deeper, something impatient beyond his interest in Jansen's surfacing memories. For his part, Jansen had not talked this much to anyone in a very long while, and he'd never shared these stories, not even with Elly or the kids. Sharing would have meant deliberately remembering everything, which even the drinking couldn't deal with. Here, though, that self-imposed restriction was as pointless as the rest of it.

"There was a game we used to play," he said. "Worked best in the winter too, only we didn't need snow for this one, we needed ice." He pointed ahead of them, toward a broad white line painted on the ground. "That's the border, near as anybody could figure. Ground got good and icy, you'd take a run and throw yourself down, and *slide*, like you're sliding into a base, only you're sliding right into the GDR." He laughed outright at the memory. "Then you'd get up and run right back across the line, safe in the good old American Sector. The Krauts used to watch us and just laugh themselves silly."

Richter said musingly, almost to himself, "All those good times . . . and all the things going on just under the surface." Jansen frowned, not understanding. Richter went on. "More than a hundred thousand people tried to escape into West Berlin from East Germany in the twenty-eight years the Wall sealed it off. Did you know that, Henry?"

"Knew it was a lot," Jansen said. "Didn't know it was that many—thought the big rush was all before the Wall."

"It was. But another hundred thousand, afterward. Most went to jail. Maybe five thousand made it through. And a lot died. But you were here. You know that."

Her dark hair, her pale-blue eyes, the little sound she made at the last, dying . . .

"Yeah. I do."

Richter had turned away, looking toward the point where the blackness slashed down forever on the East German apartment buildings. But his voice was clear and precise as he said, "Different organizations have different estimates. When the Wall fell, when Germany was reunited, the East German state wasn't in any hurry to release records that made them look like the killers they were. We've had to build up a database one case at a time, literally. One escape attempt at a time. One body at a time. Counting the heart attacks, the wounds that turned fatal on the other side of the Wall, the ones who just disappeared forever, the babies smothered trying to keep them quiet. Officially—you check the encyclopedia articles, the tourist handouts—only 136 people died. But we're figuring twelve hundred, minimum. Not that we'll ever be able to prove half of them." His voice was calm and almost expressionless, utterly dispassionate.

"We," Jansen said. "Who's *we?*"

Richter laughed suddenly, warmly, with a touch of embarrassment as faint as his accent. "I'm sorry. I forget not everyone is as obsessed with this as I am. We is the August 13 Society—I do fundraising for them in the States, and volunteer work for them when I'm here . . . I mean, *there.* Real Berlin. We're actually trying to document every case where people died trying to cross, not just the Wall, but the entire East-West border—to memorialize them, make them real for everybody. So they won't be forgotten again."

Jansen nodded, but did not respond.

Richter said presently, "What I can't figure out is the connection between all three of us—you and me and our absent Russian. Before you showed up I thought I'd driven into a rail, that maybe I was dead and this was Hell; or else maybe I'd stroked out and was in a coma somewhere while my imagination played really bad games with me. But those two possibilities would exclude you, so cross them off the whiteboard . . . which leaves nothing. I've never before met either one of you, and you were both long gone from Berlin by the time I came back. So what's the link?"

"What's if it's just . . . I don't know, random. Coincidence."

"I don't buy that. I'm a mathematician, Henry. Anyway I *was* a mathematician, before I put together my little software company. This place may be impossible, but the odds against a common pattern when two of the three of us have an obvious connection? Maybe not totally impossible . . . let's just say *highly* unlikely."

Jansen said, "We sort of have the Wall in common. But it isn't the same. You obviously know a lot about it, what with this Society thing you do. But it's not like you ever served here. You didn't live with it every day, like us. You weren't ever *on* the Wall—"

"No," Richter agreed. "I wasn't."

To Jansen's eye, Richter seemed suddenly tense and hesitant, like someone trying to avoid making up his mind.

"Well," Jansen spoke up. "What is it? You going to shoot that bird or let it fly?"

The tall man nodded. "Interesting choice of words."

"My stupid mouth is half the reason I'm divorced. What'd I say this time?"

Richter hopped off the sandbags and walked a few steps before answering. When he did, his voice was dry and tight. "My mother was a Berliner."

"Yeah, you said you were born here. So?"

"*East* Berlin, Henry. She died on the Wall."

Jansen wanted to run again, like before, but his legs wouldn't get him down off the barrier. If he couldn't run, maybe he could scream?

Not your hell, maybe, you poor bastard. Definitely mine.

When he finally found words, they surprised him. "You don't sound like you're sure."

Richter turned and looked at him oddly. Jansen wondered if something unheard in his voice had given him away. He was about to speak again when the tall man finally answered.

"The records are all scrambled—when there are records at all—and they mostly don't have names in them, just scraps of facts and description. An address here, an occupation there, a set of initials, shorthand reports of a thousand disconnected, meaningless conversations . . . it's a jigsaw puzzle with most of the pieces missing. I've been digging through the archives for a long time, learning how to read what's there *and* what's been omitted." His mouth tightened. "She died on the Wall, all right. The pieces of the picture are there."

"But you aren't certain."

"If you're asking me whether I have the *Stasi*-stamped file folder to prove it, no." Bitterness colored Richter's voice, and something Jansen couldn't begin to put a name to. He watched as the tall man stared fiercely at the ragged fringe of East German buildings that were visible from here.

"I never knew her," Richter continued. "My step-parents were friends with my mother, and they brought me with them when they got out of East Germany in 1960. It was her idea. She wasn't well—pregnancy and childbirth had been rough—and anyway she knew it would be easier for them, because they'd had a baby who died and they still had the right papers. The idea was that my mother would make it out on her own when she got better, and we'd all be in America together." His faint smile was small and young. "Only they built the Wall, and things didn't work out. She never showed up. One letter made it: nothing else. The Bruckners raised me on their own, in Wisconsin. They were good people. I can't complain."

"What about your father? Where the hell was he?" Unsummoned, there was a vision of Arl in Jansen's head, crying into Elly's arms because Larry had left without so much as a note two days after the little pink dot on the dipstick changed everything.

"Apparently I'm the by-product of a little too much Pilsner at a college party. She never told anyone his name, not even the Bruckners, not even with all the pressure of being nineteen and pregnant in a police state where social pressure favored abortion. All I know about *der fehlende vater* is that he must have been tall and blonde, because according to my stepparents nobody in my mother's family was. It had to come from somewhere."

The woman at the Wall. Got to be his mother. Goddamit, goddamit, tell him what you saw, you stupid fucking coward . . . but maybe I don't have to. Maybe, maybe if I just shut up he'll talk about something else.

Where the hell's Gavrilenko?

At the same moment, Richter said "Enough with my sob story. I seriously don't think your Russian's coming. Let's go find him." He started off without looking back.

"Hold up," Jansen said, easing down off the sandbags. His knee had stiffened while he was sitting. "Old guy, here. Anyway, maybe we shouldn't be in such a hurry."

Richter stopped and looked at him quizzically. "Why not?"

Tell him you saw his mother. Tell him you saw her die. Twice.

"No reason." Jansen stared into Richter's eyes. How could he have missed how much they looked like hers? "It's just . . . what if we take a different route than he does, coming here, and we miss each other?"

"Then we'll come back. Anyway, there's not a whole lot of *there* over there. Come on," Richter said, and this time his grin was a young boy's. "It's not icy, but I bet we can imagine we're sliding across the line."

The Wall on this side ran behind houses that looked like an abandoned stage or movie set: if the west side looked as though every inhabitant had suddenly left town, but might return at any second, here the air of a forced and permanent evacuation was glaringly inescapable. Doors and windows were not merely boarded over, but bricked up as well; many buildings had been demolished, and the rubble—often topped with barbed wire—left in place, to block any passage to the Wall. There were warnings, genuine or not, of minefields—Richter translated the signs for Jansen—and the whole effect was of desertion and neglect. The two men walked close together, automatically speaking in low voices and moving at a pace tailored to accommodate Jansen's slower steps.

Chickenshit. You could walk faster. You're just afraid of getting there.

Jansen asked presently, "You got into it, this August thing, because of your mom?" But Richter shook his head.

"Not exactly, not the way you mean. My stepparents wanted me to grow up to be a good American, so I was assimilated as hell. They told me about my mom—her name was Zinzi, by the way—but not much else, not until I was older. I definitely had the American habit of not thinking about the past very much, and certainly not some faraway European past that might as well have been in an old library book, as far as I was concerned. My head was all forward, all the time. I went to a good college, studied math and computer programming, got naturalized, taught for a while. I was an assistant professor of Mathematics at the University of Wisconsin when I came to Berlin to drink dark beer and knock down my own piece of the Wall and wound up meeting Annaliese instead. Hah. Hey, I never asked—you married?"

"Already told you I was divorced. Twice, actually."

"Oh. Sorry."

"Don't be. Just the ways things are." Jansen felt his heart thudding harder in his chest. "My first ex used to say I was a coconut in a world of bananas. I can hurt people just bumping into them."

"Colorful. Any kids?"

"Two daughters. They hate my guts too, but the pregnant one hates me worse. So there's a bright spot."

Richter stopped walking and turned to face Jansen. "Even if things righteously suck with your kids, I'm sure you remember when they were little. So maybe you'll get this. When Jacob—my son—when Jacob turned six months old, the same age I was when I was brought to America . . . I remember, I looked down at him in my arms, burping bubbles and trying to eat my shirt buttons, and I tried to imagine what Zinzi Richter would have said if she could have seen him, her first grandchild. And I thought how lucky I was to be able to tell him everything my stepparents had told me about her, even if it wasn't all that much. Then I started thinking about all the people who wouldn't ever know what happened to their grandparents or their parents, and I'd read about the August 13 Society, and one thing led to another. I'd started up my company by then—we do case-management software for big legal firms—and our code was pretty useful for what the Society does, so I had an in. And here I am." He smiled crookedly, spreading his hands.

"Makes sense," Jansen said.

"You should tell Jacob that. He thinks I'm crazy. My mother really is just a page in a scrapbook to him. He's going to be fifteen next June, and what *he* likes about coming over here is that he's tall enough now to get away with telling the local girls he's really seventeen."

They started on again, both of them unconsciously keeping to the right side of the road, away from the darkness they could see on the other side of the decayed and empty buildings. To Jansen it definitely seemed closer here, which bothered him. He thought of the suddenly open door back on the Axel-Springer-Strasse, and the words *herding us* passed through his mind.

Richter said, "You can tell I'm nervous, because I'm talking too much."

That surprised Jansen. "You don't *act* nervous."

"Quaking in my Nikes. Not the slightest sign of danger since I showed up here, but this place is really starting to creep me out. Hence the talking."

"So talk," Jansen said firmly. "Tell me more about your kids."

"I'd rather listen. Tell me what you do."

Jansen grunted, waved the question away.

"No, seriously."

"Nothing important. I remodel stuff. Kitchens and bathrooms, mostly. One-man gang, hire extra help when I have to. Been doing it more or less since I left the Army."

"That's good work," Richter said. "You do your job, and then when you're finished, when you look at what you've done, you get to see that you've made something better, made it work, made it beautiful. There's pride in that. You're a lucky man."

"Gavrilenko called me that too," Jansen said slowly. "I don't think I'm so fucking lucky." Richter regarded him curiously. Jansen said, "I'm good with my hands, with wood and tile and plastic piping, but that's it. Sinks and toilets, cabinets and countertops? Sure. People? Forget it. My exes, my kids, they're all right about me. Since I got back from Germany, I can't think of one damn thing that's gone right, except work. Not one damn thing in forty years."

Richter said, "It's the Wall." Jansen looked up in surprise. "People I work with—former refugees, their families—they tell a story that one guy who didn't make it over put a curse on the Wall with his dying breath. He made it so even if you escape, even with the Wall down and gone, there's still a curse that follows you in your life. Because you got out and he didn't."

Jansen thought *nobody ever gets out*. But what he said was, "No offense, but that's bullshit. Anyway, I didn't have anything to escape from. I did my time, got rotated to Stuttgart and then stateside. Period."

They walked a little way further in silence before Richter continued. "Maybe. But people tell stories like that because they mean something. And you said yourself that your troubles started here. It wasn't all snowball fights, Henry."

"Crap. I was a kid."

"Which makes it better how?" Richter's tone had shifted, the hint of impatience becoming more pronounced. "Jesus Christ, man, you know

I've been through the East German records fifty-seven times. I'm the guy with the damn database. So why are you dancing with me like this? Even on the official record there are at least three or four deaths that correlate with the time you must have been here. Fechter, he's the most famous, but there were others. And at least twenty, thirty more the Society is researching. Are you telling me none of that ever touched you, that you never saw anything? If not, then why the hell are you here? *What's our connection?*"

Jansen was shaking his head before Richter was halfway finished. "That's not it! It can't be it."

"*What* can't be it?"

Jansen started to turn away, but Richter squared off on him. The tall man's hands came down on Jansen's shoulders, and they were bigger hands than Jansen had noticed. He said nothing. He only waited.

Oh, God.

Jansen said tonelessly, "You can't put this on me."

"I didn't," Richter answered. "But you can take it off."

"Shit!" For just a moment Jansen couldn't breathe.

Richter's eyes were hot behind a face suddenly flattened into an unyielding mask. "I'm not an idiot. You've been wanting to tell me something since we were back at the sandbags. Spill."

"I—I don't know who it was. Just some girl, some woman . . . I never knew her name." Jansen heard the sirens and shouting, the gunfire; only by Richter's lack of reaction did he understand that the blaring cacophony was all in his head. "But I'll never forget what happened. Fuck, I still dream it."

Richter nodded him on.

"It was 1963. I was almost out, just screwing around on duty in the observation post, joking with Harding about making a midnight run to clip a little barbed wire off as a souvenir, something to take home with me. Then his eyes went all spooky and he said 'Fuck me, Lord,' just like that, quiet as if we were in a library . . . and I saw what he was seeing. This woman—"

"Wait a sec. That was the Axel-Springer-Strasse OP?"

Jansen nodded.

Richter bored in. "July or November?"

"July. I wasn't here in November."

"Tell me what she looked like."

Jansen felt himself snapping. "Don't make me do this!"

"*Tell* me."

"You have to hear me say it? It was your mother! Of course it was your mother. She had your goddamn eyes, you bastard, and she came out of nowhere on the far side of the Death Strip, and maybe she would have made it if she were a little faster, or maybe she wouldn't, I don't know, I only know it was like they were *playing* with her, like they could have cut her down at any time, but they waited until she was halfway over the top. Then somebody took her out with a single shot and she lay there on top of the wall for two hours, *two fucking hours*, bleeding out, never making a sound until the end, and the whole time I . . . the whole time . . ."

He turned his head, unable to bear looking into Richter's face.

"I wanted to go to her. Harding wouldn't let me. I did call the NCOIC and scream for a doctor, for help, for somebody, but nobody came. Nobody came. It was just me and Harding, and he wouldn't look. But for the whole two hours I did. I saw her die."

Richter's hands closed once, briefly. They seemed to sink past flesh and muscle to leave their fingerprints in his bones; yet, strangely, Jansen felt no pain at all. When Richter let go and lifted them away, something iron went with them that Jansen never tried to name.

"Yes," Richter said without expression. "I thought that might have been the one." He turned away.

"That's not all," Jansen said to the tall man's stiffened back.

Richter slowed down, but didn't stop.

"Here's the thing." Jansen had to raise his voice as the other man moved away. "You fell asleep in your car, and you woke up here in this theater set, but you didn't get to see the play. Me, I had to watch it all over again. So did Gavrilenko, from his guard tower. The run, the bullets, her death on top of the Wall. Everything. Do you hear me? *I saw your mother die all over again* . . . and when it was over I saw her climb back down, just like she was getting ready for another show. *That's* why Gavrilenko and I were supposed to meet. I don't know why I'm here, I swear to God I don't, but whatever I've done wrong in my life I can't possibly deserve having to see that again—and you don't want to see it either. Trust me on that!"

Richter stood still and said nothing for what felt to Jansen like a very long time, but which was certainly only seconds. Then he heard Zinzi Richter's son say, simply, "Huh," and had to hurry to catch up with the tall man as he walked, with quickening strides, toward the darkness.

The guard tower had looked considerably more impressive and ominous from a dingy room in a crumbling apartment house across from the Wall than it did at close range. At once splintery-new and yet already rickety, it had far more of an agricultural air than a military one, looking somewhere between a flattened silo and a hayloft. Jansen felt that there should have been a weathervane on its squared-off roof.

Richter stopped in his tracks so suddenly that Jansen bumped into his back before he could halt himself. At the foot of the tower stairs stood the ghost of Zinzi Richter.

Ashen, slender, with dark auburn hair limp against her skull, as though with sweat, she paid absolutely no attention either to Jansen or to her staring son. All her concentration was directed up the single flight of rusted metal steps to the doorway where a big old man stood hugging himself as he rocked erratically against the doorframe. Zinzi Richter made no attempt to go up to him, but simply stood waiting at the foot of the stair.

"That's her," Richter whispered. "The Bruckners had one photo. Oh my God."

As though she had put on her Sunday best for the occasion, the ghost looked as clear and solid as any human being whose heart still jumped in the cage of her ribs, still ordered blood out to her fingertips and back through her throat and her thighs. Richter took a step toward her, but this time it was Jansen's hand clamping hard on his arm. Jansen said softly, "Wait. She's here for *him*."

Through binoculars—the closest acquaintance he had ever had with Leonid Leonidovich Gavrilenko over the Wall—Jansen had always seen the Russian as bull-featured and powerfully built, with an undomesticated mass of heavy black hair that stood up crazily on either side of his broad, high-boned face when he pulled off his knit woolen cap. The man he saw now had none of that force, nothing of that implicit swagger: he only slumped against the door frame, his lips moving as though in prayer. Jansen thought, *He's old*; and then, *No, I'm old, and I don't look like that. What's happened to him?*

"That's why he didn't come to the checkpoint. He can't come down," Jansen said to Richter. "*She's* there, and he's afraid of her."

Richter ignored him. He pulled away from Jansen's grip and approached the ghost of Zinzi Richter, plainly trying not to run to her. He said, "Mother, it's me, I'm your son. I'm Bernd." He tried to take her hands in his, but she did not move, or look at him, or respond in any way. She stayed where she was, looking up the stair at Gavrilenko.

Jansen said, "Ben." A strange calmness was upon him, as though for the first time in his life he actually knew what to do. He said, "Ben, we have to go up there."

Richter turned to him, so determinedly *not* crying that Jansen felt tears starting in his own eyes. "I can touch her—I didn't know you could touch ghosts. But she doesn't see me, she doesn't even know I'm here. I don't understand."

"She's waiting for Gavrilenko," Jansen said. "She'll wait forever, if she has to. You want to find out what all this is about, we have to bring him to her. Now."

The last word snapped out in a tone that surprised him; he hardly

313

recognized his own voice. But it seemed to help Ben, who managed to get hold of himself and follow Jansen as the older man started up the guard tower stairs. *Well, I did make it to corporal before it was all over. Might have made sergeant if I'd stayed in. Things I could have been.* Jansen looked back once at the ghost. She had not stirred at all from her position, nor changed the direction of her gaze. *Holy shit, the Russian's treed, is what it is. She's got him treed.* He could not control a swift shiver.

Near the top of the stair he looked away from the tower and saw the darkness closing in, pitilessly paring away everything that was not itself.

The guardroom door was open. Gavrilenko backed away as Jansen and Richter came in, still seemingly holding himself together with both arms. In a rough, throaty grumble, a ghost itself of the striding peasant vigor Jansen had heard over the phone, the Russian said, "Unavoidably detained, Rawhide. Trouble on the range, I am afraid."

"You have to come down to her, Gavrilenko," Jansen said. "It's time."

"Is time, is time." Something of the jovial telephone derision flickered in the Russian's gruff voice. "Now you are sounding like a priest come to walk me to firing squad. No, Rawhide, I do not go with you. I stay here until she goes away. I can stay here." He rose shakily to his full height, arms firmly folded across his chest.

"Leonid," Jansen said. "That woman down there—the man with me is her son. Talk to him."

Gavrilenko turned to face Richter. His still-powerful face had gone grayish-white, making the beard stubble stand out starkly, like the last stalks of a gleaned-over wheat field.

"Her son . . ." Gavrilenko did not move, nor take his eyes from Richter's face for a long moment; then, to Jansen's astonishment, he began to smile. His teeth were remarkably white, unusual for an East European of his generation. He drew a short breath and recited, in the classic half-chanting Russian style, "*After the first death, there is no other.* Mr. Dylan Thomas, English poet."

When there was no response, Gavrilenko repeated, "He understood.

Shakespeare, Pushkin, they did not understand so well as Mr. Dylan Thomas." He seemed unable to take his eyes from Richter. He said suddenly, "Your mother—I knew her." The smile drew his lips flat against the good white teeth. "This one—" he jerked a thumb at Jansen—"he only sees her dying, no more. But I . . . I saw her living—she was good at living, Zinzi. Only a short time, we had, but we made of it what we can. *Could*—what we *could*. You see, I forget my English so soon." The wide smile still clung to his lips, fading only slowly, like the shape of a cloud.

Richter's face was also taut, but his eyes remained steady and composed. He said quietly, "You were not my father."

Gavrilenko sighed. It was a long, slow sigh, almost theatrically Russian, and its wordless tone carried the suggestion of sorrow at once too deep to be born, and too hopeless to be worth bothering with. "No, I am not your father—that was some student, she told me, gone off to the West before she even knew she was pregnant. But I could have been. For three weeks, I could have been."

It was not said boastingly or mockingly, but was somehow part of the sigh. Jansen thought about Arl's vanished husband and had to shake free of a sudden spasm of pure rage. "You helped her plan that run, didn't you? Had to be someone who knew the triggers, the timing."

"I do more, Rawhide. I show her the weak places, I show where the big searchlights are, where the VoPos hide—everything I know, she knows." His voice had taken on the same singsong quality as when he quoted the Thomas line. "She had a little money, not so much. I spread it among the VoPos, everybody getting something—so when she runs we are all turning into very bad shots, you understand? No big deal, everybody getting something." He clasped his big hands at the waist, like a child set to recite at school. To Richter he said, "I do all that for Zinzi Richter, for your mother. Because she was funny, and I liked her, you know? Also, I was young."

"Because you were screwing her and taking her money," Richter said harshly. "You used her."

"So? She is using me too." Gavrilenko appeared genuinely indignant. "You think she sleeps with me out of love? *Chort*—she knows what she does, and so did I. She comes to me, straight to bed, down payment, right? Was a bargain, and both kept our word." He laughed abruptly. "Like I said, young."

Jansen said, "Something obviously went wrong."

Gavrilenko was silent for a long time. He did not turn away from them, but he ceased to look directly at Richter, and his glances at Jansen had become defiantly despairing. He said finally, "The Stasi, Stasi, KGB—eyes everywhere, even when you know they have eyes. The day she makes her run . . . suddenly, no VoPos I recognize, no VoPos I pay money to, whole new crowd. Stasi agents, every one—I know this. What to do? I want to warn her, but I am on duty, they have made sure I have no chance. You understand?" He was glaring at them both now, looking more like an old bull than ever. "You understand? I had no chance!"

After a moment he shrugged, long and deliberately. "Also no choice." Now he clearly forced himself to meet Richter's eyes, and the physical effort was visible on his face. He repeated doggedly, "No choice."

Richter's silence was more than Jansen could bear. He had to speak. "So you shot her. She trusted you, and you killed her."

"*They were watching me!*" It sounded as though Gavrilenko's throat was tearing from the words. "All of them, firing wide, missing and missing, *watching*, looking like this—" he mimicked someone stealing covert side-glances—"waiting for *me* to shoot and miss, so they know I am traitor. Her or me, and what would *you* do, brave Rawhide?" He was breathing like a runner whose strength has ended before his race. "Sweet, funny little Zinzi, nice girl—you tell me what you would do, eh? I wait."

Neither Jansen nor Richter responded, nor did they look at each other. For his part, the constant image in Jansen's mind of Zinzi Richter's doomed attempt to reach her baby kept being replaced by one of his own daughters. Outside the guardroom door, the edged darkness was slicing in closer, while through the window, in a strangely dizzying sweep, he could see back across the Death Strip and the Wall to the apartment where he had spent much of two years staring at this very room.

"I wait," Gavrilenko repeated, and this time it was not a mocking challenge. This time it was soft and urgent, almost plaintive, as though he really did want an answer, was in desperate need of any reply at all, For a third time he said, "I wait to be told what I should have done. Speak, wise Americanski friends."

"That's a comedy word," Jansen said. "Nobody uses that anymore."

Then Richter answered him at last, his words falling like the muffled strokes of an old clock. He said, "Mr. Gavrilenko, I have to thank you. If your guilt were not so great, if you had just been an agent, a VoPo, who shot my mother and went off to lunch, it would never have dragged you here to see her again. It would never have called to Henry's guilt, or to my own guilt for being born, and causing her death . . . her stupid, stupid, needless death." For those few words there was a sound in his voice like claws on stone, and his hands kept opening and closing at his sides.

"You can't think that," Jansen said. "She could have died the exact same way, even if you hadn't been born. Believe me, you do not want to spend your life thinking—"

Richter cut him off. "What I think is not important. We're here, and this has got to be why we're here. What we *do* now is what matters. We go down to my mother, to look into her face. All three of us. This is not a request."

He looked sharply at Jansen, who nodded. But Gavrilenko backed away, shaking his head, saying, "No, *no,* I cannot, will not, no, never possible." He wailed and struggled frantically when Jansen and Richter caught hold of his flailing arms and literally dragged him out of the guard room. Old and ill, half-mad or not—his eyes were rolling as wildly as those of a terrified stallion—he was still stronger than either of them alone, and their cramped passage down the guard tower's stairway was a battle. Jansen had a bloody nose by the time they had the Russian near ground-level, and Richter's shirt was splitting down the back seam. Through it all, Gavrilenko wailed and cursed in an absurd and piteous mix of Russian, German, and English, going utterly limp at the last, which meant hauling him the final few steps like a side of beef or bale of hay, until they were finally able to dump him at Zinzi Richter's feet and step back, breathless and exhausted.

The ghost saw them.

On her plain, unremarkable little face the joy of Richter's presence, his existence—the *fact* of him—leaped up like a flame in dry grass. Seeing this recognition, the tall man took her hands between his, bowed over them, and began to cry, almost soundlessly. She drew her hands free and held him close; but over his shoulder her eyes met Jansen's, and he actually staggered back a pace, shaken by the depth of the sorrow and sympathy—sorrow specifically for him—that he read there. He heard himself saying aloud, in absurd embarrassment, "Hey, it hasn't been as bad as all that. Really." But it had been, it had been, and she knew.

Then she gently released her son, and knelt down beside Gavrilenko, where he lay on his face, hands covering his eyes. With her own hands on his upper arms, she silently coaxed him to face her. Gavrilenko screamed once—not loudly, but in a tone of pure terror, and of resignation to terror as well, like a rabbit unresisting in the clutches of a horned owl. He scrambled to a sitting position, his hands now flat on the ground beside him, face dazed and alien. The ghost commanded his eyes as she had Jansen's—how long ago?—holding them in thrall to her own, seeing through them and past them, down into uttermost Gavrilenko, his body shaking with the need to hide his eyes again but unable to do so. He whimpered now and then; and still clung to himself.

By and by he began to speak. "After first death, really is no other. You and me, Henry—you remember us? Two tired, lonely, nervous boys in uniform, pretending to be men, doing job . . ." He rose slowly to his feet. "I kill so many people since then—you know? Easy, really. *Easy.* Killings, I am telling you honestly, but no *deaths* . . . not after her." He did meet Zinzi Richter's quiet eyes then, though again Jansen saw the physical shock spread through his body. He said, "Different, you understand?"

Jansen asked, "You stayed in the army? No . . . what, you were KGB?"

"Oh, please, no KGB anymore," Gavrilenko reproved him. "In new democratic Russia, FSB—execute you with new democratic pistol. No, Henry, I did my time in private enterprise. Big capitalist, all American values, even before it was common. You would be proud."

"The Mafia." Richter's voice was tight and thick, for all its evenness. "You worked for the Russian Mafia. You killed people for them."

Gavrilenko grinned at him like a skull. "Kill for the Mafia, kill for Mother Russia—what difference? I was an independent contractor, just like American plumber." He nodded toward Jansen. "I went here, I went there, fix the sink, the toilet, go home, rest tired feet, watch the TV." He spoke directly to Zinzi Richter now, to no one else in the world. He said, "This is your blessing. You made me so."

Something he couldn't guess at made Jansen look away, and he fancied that he could actually see the darkness moving in around them if he watched it closely enough. From where they stood, nothing was visible now but the tower, the Wall in one direction, and the dark wall itself in the other . . . and after studying it, when he looked again on Gavrilenko he saw something that he could not have been expected to recognize, yet felt he should have seen from the moment he and Richter had entered the guardroom. With a sudden surge of wonder and pity, he whispered, "Leonid. You're like her . . ." He was trembling, and it was hard to get words out, or to remember what words were.

Gavrilenko shook his head slowly, heavily. "Not like her. She is long dead, forever young, forever innocent. While Leonid Leonidovich Nikolai Gavrilenko lies in Petersburg hospital, Walther PPK bullet in coward's brain." He grimaced in bitter disgust. "So many heads, so many bullets, one to a customer . . . only Gavrilenko, pig-drunk, old, sick, shaking with fear, cannot even kill himself decently . . . coward, coward, pathetic . . ." There were a few more words, all Russian.

The ghost of Zinzi Richter spoke then, without making a sound. Picking up her blue duffel bag, she looked at the three of them and mouthed a single word, rounding it out with great care and precision. Jansen could not read her lips, but Richter nodded. His mother gestured broadly, intensely with her free arm: pointing first toward the crouching, stalking darkness, then toward the Wall, unmistakably inviting them all to run with her while there was still time. She mouthed the silent word a second time.

Jansen and Richter both sensed Gavrilenko's decision before he even turned. They clutched at his arms, but he broke free with a frantic, wordless cry and dashed away from them, lunging and stumbling back toward the East Germany of their memories. Richter, quicker off the mark than Jansen, almost caught him at the inner wall; astonishingly, the old Russian hurled himself at it like a gymnast, leaping to catch the top, and was up and over it and straight into the darkness without hesitating. He vanished instantly, like a match-flame blown out, leaving no sound or glance behind him.

Richter stopped, staring at the edge.

Jansen joined him, and they stood together in silence for some minutes. The darkness, if it did not retreat, at least advanced no further. Jansen said finally, "You really think it was him that brought us here? It wasn't your mother?"

"I have no idea," Richter said, turning away from the void. "Maybe we all did it."

Jansen looked at the ghost of Zinzi Richter, waiting for them by the guard tower, forming for a third time the word he could not understand. "What is that?" he demanded of Richter. "What's that she's saying?"

Richter smiled. "*Freiheit*. German for *freedom*."

Abruptly Zinzi Richter turned and began to run, heading once again for the Death Strip, and Richter ran after her, his face as bright and determined as the face of any small boy racing with his mother. Jansen came panting in the rear, no better conditioned than the average sixty-six-year-old kitchen remodeler, but resolved not to be left behind in this place, to find his way back to a maternity clinic in Klamath Falls, Oregon. *Arl . . .Arl . . .I'll be right there . . .*

The spotlights came on, and the gunfire began.

Crossing the Death Strip, Jansen placed his feet exactly in Zinzi Richter's tracks, as her son was doing, and hunched down as low as he could, even as the rifle shots kicked up gravel close enough to sting his face and twitch at his shirt. He tried to shut the awareness out of his consciousness. *Real bullets? Memories of bullets? Ghost bullets, fired by ghosts back in 1963—God!* And then, despite a sudden blossoming fear of dying where he didn't belong, a single thought consumed him. *It's not enough to follow. I've got to get there first.*

Just as Gavrilenko's old legs and big old hands had taken him over the inner wall without assistance, so Jansen's legs, when called upon, somehow responded with speed that did not belong to him, and never had. He passed up a surprised Richter and forcefully crowded past Zinzi Richter as she set her ladder's hooks, stopping only long enough to pull the wire cutters from her duffel before starting to climb. Up the shaking rungs, atop the Wall, he worked faster than she could have, snapping wires real enough to tear his face and hands in half a dozen places. Then they were there with him, the mother and the son, and he swept them before him through the gap he had created, holding their hands as they eased themselves over the other side. He turned his back on the gunfire, covering both his charges with the width of his own torso, breath pulled deep into his lungs as if he could somehow expand to shield not just these two, but everything in the world. He felt their fingers slip away from his and he smiled.

The rifle fire kept up, but Jansen didn't move, thinking *shit, if the Krauts didn't fire in damn platoons, they'd never hit anybody.*

He heard the one sharp crack they say you never hear, and closed his eyes.

∞

Arl, hugely pregnant and wheezing with the effort, was trying to keep him from falling out of bed in what must be the clinic's emergency ward. There were half a dozen beds around him, most empty, a couple with curtains drawn around them and nurses coming and going. Jansen caught himself, scrambled crabwise back onto the bed, said, "What the Christ?" and tried to sit up. Arl pushed him back down, hard.

"No, you don't—you stay *put*, old man." There was relief in her voice— he caught that, having looked long for such things—but also the same dull rancor and plain dislike that colored their every conversation, even the most casual. "You're staying right here until Dr. Chaudhry comes."

"What happened? The baby?"

"The baby's all right. I'm all right too, thanks." That wasn't just him, he knew; everybody asked about the baby first, and it was starting to piss her off as she neared her term. She said, "They found you on the floor in the waiting room. They thought it might be a stroke."

"Oh, Jesus. I just fell asleep, that's all. Been staying up too late watching old movies. I'm fine, shit's sake." He looked at his hands and wrists, saw no barbed-wire wounds, and started to get up, but she pushed him down again, and he could feel the real fury in her hands.

"You *stay* there, damn it. A lot of people think they're just fine after a stroke, and they get on their feet, take a few steps, and bang, gone for good this time." Her face was sweaty with effort and anger; but he saw fear there as well, and heard it in her voice. "On good days I can just about stand you, and on the bad ones . . . God, do you have any *idea*?"

"Yes," Jansen said. "Matter of fact."

Arl drew a long breath. "But when I saw you . . ." Her voice caught, and she started again. "I realized right there, I am not ready to have you gone, I'm *not*. Not you too, it's too damn *much*, do you understand me? Don't you dare die on me, not now. Not fucking *now*."

Jansen found her hand on the bed, and put his hand over it. She did not respond, but she did not pull the hand away. "You look like me," he said. "Gracie's all Elly, but you've got my chin, and my nose, and my cheekbones. Must have really hated that, huh?"

The smile was thin and elusive, but it was a smile. "I hated my whole face. Most girls do, but I had reasons." She looked down at their hands together. "I even hated my hands, because they're too much like yours. I'm okay with them now, though, more or less."

Jansen said, "You're like me. That's what you hate." Her eyes widened in outrage, and she jerked away, but he held tightly to her hand. "What I mean, you're like the *good* me. The best of me. The me I was supposed to be, before things . . . just happened. You understand what I'm saying?"

Arl was beginning to frown in an odd way, staring at him. "You sure you haven't had a stroke? I wish the doctor'd get here. You talked while you were out, I couldn't make anything out of it, except it was really weird. Like you were having a weird dream."

"Not a stroke," Jansen said. "Not a dream." He did not try to sit up again, but kept his eyes fixed on her. He said, "Just someplace I needed to be. Don't ask me about it right now, and I won't ask you about stuff you don't want to tell me, okay?" She did not reply, but her hand turned slightly under his, and a couple of fingers more or less intertwined. "And I promise I won't die until you're finished yelling at me. Fair?"

Arl nodded. "But this doesn't mean I actually like you. Just so you know that."

"Fair," Jansen said again. He did withdraw his hand from hers now.

Dr. Chaudhry came in, a brisk young Bengali with a smile that was not brisk, but thoughtful, almost dreamy. He sat down on the opposite side of the bed from Arl and said, "Well, I hear that you have been frightening your good daughter quite badly. Not very considerate, Mr. Jansen."

"I'm not a very considerate person," Jansen said. "My family could tell you."

"This is something you must change right away," Dr. Chaudhry said, trying to look severe and not succeeding. "You are going to be a grandfather, you know. You will have responsibilities."

"Yeah," Jansen said. He looked up at the lights on the ceiling then, and let Dr. Chaudhry count his pulse.

ABOUT PETER S. BEAGLE

PETER SOYER BEAGLE is the internationally bestselling and much-beloved author of numerous classic fantasy novels and collections, including *The Last Unicorn, Tamsin, The Line Between, Sleight of Hand, Summerlong, In Calabria,* and, most recently, *The Overneath*. He is the editor of *The Secret History of Fantasy* and the co-editor of *The Urban Fantasy Anthology*.

Beagle published his first novel, *A Fine and Private Place*, at nineteen, while still completing his degree in creative writing. Beagle's follow-up, *The Last Unicorn*, is widely considered one of the great works of fantasy. It has been made into a feature-length animated film, a stage play, and a graphic novel. He has written widely for both stage and screen, including the screenplay adaptations for *The Last Unicorn*, the animated film of *The Lord of the Rings*, and the well-known "Sarek" episode of *Star Trek*.

As one of the fantasy genre's most-lauded authors, Beagle has received the Hugo, Nebula, Mythopoeic, and Locus Awards as well as the Grand Prix de l'Imaginaire. He has also been honored with the World Fantasy Life Achievement Award and the Comic-Con International Inkpot Award. In 2017, he was named 34th Damon Knight Grand Master of the Science Fiction and Fantasy Association for his contributions to fantasy and science fiction.

Beagle lives in Richmond, California.

About Meg Elison

MEG ELISON is a California Bay Area author and essayist. She writes science fiction and horror, as well as feminist essays and cultural criticism. She has been published in McSweeney's Internet Tendency, Fangoria, Fantasy and Science Fiction, Catapult, and many other places.

Her debut novel, *The Book of the Unnamed Midwife* won the 2014 Philip K. Dick Award. Her novelette, "The Pill" won the 2021 Locus Award. She is a Hugo, Nebula, and Sturgeon Awards finalist. She has been an Otherwise Award honoree twice. Her YA debut, *Find Layla* was published in fall 2020 by Skyscape. It was named one of *Vanity Fair*'s Best 15 Books of 2020. Her parasocial thriller, *Number One Fan* was published in summer 2022 by Mira Books.

Elison is a high school dropout and a graduate of UC Berkeley.

About the Artist

Stephanie Law's work is an exploration of mythology mixed with her personal symbolism. Her art journeys through surreal other-worlds, populated by dreamlike figures, masked creatures, and winged shadows. In her early career, she worked with various fantasy game, magazine, and book publishers as an illustrator. She created the Shad-owscapes Tarot, a best-selling deck that has been translated into more than a dozen languages, and she is the author of the watercolor tech-nique book series *Dreamscapes*. She currently focuses on working with galleries for showcasing her personal work and with botanical gardens and environmental organizations for her botanical art, while continuing to publish such projects as her recent art book *Descants & Cadences*, which features her aesthetics of mythos woven with movement and the natural world, and *Succulent Dragons*, which combines her love of the intricate patterns of nature and whimsical fantastical creatures.

Law lives in the San Francisco Bay Area.